J.L VAMPA

The Exorcism of Faeries

A DARK ACADEMIA NOVEL

For more information, address: jlvampa@jlvampa.com.

First Edition April 2025

Cover by J.L. Vampa — www.jlvampa.com
Character Art: Natalia T @eruaphora
Faerie Art: Nicoleta Dabija

Hardcover ISBN 9798330624898
Paperback ISBN 9798330651139
Ebook AISN B0DMZP8MDT

WORKS BY JL VAMPA

The Queen's Keeper
Secrets of a Nomad Ghost
Exquisite Poison Anthology: One Pirouette
Stolen Magick
Gloam Hollow: A Cozy Witch Mystery Series
The Exorcism of Faeries

THE SISTERS SOLSTICE SERIES

Autumn of the Grimoire
Winter of the Wicked
Spring of Ruin
Our Lady of War: a villain origin story
Summer of Sacrifice
Lovers Novella

The
Exorcism
of
Faeries

J.L.
VAMPA

*It will last
until endless
future times*

-Motto of Trinity College Dublin

Dublin Journal of Medicine
1990

The Irish Plague—the first case originated in Patient Zero in Dublin in the year 1987. To date, the Irish Health Protection Surveillance Centre (HPSC) has made great strides through their employment of various organisations working to eradicate the Irish Plague of Unknown Origin.

5th November 1993

He always reads standing in front of the shelf, one hand shoved in his pocket until it's time to flip the page. It's the first thing I noticed about him, while I was supposed to be studying. Instead, I watched him move from shelf to shelf and book to book. I had no idea at the time that I would one day meet him and he would change everything.

We would change everything.

-Excerpt from the diary of Ariatne Morrow, found in the wreckage at Ground Zero

The Sick Rose

O Rose thou art sick.
The invisible worm,
That flies in the night
In the howling storm:

Has found out thy bed
Of crimson joy:
And his dark secret love
Does thy life destroy.

-William Blake

ATTA
SEPTEMBER 1993

Moving a corpse in the rain is such fussy, slippery business.

Fat drops slipped into Atta's eyes as she hauled along the cadaver by moonlight, rigour mortis making her efforts all the more difficult. She couldn't see the mud sloshing up her tweed trousers and camel trench any more than she could make out the face of the dead man twice her size.

"These were new boots, you bastard," she gritted out as she pushed him up against the back of her car and smashed her hip into his weight to hold him there.

She knew it wasn't his fault. The dead don't control the weather.

Attempting to keep him in place, she wrangled the keys from her pocket and jammed the correct one into the lock by feeling alone. Her fingers had gone quite numb, but she managed to get the boot of the old '77 Granada to spring open.

This was not her first experience with a corpse. No, that had occurred twenty-five years prior, at the tender age of three. Nor was this her first time slinking away with a corpse into the night. Though she usually had a gurney with which to move them. Tonight had been less than ideal. Nothing had gone to plan.

Though Atta was nothing if not clever.

The edges of her vision darkened, a familiar fog rolling in. She winced and the cadaver fell forward against her, his chest colliding with her shoulder and knocking her back a step. Grunting, Atta willed the sharp pain in her head to go away, its ghastly hallucinations with it.

For once, it blessedly did.

But the body slipped from her grip, thunking to the asphalt as Atta hissed a curse. Grateful as she was for the broken streetlights and ominous clouds obscuring the car park and, therefore, her dark deeds, she wouldn't make it to Achilles House before dawn if things continued progressing at the rate they were. She should have waited for a clear night—or early morning, as it were—but this John Doe had been too good to pass up.

Atta bent over double, sloppily wrapping her arms around the fallen corpse's middle, and heaved his torso up. Grunting and cursing in a way that would make her mam toss holy water at her, she dragged the dead man up against her chest, muscles screaming.

Maybe she should join a gym.

She almost dropped him again when she snorted at the absurdity of such a thought.

Alas, Atta managed to drag him along.

"Almost there," she encouraged herself through the strain.

Something about the way his heels scraped against the asphalt as she tugged at him was making her nauseous. Viscera and bone beneath a scalpel or bone saw never made her bat an eye, but this was different. She shouldn't have been able to hear the disturbing *shush* of it over the rain, but the deluge was finally slowing and the sound of skin on road felt too human.

No matter that there was nothing human about this man. Not anymore. His soul had gone off to wherever souls go, to haunt or to hallow.

Atta managed to get his shoulders into the boot of the car before he slipped again, and she bit back a cry of frustration. The rain slowed to hardly a drizzle and the full moon broke through the clouds with enough silken light for her to make out the crumpled, nude body, his chest hastily sewn shut.

Another *Unidentified Deceased*. One more for the pile of bodies in the overrun morgue.

Atta'd been the one to accept him, tag him, and run the preliminary procedures according to protocol. She'd planned to put him with the rest, to be picked up by the gravediggers coming in the morning to take them to the incinerator—as was expected of her. But, come closing time, everyone else had left, and Atta *needed* to know more about the inner workings of the John Doe. Her fingers had *itched* with the desperation to investigate.

Thus, she'd snuck him down to her hidden, makeshift laboratory beneath Gallaghers' Morgue which she'd outfitted with discarded tools received from Achilles House as payment, and began her research with exhilaration in her veins.

With his chest cavity open, all had appeared as expected at first glance. Blood blackened by the Plague, organs failed from the infection.

That was when Atta saw it.

The blossom sprouting from his lungs.

Not a phantom or a trick of the lamplight. Not even a

seedling-looking thing one could pass off as an abnormal growth of some sort. No, it was a macabre bloom of foreign flora that had taken root in the man's lung, and flowered.

Rain sluiced down Atta's face, dripping off her lashes. She tore her eyes from the sodden, sewn chest and told herself not to pull that flora from her pocket. Not right now. It was surely already soaked, and she never should have removed it from the body in the first place. Yet, it didn't look anything like the thousands of botanicals she'd studied in her coursebooks or those in her grandfather's journals that she grew up with her nose shoved in.

But what was done was done.

Refusing to look at him any longer, Atta heaved and pulled and pushed until she got the corpse shoved into the boot and shut the lid, hopping to press down on it with all her weight like an overfilled suitcase before it finally clicked closed. Huffing, she slid into the front seat, wondering just how sore she was going to be later.

It took three tries for the car to start.

At least the exertion meant she was no longer cold. Still, Atta flicked the heater to full blast in the hope it would dry out her boots some. It made a horrible hissing sound as if mocking her, and blew out only cold air. Atta slammed her fist down on the dash and the whole of the air system shut off.

"Fecker," she muttered and threw the persnickety car's gear in reverse.

The streets were still dark, but the flickering dash clock read 5:42 and the sky would begin to lighten all too soon. As she drove, Atta pictured the corpse wobbling and twitching in the boot of the car with every bump in the road, but she hadn't a second to spare for thoughts of her blasphemy against the dead. She suppressed a laugh. That ship had long since sailed to the Americas.

Nearing her destination, Atta switched off her lights, pulling onto a short gravel drive concealed by a copse of black alder trees.

The first time she'd made this trip, she'd taken the tooth-leafed trees indigenous to Ireland as a sign of good fortune. As a sign that she'd made the right choice.

This morning, they looked like they were mocking her.

Atta bared her teeth right back at them and pulled her car around the back of Achilles House, with its imposing arches and ribbed vaults. Its rough, uneven stone and mullioned windows.

It was a beautiful building, she couldn't deny that, even if it was unnerving. She slid out of the car, not bothering to close the door, and popped the boot. She'd parked in a way that offered a tidy view of the corpse, and she unwrapped the canvas sheet like she was presenting a gift.

Satisfied, Atta approached the Gothic doorcase that perfectly matched the one facing Merrion Square. Not that she or anyone else ever approached from anywhere other than the concealed back.

Atta banged the open-mawed gargoyle knocker on the thick, polished black wood of the Achilles House door. A long moment passed before she heard the scratchy swivel of a peephole cover sliding against woodgrain. It dropped quickly back into place, and the door creaked open, an increasingly familiar mask coming into view.

They all wore the same plague doctor masks at Achilles House, a clear sign they belonged to one of the secret societies at Trinity, but this anatomist's was a variation of the classic leather beak and goggles. His mask was stitched in red instead of black. Though Atta had seen some stitched in white as well. It was a way of identifying a ranking system, she presumed.

Gilded as he was by the warm light of the House interior, the black blood on the anatomist's leather apron looked thick as pitch. He said nothing, the gaslamps framing the door glinting in his round metal goggles as if he was blinking at Atta behind them. He upturned his chin to reveal a dark throat. "Yes?" His voice was muffled by his mask, but easy enough to make out.

"I've another cadaver for you."

"I'll send someone out." This Red Stitch never minced words. None of them did. "Payment will be your usual rate."

He made to close the door, but Atta reached out and pushed against it to find another Mask had joined them, hovering in the foyer. Atta couldn't tell the colour of this one's stitches, but it wasn't red, black, or white. Curious.

"This Infected is different," she rushed to say. "He showed signs of—" She realised she hadn't the faintest idea how to explain it. "His lungs had a growth. One of botanical origin."

The stoic demeanour of the man behind Red Stitch shifted. An unidentifiable thing in his shoulders—a bit like the first twitch of a spooked horse. His posture corrected, and Atta considered maybe she was just seeing things. He shooed away the Red Stitch and met her in the doorway.

Gold. His mask was stitched with shimmering gold.

"Now that is downright mad," he said, his voice low and menacing, proper and lilting, screaming of old Irish money.

Willing herself not to lash out at the insinuation she'd heard too many times in her twenty-eight years, Atta took a breath before speaking. "I– Sir, I am not *mad*. I know what it is that I saw."

Did she, though? She reached into her sodden coat pocket and felt the flora. It was real.

The pain began in her temple this time, a dull thing, growing sharp fangs, and she dropped the blossom to the recesses of her pocket again.

The Gold Stitch came out onto the steps, closing the door behind him and looking over Atta's shoulder at the corpse in the boot of her car. "Why, pray tell, would you open a cadaver? We cannot provide payment for a desecrated corpse."

Atta's trepidation began to boil into something hotter, volatile. "I've done no such thing. I'm well-versed in postmortem arts and autopsy. It's why I'm able to help you at all." She stood straighter when he looked down his crooked beak mask at her. "I use the very instruments given to me from Achilles House, and I only mean to get to the bottom of the Plague, as you do." She lifted her chin and added, "*Doctor*," for good measure.

The Gold Stitch hissed. "What *instruments* given to you?" His words were thick as sludge and something writhed within them.

"I requested them. Instead of money," Atta explained simply.

"Requested them of whom?"

Not that she knew any of their names or had seen any of their faces, but she knew it was a White Stitch and who knew how many of those there were? Regardless, Atta had no intention of snitching on anyone, but her silence was damning enough. She'd only ever dealt with the same man from tonight and a White Stitch gangly lad.

"I see," the Gold Stitch said slowly when she never responded. "There will be no payment for this cadaver, and you will return all of the instruments in your possession immediately."

Atta's pulse beat quickly in the hollow of her throat, and she fought against the desire to growl the words as she spoke. "With respect, they are mine now. I provided you with corpses, and they were my payment." It had mostly stopped raining, but she knew she still looked like a drowned rat and it wasn't likely to help her case.

The Achilles House doctor took a step closer and Atta clenched her fists at her sides. He towered over her, but if she cowered, she would lose her only access to the tools she needed. It wasn't like her mam was sending autopsy supplies in her care packages or that she could steal them from the morgue where she worked.

Unlike the surplus of unidentified bodies piling up at Gallaghers' Morgue, tools would be quickly identified as missing.

"You will return them, or I will have them confiscated." She had to look up to meet his gaze. "And we wouldn't want the Provost of Trinity to discover what their upstanding student is doing, cutting open bodies illegally. Now would we?"

Atta ground her teeth together. How did he know she was a student? Or was it just a lucky guess? "Why would I care if you speak to the provost, hm?"

He leaned against the doorframe and the lazy mannerism made her hate him even more. "You have textbooks in the front seat of your car." He nodded his mask toward where she'd stupidly left her door ajar, the overhead light illuminating the six textbooks she had stacked there. "You seem a bit *old* for secondary school. Undergrad, even." His head tilted to one side, the movement birdlike and unsettling. "Graduate student, then."

"Just take the body and give me my payment," Atta snapped.

The Gold Stitch turned around and walked inside, slamming the door shut in her face.

Atta snarled at the gargoyle knocker and kicked the gravel, allowing herself a small tantrum. She was halfway to her car when a side door opened and a Black Stitch came out, lugging along a gurney. Unlike the metal and vinyl ones at Gallaghers', the Achilles House mortuary cots were *old*, like they'd been stolen out of an abandoned insane asylum in 1893.

He loaded the body up as Atta watched, and Red Stitch came back out to give her payment. "The crotchety one changed his mind, did he?" The Red Stitch didn't answer her, he merely turned on his heel and walked back inside. It was all over in the span of a couple of moments, and Atta was alone outside in the drizzly cold again.

An uneasy feeling slipped into her veins, thinking of how the gangly White Stitch lad might fare if they put it together that he was the one who usually came out to pay her.

It wasn't her business.

Cold, tired, and annoyed, Atta returned to her car and she flipped open one of her textbooks, hiding the cash inside nestled next to a diagram of the external morphology and internal anatomy of a *Hyacinthus Orientalis,* or Midnight Hyacinth.

"Cash is useful," she told herself as she drove toward campus. It was, of course, but autopsy instruments were necessary for her, too. Familiar friends. The tools she used to conduct her research.

It wasn't as if she'd had her own when she moved from Galway back to Dublin—she'd always simply used the ones in her family's mortuary, and when her father called in a favour and got her the job at Gallaghers' Morgue, she'd begun using theirs.

A few days after moving back to Dublin and starting at Gallaghers', Atta overheard a couple of transport guys talking about an arm of the hush-hush Plague Research epicentre referred to by the public as 'the Society.' According to the transport lads, they'd opened to find a cure and needed more specimens to conduct their research.

Atta saw an opportunity.

The first time the House door opened, and a masked man holding a sternal saw asked, '*How much?*' for a corpse she'd pilfered from the pile of *To Be Burned*, Atta had taken that opportunity just a bit further, striking a deal.

Giving up her tools was going to be painful. She couldn't very well allow herself to be expelled or thrown into prison. She would just have to cope. Save up her meager salary and purchase her own instruments. Stay after hours and borrow the morgue's.

The goal had been to save up for her own place, to live off campus so she didn't have to hope that Siobhan and Seamus Gallagher never ventured into the basement supply closet she used as a makeshift lab. That wouldn't be easy to accomplish while handling her class load, but it was at least a minor possibility while making extra money thieving for Achilles House.

The semester had only been underway for two weeks and Atta was already behind in her studies. Maybe keeping Gold Stitch and his anatomists happy would help her in the long run.

SONDER

A splinter lodged itself beneath his skin as he slunk back from the window. Sonder lifted his plague doctor mask and yanked the damned sliver of wood out with his teeth. Tossing the mask onto the pile of papers atop his desk, he made for the dank corridor, sucking at the little red bead of blood that bloomed on the pad of his finger.

"Gibbs," he said by way of greeting as he strode into his quiet corner of Achilles House. "Did you give someone medical tools as payment for cadavers?"

Bernard Fitzgibbon was kind, with big brown eyes and a mind for statistics and organisation, but he was a sheepish young man and had a habit of making a right bags out of just about everything. It drove Sonder out of his skull. He wanted to throttle sense into the lad.

"Ye'." Gibbs risked a fearful glance at Sonder before returning his attention to his desk, his glasses slipping down his nose where he was hunched over an open ledger. "That pretty, macabre girl? She asked me for them instead of money, and I thought saving the House some cash would be a good thing," he stammered.

Sonder looked over his shoulder out into the hall. There were always rats listening. Reporting back. Maybe if he spoke slowly, the lad would understand. "You know anything at the House must be disposed of properly."

Gibbs finally looked away from his ledger, but he still didn't look him in the eye. Sonder couldn't fathom what in hell he did in those ledgers all day, but it benefited Achilles and its overlords while the rest of the anatomists stayed busy with their hands dirty, so he kept Gibbs around.

Sonder heard the back door finally bang shut and the girl's tyres crunch down the gravel. He crossed the small room to Gibbs, hauling him up by the arm despite his half-hearted protests. "You need to get out of here." Sonder pulled him along, the blood on his leather apron smudging Gibbs's pristine white shirt. "If Walsh opens his mouth about what you did, retribution will be expected."

"I'll leave," Gibbs whispered shakily. "Just please let go, you're getting gore all over me!"

The lad followed him down the front stairs. "I left a perfectly good cadaver to save your sorry arse," Sonder muttered over his shoulder, "so I think you can handle a smudge or two." He made quick work of unlocking the front door and shoved it open onto empty Merrion Street. "Cross the park," he instructed Gibbs, his tone as clipped as his patience. "It'll get you out of sight faster. You were feeling ill and left early today. I haven't seen you since midnight."

Gibbs stepped out onto the footpath, and Sonder yanked him back, grabbing a white-stitched mask off the coat hook and slamming it into his chest. "Put this on, you eejit. It's nearly dawn."

Gibbs did as he was told and started for the park across the way but turned back, fiddling with his glasses underneath the mask to make it fit properly. "Why did you help me? I thought you hated everyone."

Sonder debated telling him the truth of the pain he'd see if someone snitched, but he didn't know Gibbs that well, and he really did make a mess of things. "I do." He clapped him on the shoulder. "But I hate ledgers and don't relish the idea of having to handle them if I sack you. Now fuck off."

He hated that Gibbs had looked so grateful. Too grateful— like nobody'd ever been there for him before, and now he was going to think Sonder would be.

Gibbs managed to get his mask in the proper place and nodded once before bounding across the street and into Merrion Square Park with a gait that led Sonder to believe he'd never taken off at a run in his life. He could just make out Gibbs's shadowed form as he *flopped* over a bed of tulips, and Sonder winced, turning to go back into the House.

"Doctor Murdoch," came Dr Lynch's voice just as Sonder closed the massive oak door. The doctor eyed him keenly, from his soiled apron up to his face and Sonder tried not to clench his jaw. "How is your autopsy going upstairs?"

The bastard investor hardly ever stopped by, and certainly not in the pre-dawn hours of the morning. He'd always hated Finneas Lynch, from the first moment they were shoved into Briseis House together in grad school just like their parents and grandparents before them.

Sonder slid his hands into his pockets. "My current corpse is rather ripe. Too ripe to be of much use." *Here, anyway.*

The doctor's moustache twitched, but he nodded. "Anything of note?"

Plenty. "Not a thing," he lied smoothly. "This Infected appears exactly like the last dozen corpses I've studied."

"Take heart, Murdoch!" Lynch said it so forcefully that Sonder found himself grinding his molars together despite his efforts. "You will find answers soon." The heels of his shoes scuffed across the floorboards as he walked away, calling over his shoulder, "The Plague cannot win forever!"

No, not if Sonder Murdoch had anything to say about it. He wanted that fresh cadaver, though. The one that had the girl spooked. The one she'd, intriguingly enough, cut into herself.

"Doctor," he called back, and the man paused, already halfway to whichever rat he was collecting information from this time. "Don't distract my anatomists, hm? They're busy." And they didn't need Agamemnon Society's fucking lackey weasling around.

"Yes, yes." Lynch waved a hand dismissively. "In and out, mate."

Sonder flipped his middle finger at the bastard's back.

Taking the steps two at a time, he reached the landing and rubbed his hands together like a bonafide mad scientist, a blasphemous grin plastered to his face. Standing over the flayed corpse on his examination table, he couldn't help the staccato of his heartbeat. How could he react any other way when there were *vines* wrapped around the man's spine? *Vines.* Clawing their way up toward his heart—one even reaching for it. As if it was almost, *almost* there before the man died.

"You're coming home with me tonight, it would seem, my friend."

Still, as he prepared his corpse for the trek to Murdoch

Manor, he couldn't help the niggling feeling at the back of his skull about the body the girl brought in. Cursing his curiosity and impatience to wait until after a solid night's sleep, he left his corner of Achilles House behind and crept down to the chill chamber. It had been a good half hour since the girl dropped the cadaver off. Certainly, Walsh in Records would have catalogued the newest body by now, and probably already left for home, with any luck.

Sure enough, the body was in the closest chill drawer, front and centre. Sonder was surprised to see he'd not been cut into as haphazardly as he'd thought. The fresh autopsy incision certainly hadn't been done with the precision of anyone in Achilles, but it wasn't a complete hack job. The stitches, however, were bordering on archaic. A rushed endeavour.

Sonder moved around the body, taking mental notes of everything he could, pausing at the toe tag Walsh had written so recently that the ink was still damp.

John Doe #452, shows signs of Stage 3 Infection

A low whistle built within Sonder until he let it out. *Stage 3.* That meant another Infected with signs of flora.

A smile crawled across his face so wicked that his mam would turn over in her grave.

ATTA

The dash clock blinked 7:06 and Atta swore, whipping her car into the farthest spot from her dorm. If she hurried, she'd have just enough time to shower, change, and make it to her 8:00 Biodiversity lecture. Provided Imogen or Colin wasn't hogging the bathroom. Or one of the degenerates they dragged home. There were no sounds of running water coming from the bathroom when she passed by, so things were looking up.

Atta tossed her bag onto her bed and gently extracted the flora she'd plucked from the cadaver's lung. Unwilling to repeat her earlier reaction to it, she left the blossom wrapped in wax paper and tucked it away in her desk drawer to inspect later. She grabbed her robe and rushed for the bathroom before one of her roommates could sneak in.

Rather than stripping down, Atta decided to hop in the shower fully clothed and let the hot water wash most of the mud and guck down the drain. It was a heavenly sort of hot burn after the drenching of cold rain. Summer hadn't fully gone, but it was certainly well on its way out.

Atta wrapped the sopping clothes in a towel and shoved them under a cabinet to retrieve later when no one was home. She'd just returned to the shower and was washing her hair when the bathroom door opened wide, bringing with it the sounds of humming and snatching all the warmth from the steam.

"Christ sake," Atta bit out. "I'm in the shower."

"Just me," Imogen's voice sang.

Atta scrubbed shampoo into her long, chestnut locks, attempting to keep her irritation at bay. "You're up early," she commented rather stupidly. On principle, Imogen didn't rise before 10 a.m. and probably hadn't had a class before 11 a.m. since she was able to choose her own schedule.

"Up late." Imogen's words were a tad slurred. Probably had been since late last night.

"Ah."

Atta could tell by the lack of sink and drawer commotion that Imogen was likely undressing. Or taking a piss. She sighed. Having roommates wasn't her cup of tea. Granted, between undergrad and moving back home, she'd never lived alone before, but she didn't need to experience it to know it was preferable to sharing a bathroom.

A cold burst of air made her squeal as the shower curtain was yanked back. "Imogen!"

"Can you see this?" She ignored Atta's protests, pointing to a very visible lip-shaped spot on her neck that was mottled purple.

"Clear as day." Atta shut the shower curtain and huddled under the hot water, but not before she'd noticed what her roommate was wearing. "You really shouldn't be going to parties, Imogen."

"Blah, blah. There aren't any restrictions against *parties*."

Atta turned off the water and grabbed her towel, wrapping it around her body and stepping out onto the plush bath mat she purchased herself after one of Colin's buddies puked on the old one. She often asked herself why her roommates were pursuing a postgraduate degree at all.

Colin, she surmised, was trying to get back into his father's good graces—and bank account. Imogen, she wasn't sure about. Scared of going out into the real world, maybe.

Atta had been outside the collegiate bubble for six years after undergrad and could confirm it was not all it was cracked up to be, Plague or not.

Imogen was studying the hickey in her reflection. "Could I borrow one of your frumpy turtlenecks to cover this?" She looked at Atta in the mirror, golden hair still perfect but her makeup clearly in disarray after a night of doing things Atta didn't care to consider.

"My turtlenecks are not frumpy."

"Em, okay," Imogen snorted.

Atta let it go, pushing at the more serious matter Imogen had skated right past. "There may not be any *rules* against gatherings, but it's still unwise to spend your time out at night with loads of people until we understand more about the Plague."

"You're such a buzzkill. They say that's not even how it spreads." Imogen rolled her eyes and began removing her shirt with enough difficulty that it was clear she was still sloshed.

She wasn't wrong, though. The Health Protection Surveillance Centre had deployed several arms of their organisation, such as Achilles House, to study the Plague after the first patient succumbed to the strange disease. Many of those arms of the HPSC are quiet shadow organisations the general populace knows nothing about—it's a wonder Atta even heard about Achilles House at all—but all findings are reported to HPSC. Though they have certain precautions advised in Dublin, they have made it clear the Plague does not pass to individuals as a communicable disease does.

In the last six years, that's about all the HPSC has announced.

If they discovered the flora, she suspected that could all change very soon.

"Imogen," Atta pressed, looking away from her roommate's bare breasts in the mirror. "This Plague is only going to get worse. You can't just keep putting all of us at risk. No, it doesn't spread like a virus, but it's too much of a risk to be swapping bodily fluids with people and coming home to drink out of the milk carton." Atta *loathed* that Imogen did that, like a child.

She wrinkled her nose at Atta in the mirror. "How do you know it's going to get worse?"

Atta thought of the foreign flora hidden away in her desk drawer, a melody singing in her blood, calling her to study it with her lenses. "Just stop going to parties all the time. You're here to learn, anyway."

Imogen groaned and turned around to face her, where she was dripping on the mat. "Were you more fun in undergrad? When you were young?" She made one of those idiotic faces reserved for D4 girls and girls drunk on Daddy's money. Which was amusing because Imogen only pretended to be either one of those things. Sometimes both.

"Oh, look," Atta droned, "you made it nearly twenty-four hours without referring to my elderly age."

Imogen giggled, and Atta left before she had to watch her roommate undress any more than she already had.

At least she hadn't been forced to share a room with anyone since her second year. Even still, she'd learned the hard way to take the extra second and spin the lock on the knob. The first night the three of them had spent in the suite, Colin came home from some *Welcome Back* party and walked in on Atta changing. She still wasn't quite sure if he'd been that hammered, thought it was his room, or assumed he could fall back on either of those as an excuse if need be. Atta, in nothing but a bra and black stockings—ironically her current state of dress again—had kneed Colin in the groin and toppled him howling into the hall. The lock became her new best friend and Colin had just started speaking to her again a week ago. Not that he provided her with any titillating conversation she'd been missing out on.

Her insolent roommates were worth the headache in regards to the view living with them afforded her. Slipping on a brown and taupe plaid skirt, Atta fastened the tortoise buttons as she looked past the trees toward Front Square, with its Gothic stone buildings and proud bell tower. She remembered walking through the arch of Campanile ceremoniously upon her first graduation from Trinity in 1987, her father's bright smile and the click and whir of her mother's camera.

That was before her father's accident. Before the Plague. Before they needed her back in Galway.

Atta shook her thoughts loose and dropped her attention from the view beyond down to the half-written essay on her desk and several crumpled attempts at a re-write. She didn't have to think about that until after classes and her shift at Gallaghers'. The essay wasn't going well, but she'd compiled a lovely botanical journal in the process, and ran her fingers fondly over a purple blossom pressed flat and forever beautifully dead in wax paper, a scrawled description below it.

Bottom lip tucked between her teeth, Atta opened her desk drawer and pulled out the flora coated in black, diseased blood. Gingerly, she pulled back the top layer of wax paper irrevocably smudged and wondered if she had time to clean up the flower and press it. A quick glance at her antique desk clock pushed that idea away. Regretfully, she returned the flora to its hiding place for later.

Blowing a breath past her lips, Atta slipped on her softest black turtleneck, her favourite tweed blazer and comfiest pair of black Oxfords. She buckled the thin band of her watch, refusing to look at the time again because she knew it wasn't enough. A quick run of a brush through her still-damp locks was going to have to suffice. It was still drizzling out, anyway.

Books shoved into her leather satchel, Atta snagged Imogen's umbrella from the coat rack by the suite's front door and rushed down the stairs of their building, waving *hullo* to one of the neighbours on her way out.

ATTA

S tudents milled about campus, walking to their various lectures and activities, still buzzing with the excitement of a new year at Trinity or the start of adult academic life at all. It was always easy to spot the Freshers. They spent the first term oscillating between pure joy, hugging their books to their chest with a skip in their step, and twitchy exhaustion, bookbags weighing down their shoulders, a wild-eyed caffeine buzz coating them like a dark aura.

A lone brown leaf crunched under Atta's shoe and she smiled. The trees hadn't yet changed, still hanging onto the last breath of summer, but the air was crisp and the drizzle had gone for the time being. She was one of those peculiar students who felt the thrill of academia every year, all year long. The last six years without hallowed academic halls and papers to write and books to study, she'd felt adrift. That didn't mean she hadn't still written papers, and conducted her own research, and read countless books, but it was different to be surrounded by a place, by a people group dedicated to the pursuit of knowledge, especially in a time such as theirs.

When Atta attended Trinity for undergrad, the Plague was but a distant scare. A sickness violently befalling a few select individuals here and there. Partway through the summer after her graduation, so many cases had popped up that the powers that be erected HPSC's secret places of science, medicine, immunology, and research. Very little was known about this organisation and its advancements in dispelling the Plague had been minimal.

Atta was not one to accept when things were on a '*need to know*' basis, so she'd spent a great deal of time in the fall of '87 researching the researchers. She wasn't able to discover the name of the shadow organisation, only the fact that they knew very little about the origin of the Plague. What they *had* discovered was a peculiar spore had been found in Patient Zero during the initial autopsy prior to incineration.

A spore of unknown origin.

A spore that sent Atta into a six-year-long obsession.

She did not for one moment believe the spore was bacterial. Nor did she think for one moment that Achilles House didn't already know that. They had to, or she'd made a grave error in taking that cadaver with the flowering lung to them.

Another student brushed past her, knocking into her shoulder without a backward glance. She was loitering in front of the lecture hall doorway after all, with only seconds left until class began.

The pain began at the base of her skull, pulsing up and forward, sliding down over her eyes in a ghastly hallucination. A young woman reclined in a cracked vinyl chair, like the kind in an old 50s-style kitchen. A small television, antennas erect, glowed with static snow. The walls were bare behind the girl, save for a slash of creeping vines. Something between

Acanthus Spinosus and English Ivy. The hallucination wrinkled and shifted, and Atta saw the vines crawling down the girl, her hands limp at her sides, nailbeds bruised. No, the vines weren't crawling along her—they were *part* of her, making up her spine, her head pulled off her neck and held aloft by the vines, her lifeless, glossy eyes open.

Atta gasped, and the images cleared, the sharp pain receding to her temples. It would be a nasty migraine, she expected. She should have gotten more sleep. Grabbed coffee. Stolen one of Imogen's stimulant pills.

Shaking it off, Atta bustled in and slid into one of the last seats available in the back, the worn wooden desk and chair combination groaning as she did so. She always wondered just how many students had learned at these desks over the years. If the right information was sought out—the year these particular desks were brought in and how many students had taken the classes in this hall—she could arrive at an answer, but there were more important things to think about. Namely, the professor at the chalkboard addressing the small group of students and directing them to open their Biodiversity textbooks to Page 394.

Removing her notebooks, pens, and textbook from her satchel, Atta laid them out neatly as the professor began etching out the various parts of a vascular plant on the chalkboard. The diagram on Page 394 of the textbook had a similar sketch, though more refined and really quite beautiful. Beside the fern, the professor jotted down terms, his chalk tapping against the blackboard with each new letter stroke and kicking up enough chalk dust that a girl in the front row sneezed. When the professor turned back to face the rows of

students, Atta began to scribble down what he'd written before
he commanded they all do so.

Xylem

Phloem

Sporophyte

The rest of the class had their heads bent low over their
notebooks, scribbling furiously as the professor droned on and
on about the defining characteristics of vascular plants, their
tissues and phases, but Atta merely listened, letting the lecture
confirm what she'd already known since she was a little girl.
Since her grandfather began teaching her the intricacies of
botany when he wasn't teaching her how to autopsy a body.

By the time class let out, Atta had already drawn her own
sketch within the textbook and a two-page spread in her
notebook just above the assignment: *a 3,000-word essay on
Vascular Phases due September 12th.*

At least one of her classes was a breeze. Though Intro to
Biodiversity was a beginner's course, her undergrad studies had
been vastly different. To pursue her Masters in Biodiversity, she
was required to have the basic courses on her transcript, and
Atta didn't mind having a refresher that directly correlated with
her personal projects. Not that she had much time for those.

Back out on the green, she checked her watch. Her next
class wasn't until 2:00, and she might have enough time to grab
a bite to eat before heading to the library. She had two
assignments due by week's end and one of them was going
quite poorly if her desk in the suite was to be used as evidence.

Though the Dining Hall was an 18th-century stone building
one would expect to see Mr Darcy lurking in while Lizzie
dances, only lunch was served there, and Atta arrived at the

technical time for Second Breakfast and not quite Elevensies and certainly not Luncheon.

Electing to go into The Buttery, Atta filled a cafeteria-grade bowl with the crushed remnants of Banana Bubbles Cereal and poured in a bit of milk that was probably borderline expired. She sat down at the edge of one of the long tables, only a handful of other students milling about. Something smelled delicious next door and she wished she'd gone to the library then gone into the Dining Hall for lunch instead. After stirring her unwanted cereal for a minute, she decided to just discard it and check her letterbox. It was rare to find anything in there after the first week of classes, what with all the *Welcome Back!* news and flyers asking students to join various clubs, so she only checked it every couple of days. During undergrad, her mother sent care packages monthly and Atta was feeling a bit homesick, finding herself hoping her mam would continue that tradition through grad school.

Alas, there was only a flyer for a student play being put on in a couple of weeks and a red envelope. Curious, she ripped it open to find it was a summons to see her student advisor, Mrs O'Sullivan, as soon as possible.

Atta sighed, folding the flyer and note to stow them away in her satchel. So much for her much-needed study time in the library.

Mrs O'Sullivan's office was a long walk across campus on the opposite side from the Botany building. The weather was shaping up beautifully, though, a crisp breeze teasing at her hair. Atta slipped on her headphones and clicked play on her Stowaway. The mix-tape of her own making made the walk even more pleasant, the notes of Chopin's Nocturne Op. 27, No. 2 putting her mind in the perfect place to contemplate her private research. She would go to meet with her advisor and take notes in her 2:00 lecture until her hand hurt, then she could check on her cadaver beneath Gallaghers' Morgue in between her shift duties.

Atta was almost at the student offices building when she first noticed the new signage.

Be Vigilant. Inform HPSC of any Plague symptoms immediately, by phoning the hotline.

Atta shook her head. It would help if they knew what those symptoms *were* before it was too late.

In the early days of the Plague, the whole of Dublin entered a dangerous Group Think somewhere along the treacherous lines of: It could never happen to me. And, in their defence, it hadn't happened to most. But who it did happen to was usually unexpected and wholly unpredictable. The sickness did not breed in lower-income areas, it didn't happen to those who were in close contact with the Infected, and it didn't always happen to those in pre-existing poor health. It was an enigma. A curious, confounding disease that began with an unidentified spore in Patient Zero and spread how it saw fit, making the Infected first mildly ill, then quickly fading into organ failure and eventually death, their teeth coated in the black blood and bile they coughed up.

The spore.

The black blood.

Those were the things Atta zeroed in on.

"Morning!" Atta was greeted by a cheery woman behind the front desk as she entered the Admissions Office in House 5. "Where can I direct you?"

"Mrs O'Sullivan's office, please."

"Sure thing, love. Name?"

"Atta—" She caught herself. "Sorry, habit. Ariatne Morrow. Grad student, Botany."

The bubbly brunette picked up the receiver of her phone while Atta turned to look out the windows, studying the students as they walked by down below, Campanile standing sentry and HPSC notices in their hands.

If Achilles House or *someone* could discover what all the Infected had in common, it would make things much clearer. Atta thought the notices from HPSC were most likely bogus, created to lull the general populace into thinking they were accomplishing something with their research. In turn, if that was the case, it meant they'd actually accomplished nothing.

The thought was depressing.

"Miss Morrow?"

Atta turned to face the desk clerk.

"Mrs O'Sullivan will see you. Third door on the right."

She found it easily enough having been there before, and went in the open door, preparing herself mentally for the number of cat figurines crowding the small office.

"Hello there," her kind, lovely and round advisor greeted her. "Have a seat Ariatne." Mrs O'Sullivan smiled, gesturing to the only other chair in the cramped office.

"Oh, it's Atta," she corrected, avoiding eye contact with the creepy cats. Atta loved cats as much as the next reclusive, bookish girl, but she drew the line at figurines.

Dropping her bag to the floor, she took a seat on the upholstery that hadn't been updated since at least the early 70's. It was a horrid shade of pink, situated across from a porcelain cat statue posed mid-paw cleaning.

"No one calls me Ariatne except for my gran, and that's only because I was named after her."

The advisor opened a file in front of her with Atta's Christian name stamped on it in ink slightly smudged on the *w* of Morrow. "See now, I thought you were named after Agatha Christie's heroine."

"Ah, nope. That is spelled with a *d*, not a *t*. But if you ask my gran, she'll tell you Ariadne Oliver was named after her."

Mrs O'Sullivan chuckled. "Your gran sounds like a delight."

"She is." Atta fiddled with her thumbnail. "Em." She cleared her throat and sat straighter. "I'm sorry, but I'm not sure what I'm doing here."

"At Trinity?" Mrs O'Sullivan's brows met in the middle over her red cat-eye glasses. Atta was wildly out of fashion herself, but she was certain those glasses had been purchased in the same year as the chair she was sitting on.

"No, in your office."

"Oh!" The advisor bopped and bobbled in her seat. "Right. Well, dear." Fitting her fingers together, she set her hands on Atta's file and looked at her with what had to be pity. "I'm afraid it isn't good news."

A thousand thoughts assaulted Atta. Her father had another accident. Her mother was dead. The Plague was shutting down Trinity—

"The majority of your funding was not approved."

Atta uncrossed her legs and sat forward. "What?"

Mrs O'Sullivan lifted a hand placatingly. "Not all of it, but the larger portions we were hoping for were denied. The grants and scholarships."

"I— I don't understand." Her voice was breathy, like a laugh, the hysterical kind that follows horrific news because the brain shuts down and leaves only mania. "I received near-perfect grades in undergrad."

"Yes, Ariatne—"

"*Atta*," she snapped. "Please."

"Right, yes. Of course. *Atta*. Your grades were outstanding, but that was six years ago."

"So?" *Fuck*, she was being rude. "Sorry." She squirmed in her seat. "I'm sorry. I just don't understand."

The look she received was even more pitiful than before. "There are a lot of young people vying for that money, Atta. What have you been doing for the last six years? Your paperwork says you've been working in a morgue and that you have the same position here in Dublin.

"It— It's the family business," she stammered, feeling light-headed.

"Right, okay. But it has nothing to do with your undergrad degree or your master's program." She looked down at the file on her desk and back at Atta over her glasses. "It says here your undergrad degree was in Folklore with a Religion component?"

Atta's mouth was too dry to speak, but she managed a small nod.

"That makes your pursuit of postgraduate studies in botany seem more recreational than vocational. Do you understand?"

Atta *understood* that she'd like to punch Mrs O'Sullivan in her ruddy throat.

"The point is, it doesn't look good to the powers that be. You have been denied."

"Is it hot in here?" Atta pulled at the collar of her turtleneck, looking around—for what, she wasn't sure. A window to throw herself out of?

Mrs O'Sullivan rose and poured a glass of water from a pitcher in the corner decorated with little black cats, sliding it across her desk to Atta. "We have a couple of options."

"Oh?" Atta held the glass just to feel the coolness against her palms.

"You could always see about taking out a loan."

A snort escaped before Atta could stop it, a dribble of the water sloshing out onto her tights and seeping through to her leg. "I don't make enough money to qualify for something like that."

"What about your parents, then? Perhaps they could help out. They're business owners, yes?"

Atta blinked at the well-meaning woman who clearly grew up without these types of problems. Without having to pray for ends to meet or wondering where the next meal might come from. "There isn't a lot of money in caring for the dead." She looked down into the water, watching the ripples keep time with the pulse in her hands. "You're thinking of funeral homes." —that rip off the bereaved for their own benefit. Thankfully, Atta kept that last part to herself.

"I see." Mrs O'Sullivan's pink lips pursed together in thought. "There is one more option." Atta brightened and Mrs O'Sullivan held out her palms. "Classes have already been in session for a couple of weeks, so I don't think it will be possible, but we can see."

"Anything. I'll do anything to stay here." To stay in a place of knowledge and books and information. Where her inquisitive research can delve deeper.

Mrs O'Sullivan sighed. "We do have jobs on campus."

"But I already have a job." One she couldn't give up. It

would defeat the entire purpose of what she was after. Or, at least, cut off her access to what she needed.

"And does it make you enough to pay tuition?" Mrs O'Sullivan had lost her benevolent constitution.

"No. You're right. Go on, please."

"There are Teacher Assistant positions that offer a significant tuition discount in lieu of payment, as well as boarding and three hot, three cold meals a week available at The Dining Hall or The Buttery."

Atta's heart rate began to slow. She didn't know how she could swing a full course load and two jobs, but she would figure it out. There was still hope.

"It won't cover everything, but it's a massive start."

"Yes. Of course." Atta scooted to the edge of her seat. "I'll do it."

"I don't know that there are positions available, but you paid some upfront to be enrolled"—she checked her records for the amount Atta already knew, her entire savings—"and that covers you for a couple of weeks." Mrs O'Sullivan looked at Atta solemnly. "Go to the rest of your classes today and I will see what I can do."

Numbly, Atta left House 5 and walked back across campus in a daze. If she kept her job at the morgue and pilfered bodies for Achilles when she could, it might be enough to cover what the TA position couldn't.

If Mrs O'Sullivan even managed to find her a TA job at all.

SONDER

"Why is the tongue removed during an autopsy?" Sonder slid one hand into the pocket of his trousers, waiting for the 'best and brightest' of his students to answer.

Predictably, it was the brown noser always up his arse at Achilles and now in class, Tom Walsh, who spoke first. "In order to examine the oral cavity thoroughly."

Walsh was the only student who didn't cower in Sonder's presence. The lad was annoying for it, but he certainly studied the material.

"Correct. Once the tongue is removed to better access the oral cavity, what should be done next?" Walsh had a bright-eyed, bushy-tailed look about him and opened his mouth, but Sonder frowned, speaking before the lad could. "Anyone else?"

Classes had only been in session for a fortnight, but Sonder was already itching to be through with lectures and onto the more hands-on portion of his teaching.

"Document?" a quiet girl in the front row suggested timidly.

The classes at Trinity were small. It was a better way to teach, certainly, but it always meant the students were so *near* to his person. He wished this mousey one with the sweetheart face and doe-eyes would sit in the back row. She was clearly terrified of him. He wondered how she'd ended up in his course in the first place, and predicted she would be the first to vomit when they moved on to real cadavers.

His fingers twitched, wanting nothing more than to get classes over with and head back to Achilles House. To the body waiting for him. *Stage 3 Infected.* A thrill shot up his spine. He was so close. If only he could encourage the infection, coax it into Stage 4 somehow—

"Note any abnormalities," another student's voice broke into his thoughts.

"Correct. And?" Sonder looked over the faces, not registering any of them.

"Take tissue samples for further analysis." *Fucking Walsh.*

"Good." Sonder strode to his desk and put on his wire-framed glasses, looking down at his notes nearly lost in the disarray. "Read chapters 7-10 and have a 4,000-word essay on my desk by Tuesday."

The entire class groaned, but he didn't care. Easy work meant weak minds, and he didn't teach imbeciles.

Which reminded him he needed to check in on the mess Gibbs had made—ensure the instruments were properly returned by the cadaver girl.

"All right, fuck off then." He made a shooing motion and dropped his glasses onto the mess of papers, shucking his tweed jacket and rolling the sleeves of his shirt up his forearms.

As soon as they'd all filed out grumbling, Sonder strode

through the glorious, mystical corridors of the Medical Building toward the teachers' room. Met with the scent of burnt coffee, he picked up a stale doughnut and considered powering through the disgusting taste of it, but reconsidered the desecration of his palate and threw it in the rubbish bin since he'd already touched it. One didn't cut open the number of bodies he had without being forever altered by the disturbing transference of bacteria.

At least he was alone in the room.

Sonder was pouring the sludge some intern or TA had made hours prior into a loathsome paper coffee cup when he heard the irritating click-clack of high heels on the floor out in the hall. Sure enough, the sound came closer until the intruder was upon him.

"There you are!" He turned to find Mariana O'Sullivan in the doorway, her ample chest heaving.

"Walking around campus might be easier if you didn't wear those." Sonder pointed one finger at her gaudy pink heels, the others wrapped around his coffee cup that he took a sip from and immediately regretted the act.

"You're delightful, Professor Murdoch." Mariana pursed her lips at him. "I've been looking for you because I have a proposition."

"Ah, Mariana. I'm not going to sleep with you. I've told you a thousand times."

"Would you shut up and sit down?" She said the words sharply, but she did blush. At least Mariana wasn't afraid of him. She had been his student advisor when he was after his PhD, just a young pup herself back then, one of the only people still in his life who'd truly known him *before*.

Irritably, he did as she asked and dropped into one of the leather armchairs by the hearth, crossing one long leg over the other. "Can we make this quick?"

"You know," Mariana plopped into the chair across from him, "you're too old for this insolent behaviour. Christ, you're a grown man, Sonder." She leaned forward and inspected his chin. "You've even got grey hairs there in your stubble."

"Mariana," he warned through his teeth.

"I'm only saying you could do with some cheer. Your students think you're The Dullahan."

Sonder snorted. "I might, on occasion, remove other people's heads for scientific purposes, but I do not remove my own." He took a sip of the bitter coffee and made a face, discarding the cup on the side table. No self-respecting man should use a *paper* cup. "Besides, carrying my own head around with me would be a hassle, and the last time I rode a horse was as a child."

Mariana sighed through her nose and he just noticed a file in her hands. "What's that?" He gestured toward it, already regretting sitting down with her.

She laid it flat on her lap all squeezed up tight in her pencil skirt and rested a hand on it, her wedding band glinting in the firelight. "This is the file for a student I think should be your assistant."

She'd shocked him, he'd grant her that. "I think you have me confused with someone else."

"Just listen—"

"I don't need a TA."

"She's a grad student, not in the medical college, but she's truly a gifted mind—"

Sonder stood abruptly. "Fuck's sake, Mariana. Why would I

want a TA that isn't even in my area of academic expertise?" He turned, his back to the fire. "Has she ever even taken any of my classes?"

Mariana squirmed and he knew the answer. "No, but she is well-versed in postmortem sciences."

Sonder arched an eyebrow. "What *is* her area of study, then?"

"Botany."

Sonder barked a laugh, and Mariana grimaced. "You're joking."

"I'm not. She is a gifted young woman. Ariatne Morrow is her name." She tossed the file on the side table near Sonder's discarded coffee. "Have a look. She was raised in a mortuary her parents own and has worked there full-time for the past six years, after undergrad."

Sonder squinted at the closed file, then back at Mariana. The student was a bit older than most, at least. "I don't need any assistance."

Mariana tilted her head to one side. "Just let the girl make your copies and bring you coffee. Then, she gets the tuition she needs, and you can do some good."

Sonder glared at her.

"She even works at a morgue here in Dublin now to offset her expenses."

Now that was intriguing. . . He tried to keep his features even, but judging by Mariana's wobbly expression, he assumed she was becoming borderline scared of him like everyone else. "A botanist with a background in postmortem sciences."

Mariana gave a terse nod, her hands folded together in her lap.

Sonder turned from her to face the fire, one hand on the

mantle, and a thought struck him. He spun slowly back to face Mariana. "You know, Mrs O'Sullivan, I think we can work something out."

She beamed at him. "Wonderful!"

An Old Irish Poem

It is said they are but lore.
It is said they are but demons.

This is but a plague.

Wayward spirits.
Ghosts.
Spectres.
Ghouls.

The truth beckons

Tick flick tick
The clock keeps time with the candle
Until they all get sick

Wax slides down the gilded stick
And the Fae invade with bramble

ATTA

Most people don't realise how hard it is to close a dead person's eyelids. It's not like in films. They often spring back open.

Closing the eyelids of an Infected is even more disconcerting.

Atta hadn't squirmed away from a corpse since she was a child—she knew the spirit was gone and the body was just the coat left behind—but there was always something mystifying about the Infected. Almost like there was something *other* left behind. Something alive, but inhuman. She knew in her heart of hearts it had to be related to the flora.

After finishing bagging and tagging for the day, all she had to do was document the necessary details for the Identified—both naturally occurring deaths and the Infected—and then double-check the list of *TBBs*. It was a shorter list of bodies to be burned than usual, which was a good thing in the grand scheme of things, but it meant there were only a couple of Unidentified Infected and Atta *really* needed one to take to Achilles House after last night's debacle.

It was possible she could take the one she had down in the basement, but it had been out of the chill room for hours already. It wouldn't be a viable option. In fact, she needed to hurry with her duties because the corpse could very well turn by the time Siobhan and Seamus left for the night.

As quickly as she could accurately manage, Atta finished her duties. At the last second, she decided to document both Unidentified Infected. It was too risky to take one of only two.

Peeking out into the corridor, she heard Seamus's bone saw in the autopsy room down the way and Siobhan's voice echoing from the front as she spoke with someone. A widower perhaps, or a lawyer. She couldn't quite tell.

Cautiously, Atta tiptoed toward the back and took the steps down to the cellar in twos, nearly tripping and breaking her neck.

"Hello, you," she murmured to the cadaver awaiting her in the supply closet-turned-laboratory.

She'd chosen this one for herself because of his eyes. The veins in them had gone grey, and it intrigued her. It was something she hadn't noticed in another Infected before.

Atta flicked on her overhead light, the hum of the fluorescent bulb filling the small space, then slipped on her head light. It was an ugly thing, but how else was she to see in such a dank space?

The body, prostrate before her, looked innocuous upon first inspection with its chalky pallor and vacant eyes. But she knew underneath the flesh, there would be more signs of decay from the Plague. She lifted her scalpel and set it just below the clavicle, slicing to the man's sternum, a thin incision immediately tracing her movement. Atta paused, leaning in closer. . .

There was something on his neck.

"My god," she breathed.

His veins had gone black, just a little, spidering out near his jugular, like fungal mycelium. It made sense that the veins would appear black considering the blood darkened, but she'd never seen it visible through the skin before. In fact, the skin was almost translucent in some areas.

Her heart pounded with the idea that she was on the cusp of a major discovery. She moved the scalpel to the other shoulder, slicing toward the first incision, then sliced with careful precision, dragging the blade down toward the pelvis.

"Atta!" Siobhan's voice echoed down to the cellar and Atta's scalpel slipped. "Are you down there, hun?"

"Yep!" Atta skittered out of her hideout like a frightened arachnid. "I'm here!"

"Phone for you! I think it's that twat you live with."

Atta coughed a laugh. Perhaps she'd been a bit too open with her employers. She wiped the black blood off her hands as best she could, but it was caked under her nails. Not wearing gloves was foolish, but there hadn't been any cases of transference from an Infected corpse to a live host a couple of days after death, so she wasn't worried about that. However, she should probably be more concerned with the cleanliness aspect or—possibly—the illegal dealings she was hiding under her employers' morgue.

Sometimes the lines of laws and normality needed to be smudged a little—with black blood, evidently.

"Hello?" she breathed into the telephone when she made it upstairs. "Imogen?"

"Colin."

Atta tucked her lips between her teeth. So *Colin* was the twat. "Hey."

"You got a call from your advisor. She said it was important."

"Yeah, thanks, Colin. What's the number?"

"You got paper? I don't have all day."

"You're a real ray of sunshine, you know that?"

"Fuck off."

"Wait. Yes, I have paper." She did not.

Colin rattled off the number one time, and the phone clicked. Thank goodness Atta had a decent memory. She glanced at the clock. 4:55. The offices would close any minute.

Atta dialled the number quickly and set to picking the dried blood from under her fingernails.

"Trinity Student Offices," a chipper voice came over the line.

"Yes, this is Atta Morrow for Mrs O'Sullivan."

"Hold please."

Atta tapped her foot against the linoleum and twirled the curly phone cord with her finger. Siobhan came up behind her, speaking loudly at first, then lowering her voice when she saw the phone sandwiched between Atta's shoulder and ear. "We're headed out, hun. Lock up after the *TBB* van?"

Atta nodded and wished her employers a good evening.

"Atta!" Mrs O'Sullivan's voice came over the phone cheerfully and Atta stood up straight. "Have I got good news for you."

The advisor rushed through the name of a professor, a classroom, a building, and a time, and instructed Atta to come by her office again in a couple of days to get the keys to her new place.

"TAs all cohabitate in their respective college's House, near the professor's office. It helps with late-night grading and things of the sort."

A vague map of campus etched itself in Atta's mind and she tried in vain to calculate how having all of her classes in the Botany building was going to work with living and working around the Medical College's buildings. Maybe she was mistaken about the location.

"Professor Murdoch doesn't often stay on campus late, so you won't likely need to be close by, but the lodging included with the position is only in the TA Houses. Yours is called Briseis House." She rattled off another building and location and Atta looked around frantically for a pen and paper, momentarily distracted by the interesting name of her new student accommodations.

It was what she got for being an arse and lying to Colin about having a pen handy.

"Thank you, Mrs O'Sullivan. I don't know how to repay you."

"Just keep your grades up and don't let Murdoch scare you off."

Scare her off? A horn blared out the back door and Atta jumped. "Yes, of course, Mrs O'Sullivan." She looked over her shoulder at the door. "I have to be going now."

"See you, dear."

Atta hung up the receiver just as a meaty fist banged on the back door, rattling it on its hinges. "Bring out ya' dead! Bring out ya' dead!" The voice outside was muffled, but he used the same crass joke every night and every night it made Atta laugh. *Monty Python* had been a favourite film of hers growing up.

"You'd think that would get old," she said to Carl by way of greeting and the big oaf grinned.

"Nah." He lumbered in past her, looking at the body count list she handed him. "Whatcha got for me? Only two *TBB*s tonight?"

Atta nodded, already wheeling one toward him.

"Think the Plague is lettin' up then?"

"I don't think so, Carl." She said the words gently. Carl had lost his sister to the Plague a couple of years prior, and it was why he began working for the service that incinerates the bodies in the first place. He'd told Atta his life's story her first shift at Gallaghers' before term began. He was a sweet guy and she didn't want to upset him, but saw no point in lying to him, either. Lies were a rare currency meant for the Garda and politicians and pricks like Colin to keep them out of your business—but you had to know how to wield them. That's what her gran taught her, anyway.

"Well, fuck me into next week." Good ol' Carl. He wheeled the first body out to his transport van while Atta wheeled the second out behind him.

As soon as Carl's taillights faded into the fog around the dark street corner, Atta locked up Gallaghers' tight like a fort and crept back downstairs to her John Doe.

Scalpel in hand, she completed her incision from earlier, but as she reached for her rib cutter, she realised two discomfiting things. She didn't have a body for Achilles. And she needed to return the very cutter in her hands.

It was likely she wouldn't receive much payment for the cadaver as it was since she'd sliced the man open and he was rather ripe already.

At least she had a gurney available this time.

Sadder than was warranted or sane, Atta checked the perimeter of the morgue and wheeled the body and her medical bag of precious tools out to the boot of her car.

SONDER

T he ice clinked in his glass as Sonder took another sip of whiskey, draining it. He sat on the edge of his desk and unbuttoned the collar of his black shirt—it was bloody anyway. The manila folder on his desk stamped with ARIATNE MORROW glared up at him. He'd yet to open it and debated doing so, but the whole thing rather annoyed him.

Reluctantly, he lifted one edge, about to flip it open, when he changed his mind and threw the whole damned thing into the rubbish. If Mariana hadn't made copies for her records before giving him the file, it was her own fucking fault.

Eyeing the flayed corpse across his lab, he poured himself another glass from the most expensive bottle he had stored at Achilles House. One of three his father had been saving for special occasions he'd never get to see.

Sonder, however, did have occasion to celebrate tonight.

That Stage 3 corpse had left him one step closer to proving his hypothesis correct.

After he'd cut apart the sloppily stitched sutures, he'd been greeted by exactly what the pretty girl mentioned last night. There were signs of flowering in the lungs. And the heart.

Sonder swirled the amber liquid in his glass and strode over to the body, looking down into the open chest cavity.

In fact, he could tell precisely where the girl had hastily torn out a bit of the flora for herself. She'd failed to take the root, instead ripping off the stalk, like one might carelessly rip a hellebore bloom from a garden. She hadn't mentioned the heart, and the bud there was so fresh, so new, he suspected it wasn't there before and half-expected it to grow before his very eyes. If he kept it under the correct conditions, it just might.

Tyres crunched on gravel outside and Sonder moved to look out the window, staying hidden so he didn't have to don his infernal mask. Watching from behind the curtain, he recognised the car. An old 70's something or other in the exact shade of brown as his favourite shoes. Her face sprang to his mind, unbidden, before she even stepped from the driver's side in a plaid skirt.

Christ sake. He hated the way he noticed the fit of it over her hips as she walked to the back door of the House and banged with the knocker. He couldn't see her expression clearly from the second floor, but she sure beat the hell out of that door, the sound meeting him from both outside the window and up through the House. She had a medical bag clutched in one hand. An old style from the 50's, and he felt a stab of envy for it. A thing of beauty. Presumably, it was filled with the instruments he'd demanded she bring back.

She glanced up suddenly, looking right into his window, and Sonder slunk back into the shadows to grab his mask.

ATTA

H er mood had soured considerably by the time she made it to Achilles House.

Hauling her doctor's bag out of the passenger seat, she stalked up to the back door and banged the gargoyle knocker against it with the full force of her ire.

A curtain twitched from somewhere up on the second floor and her attention shot to it just in time to see someone scurry back into the shadows.

The door groaned open and Atta scowled up at the Black Stitch Mask who greeted her.

"Here." She shoved the bag of tools into his chest with enough force that he grunted. "I want that bag back. And there's a body in the boot of my car."

The Black Stitch said nothing, only turned and went inside. Atta waited on the front step with her arms crossed, looking up at that window where someone had been spying on her. It was late and she was cold and wished they'd just hurry up.

A few moments later, the silent Black Stitch came back out and unceremoniously handed her the bag. She popped the boot open and tossed her grandfather's old medical bag into the passenger seat while the Society bloke hauled the body out and dropped it onto a gurney he'd dragged out the side door behind him. It made a racket on the gravel and Atta wondered what the passerby might think—bodies coming in and out at all hours—if the back of the House hadn't been tucked up in a copse of trees unseen from Merrion Square.

Atta leaned against the bonnet of her car, ankles crossed and her coat pulled tight around her while she waited anxiously for her payment, hoping the Gold Stitch prick wouldn't tell her never to come back after bringing two opened bodies. It wasn't like she'd removed any vital organs or anything. She'd done them a favour, really, getting the process going.

The White Stitch gangly lad came out then, handing her an envelope.

She opened it quickly and thumbed through it. "This is half what I should be paid," she called to his retreating form.

He turned around and shrugged. "It was cut open and tampered with. That's not the deal."

"The *deal* is I bring you cadavers."

He shrugged again and walked wordlessly back inside, slamming the door shut.

Grinding her teeth together, Atta shoved the cash into the pocket of her blazer and made to open the door. A movement over the bonnet of the car made her jump. It was Gold Stitch, looking menacing in all black and his plague mask.

"*Jesus*," she muttered, clutching her chest.

"You're the girl who seems to enjoy bringing me open bodies," he said.

"I'm the woman who helps you further science." *Arsehat.*

He stepped around the front of the car toward her, and Atta

backed up, holding her keys in her hand the way her father taught her, pointy ends out between her fingers.

She watched him slide his hands into his pockets, and the mask tipped down like he'd noticed her makeshift weapon. Then he chuckled, a low rumble like the roll of distant thunder. "I'm not going to hurt you."

That was exactly what a psycho would say. "What do you want?" she bit out.

"I need a body."

Atta scoffed. "I just dropped one off. You obviously saw that from where you were lurking in the trees like a murderer."

He laughed again and the sound of it licked up her neck. "I need another."

"I didn't even get paid enough for that one. You'll get another when you get another."

"You cut them open."

He didn't formulate it as a question, so she didn't answer.

"Sloppily," he went on, "but you open them."

"My technique is none of your damn business." She took another step back when he took another forward.

"I'll pay you handsomely."

She hated that her face probably betrayed how much she needed the money. How much she wanted to say no, not give into coercion, but there was still the rest of her tuition to consider, and what if the TA position didn't work out?

"What's the catch?"

He shrugged. He had nice, broad shoulders, and she shook that thought loose. "No catch."

"I don't believe you." She raised her chin and got the distinct feeling he was grinning at her behind that mask like a wolf.

"Fine. I need another corpse like the one you brought in yesterday. One with signs of flora."

Atta's pulse beat loud in her ears because she'd only heard one thing: she was no longer expendable.

"Then I want my instruments back."

Beneath the glow of the Society's gaslights, she watched the small V of exposed flesh at his shirt collar and his throat as he swallowed, as he spoke. "Bring me what I need and I'll give you the best tools money can buy."

———

God, she was exhausted. And she hadn't even studied or actually begun her TA job.

Had she even eaten today? Maybe some cereal crumbs, but she honestly couldn't remember if that was yesterday or today and she had to meet her new professor-employer in less than ten hours.

Atta pulled into the car park and groaned. Maybe Imogen had some leftovers she could bum off her.

Leaving the empty doctor's bag on the floorboard, she hauled her heavy satchel onto her shoulder and began the climb of three flights to her suite.

Halfway up, she realised she was going to have to move now. Locate boxes and pack amidst all the other things she had to do and leave her beautiful, picturesque view of the campus. Atta dropped her satchel to the stairs and hung her head.

"Deep breaths."

She ascended the rest of the steps, her bag thunking along behind her because she was too tired to carry it any further.

Two guys in band t-shirts sandwiched a pretty, punk-looking girl—an obvious Kurt Cobain fan—as they watched a horror movie in the common room. One of them waved at Atta, but she ignored it. He'd asked her out twice since the start of term and she couldn't even recall his name. Chad or Brad or something. As much as she, too, loved Nirvana, the lad's grunge obsession and hairless face did nothing for her. She'd never really been attracted to men her own age, let alone one who'd hardly been considered an adult save for a handful of years.

When she unlocked the door of her suite and went in, Atta found Imogen sitting at the tiny island between the kitchenette and the living area, munching on cheese and crackers.

"Did you have dinner?" Atta asked, leaving her bag by the door along with her Oxfords and the umbrella she'd stolen from her roommate that morning.

Imogen gestured to the poor-grad-student version of a charcuterie. "All I've got. Colin conned some poor girl into making him spaghetti. Leftovers are in the fridge if you're willing to face the wrath."

Atta reached for a cracker and popped it into her mouth. "No, thanks. I've had enough Colin for a lifetime already."

Imogen giggled and pinched a piece of cheap cheddar between her fingers.

"Hey, what do you know about a Professor Murdoch?"

Imogen tipped the last of her wine into her mouth, her lips purple when she finally responded. "Dr Frankenstein?"

Atta pulled down a clean wineglass, the fancy kind Colin's parents bought for him before they wrote him off. "Is that what you call him?"

Snatching the wine bottle straight out of Atta's hands,

Imogen poured another glass for herself. "That's what everyone calls him, babe."

"Why is that?"

"He's just so. . ." Imogen visibly shivered. "Spooky."

Atta watched her roommate warily, reclaiming the bottle and pouring the last of it—which wasn't much—into her own glass.

"Did you know he's the youngest professor to have so many accolades in the history of Trinity? He's only been here a few years, I guess right after your undergrad days, but he"—she flipped her hand around like a dead fish—"came up with some *thing* to do with postmortem stuff, and the board was beside themselves."

"Postmortem *thing*?"

"Yeah, he's the professor of some grotesque study area."

Atta chewed on her bottom lip, one hip against the counter, wondering how Imogen received scholarships for graduate studies, and she was about to be working her fingers to the bone for her tuition. "You're going to have to give me more than that."

Imogen scoffed and eyed Atta with disgust, all their camaraderie used up. "I don't know all that gross stuff. That's your area of expertise, not mine."

She couldn't think why Trinity would have her TA for someone not in her area of study after the whole grant denial occurred because of it, but it did not behoove her to scoff in the face of serendipity or good fortune. The only kind of fortune she knew: dumb luck.

"Anyway," Imogen went on, smacking on a piece of Coolia cheese and adding a dried fig to the jumble in her mouth, "I guess all that renowned stuff the prof did was before the

Plague. He's a doctor of some kind, but he actually gets really pissed if you call him that."

"Call him what? Dr Frankenstein?"

Imogen chewed her bite of food so grossly that Atta wanted to slap it out of her mouth. "No, as in pissed if you call him *doctor* at all."

"Strange," Atta mumbled. "It's usually the other way around. Doctors love to have their arses kissed."

Imogen shrugged. "I dunno. Now he lives in a huge creepy house on the outskirts of Dublin, Murdoch Manor, like a total Boo Radley."

Atta had to give her roommate credit for even knowing who that was.

"And he's so mysterious and broody and completely fuckable in the most scholarly way, but no one will go near him." Imogen shivered again. "Not like that, anyway. He's too. . ."

"Spooky?" Atta finished for her sarcastically. But the tone went right over Imogen's head and she pointed a pink fingernail at her as if it was the first time the adjective had come up to describe the prof.

"Yeah. *Spooky.*"

Atta made a mental note to scrounge up her course catalogues and see if she could learn more about this Professor Murdoch before she was expected to meet up with him in the morning. It had already been a long, insane day and she still had assignments to finish. "I'm headed for bed."

"Sweet nightmares, you freak."

Atta didn't care to respond. Imogen wasn't really that far off.

Taking another bite of sharp Coolia and a bushel of grapes

for the ever-so-long trip down the hall to her room, she saluted her roommate and left the kitchen.

Before beginning on her studies, Atta pulled out the little piece of wilted flora from her desk and found her course catalogue at the back of the desk's bottom drawer. She twirled the broken stem of the foreign lungflower, relieved it wasn't giving her another migraine as she sprawled out on her bed and flipped through the glossary of professors.

There he was:

Dr. Sonder Murdoch, PhD

Imogen was right. Professor Murdoch was horribly attractive, in a scholarly way as she had put it, with piercing eyes, a cut, stubbled jaw, and brown hair so artfully careless it was begging to have fingers run through it. There was something strange and mysterious about him, as Imogen also mentioned, and Mrs O'Sullivan alluded to as well, come to think of it. But Atta found it alarmingly alluring, more than anything.

Shaking off those unhelpful and inappropriate thoughts, she read the rest of the description under his photo:

Doctor of Medicine, specialisation in Pathology

TCD Class of 1977 Morbid Anatomy and Greek Studies;

1983 Discipline of Histopathology and Morbid Anatomy

Professor of Morbid Anatomy, Pathology, Autopsy

Atta didn't know much about pathology aside from what she'd taught herself out of curiosity about the Plague, but it was hopefully enough to help grade papers or file things and make copies—whatever it was TAs did.

ATTA

tta stared up at the entrance hall of the building with its mix of Neoclassical limestone columns and Gothic stone architecture. Her nerves were frayed by the idea of meeting Professor Murdoch and her trepidation gave the Medical Building an air of eeriness she'd never felt there before.

Atta hadn't many occasions to enter the Medical Building, but she'd toured it before undergrad, her father beside himself over the stunning domed roof of colourful brickwork. It was a masterpiece of a building in her eyes as well, second only to The Long Room—her heart of hearts. Sure, The Berkeley was great as far as libraries went, but The Long Room was unmatched. There were rumours that Trinity planned to rope off the study tables and the books to protect the sacred texts, and though she saw the logical side of that, it made her inexplicably sad to consider losing time huddled in the stacks at an old table, surrounded by tomes and bent over open pages.

She made a mental note to study there as soon as possible,

then climbed the steps to the second floor of Medical College where she'd been told to find Lecture Hall 26.

It was a smaller classroom, much like the others at Trinity, but it was larger than those in Botany College.

One hand raised to knock on the open door and alert the man bent over at his desk, Atta caught a glimpse of the clock on the wall behind him. She was early. Before he could look up and notice her, she decided to back out and wait in the hall for another few minutes, but the opportunity to openly study her new employer—for all intents and purposes—in live and living colour was too hard to pass up.

She couldn't see his face, not with him scribbling on the papers in front of him, but she noted the crisp white of his shirt, his hair a semi-tamed mess of chestnut brown waves and just long for some of the ends to spill forward and conceal his brow as he looked down. His jacket was a lovely forest green tweed Atta was instantly envious of, but then she saw the elbow patches and contemplated stealing it, though it would be far too large for her. She was no tiny waif, but even seated she could tell Professor Murdoch was tall and lean, but broad-shouldered.

"Are you going to come in or just stand there and lurk?" he asked without looking up from his work. His deep voice, like the smooth burning warmth in the first sip of whiskey, startled her, and Atta almost tripped trying to appear like she'd just arrived.

"Yes, of course." It occurred to her that she'd said something similar to his words last night to a creepy man watching her, but then Professor Murdoch looked up and Atta lost all rational thought. A curl of his hair slipped over his forehead as he removed a pair of round, wire-framed glasses to regard her with disinterest.

She continued down the few steps past rows of desks and he stood, coming around his desk to meet her. When she made herself look up to meet his gaze, his brows pinched in the middle, just for a second, a note of something she couldn't quite place lighting in his hazel eyes before he smoothed his face back into indifference.

"I take it you're Ariatne Morrow."

"Yes, sir." She shuffled her books to one arm and held out a hand. Professor Murdoch removed his right hand from his pocket and shook hers firmly. Atta gave the sourpuss a point in his favour for that. Actually, something about him was familiar, only she couldn't quite place it. "But please call me Atta."

Murdoch nodded once and moved to sit on the edge of his desk, his arms crossed in front of his chest.

Jesus of little Nazareth. No wonder Imogen had given her crass description of the man. Atta was not usually one to be distracted by a handsome face, but it took a great deal of effort not to soak in every detail of him. That photo in her course catalogue had not done the good doctor justice. The stubble on his jaw was just the right amount and the lines etched next to his eyes made her think he hadn't always been so sombre as his reputation made him out to be. She thought if he smiled she might *actually* go weak in the knees.

All right, Jane Bennet, get your shite together. You are a Lizzie, damn it. And this man is no fucking Darcy.

"Atta," he repeated, boredom coating his cold demeanour, "I don't need a TA."

Her juvenile infatuation dissolved as her heart sank, anger boiling up to take its place. Before she could say anything, Murdoch went on.

"But Mariana O'Sullivan is an old friend of mine and she tells me you're quite gifted."

What was she supposed to say to that? '*Yeah, I truly am*'?

"I also understand that you haven't taken any of my courses and you are in Botany College." His eye crinkled with what she took as revulsion, and she fought the urge to baulk and call him a dick.

"That's correct. But I was reared on autopsy. I've worked in a mortuary since I was legally old enough to. Earlier, actually, but, you know, child labour laws and all that—" She trailed off with a nervous laugh, and Murdoch blinked at her, sitting there still as a marble statue of a Greek Tragedy hero.

Atta's books were becoming a burden to hold along with the effort of not sounding like a babbling idiot, so she set them on the closest desk. "I'm well-trained in postmortem arts. I understand that's what most of your courses centre around?"

He offered her the barest of disinterested nods.

"Good. I'm certain I can keep up with whatever it is you need. I don't know a great deal about pathology, per say, save for what I've taught myself, but I'm a quick study. I'm sure that I can help grade or make copies." She pushed her hair back from her face. "Grab your coffee—"

"You taught yourself pathology?"

"I— Em. Well, yes. Again, not a great deal, but working in a morgue at the height of a rampant Plague no one understands. . . Well, it left me curious." *Christ, someone make her stop rambling.*

"Curious?" the professor pressed, but a little thrill went up the back of her neck because he didn't look quite as bored anymore. Maybe he wouldn't regret this after all. It shoved a modicum of steel into her spine and she felt more like herself.

"*Tick, flick, tick. The clock keeps time with the candlestick until they all get sick,*" Atta recited a portion of an old folklore rhyme. "Isn't that how it goes?"

That pinch of his brows came again, this time he didn't bother smoothing it out. "I believe it is, yes."

"Well"—Atta lifted one shoulder, dropped it—"I don't want to get sick."

She was nearly ready to squirm beneath the intensity of those eyes of Murdoch's when a "*Yoohoo!*" came from the doorway.

"Oh, *yoohoo*! There are the two of ya'." Mrs O'Sullivan beamed from the doorway, giving them a wave so big it was as if she were attempting to land a plane. "Lovely, lovely," she repeated with each step as she descended them rather perilously in her pumps.

By the time she reached the front of the class, Murdoch was already back behind his desk, taking off his jacket.

"Make it quick, Mariana. My class is about to begin."

An exceptionally punctual student was summoned by his words, sliding into a seat at the back of the lecture hall. Without looking up from the shuffling of his papers, Murdoch said loudly, "I won't bite again, Miss Murray. You can return to your normal seat."

"*Sonder*," Mrs O'Sullivan censured under her breath. "You can't say things like that to students. People will get the wrong idea."

"*People* are imbeciles. Don't be churlish, Mariana. The girl gave a stupid answer last week, and now she's frightened of me. You're the one who told me to be nicer."

"Evidently, you don't know how to do that."

"I am but a tragic lost cause."

Atta got the distinct impression they'd both forgotten she was there. Miss Murray, it would seem, was slowly and rather shakily relocating for a desk in the second row.

Atta felt a cold hand wrap around her wrist and she turned away from the poor student, looking instead into Mrs O'Sullivan's heavily mascaraed eyes.

"Come with me, dear. I have the key to your new student accommodations." She flicked her attention over her shoulder to Murdoch's back where he was writing on the chalkboard. "That is if this is all working out?"

The professor didn't bother turning or answering the question directly. "Be at my next 10 a.m. lecture, Miss Morrow."

Mrs O'Sullivan pulled Atta along before she could ask when that was or even what course. And what if she already had a class at that time? Oh, this was a mess.

"Wait, my books." She pulled out of Mrs O'Sullivan's death grip before they got up the gallery stairs and snuck back to retrieve them.

Out in the hall, Atta asked when the next class was.

"Unsure, dear. I'll look into it and give you a ring." She produced a key from the pocket of her too-tight blazer. "You will be in Room 4, Third Floor of Briseis House. It is located not far from your current accommodations, so I trust the move won't be too difficult." She set a folded paper on top of the key in Atta's outstretched hand. "That is a map with Briseis circled, but it's just 'round the corner. I'll point you in the right direction."

Outside, the campus was bustling with students, a hint of the approaching autumn on the wind, stirring the leaves that would soon lose their chlorophyll and show the world how beautiful it is to die.

————

Briseis House, in all its stately, Gothic stone didn't look all that different from her grad suite with Imogen and Colin, but she was still sore over losing the view from her old room.

"Sure you wanna do this?" Imogen dropped the box she'd hauled from Atta's car unceremoniously at her feet. She should have given her the bags of clothes to carry.

"I don't have a lot of choice anymore. The ball is already rolling."

Imogen shrugged. "Your funeral."

"Encouraging speech, Imogen."

The girl bent to pick up the box she'd set down, using her back instead of her legs like an amateur. Alas, Imogen only had to worry about how shiny her hair was, not how to carry dead weight.

"Here, let me help you with those." They turned to find a young man about the same age as Imogen—let's face it, the same age as every grad student but Atta and the middle-aged man in Geology College. He was a handsome lad with warm brown skin and even warmer brown eyes lined with enviable lashes and black hair shinier than even Imogen's. He wore thick-framed glasses, and he was fairly gangly, not quite filled out yet despite his age that Atta would peg at about twenty-three. He wore jeans and a Trinity College hoodie, nothing out of the ordinary, but he gave one glance at Imogen, and Atta almost snorted. The lad probably hadn't realised Atta even existed. She wasn't blonde, busty, and long-legged, after all.

Most young men hadn't yet realised the appeal of soft curves and more to grip.

To Atta's immense surprise, Imogen wasn't an arse to him.

"That's so thoughtful." She kicked the box toward him and he scooped it up, struggling only minorly less than Imogen had.

"No problem at all. The name's Bernard Fitzgibbon. But everyone calls me Gibbs. You moving in here?"

He directed the question at Imogen, but Atta answered. "I am. I just took a TA position. I'm Atta. That's Imogen."

Gibbs finally looked at her and the box slipped from his hands, but he caught it at the last second. "Sorry about that," he laughed awkwardly. "So, you're the one that took the position for Dr Frankenstein— Em. Sorry. Professor Murdoch."

Imogen laughed, inspecting her nails. "Told you everyone calls him that."

"Get the door, Imogen," Atta gritted out, juggling her box.

In no rush at all to follow directions, Imogen sauntered slowly toward the door and Atta addressed Gibbs. "How did you know it was me that took the position for Murdoch?"

"Oh." He balanced the box on his knee and pushed his glasses up his nose. "I do some work for him sometimes. Just" —he shrugged, adjusting the box in his grip—"calculations, stuff like that. Word gets around fast here."

Gibbs let her enter the dorm first, and they stepped into a common room that was far more polished than her previous one, outfitted with a pool table, a kitchenette, and a media corner. Imogen ran off to take a cider from the well-stocked fridge.

"Tell me I didn't kick you out of a job," Atta said to Gibbs as they climbed the stairs toward her floor. "I didn't realise

Murdoch had an assistant already. He told me he didn't need one, but I thought he just didn't want one."

"Oh, no, no." Gibbs shook his head and she worried his glasses might fly off. "It's nothing like that. Finally, that empty room on our floor will be filled."

"Wait, 'our' floor? I'm in your suite?"

"Sure are." He beamed at her and Atta decided she liked the lad. She could use some of his enthusiasm in her life. At least he hadn't brought up her age. Though reminding herself she was going to end up a veritable Dorm Mother was a tad depressing.

"The suites work differently here than any of the other dorms," Gibbs went on, leading the way. "Each suite is an entire floor. Murdoch, Vasilios, Lynch, and Kelleher all stayed on Third when they were postgrad students, and it became a time capsule of sorts because their parents and grands stayed here before them. We're all TAs here, and the suites are all split around three separate common rooms, one on each floor. Only Second and Third have two bathrooms, so you lucked out only having to share with one of the three of us."

They walked through another common room that rivalled the setting of a fancy French ski resort. It was more a cosy library and bar than anything else. The hearth logs weren't lit, but she could easily picture herself snuggled up on one of the comfy couches in front of the bookshelves to study by the fire come winter. Maybe leaving her picturesque view wouldn't be so bad after all.

"And you are TA for. . ."

"Lynch. Domhnall assists for Kelleher, and Emmy assists for Vasilios. The TA room for Murdoch has always been empty, though." Gibbs kicked open the door to what must be their suite, and Atta followed him in. "It might be a bit dusty in there." He dropped the box onto a round coffee table in the middle of the small sitting area and pointed to one of the four doors. Two of the others stood ajar but were empty of students. One had cream walls covered in a chaotic array of band posters and shelves of esoteric knickknacks, films, and records. The other room was a whirl of clothing on the floor and the bed, the only decor a poster of a bikini-clad woman Atta didn't recognise.

"Oh, this one's mine." Gibbs smiled and bopped over to open his door. It had taupe walls, a little brown desk and not much else that she could see. "I'm not here often," he explained bashfully. "And I've never been one for *stuff*."

"I respect that." Atta set down her box by her door and looked at the grain of the dark wood for a moment.

"You okay?" Gibbs asked from behind her.

"Have you ever felt like your life is about to change all of a sudden? If you do one little thing?"

"Like open a door?"

"Yeah. Just like that." She looked over her shoulder at her new roommate.

"Atta, I think your life changed when you said yes to assisting Dr Frankentstein."

She definitely liked this lad. "I think we're going to get along just fine, Gibbs."

"Good." He smiled. "I'll head down and bring up more of your boxes. You settle in."

Gibbs bustled off with more energy than Atta had dreamed of having since before she was that age.

With a deep breath, she took the brass knob in her hand. A *zing* went off behind her eyes, and she almost doubled over.

She was no longer herself for an instant, but a beautiful, stunning young woman with flowing auburn curls down to her waist, laughing as she opened this very door. The hallucination jumped, like a bad movie edit and the woman was older, shrouded in white, her veins black and pulsing as she lay on a bed. Atta sucked in a breath and it was all gone, dissipated into fog.

"Jesus." She pressed her palm against her breastbone and willed away the anxiety that inevitably came with the migraines. Lips in a thin line, Atta reached for the doorknob again and twisted.

Her headache was immediately forgotten. The room was painted in a wrought-iron green, like a misty Fae Forest at dusk. One wall was solid bookshelves as loved and worn as the dark oak floors they matched. In the far corner was a small bed, naked save for a standard-issue mattress. Next to it, a window overlooked the Rose Garden and the Medical Building. There were just enough trees bordering her view that it would certainly give her old window-view a run for its money once the leaves changed. Perhaps there simply were no bad views at Trinity.

Atta ran her fingers over the desk situated under the window sill, imagining all the studying and sketching she would do there. It almost made her want to let her job at the morgue go—to throw herself, finally, fully into her studies. But she'd agreed to too much, needed too much, had too much darkness in her heart to be a proper academic.

Gibbs came bumbling back in carrying another box and a bag of clothes dragging behind him. "I couldn't find your friend." He looked around her room. "Where do you want these?"

"There's fine." She pointed to a cobwebbed corner. "I think it's safe to say we've lost Imogen's help."

Gibbs set the boxes down and dusted his hands together. "You don't have much stuff. What say we knock it out and I've got a couple of things to take care of after my next class, but then I'll take you to meet Emmy and Dohmnall. They always go to the pub off Poolbeg on Wednesday nights. Vasilios and Kelleher usually have them working their arses off the first half of the week."

"Sure," Atta smiled. "That sounds great."

SONDER

A knock sounded on Sonder's office door and he looked up from marking papers.

"Lynch asked me to bring you these," Gibbs walked in wielding a sealed brown folder.

"Just put it over there," he gestured with the end of his pen toward a stack of things he didn't care to look at.

The lad stood there staring at him, so he reluctantly leaned back in his chair, the rich leather protesting. "What is it?"

"Your new TA."

"Use complete sentences," he prodded impatiently. Gibbs scuffed his runner across the carpet before fiddling with Sonder's blown glass whiskey decanter. "Stop touching that."

He only moved his ironically idle hands to the polished mahogany of Sonder's bookshelves. He took off his glasses and watched the lad. "Gibbs. Why are you still here?"

His grubby hands moved toward a vintage, leather-bound copy of *The Iliad,* and Sonder jumped up. "Stop touching things!" he boomed. Gibbs's hand shot back like he'd been burned, his eyes wide. "What do you *want*?"

"Th–the girl. The one who—" His words broke off and he glanced at the open office door, his voice lower when he continued. "The one who sells us cadavers. She's your new TA."

"Jesus Christ." Sonder pinched the bridge of his nose. "Tell me, do you smoke?"

"Em. At the pub, I guess."

Sonder rose and fastened the middle button of his jacket. "Get the door."

Gibbs did as he was instructed and Sonder went to the sideboard. "I take it you've officially met Miss Morrow, then?" he said as he poured a finger of whiskey each into two glasses.

"Yes, sir. She just moved into our suite on Third at Briseis."

Sonder's hands stilled mid-pour. "In the green room?"

"Yes, sir."

Sonder sighed. "Stop with that 'sir' shite."

"Sorry."

Sonder handed him the glass of whiskey. "You're a squirrelly lad, aren't you?"

Gibbs eyed the amber liquid in his glass. "Em. It's 1 p.m."

"And? Aren't you in college, for the second time? Live a little."

Gibbs shrugged and took a sip. Sonder tried not to laugh when he wheezed. "Ugh. That *burns*."

"That'll put hair on the chest of even the most Irish of men." Sonder clapped him on the shoulder and retrieved his cigar box from the drawer of the sideboard. He opened it and told Gibbs to pick what he'd like.

"Are those brown cigarettes?"

"Cigarillos," Sonder clarified, biting back his horror at this uncultured swine. Handing one to Gibbs, he took one out for himself. "Thin cigars."

It was clear he had never experienced cigars. Sonder had half a mind to pull out a pipe and see what he would do. Instead, he withdrew a matchbox from his trouser pocket to light the cigarillos for them both and gave Gibbs no instruction. Call it an experiment. A curiosity.

One go at it and Gibbs was coughing, banging a fist against his chest. "Jesus," he gasped.

"You're supposed to puff it, not inhale it," Sonder told him calmly, pointing to a pitcher of water on the sideboard.

Gibbs filled a glass and returned to his seat with watery eyes. "How do I do this?"

"Good on you not giving up." Sonder unbuttoned his coat and sat opposite him, showing him how to puff a cigarillo correctly. The professor in him took it far enough to show him how to properly use a pipe and chase the puff with a sip of whiskey.

"Are we bonding?" Gibbs asked stupidly when he finally got the sequence down.

"Christ." Sonder sighed through his nose, finishing his cigarillo and laying the stub in a crystal tray. "Please don't make me smack you in your stupid mouth." He leaned back in his perfectly broken-in leather cigar chair. "You came here to talk about Miss Morrow."

"She has the room right across from mine."

A vicious warmth burned up Sonder's chest. He hated that was the first thing Gibbs said. The idea that this moronic, adolescent *child* would daily have access to Atta's room filled him with a peculiar fury.

Fucking hell, what was he thinking? Sonder shook the absurd emotion off. "And?"

"Oh, it's only that. . . Well, wasn't that your—"

"Stop there," he cut the lad off. "None of that is your concern. Now, if you would please spit out what your concerns *are* then I can go on marking papers and be where I need to be this evening."

Gibbs tapped his cigarillo into the tray incorrectly, ashes blowing everywhere. If he took another puff, the flavour would be all wrong now. "Right. I'm just concerned I might slip."

"Slip?"

"Say something or do something that makes her realise who I am. Or that you will and she'll figure out we're part of the Society."

"She's clever, Gibbs, but she has no reason to connect those dots. Keep your distance from her and we won't have a problem."

"Oh." He looked down into his drink. "It's just— She's really nice and very pretty—"

"*Not* an option." Even Sonder was surprised by the amount of venom in his voice.

Gibbs set down his glass and stood quickly, all the apprehension they'd erased drawn back in thick, jagged lines. "Right. Of course. I'll be going, then."

The door clicked shut behind him, and Sonder leaned his head back against the top of the chair, loosening his tie. He spent entirely too long contemplating if Ariatne Morrow and her knowledge of the macabre and botanical was going to help him or royally fuck him over.

He supposed he would find out in the morning.

ATTA

I t didn't take long to unpack all of her belongings. Within just a couple of hours, Atta had the room situated exactly the way she wanted it. In the organisational compartments of the well-worn desk, she'd staggered her grandfather's gold microscope, her hand lenses, and rolls of wax paper tied up in twine, her instruments right where she could admire them. Amongst those, she'd placed a few of her favourite bundles of dried flowers and bottles of pins, matches, and annotation tabs. Her collection of the few fiction books she'd brought with her to Dublin was sandwiched between a Venus Italica statue and a bust of Elizabeth Barrett Browning, their vintage leather and gold spines complimented by her grandfather's old clock and her grandmother's golden candelabra.

Feeling lighter than she had in weeks, Atta slid her plethora of Botany, Folklore, and Religious Studies books onto the shelves next to her bed, one by one, relishing the *shush* of each and the immense pleasure of spines perfectly aligned.

In the middle of each row of books, she situated her specimen display boards. One of moths, their wings pinned to black velvet, one of bees, their wings pinned to taupe velvet, and one of dragonflies pinned to olive velvet. Atta ran her finger gently over a wing of the *Seabhcaí an Fhómhair*. Really, the insects and blossoms in her room were all the organic matter she had with her of Galway, and they brought her comfort.

All that was left to put away after her precious books and research materials was her limited wardrobe of tweed, plaid, wool, and corduroy, all in neutral colours. Those she stowed away in the small wardrobe, and her books had only filled up a third of the shelves, so she ended up using the bottom row for her shoes and another row for her woven jumpers and waistcoats.

Intermingled here and there, she set out the rest of her oddities. A bust of Marie Curie, a few extra candlesticks for if the power ever got fussy, a skull she'd managed to rescue—or was it steal?—from her parents' morgue when they'd been called to pick up remains unearthed at a building site, and her first botanical research journal she'd compiled with the help of her grandfather.

Once she had her dark floral sheets on the bed and her grandmother's old lamp situated on the desk, Atta stepped back and admired the room with a small smile.

Maybe this would all work out after all. She supposed she would find out in the morning when she actually began assisting Professor Murdoch.

Thoughts of him and autopsy reminded her of the lungflower tucked away in her desk drawer, and she ventured to pull it out. This time, as soon as she folded back the wax paper, her nose burned, and a sticky sweet scent like honey filled her senses a second before the pain seared through her,

her brain feeling as if it was being cleaved in two. Splotches of black dotted her vision before everything went white, then lush green, then filled with the screams of a dying man.

Atta dropped the flower to her desk and stepped back, the pain and hallucination receding. She tried to catch her breath, not let it get to her.

What would happen if she tried to look at it with her lens? She had to find out. Nodding resolutely to herself, Atta took her most powerful lens and poised it above the flora, careful not to let her skin come into contact with it.

Beneath the powerful Hastings lens, the flower looked nearly like Hemlock, only each tiny petal had markings, almost like a thousand box tree moth wings, black at the tip, bleeding out into tan until it came to a crimson dot. The effect made the flower, at a distance, appear to be a moody garnett shade.

Chewing on her lip, Atta pulled out her research journal for all things Plague-oriented and jotted down her notes. Using the wax paper and tweezers so as not to touch anything, Atta taped the flora into her journal for preservation. With everything safely stowed away at the back of her desk, she glanced down at her watch and jumped. She was due across campus at class in twenty minutes.

Snatching her satchel, her duster coat, and the two textbooks she would need for Fundamentals of Ecology, she rushed from the suite, barely remembering to lock her new front door.

———

After class, Atta headed straight for the library to study. By the time she left, the sun was behind the horizon and Gibbs met her at the door of their suite.

"Dony and Emmy are already at the pub," he explained in one long breath. "Let's go!"

Gibbs's enthusiasm for life was infectious and Atta couldn't help but feel lighter around him.

It turned out the group's usual pub was one of Atta's old favourites from undergrad—Mulligan's, just off campus. It was a brisk but lovely walk there chatting with Gibbs, and they were greeted enthusiastically by two individuals already there and nursing drinks.

"A *girl*!" the young, vibrant woman said, jumping up and hugging Atta. "Thank Christ! It's always smelly lads in our place." She scrunched up her nose and Atta took an instant liking to her, just as she had with Gibbs. The stunning woman stuck out her hand, glossy red hair swaying and crystal-blue eyes glittering. "Emmaline Quinn, at your service."

Atta chuckled and shook her hand. "Ariatne Morrow, but call me Atta."

"Then call me Emmy." Her spray of freckles accentuated her smile.

"Grand to meet you, Atta," the sporty-looking lad sitting at the table said with a big, welcoming grin. "I'm Dony."

With the pleasantries out of the way and drinks ordered, the conversation came more easily than Atta expected.

"I thought that other room would stay empty forever," Dony said between sips of Guinness.

"I have to agree," Emmy put in, popping a couple of peanuts into her mouth. "I never thought Dr Frankenstein would hire a TA." She looked at Atta apologetically. "No offence or anything."

"Oh, none taken." Atta ran a finger around the rim of her glass. "He's sullen and has a reputation, but I think it'll be all right."

"He's a prick," Dony put in uselessly.

"He's not all bad," Gibbs jumped to Murdoch's defence to everyone's apparent surprise, and Gibbs looked down at the scarred table. "I mean, he's not the greatest, but give the man a chance."

Dony snorted something, his speech already fairly slurred. Emmy flipped her hair over one shoulder and bustled off to order another round, ignoring Gibbs.

"Do you all know the professors fairly well, then?" Atta asked when she returned.

"I wouldn't say we know them much at all," Emmy offered, smiling her thanks to the lad behind the bar who made their drinks. "We know *about* them, sort of as caricatures, I guess."

"We know they like to drive us into the ground," Dony groused into his glass.

Gibbs frowned at Dony and turned to Atta. "We are their assistants and we do our jobs. Lynch is Faculty Dean of Health Sciences, so I stay rather busy in that department, but he's also Professor of Applied Social Research which is my college."

"Dr Marguerite Vasilios," Emmy announced regally, "is Professor of Psychology and Mental Health." She pressed her fist against her chest to stifle a burp. "Oops, sorry about that. Dony?" she prompted and all of their attention swivelled to him.

"You're really pretty, Atta," he slurred and Emmy punched him in the arm.

"He's a dick when he's had one too many," Gibbs explained

apologetically. "He TAs for Professor Kelleher, Pharmaceutical Sciences."

Atta nodded along, feeling a little out of place.

"How old are you?" Emmy asked at random, though there was no malice or judgment in her tone. "I took a few years off," she explained before Atta could answer. "So everyone is younger than me. You seem about my age." She smiled, her cupid's bow lips flushed with drink. "I'm twenty-six."

A tinge of relief flooded Atta, to room with someone not only kind and welcoming but closer to her age than all the other students. "I'm twenty-eight."

"I knew it!" Emmy smashed her glass against Atta's creating a tidal wave of Guinness and whiskey. "This is going to be nice, having you around."

They spent the next couple of hours drinking and getting to know one another before Gibbs responsibly ordered everyone food and coffee to sober them up, and they walked back to Briseis House together.

Gibbs and Dohmnall claimed they were going to play some video games out in the common room while Emmy followed Atta into her room, looking at all her books and oddities.

"You are an intriguing woman, Atta." She smiled at her over her shoulder as she inspected the moth display. "I hope you know that's a high compliment."

"I appreciate it. I never really fit in anywhere, so I tend to stick to myself."

Emmy plopped down on Atta's bed, leaning against the pillows. "Fitting in is all a masquerade, anyway. Quality over quantity is my motto. I tend to stick to myself, too. You seem all right, though."

Atta laughed, sitting down in her desk chair. "You seem all right, too."

"Are you ready for tomorrow?"

Atta shrugged. "I don't know what to expect, but I'm sure it will be fine."

Emmy nodded thoughtfully. "Just be sure to wear something sexy."

Atta screwed up her face at her new roommate. "I want to command respect."

With a snap of her fingers, Emmy pointed at her and winked. "Exactly."

"So," Atta explained slowly, "coming off as *sexy* is not my aim."

Emmy rolled her eyes and sat up on the bed. "I didn't say *slutty* or that you have to fuck him. It has very little to do with who the man is, anyway. It's about *her,* the woman in the scenario. When a woman feels sexy, she feels confident and in control. It puts a spell on men. It has *nothing* to do with sex and everything to do with power. It's just another tool in a woman's arsenal." She laid back, resting on her elbows. "You clearly have the brains. *Make* people see you."

Atta considered Emmy's point for a moment, understanding her new friend wasn't insinuating she should degrade herself to gain a man's respect at all. "Show them where to look without saying a word," she mused.

Emmy howled. "Exactly that! And I don't mean your tits. Your fucking *aura,* Ariatne Morrow. It's a good one." She winked again and Atta half fell in love with her. She'd never had a female friend that was a woman's woman. A supporter, not an insecure girl always lurking in the shadows waiting for an opportunity to make your life a living hell out of jealousy.

"You're wise for your years, Emmaline."

She preened, lacing her fingers together and resting her chin on them, batting her eyelashes. "Now, show me your sexiest librarian look."

After three glasses of wine, too many outfit changes, and a sore stomach from laughing, Atta beamed, looking at herself in the wardrobe mirror.

She wore a chocolate brown pleated skirt just short enough to show off her shapely legs, paired with a deep cut, tulip-collared blouse under a woven sleeveless pullover. She'd added her favourite forest green wool blazer and her (slightly) heeled lace-up Oxfords with patterned Argyle socks. Atta did not for one moment believe anyone would find her outfit *sexy*, but she felt unstoppable.

"I think this is it."

"Completely agree," Emmy said emphatically. "I'd salivate over you if you were my librarian. *Lads!*" she called, and Dony and Gibbs shuffled in, half asleep. "What do we think of Atta's outfit?"

"Oh– Well, it—" Gibbs stammered perking up as soon as his attention landed on Atta, eyes wide behind his glasses.

"It's. . . You look—" Dohmnall's face went beet red. "Incredible. . ."

"All right, that's enough. Get out." Emmy shooed them away. "Exhibit A: A woman's confidence makes putty of lesser lads and commands the respect of men."

Atta did *feel* incredible. But that might have been the wine.

ATTA

Nursing a hangover on the day she was meant to
begin her new assistant position for the severe
Professor of Morbid Anatomy was not ideal.

A hangover always made the migraines worse, too.

Atta knew better than to drink whiskey and Guinness at the
rate of college kids, let alone chase it with three glasses of wine
and little sleep. The night had been fun though, far more fun
than Atta had expected it could be. She was actually looking
forward to sharing a suite with Gibbs, Domhnall, and Emmy.
Especially now that she knew the scales weren't tipped too far
to her side concerning maturity, and she felt bolstered by
Emmy rather than the competitive *girl world* most women
lived in that Atta found disturbing.

There were clouds rolling in, but for the time being, the sun
was shining over campus, the breeze was crisp, and the walk to
the Medical Building from Brieseis House was short but
beautiful.

The coolness of the building's interior sent a chill up Atta's
arms, and she wondered idly when the college would switch on

the heat. The corridor leading to where Mrs O'Sullivan said Murdoch's office was located was significantly warmer, and she discovered upon reaching said office that it was because he had a lovely fireplace there.

She knocked politely on the open door just as she had on the open door of his lecture hall when they first met a few days earlier. He was standing with his back to her, one hand in his pocket, the other holding an open book. Again, she was struck by the familiarity of his stance, and again, she couldn't grasp where that familiarity came from. It was a distant thing, far off and fuzzy. It was going to drive her mad until she figured it out.

"Come in," he said more to his book than to Atta. He didn't seem to often look at people when they entered, and it irked her.

"I know I'm a little early," she said as she came in. "Mrs O'Sullivan said I could find you here before class and I thought we should discuss what it is you'd like for me to do today."

"One moment," he murmured, again more to his book than to her.

He was completely engrossed in what he was reading, and Atta couldn't help but wonder what it was. Finally, he slid that hand out of his pocket and flipped the page reverently. It almost felt like she was intruding on a private moment, something special and intimate. Or was she captivated by seeing this surly man be so gentle with the book, that page-turn almost romantic. . .

Murdoch clapped the book shut and Atta jumped at the sound, her romanticism dissipating like faerie dust.

"Have a seat, Miss Morrow." He turned and gestured toward one of two fine leather chairs opposite his desk.

She dropped her satchel to the floor and stacked all her

textbooks on an end table. Sitting in the left chair, she smoothed out her pleated skirt that was frankly too short for sitting without the cover of a desk. "This is a lovely office, Professor."

As a rule, Atta did not hand out empty compliments. Murdoch's office truly was stunning. Dozens of anatomical sketches, skeletal renderings of various creatures, and one large Doctor of Philosophy diploma hung in simple frames between two glass-enclosed bookcases taking up the entire charcoal grey wall behind Murdoch's mahogany desk. To Atta's left there was an antique sideboard with a beautiful glass decanter of what was most likely expensive whiskey and an old globe, the sepia-toned kind that bore depictions of the old world. Across the room was a small hearth, a fire steadily burning and casting the space in a warm glow.

Despite the perfect order of everything else in the room, particularly the bookshelves, Murdoch's desk was a flurry of chaos. It was mostly papers and pens, a gaslamp, and a few scattered books, but there were also three coffee mugs—not the paper takeaway kind—and an expensive-looking pipe on display. Ah, that was it, the scent lingering along with the parchment and leather aroma of books and stale coffee: pipe tobacco. A smoky, sweet scent, like old books, spices, and deep woods.

Professor Murdoch did not respond to Atta's compliment, he merely sat in his chair across the desk and watched her until she nearly squirmed. She hated that he made her feel like she could come out of her skin.

"I thought we could discuss what it is you'll need me to do today and going forward," she repeated her earlier statement when his gaze became too much. He certainly didn't have trouble keeping his eyes on her while *not* speaking.

Murdoch laced his fingers together and set his hands loosely on the mess of papers in front of him, like a ribcage splayed on parchment. "For the next few weeks, I'd like for you to simply observe."

Atta blinked at him, certain she'd misheard. "I'm sorry. Observe?"

"Yes."

"For a few weeks? That's more than half what's left of the term, Professor."

"Yes."

Maybe she was too hungover for this, but she was getting pissed. "Then what?"

"Then, maybe we can discuss you making some copies for me, or fetching coffee like you so generously suggested the other day."

Nope. Not just hungover.

Atta shifted in her seat. "Let me get this straight. You need me to observe your classes before I can even be allowed to make copies for you or bring you *coffee*?"

He didn't even move, let alone respond.

A bitter laugh escaped her. "Unbelievable."

"You know," Murdoch said, leaning forward on his elbows, his clasped hands sliding across the desk closer and closer to her with the movement, "most students would find this the easiest way to free tuition, not complain about it."

"I'm not most students," she shot back, failing to keep the ire from her tone despite the flush rushing up her neck.

"You've never taken my courses, Miss Morrow."

"I don't need to take a course to know how to make copies

of Page 45," the pitch of her voice rose there at the end, making her accent thicker, and she took a deep breath when one of Murdoch's eyebrows dragged upward. "I have been performing autopsies since I was practically a child. It's wildly inappropriate how young I was the first time I cracked a rib cage open. I've studied pathology myself for six years, and I might not know every detail of your courses, but I'm uniquely qualified in that regard to at least make *copies* of the damned diagrams."

"So I've heard."

Jesus, she wanted to slap the brooding right off his face. "Do you want to see my CV?"

"I already have that. What I don't have is proof."

"I don't understand. Do I really have this position or not?"

"You have it as a favour to a friend. If you have it for being actually useful remains to be seen."

Common sense told her to rein in her temper. To take the easy way. To listen to the handsome, infuriating professor holding her fragile future in his hands. But she'd never been very good at things like that and the fire was hot and the scent of his lingering tobacco smoke was intoxicating.

"You know, these students are all spooked by you, but I don't think you're scary. I think you're just a bastard."

One side of his mouth twitched and Atta stood, unable to sit there a moment longer.

"I think I need to go." Her words hardly carried. If she'd said them above a whisper, she would have shouted them.

She was halfway to the wrong dorm when she realised she'd left her bag and books and probably the whole of her tuition in that office.

Sitting down on the nearest bench, she wilted, pushing

against her eyelids with her fingers. The scent of cigars and books—the scent of *Murdoch*—was still cloying with her senses, embedded in the fabric of her clothes.

This time, the migraine that came from nowhere and everywhere brought a song, student passersby disappearing, replaced with synesthesia in shades of warmth, nostalgia and a forest in winter.

God, it was beautiful. Tears sprang to her eyes, but she couldn't make them stop, the fog only breaking long enough for her to see strong, slender fingers gliding over an old piano, the notes filling up her soul before she could see her bare legs in a tub, covered in suds, a melodic voice reading her fairytales.

Then everything was slashed in red. Garish gashes of black blood, the notes cut short, a scream tearing through her so forcefully she thought it must be real—now. Everything trembled, the world shaking, crumbling. It all went black and Atta gasped, opening her eyes to see students on the green staring at her.

Tears streaming down her face, she ran for Briseis House, ripping off her clothes as soon as she hit the door to the suite. She needed *away* from the scent of that man.

Showered and changed, Atta realised she had to go back. Every iota of her coursework was in that office.

Tomorrow. She'd go back for it tomorrow. When Murdoch was in session.

SONDER

"Would you pay feckin' attention?"

Sonder dragged his gaze from Miss Morrow's belongings and focused on Nolan Kelleher's disgruntled face. "You drone on so much, I stopped listening."

Kelleher's nostrils flared. The two of them had never been close, despite living together for the better part of six years almost a decade ago in Briseis. It was amazing how much could remain hidden within the same walls when no effort was put forth.

Sonder, however, had put forth quite a lot of effort back then to sift out all Kelleher's secrets. Being an integral part of a secret society would do that to a man, make him thirst to fill his arsenal with the secrets of his fellows—just in case.

"Rochford wants your work to have results sooner rather than later. He's getting impatient, pressing Lynch and me to put pressure on you."

"Is it grand being Rochford's lapdog? Does he scratch you behind your ears and offer you treats?"

Kelleher's ears were turning red and Sonder suppressed a smile. "Just because your proposition for Achilles House was accepted and my ideas were not, does not make you better than me, Sonder Murdoch."

"There, there, Kelleher. Don't get your knickers in a twist." Sonder stood and rounded his desk, unintentionally pulled toward Miss Morrow's things on his side table. "Message received." He made a purposefully disrespectful and flippant hand motion for Kelleher to leave. Which he did, in a huff.

Sonder closed and locked the door before returning to the abandoned satchel. For a long moment, he stared at it. And then he was opening it, pulling out a notebook, then another and another.

An hour and two glasses of whiskey disappeared before he realised how engrossed he'd been. Ariatne Morrow was no dolt. Her notes were thorough, her sketches clean, her ideas unique. To his surprise, his favourite pages were the ones where she had clearly been distracted or bored in classes he surmised were too simple for her and she'd drawn little fairytale creatures. Wills-o-the-wisp and trooping faeries, gargoyles and dragons.

One notebook was entirely filled with abstract ideas about the Plague cadavers she'd cut into and had no idea he knew about. Her observations were astute and accurate, but her foolishness to carry around anything of the sort. . .

He came to his senses and put everything back in order, but paused to look over the book titles in her bag, chuckling when he realised none of them were textbooks, but fiction titles. *The Iliad, To the Lighthouse, Vanity Fair*, a new title: *The Secret History*, and only one he had not read himself: *The Canterville Ghost* by Oscar Wilde.

Sonder scribbled the title on his blotter and left for a night at Achilles House.

ATTA

"Uh oh." Emmy caught Atta in the common room on Third of Briseis House, staring into the fireplace. "Today didn't go so well?" she ventured, sitting down next to Atta on the sofa.

"He's a bastard."

Emmy rubbed a small circle on her back. "We tried to tell ya', hun."

"I can't be kicked out of Trinity," Atta said quietly. Emmy's hand disappeared and then her presence after it as she went to the common fridge and pulled out a half-drunk naggin of whiskey.

She handed it to Atta. "Sip, then spill."

Immensely grateful for Emmy's calming presence, she twisted off the lid and considered a sip of the cheap liquor straight from the bottle, but then remembered the Plague and the body she'd dropped off to feckin' Gold Stitch after her miserable shift at Gallaghers'. "Cup?"

Emmy laughed her deep, husky chuckle and left, returning with a fancy champagne flute.

Atta filled it to the brim, lying to herself that the germs were only on the lip of the bottle, not in the liquor because of the alcohol content. She took a gulp, and Emmy snatched the flute, doing the same.

"There we are. Now, spill."

"Murdoch said I have to just sit in his classes and observe before I can even make copies or fetch him coffee."

"*Prick*," Emmy interjected supportively, taking it upon herself to drink half the flute of whiskey.

"And then I called him a bastard and stormed out."

Emmy gaped at her. "You did not."

"I did."

"I don't know if I should be really fucking proud or horrified."

Atta melted into the sofa, palms up on her knees. "I think both."

"Definitely both."

"What am I going to do, Emmy? I can't lose this tuition." Perhaps she shouldn't have let her desperation show, but it was too late to pull the words back in.

"And I can't lose my only female roommate." Emmy bumped her shoulder with her own. "It'll work out."

They sat in silence for a long time, draining the whiskey and moving on to cider and Tayto's. Dony showed up with a group of guys smelling of sweat and the rugby pitch, taking over the sofas with no regard for the women already there.

"Gross," Emmy muttered, hauling Atta up. "You know," she said as they headed for their suite, "he's a fantastic lecturer."

"Who?" Atta asked, too tipsy to put much together.

"The bastard." Emmy opened their door.

"Murdoch?"

Emmy locked them in and proceeded to put a kettle on. Thankfully, it was just the two of them since Gibbs was off doing whatever it was he did in the evenings.

"Yes, Dr Frankenstein. Loads of students flock to his open lectures." She pulled out a pot of something that smelled delicious as it began to heat on the stove. "I went to his seminar on Greek Tragedies, and it was—" She broke off, shaking her head, copper braid swaying. "He had this whole monologue about Achilles and his tortured relationship with Patroclus, the way he so savagely mourned Patroclus's death and wanted his bones mixed with his after he, too, perished." Emmy paused and pressed a palm to her chest. "It was moving. Otherworldly."

Emmy brought Atta a cup of tea leaves, and she wrapped her fingers around it, though it didn't yet have any hot water.

"His take on the tragedies through the lens of morbid anatomy was profound as well," Emmy finished, stirring the pot and flicking off the heat for the kettle.

"Why doesn't he like to be called '*doctor*'?" Atta asked as Emmy poured steaming water over their tea leaves. "My old roommate told me that."

"No one knows exactly. All I've heard is that on the first day of class, he declares to all his students that his patients are dead, so don't call him Dr Murdoch."

Atta stirred a spoonful of sugar into her tea, watching the crystals dissolve and contemplating what would cause Murdoch to take such a stance on his hard-won title. There had to be some reason and she surmised it was likely tragic.

They passed the rest of the evening and late into the night

speaking of other things besides Murdoch and college, drinking tea and dozing in between conversations on Emmy's bed.

Eventually, Atta startled awake from a dream of jagged, sharp teeth and the screams of a man she felt she knew.

Sweaty, hungover—again—and disconcerted, Atta made her way to her room, but it only made the nightmares worse.

The bell it tolls,

Its song eerie,

Twisting my velvet bones.

Every hour, it rings.

A reminder that it's almost time.
Time for the man in coats of moonrise
to begin his lurking.

Seven. . .eight. . .nine it tolls.

I no longer attempt to hide.
Hiding doesn't suit me, anyway.

SONDER

"Thought you might be back for those."

Ariatne Morrow jumped out of her skin, two of her textbooks dropping to the floor of Murdoch's office and he was glad she didn't catch his smirk.

Still, he strode to pick them up before she could and set them on her teetering stack. She looked up at him like he might murder her, so he stepped back, looking away from her pretty green eyes toward the huge satchel she always lugged around but had left in his office for the last two days. "What have you got in that bag if you're carrying all those books around?"

She looked self-consciously at her bag, her freckled cheeks turning pink.

Christ. He moved to put his desk between them.

"Not that it's any of your business, but I keep lots of notes and sketch pads and"—she tucked a strand of hair behind her ear, hugging her books to her chest—"I enjoy reading for recreational value, too."

"How many recreational books do you have in there, then?"

"Two."

Liar. Sonder felt his body heat, and he cleared his throat. "Are you staying for class this time, Miss Morrow?"

He could tell by the way her eyes darted around then landed on him with ire, that she wanted to say no. Surprising him yet again, she nodded. "Yes. But I will not just sit there and observe."

Her notes and sketches proved that was a vast waste of her time and intellect, but admitting that to her was too volatile a thing. She had the brains and hadn't been exaggerating her knowledge base, but she was naïve enough to leave earth-shattering notes in his office for nearly two days. It probably never even occurred to her that he wasn't honourable enough not to look at them.

With any other student, he wouldn't have. Would never have considered it. But Ariatne Morrow was something different. She did something different to him. Ever since he made the mistake of opening that first notebook, all he'd wanted to do was crack open her mind and swim in it.

"All right." Her face brightened at his agreement and he leaned back in his chair, tapping the end of a pen to the mahogany of his desk. "But you'll take the quiz with the class today."

He expected her face to drop, but there was a challenge in her eyes. Perhaps a thrill, too.

"If you pass it, you can make my copies."

God help him, she snorted. "If I pass it, I get a chance to prove to you I know what the hell I'm doing."

Sonder ran his tongue over his canine and she met his stare, defiance in the set of her jaw, her lips. He rose and held out his hand. "Deal."

He could have sworn she winced when her hand clasped his.

ATTA

F uck fuck fuck.

She *knew* this.

Atta chewed on the end of her pencil, feeling Murdoch's eyes boring into her profile as she hunched over a desk in the front row. Apparently, it would be *her* desk if she managed to keep this TA position.

She didn't do wonderful under pressure. It was more that she didn't do well off-schedule. That was a stupid, stupid thing to be—the woman who can't roll with the punches—but she'd already missed two assignments for classes because Murdoch had her books in his office, and now she was missing another entire lecture because she'd agreed to take a stupid quiz.

Oh, no. How had she just realised her class schedule collided with Murdoch's? *Oh, god.*

Atta pulled air in through her nose and blew it out slowly through her mouth. If she didn't have this position, she wouldn't have any classes to attend, anyway.

Focus on the task at hand.

Once she managed to calm herself down, the quiz was a cakewalk.

1. **IF A PATIENT DIES OF HEMORRHAGIC COMPLICATIONS, WHICH SHOULD BE PERFORMED FIRST?**

Atta marked **B:** TAKE PHOTOGRAPHIC DOCUMENTATION PRIOR TO BLOOD DRAINAGE

2. **THE PANCREAS IS MARKED IN DARK BLOTCHES RESEMBLING A PATTERN. WHAT IS THE CORRECT DEDUCTION?**

D: AUTOLYSIS

3. **WHAT METHOD SHOULD BE USED FOR HEART DISSECTION IF THERE IS SUSPICION OF INFEROSEPTAL MYOCARDIAL INFARCTION?**

C: REMOVAL OF THE INFERIOR WALL OF THE RIGHT VENTRICLE

Atta flew through the rest of the answers, confident she missed —at most—two, and turned her paper in at Murdoch's desk.

"Stick around after class," he told her quietly without looking up from his book. She noticed it was the same one he'd had in his office and her desire to know what had him so captivated pulled at her once more.

A few moments later, he told the students they had only one

minute left to finish marking their answers. When the time was up, he rose and flipped through the papers before he proceeded to throw them all in the rubbish save for one, which he left facedown on his desk. Murdoch moved to address the confused class of about fifteen students and Atta.

"This is not secondary school. I will not be giving any other quizzes or tests aside from the final, which, in this course, is to perform a full autopsy on your own with the parameters given. We've gone over enough prerequisites and it's time we dive into the true material of this course."

A pasty lad with sandy blonde hair raised his hand.

"Mr Murphy, do you raise your hand to interject your thoughts into a conversation with your peers?"

The lad blinked at him. "No, Professor."

"Then let us be intellectual peers here as well. That's the aim, anyway." Murdoch walked a slow line in front of the class, one hand cutting the air as he spoke. "The first two weeks are meant for introductions and syllabi and all of college's damned requirements. Now that we have that shite out of the way, I want this to be akin to supervisions more than lectures. When we don't have our arms elbows-deep in cadavers, this course will be conducted as small group, intensive discussions." He stopped pacing and nodded at the lad who'd raised his hand. "Now, Mr Murphy, go on, then."

Everyone turned to look at him and his cheeks developed splotches of crimson. "I only meant to ask why we took the quiz at all if you were just going to toss them out."

"Because the order in which you turned your answers in, is the reverse order of who will get their hands dirty first."

All the students looked at one another sheepishly, and Murdoch went on. "Those whose hubris or over-studied minds led them to turn their quizzes in the quickest need to understand they don't know everything. That there is much to be deduced by observation and employing an irritating level of patience." He clasped his hands behind his back and took up pacing again. "Those who took their time or perhaps had no knowledge of the material, well, they need the most exposure to corporeal subjects and a chance to be thrown to the wolves to knock the apprehension from their bones."

Something in the air changed. It felt charged with that distinct dopamine hit unique to academics at the height of study.

Atta could see it then, why he had been granted such accolades before the age of forty. How this professor was so gifted to teach, such a powerful lecturer, even if all his pupils were frightened of him. Professor Sonder Murdoch was the cliff-jump that terrified, the majestic wolf that captivated, the risk you knew might kill you, yet you couldn't pass it up.

Murdoch began writing on the board, his handwriting the sloppy mix of tight cursive and adolescence that indicated either a certain level of genius or psychopathy. When he moved out of the way, he'd listed the students in order of who had, Atta assumed by his explanation, turned their answers in last to first.

Her name was absent, as she'd expected considering she wasn't one of his students, but a thread of disappointment still knotted in her stomach.

"Read chapters 17-20. If you have something against standard-issue surgical gowns, I suggest you bring your own to class and don't wear your pretty shoes. Now, fuck off, the lot of you."

The students filed out, and Atta was left trying to determine if she should sit at her desk or stand. Sitting made her feel too much like a fledgling fresher, so she stood.

Murdoch reclined on the corner of his desk, one foot swaying as he looked over Atta's answers. He scrubbed a hand over his stubbled jaw as he did so and Atta looked away, trying not to fidget.

"You missed number eight." It seemed to her that his voice was deeper when he spoke to her. Far less charismatic and more guarded. "Petechiae are minute haemorrhages. After asphyxiation, they can be found not only in the heart and other organs but in the eyes and even areas like the scalp." He handed her the paper. "But our deal was to pass. And you did."

"I can do more than observe, then." She didn't form it like a question. "Prove I can do more." They'd had a deal after all.

"I will not have the integrity of my course jeopardised by your involvement or need to prove something to yourself."

"A deal is a deal," she ground out.

"And I'm not going back on that. I'm merely ensuring that you know the parameters of this arrangement. I will ban you from my classes if you interfere and I don't see that going well for you."

A couple of hours ago, she would have thought him an arrogant prick for saying such a thing, but now she saw it for what it was: a professor protecting his students.

"Professor Murdoch," Atta implored him gently, "I don't want to jeopardise the integrity of your classes. But I do want to do more if I'm here. If you just want me to fetch tea, fine, but I'd like to prove to you that I can do more if you'll grant me the opportunity."

He was close enough that the smoke and spice scent of him cloyed with her senses again, but she stood her ground as he regarded her, brows pinched. It was the most expressive she'd seen his face to date.

Murdoch rose from the corner of his desk. "Get your coat."

"Pardon?"

He was already walking toward the door and she jumped to grab her things.

"Wait, where are we going? I have class in thirty minutes." She followed him out into the corridor, nearly having to run to keep up with his long, purposeful strides.

"It's my understanding that you won't have any classes at all if this partnership doesn't work out, so keep up."

His choice of phrasing struck her as odd, but she supposed he was right.

Their shoes made a quick tattoo on stone steps as they descended deeper and deeper below the Medical Building. Eventually, they were spit out into the belly of it, surrounded by stone and iron, metal and cold. A veritable castle dungeon.

Atta had never partaken of hard drugs when everyone else had in the 70s and 80s, but she was nearly certain that *zing* felt very similar to the one that coursed through her as she took in the stone autopsy table standing in the middle of the room like a sacrificial slab; masonic, medieval.

She was still standing there, mouth agape, when Murdoch strode to the chill chamber wall of cadavers and pulled open a metal drawer. "Help me get it on a gurney."

Atta pulled her attention away from the morgue of her dreams.

She appreciated that he didn't expect her to have a delicate constitution or need to work up to handling a corpse so readily. Perhaps he actually believed her. Or maybe he was testing her. *Maybe* he knew she was essentially a glorified grave robber.

Atta laughed inwardly at the thought, though it was short-lived. She knew she was worse than even a grave robber. They only stole replaceable, earthly things, not the corpses themselves.

For science, she reassured herself as she heaved her side of the body onto the metal gurney.

Murdoch wheeled the body over to the stone table. He did not ask her for assistance in getting the cadaver onto it from the gurney, and Atta assumed he'd only been testing her vitality rather than in need of actual assistance.

With the corpse laid out, he removed the sheet with a flourish to reveal a naked woman. Or what used to be one. Young, brunette, thin, her hip bones protruding.

Captivated as always by the personhood of the deceased, the spirit that once wielded the bones, Atta approached slowly, acutely aware of the scuff of her lace-up boots against the rough stone floor. Of Murdoch halting his movement at a set of metal drawers to watch her. Of the remaining shell of a woman, prostrate on a cold table. Who used to be a child, then a girl, then a woman whose life was cut short. By what? The Plague? No, her body would be at Achilles House or in a morgue with a quick turnaround if that were the case.

She walked slowly around the woman's body, examining, taking it all in.

Someone had loved her once.

She had postmortem bruising around her wrists and ankles. On her cheekbone.

She'd loved someone once.

Her index fingernail was torn past the quick.

She'd laughed and enjoyed meals once.

There was antemortem bruising on the sides of her palms, her far-right metacarpal showing signs of fracture.

She'd read books, watched movies, listened to music once.

Her ring finger had an indention where a wedding band must have been.

She'd been married once.

Atta looked up at Murdoch, who was regarding her intensely, his hands in his pockets as always. "How did she die?" she asked him in a small voice. But it wasn't fear or intimidation softening her. No, this was her *world*. It was the sadness that made her feel hemmed in. Not trapped or entangled, but focused. Like the tragedy of someone else reminding her of what was truly important.

Murdoch dipped his chin toward a tray he'd laid out, laden with surgical instruments. "You tell me."

"I'll need a notebook," she said, her spine straightening, her mind cooling with the process, the protocol and sanctity.

"Of course." Murdoch moved to a desk off to the side and produced a clean, empty notepad and a pen.

Atta donned paper booties and a surgical gown, then gloves. The instruments were pristine, like new. They felt *good* in her hands and all faded away, even the looming professor as she cut into the cadaver and began her work.

She was around halfway through her process when a voice broke into her void of focus. "Tell me about the class you're missing to do this."

Atta paused, scalpel poised over the heart and looked at Murdoch. "That's off-topic."

He shrugged, one corner of his mouth almost twitching. "I'm only trying to help."

"Or are you trying to see if I can avoid distraction?"

He failed to stop the twitch that time, and a spark shot up her chest at the sight. "You're clever, I'll give you that." His tongue ran over his lips to moisten them and Atta looked back at the ribcage splayed before her. "Let's say it's both," he said. "So tell me what it is you were learning."

Lips pursed, she jotted down a few notes concerning the cadaver and moved on to her inspection of the lungs. "The class I missed today is studying the interactions between biological, physical, and chemical environmental components."

He was quiet for a moment, but she ignored it.

"Intriguing. And do you think those interactions play any role in the Plague?"

Atta stilled at his question. Did they? "No," she said after a moment. "I really don't."

He might have asked her more questions, but she didn't hear if he did, because she'd determined the cadaver's cause of death.

"All right." Atta finally stepped back, removing her gloves and wiping her hands with a towel from a stack of them—coarse, hospital-grade.

"Ready to report your findings?" Jesus, he looked bemused, a glitter in his eye.

As soon as she started speaking, his demeanour sobered. "She was killed. By her husband."

"Ah, ah." Murdoch stood and came to her side. "It is not the job of even a forensic pathologist to make assumptions like that." He peered over her shoulder at the cavity where a heart had once beat. Despite their surroundings, she was acutely aware of how close he was standing to her. "Tell me your concrete medical findings and that is all."

Murdoch stepped back, and Atta continued, beginning with the swelling of the cadaver's vocal cords, down to the heart with signs of pulmonary oedema, the antemortem and postmortem injuries the woman sustained, and the damage to kidney and liver.

"My conclusion is that this woman sustained injuries prior to her death that were not directly related. Cause of death was prolonged carbon monoxide exposure, leading to poisoning." She took the booties off her shoes and threw them in the rubbish bin. "And a bastard husband."

Murdoch's lips quirked to one side. "I'll bite. What is your non-professional theory there, hm?"

Atta sighed, looking at the poor woman one last time before she covered her with the sheet. "The indention on her finger, firstly. Yes, all of her personal effects were removed when she passed, but there is something about the indention that leads me to believe she'd already removed the wedding band—fairly recently. The bruises on her arms are consistent with domestic abuse, but it was the metacarpal fracture in the right hand that got me. She was trapped somewhere for quite some time, banging on a wall or door. Trying to get out. That explains the swelling and tearing of her vocal cords as well."

"But what if she merely found herself trapped somewhere, she wasn't forced there?" Murdoch challenged, all serious, all professor.

Atta considered that for a moment. She couldn't very well quote a woman's intuition, though that was the root of it. "The postmortem bruising on her ankles and wrists." Atta shook her head. "What grieving widower or anyone else who may have found her would tie her ruthlessly like a hog? It screams of ill-intent."

Murdoch nodded once and stood upright from where he was leaning on a stool. "Very good, Atta."

A flurry of moths tumbled around in her abdomen when he said her name. Praised her.

"Do you smoke?"

"No, I don't. Seen too many charred lungs."

Murdoch chuckled, a low sound that rolled like thunder in the night. She suppressed a shiver. "We all have to die some way or another. Come with me."

Atta hated that, currently, she might follow him anywhere despite being the antithesis of that kind of woman. She had self-respect, and he was—sort of—her *professor*, for Christ's sake.

Alas, she followed the man out a back door that led them to a little courtyard of stone and iron.

Murdoch leaned against the rough side of the building and handed her a file folder. "Take a look."

While she opened it and made sense of what she was looking at, Murdoch pulled a cigarillo out of his shirt pocket, struck a match, and lit it. He puffed on it, filling the chilly courtyard air with a spicy, sweet scent she would forever associate with him. At least it didn't give her a migraine this time.

The file he'd given her was a Garda report, detailing the homicide of one Patricia O'Malley.

"Christ," Atta cursed on an exhale. She slid down the wall, sitting on the cold concrete. "She was only twenty-six."

Murdoch hummed a note of acknowledgement. "She had her whole life ahead of her."

Atta read on. She'd been right. The woman was separated from her husband. She'd filed three reports of violence against him. Look what that had gotten her. The opportunity to die and be cut open by a girl trying to prove herself in the academic world she didn't even belong in.

After her third report, Patricia O'Malley was locked in a pantry, the kitchen gas on for ten hours. She was discovered one morning by a neighbour who was walking her dog near the woods and found Patricia bound by her ankles and wrists. Upon questioning, Patricia's estranged husband admitted to killing her, tying her up, and dumping her body to make it look as if she'd been kidnapped.

Eyes misty, Atta read the last line of the report aloud. "Cadaver donated by the deceased's family to Medical College, Morbid Anatomy Dept., Trinity College Dublin."

She closed the file and set it on the ground beside her. She could feel Murdoch's eyes on her, smell the scent of his cigarillo.

"Why are you here, Atta?"

She looked up at him. Felt something shift.

Things kept shifting.

"Why are you at Trinity?" he pressed quietly.

"Is the pursuit of academic excellence not enough?"

He smirked, and she hated it. Loved it. "No." He dropped the cigarillo and twisted the ashes into the concrete with the toe of his shiny brown shoe. "Not when you make postmortem diagnoses and forensic deductions like you do and yet choose *Botany* for your postgraduate studies."

The clock tower bells rang in the distance as she looked at him and he at her. Then Atta gasped.

"Fuck!" She stood up, running a hand through her hair. "How is it 5 o'clock? I'm supposed to be at work!"

Professor Murdoch said nothing as she ran off.

ATTA

12 OCTOBER 1993

The next few weeks were a blur of lectures, assignments, cadavers, fetching Murdoch's coffee, watching his students butcher their autopsies and one unfortunate trip to Achilles House.

"It's all I've fecken got," she'd groused at the Gold Stitch.

"I need one with flora. *I thought I made that clear."*

"I'm not a dunce. I heard you, but I can't make *it happen."*

The leaves had all gone crimson and russet, the candles and confections cinnamon. Walking around campus was a fever dream of autumnal wonders and still, nearing the middle of October, she knew the charm had only just begun.

Professor Murdoch, on the other hand, had lost all of his charm.

"You marked these incorrectly." He tossed a stack of essays at her.

Atta curled her lip at him but looked over the essays. She'd marked everything exactly the way he'd laid out in the *extensive* notes he'd given once he finally agreed to let her help look over students' work.

"This is exactly what you told me to do."

He finally looked at her, most likely due to the insolence in her tone more than because of what she'd said. "You used a red pen."

She blinked at him. "Red is the standard pen colour for making corrections."

"Not in my courses."

She looked at the anatomical rendering of a heart in front of him where he was correcting a student's labelling. "You use blue."

"They have enough harsh lines in their lives, Miss Morrow. They don't need any more. It does nothing but discourage."

Fine. He hadn't lost *all* of his charm. She wished he'd take those damned glasses off though. No one had the right to look that alluring with nerdy glasses and a sullen attitude.

"Can I help you with something?" It wasn't until he spoke that Atta realised she'd been staring.

"What? No. No." Shaking her head too many times, she noticed the Dublin Paper on his desk next to a mug of stale coffee. "HPSC recruits professors at TCD for—" she read, but he cut her off, standing.

"That's enough. Finish those marks by class." And he shooed her out of the teachers' room.

Most afternoons with him went by similarly, him brooding, her irritated. It had taken some time to work out her class schedule with Murdoch's, but he'd given up on her observing all his lectures and missing her own rather easily after a time. It gave Atta an odd sense of pride that she'd at least proven herself enough to keep the position.

Most of her shifts at Gallaghers' had grown slow and boring. When she asked Siobhan about it, she gave a noncommittal shrug, but there was worry etched in the lines of her worn face. She was quieter than normal. Reserved and reclusive.

"Are you all right?" Atta asked her one evening. "You don't seem yourself."

"Something's brewing, pet. I can feel it in my old bones."

"How do you mean?" she ventured rubbing at her arms that had gone dotted with chill bumps.

"Don't be worrying, now." Siobhan stood, looking older than Atta had ever seen her. "I don't think we need you on tonight, pet. Go on home, I'll be having a pint and lockin' the doors."

Atta swore she heard a childish giggle on the wind as she walked between the park and the Medical Building to Briseis House. She couldn't make out much in the dark, but there were glimmers of lights, little bursts of iridescent shimmers floating about in the park.

———

"What's going on out there?" Atta asked Emmy over breakfast one morning. There were loads of workers traipsing through campus, enough that Atta had noticed from their suite window overlooking New Square.

Emmy, curious, set down her tea and came to the window. "I don't know."

Gibbs burst through the door, carrying a crumpled copy of Trinity News. "Have you heard?"

Emmy and Atta exchanged a look before shaking their heads in unison.

He rushed over to the coffee table and spread out the paper.

"They're shutting down a section of the park." He pointed to a black-and-white map of College Park, where it backed up to a row of trees bordering Nassau Street. "It's not a large section, but they've got huge iron gates going up."

"What are they doing with it?" Emmy asked as Atta bent in to inspect the article with the map.

"They're using it to bury the Infected?" she screeched, shocked by her own uncharacteristic hysteria.

Gibbs, his eyes wide as saucers that lent her to believe he was also bordering on hysteria, nodded mutely.

"Why here?" Emmy asked, horror in the grim set of her mouth.

"They've always insisted the Infected must be burned. . ." Atta couldn't halt the onslaught of thoughts. Who were *'they,'* anyway, making these decisions? Part of her thought it had to be Achilles House, but that couldn't be it. They were a part of a larger whole, that much was obvious.

"I don't know." Gibbs sank onto the sofa, Atta and Emmy flanking him. "This is mental, right?"

Both women nodded absently, each lost to their thoughts.

When she felt she had command of her sensibilities, Atta read the full article, a knot of dread knitting together in her abdomen.

Hours later in Morbid Anatomy, Professor Murdoch was pacing around an open cadaver splayed before the class, but she hadn't heard a word he'd said.

". . .Take the Plague for example," he was saying. "It shuts down the organs, blackens the blood, resulting in death." He walked a circle around the cadaver. "But the Plague seemingly chooses at random. There are no current indications of a rhyme or reason, like a typical disease, or even pre-existing conditions

or signs of cancer"—he tossed his hand around in the air—
"foul play, nothing of the sort. The Plague has made equal men
and women of us all over the past six years."

Atta scoffed, unable to stop herself or use decorum in her
stressed state.

To her horror, Murdoch stopped and turned to look directly
at her, one brow quirked, and she froze. "Do you have
something to add, Miss Morrow?"

Atta shook her head sharply, hoping her cheeks weren't
aflame.

Murdoch returned to his route around the corpse, but Atta's
shadow self, her darker side, the one festering with all the
Plague had wrought over the last six years, that side betrayed
her. "Actually," she heard herself say, like an out-of-body
experience, "I do."

One of the students behind her snickered, the little gobshite,
and two others let out audible gasps.

"By all means." Murdoch splayed a palm in a gesture for
her to continue.

Her blood was boiling enough that it pushed out trepidation
and perhaps logic. He did that to her, this man, just like the
Plague. "The elite like to pretend that horrific events or
circumstances make them equal with lower classes, but it's
only to pacify their own conscience and lull the lower classes
into thinking they're not just existing in an open-air prison."

A flicker of something glittered in Murdoch's gaze as he
levelled her with it. "Death comes for us all, Miss Morrow.
There is no one left untouched by the Plague, not anymore."

Atta stood from her seat. "That is a cop-out. Something the
wealthy say to blur the harsh lines drawn between classes. You
said yourself that we have too many lines. The elite use blue

instead of red, but it doesn't mean the harshness is actually softened, it only portrays the illusion that it is."

She knew the class had no idea what she was referring to, but Sonder Murdoch did. And if the look on his face was any indication, she'd struck a chord. Or a nerve.

"And yet we all die," he said evenly. "Do we not?"

"Of course we do." Atta gestured angrily at the cadaver. "But nothing short of a cataclysm, nature steamrolling even the elite, can make *equals* of us all as long as wealth and power rule the world. And they still do."

"And if the Plague is that event?" he challenged.

"How can it be? You can't tell me the elite have felt the effects of the Plague as harshly as the lower class."

"Has it not killed the wealthy as ruthlessly as the poor?"

"Perhaps it has," she argued, "but is it the wealthy who are going to be helped first, or the poor?"

"Hypotheticals will not help your case, Miss Morrow."

Her head was on fire, but he looked to be enjoying himself.

Despite the inferno in her gut, Atta smiled, let it be a wicked little grin. "You've just proven my point. Just because you can't see it doesn't mean it isn't true."

"You make rash, snap judgements," he shot back with a dark, humourless laugh. "That might be acceptable in Botany, but it will not bode well in Morbid Anatomy, in *real* science."

Atta's head jerked back as if he'd slapped her. Rather than responding, she collected her things and left.

She spent the rest of the afternoon hiding in the cocoon of the library, lost to her studies, to her tapes of Liszt, headphones blocking out everything and everyone. Most of all Sonder Murdoch and the unsettling cemetery of Infected she couldn't stop thinking about.

The sun was beginning to set and her stomach growled, alerting her it was time to make her way home. Maybe she and Emmy could make cheese toasties and pretend the world was normal before her late shift at Gallaghers'.

"Good evening."

Atta looked up at the sound of the terse, gravelly voice, shocked to see Murdoch lounging on the green sofa in the Briseis common room like he still lived there. The colour made his eyes stand out, and she merely blinked at him, watching him as he rose and crossed the room toward her.

"Walsh asked if you and I would debate in every class." He tried at a smile, but as usual, it fell flat. "I wanted to apologise to you."

Atta crossed her arms. "Then do it. I'm going to be late for work."

"I won't apologise for the debate. I rather enjoyed it, to be frank. But I insulted you and it was cruel. I'm sorry."

As far as apologies went, it wasn't half bad. "I'm sorry I challenged you in front of your class."

Murdoch shook his head, a dark curl falling across his forehead. "If we were never challenged, Atta, we would never grow."

Before she could say anything, he reached out a hand, one finger gliding up the elongated spine of her collar chain, ending at one of the two skulls attached on either side. "I like this."

Turning on his heel, he strode away, one hand in his pocket and the other—the one that had just been so very close to touching her—clenched in a fist at his side.

ATTA

They fell into a delicate rhythm after the evening Murdoch apologised.

It was still tense, thrumming with something Atta couldn't quite put her finger on, but he gave her more to do, and would sometimes even carry on conversations with her. She discovered the book he'd been reading when they'd first met was a work of fiction, *The Prisoner of Zenda* by Anthony Hope. It took some cajoling, but he'd even told her what it was about, and Atta suggested he watch *Princess Bride* because it sounded similar to her.

He'd smiled then, a small thing that looked as if it pained him a bit. "I don't get to see many films."

Then, the conversation was over and they went about their work separately, Atta marking papers and Murdoch scratching away at a notepad.

"Did you read about the section of campus they're blocking off to bury some of the Infected?" she ventured a few days later when she brought him coffee between classes.

Atta watched Murdoch's jaw clench. "I did. Yes."

"It's strange, isn't it? All this time we've been told it's important to burn them. What changed? The article said the Medical College was taking part in the research to stop the Plague. Is that you? I would assume Pathology and Morbid Anatomy would be the perfect department for tha—"

"Those matters are not to be discussed here."

Atta swallowed the rest of her words and busied herself with other things until her next lecture and shift at the morgue.

By the time she made it to Achilles House that night, she was surviving off of caffeine and a petrol station chicken fillet roll she would undoubtedly regret soon. But it was worth it.

The Unidentified Infected numbers were still low. The Plague had its tendrils further into the flesh of society leaving more and more mourners behind, and Atta without subjects. There had, however, been one Unidentified that day. When Carl arrived for the TBB, she lied and told him the body had been identified, and that it would be buried in the new Trinity Cemetery. Carl left and Atta sliced, rejuvenated by the prospect of the first subject in what felt like ages.

Her heart fell when there were no signs of flora, but she still found something grossly interesting. The blood around the cadaver's heart had not only turned black but congealed into a loamy mess that resembled used coffee grounds or— Atta had gasped. *Soil.* She quickly made her notes, sewed the body shut, and hauled it into her car.

The door opened before she could finish knocking. Gold Stitch stared down at her, the light glinting off his goggles. "You haven't been here in two weeks."

"Wow. Thanks for the history lesson."

"That body better be for me."

"Isn't this whole shindig yours?"

She couldn't see his face, but she knew it was snide. "I need a Stage 3, and you know it."

This piqued her interest. "Is that what you call it—the flora phenomenon? How many stages are there? What marks the other stages?"

Gold Stitch stepped out onto the stoop, causing her to back up, descending to the gravel. She didn't like him higher than her, peering down.

"Stop asking questions." He came down the steps and walked past her to her car. She opened the boot for him and he cursed, really a rather colourful display hissed through the beak of his mask. "You opened the corpse again. A–" He abruptly broke off. "You have to stop opening them. It jeopardises the integrity of the research."

"How am I supposed to know if there are signs of flora if I don't open them, Sherlock?"

The sigh that escaped him was so long she thought it might be his final breath. "I foolishly assumed you were aware of the outward signs."

Her banter slipped away into the cold night air. "Wait. How did I miss that?"

Gold Stitch lifted a shoulder, impatience in the set of his limbs.

Had she, though? Missed it? "Do you mean the black veins?"

"Especially in the eyes."

Atta gnawed on her bottom lip. She had put that together internally, perhaps even in her notes, but it hadn't fully registered. . .

She squinted at Gold Stitch. "What's your name, hm?"

He didn't answer her, only strode back toward the door.

"Tell me your name and I'll stop opening the cadavers."

"Nice try."

He disappeared inside, and Atta tried with all her might to get as good a look as she could at the interior of the House before the door slammed shut. When it re-opened, a Black Stitch wheeled out a gurney, and the usual gangly White Stitch brought her a half-payment, more skittish than usual.

"Hey, does that Gold Stitch guy run his place?" she asked White Stitch conspiratorily.

He startled back a step. "You need to get out of here." The lad fled and Atta returned to her car, counting her money.

When she looked up from opening the car door, a masked figure was sitting in her passenger seat.

"Fucking hell!" she spat. "What in hell are you doing?"

"I told you I need a particularly plagued body," Gold Stitch said rather calmly if it wasn't just the mask muffling and distorting his voice.

"And I told you, I don't have a *Stage 3*." She threw sufficient mocking into the last words.

"Then let's go."

"Are you mental? I'm not going anywhere with you."

"Get in the car, Atta." The words brooked no argument, but that wasn't why her breath caught. He knew her name. He knew her fucking name.

"*No.*"

His sigh sounded trapped this time. "It's your car. You have the keys and I'm in the passenger seat. Who has the upper hand here?"

He had a point. Maybe.

She slid into the driver's seat and started the car, smashing a fist against the dash

His head turned slowly toward her. "Was that some sort of fit?"

Atta barked a mad laugh and it seemed to startle Gold Stitch, to her great satisfaction. "It's the only way the heater comes on. Old car."

She turned in her seat to look at him, wondering what he'd do if she reached across and ripped the mask off. Probably kill her. *We all have to die some way*, Murdoch had said.

"Where are we going?"

"The campus cemetery."

"What do you need me for?" she asked as they crossed the Liffey. "You're a big lad."

He was turned away from her, looking out the window, and he smelled of embalming fluid and cigar smoke. "I haven't told the others about the flora, and told my anatomist you mentioned it to that you were mistaken."

His honesty shocked her so much that she almost stopped the car. "Why?"

"I suspect some above me already know, but I like to keep my research close to my chest."

"And how do I fit into this?" she pressed, turning at the next light.

"Those are Botany textbooks, are they not?" He pointed a black-gloved finger to the stack of coursebooks he'd had to move to the footwell when he invaded her car.

Grappling with a mixture of flattery and fear, she said the first stupid thing that sprang to her mind because of the scent filling her senses. "Do you smoke?"

The mask stared at her for a moment, the cherry street lights reflecting in his goggles and making him look comically ridiculous. "On occasion. Why?"

"I can smell it on you."

He was silent until she turned onto Nassau. "Turn off the headlamps."

She parked as he directed her to. The streets were nearly deserted, the pub and tourist crowds calling it quits past 3 a.m. Gold Stitch opened his door first, and Atta considered shoving him out of the car and speeding off, but the massive, black iron gates loomed ahead of him, and Atta bent to peer up at the top of one through the windscreen. Then, she blew a breath past her lips.

"How are we going to get in there?" she whispered.

"You'll see."

God, she was tired. "I don't exactly have a shovel in my car."

"Yes, you do." He pointed a gloved finger again and Atta followed the direction, looking into the backseat. "Put two back there myself."

She wrinkled her nose at him. "You think you're quite clever, don't you."

"You aren't scared of me," he said, completely off-topic and sounding more befuddled than anything. "Why?"

Frankly, she was pleased she'd come off as unafraid because she was still rather terrified. Though, she supposed, it wasn't the creepy masked man or the horrible crime they were about to commit. It was the possibility of getting caught. "We all have to die some way or other, Gold Stitch."

He cleared his throat at her words but said nothing.

"There's a little phrase wise women live by. *If he wants to, he will*. It's usually more romantic than our particular scenario, but the point still stands. If you wanted to murder me, you would. Now, come on."

They exited the car in unison, both having the forethought enough to shut their doors quietly. Atta used her hip to close hers the rest of the way while Gold Stitch opened the rear door and produced two shovels. Atta walked around and he handed her one, reaching inside to pull out a lantern.

"A kerosene lantern?" she mocked. "I probably have a torch in here somewhere."

"I'm old-fashioned," he answered her, leaning his shovel against the side of her car and lighting the lamp with a match.

"Mmhmm." They both knew she was goading him, but she didn't feel inclined to stop. Judging by his status, build, and muffled voice, she'd peg him somewhere in the latter half of his thirties, possibly early forties. She'd always been enthralled by slightly older men. They knew what the hell they were doing in life. A flash of Murdoch slipped into her mind unbidden—the day he told her about the novels he'd been reading. Atta shook the memory loose.

"Old-fashioned or old?" she goaded Gold Stitch further. "Hard to tell with that mask on, you know."

They hid in the shadows and the lantern light shown in his goggles, her face reflected back at her in the flame. "I'm vintage, darling."

Blood rushed to Atta's ears and every other part of her body, but Gold Stitch merely turned and walked toward the dark cemetery, lantern in one hand and shovel over his shoulder.

Atta followed, her heart hammering against her ribs. This wasn't like sneaking a body out of the morgue under broken streetlights after the Gallaghers had left. This was a cemetery *within* the college.

"What exactly is the plan here?" She rubbed her cold hands together, looking over her shoulder as he picked a lock.

It clicked open and Gold Sitch reached for the handle. "We find a Stage 3."

"But how will we get an entire body out of here?"

"We don't need an entire body, we need a look at one and *samples*."

All the graves were fresh, the soil upturned and carefully laid in mounds atop each corpse. Atta was inexplicably saddened by the fact that none of the graves were marked with names. "Why aren't there any headstones?" she asked as they walked.

"Those take a while to be made," he answered. It was difficult to hear him out in the open. "But I would venture to say they never will be."

Frustrated and horribly unnerved, Atta reached out and snatched the elbow of Gold Stitch's black coat. He froze mid-step and turned to face her. "I can accept that you won't take the mask off or tell me your name, but if I'm going to be involved in this shite, I want to know what's *really* going on."

"I can't tell you that, Atta."

"Ignorance doesn't equate to safety."

"I didn't say it did."

"Do you even know what's happening? What all of this is?"

"I know that it's strange they wanted the bodies burned and now they want as many buried as possible," he said sharply, "but my job is to cure this Plague, not question the burial practises of the great city of Dublin."

"Does Achilles House work with the Morbid Anatomy Department at Trinity?" she said as he tried to walk away.

He only kept walking.

"An article said the government had consulted them. Are you not an entity of the government? How could you possibly find all the funding you need if you aren't?"

He spun around to face her. "You ask a lot of questions," he gritted out. "Now is not the time for a history lesson of the Society."

He stormed off and Atta picked up her shovel, balancing it on her shoulder to follow him. "Do you even know what you're looking for?" she asked when they'd gone in a circle.

"Stage 3 graves are marked with something. I don't know what. I thought it would be at least somewhat more obvious than this, I'll admit."

Atta bent down next to the plot nearest her. "Hold the lantern over here."

Gold Stitch did as she requested, and Atta stuck her hand in the grave dirt. It was moist, fertile. She spread the soil out with her fingers, inspecting it. "Closer," she demanded. Gold Stitch crouched beside her, one of his knees almost brushing her arm. "Jesus of little Nazareth," she cursed and a distinct snort came from behind Gold Stitch's mask. "This is fertiliser."

He turned to her so sharply that the leather beak of his mask almost hit her in the cheek. "To fertilise the grass for regrowth, right?"

Atta dusted her hands off and rose. "I never really go out to the graves, but I would think so. Except. . ." Her words trailed off as she pointed to the grave next to it, the dirt harder there. Much less fertile. It was easy to grow on the Emerald Isle, but. . .

Gold Stitch swung his lantern in that direction, then up, illuminating half a dozen fresh plots. Only one was the dark, black soil awaiting growth.

"Look at this," he said, sidestepping the grave to set the lantern by the head of it. He reached down and picked up something shiny and silver between his fingers, glinting in the lantern light.

"A coin?" Atta bent to take a look, and he held it out to her.

"I've never seen anything like it before.," Gold Stitch mused. "The material is less dense than expected. Shiner, almost ethereal."

"That's a hawthorn tree on it." Atta held out her hand, and he placed the coin in her palm. The second it touched her flesh, she gasped, a horrible, rasping sound in her ears.

She was instantly standing in a foggy wood, surrounded by endless hawthorns.

She was afraid.

Running.

Running from something. Or was it *to* something?

Someone was calling her name. They sounded even more frightened than she was. She could feel tears on her cheeks, but why was she crying?

"*Atta*!" The voice again, bellowing. It was familiar, that deep, resonant voice.

The tears fell harder, her legs pumping faster.

"Atta, *no!*"

She thought her gasp into the hallucination had been guttural, but this man's cry for her was rife with pure agony.

Lights were flickering in the fog. Blue, like the hottest part of the flame.

Wills-o-the-wisp she heard her own fragmented mind say. *Corpse Flames*.

She darted further into the fog, chasing one. Breath heaving, she pulled out a vial of black salt and ran harder.

A piercing scream filled the misty night, and everything went white.

"Atta!"

Someone was shaking her.

"*Atta*, wake up."

A gloved hand was on her cheek, the leather soft, the touch tender. Her eyes fluttered open, going wide when she saw the plague doctor mask hovering over her. She was in his lap, covered in grave dirt.

"Oh my god." She scrambled off of Gold Stitch and into the muddy grass. "I'm so sorry."

"Atta," he said calmly, "what happened?" He stood and made to help her up.

She didn't take his offered hand. "Nothing. I get migraines sometimes."

"Migraines that cause you to faint?"

She scrubbed at her arm. "That part was new."

"Give me the keys."

"What? Why?"

"I'm taking you home."

"But what about the body? The samples?"

"Never mind that. Give me the keys."

"No." But she swayed on her feet and he jumped to steady her with an arm around her waist. When he pulled away, he had her keys in his hand.

"Hey!"

"Let's go."

"You forgot your damned lantern. You make a terrible criminal." She scooped it up and startled when the flame turned blue, then leeched away from the wick, darting out of the lantern completely. Before she could even react, it dissipated like a spent sparkler over a different grave.

"What are you doing?" Gold Stitch groused as she jumped over one grave and then another to look at the one the flame had sent her to. *Will-o-the-wisp*, her traitorous mind whispered like the migraine-induced vision, *Corpse Flame*.

"This one has been fertilised too," she called over her shoulder. "Come here."

"We can deal with this later. You need to get *home*."

"Shut up." She saw another coin glint in the light. Another hawthorn tree. She handed it to Gold Stitch, feeling a buzz in her veins.

"We need to *go*."

"I see something." She leaned in closer, finally giving up and getting on her hands and knees. Something else was peeking up out of the soil.

Stoic Gold Stitch was on his knees beside her in an instant. "My god. Is that—"

"A mushroom."

"I don't claim to know a lot about Botany, but that isn't likely on a fresh grave, is it?"

"Not one this fresh. I'm going to take it."

His hand clamped down on her wrist as she reached for it. "Not without a mask and gloves you won't. This Plague is spreading somehow and we can't take risks."

"Give me your gloves then."

He contemplated for a moment, but eventually shucked off his gloves and handed them to her. They were too large and too difficult to work with. "I need the mycelium beneath it."

"I don't have a specimen jar big enough for that. We'll come back tomorrow night."

Everything in her wanted to snatch that mushroom and

study it. For all they knew, it had somehow managed to cling to life from where it had been upturned with the soil. She wouldn't know unless she could study the mycelium.

"Please, just— Let's get you home." His tone had a note of tenderness, enough to stall her.

"All right," she finally conceded, rising and dusting off her clothes.

She followed Gold Stitch to her car and let him drive. They spent the entire ride in silence until they turned into the car park and he parked away from other cars, turning off the ignition.

"How will you get home?" she asked.

"Don't worry about that."

They exited her car and he handed her the keys.

"Why would an Infected person sprout a plant from their organs?" Her voice was smaller than she would have liked for it to sound, but so was his, almost inaudible through the mask.

"I don't know yet. And now I'm worried about who does. Get inside your dorm."

He strode away into the dark trees, shoving his hands into the pockets of his coat.

She was unnerved by how much he knew about her—her name, where she lived—but it was her *lack* of fear of him that unnerved her even more. Halfway to Briseis House, she turned to look over her shoulder to find him in the trees, watching her. He made a small *keep going* gesture, and it wasn't until she made it up to Third that it occurred to her he'd been watching to make sure she made it inside safely.

SONDER

"Get up."

Sonder smacked Gibbs's foot where he lay in his tidy bed in his tidy room so close to Atta's.

"Gibbs. Get *up*."

"Fucking hell," he groaned, rubbing a fist at his eyes as he tried to sit up. "Murdoch? Fuck. What are you doing in my room?"

It was nice to see the lad's trepidation of him was eradicated by sleepiness. "I need to talk to you."

"What time is it?" He looked around blearily. "How did you even get in here?"

Sonder hung his mask on one of the posts of Gibbs's bed. "It's 4:56 in the morning and climbing a tree is not that fucking hard. Now get *up*."

"I'm up, I'm up." He shoved on his glasses and Sonder turned on a lamp, Gibbs squinting at the abrupt light. "What is it?"

"What do you know about Atta's migraines?"

"Atta's mig– What?"

"Christ, Gibbs. I know you were asleep but this is ridiculous. Her *migraines*. Atta has migraines. Why does she get them?"

Gibbs shook his head, hair wild from sleep. "She's never mentioned them."

Sonder squeezed his jaws together. "I need you to find out."

"You want me to spy on my roommate? Why don't you just ask her?"

"Because I can't, all right?"

"Is this Society business or Morbid Anatomy business?"

"I fucking swear. You ask almost as many damned questions as she does." Sonder rose and moved toward the window, grabbing his mask. "Just find out."

He donned the mask and ducked out the window, hand latching onto the large tree outside it before leaning back in. "Make sure she locks her fucking window, too. This was too easy."

"Most people don't climb in other people's windows like creeps," Gibbs shot back.

Sonder snorted. "I like this no-holds-barred version of you, Gibbs."

He climbed down the tree, hopping from the trunk to the soft dirt, and began the long walk back to Achilles.

ATTA

"That one." Emmy pointed to a heather-taupe knit jumper Atta held aloft opposite the exact same jumper in brown. Emmy was on Atta's bed, lying on her stomach, chin in her hands and ankles crossed. "It perfectly matches the trousers."

Atta agreed, slipping the sweater over her lace bra and tucking it into her plaid, tapered trousers. It was nice having simple, mindless girl talk. She hadn't had many friends in her life—the peculiar girl with her nose always in a book, who lived above a morgue. She found herself thankful on a daily basis that Emmy and her other roommates had accepted her right away. They didn't even care that she was older than them, though they mercilessly teased her for it when she tried to make Domhnall chicken soup when he fell ill a couple of weeks prior.

"How are things going with Dr Frankenstein?" Emmy waggled her eyebrows. "I certainly wouldn't mind all those hours you spend alone with him. What did your friend call him?"

Atta laughed despite herself, plaiting her hair into a messy braid over one shoulder. "'*Fuckable in a scholarly way*,'" she quoted Imogen with a laugh. "He's not exactly a chatty fellow most days, but it's not so bad. How are things with Professor Vasilios?"

Emmy sighed and rolled over onto her back while Atta began putting on too many rings. To clear her mind enough for sleep after her night in the graveyard with Gold Stitch, she'd painted her nails a chocolate brown and all the silver rings brought out a hint of dusky purple in the polish. She liked it.

"Marguerite is Marguerite," Emmy said. "She has this new idea—a fad she read about in the Psych Journal, I'm sure—that group therapy is more beneficial."

Atta grimaced. "That sounds terrible."

"It is. The students loathe it. Airing all their sins and kinks for their peers to assess? It's fucking mental. I don't think it's helping at all. And their papers?" She blew a breath through her lips that made them sputter together. "They hate what it's making them into."

"What's Vasilios's aim with this group therapy thing?" Atta asked, straightening the tassels on her loafers.

Emmy sat up, her cream silk robe opening to reveal part of her breast. "She claims it will help them see they aren't alone—the effect of a mediator without having one. Do you know what I mean?"

Atta nodded, slipping her arms into her wool blazer. "As in, people feel more comfortable airing grievances when there are other people around. A buffer."

Emmy snapped and pointed at her. "Exactly that."

"Does it work?"

"So far, no. But maybe it will only take more time. I think

Marguerite is blind to the fact that this type of therapy is for those in a family unit or other common life scenario, not veritable strangers in a lecture. I think she should try it in her smaller classes."

Atta nodded. "I like that about Murdoch's classes. They're so small that it's almost like being part of a fellowship. The students, by semester's end, will be rather close in many ways."

"That would be the perfect setting for group therapy, what with all those bodies you slice open and the nightmares it must induce." Emmy shivered, and Atta laughed.

"Emmy!" Dohmnall shouted from the common room. "Atta! Come out here, quick!"

The women shared a befuddled look and hurried out into the common room where Dohmnall had the telly at full blast and was uselessly hitting buttons on the remote to try and make it louder.

A sombre newsreader was standing in front of Campanile Tower, a microphone to her mouth and autumn leaves billowing behind her. Atta could see her old window, second floor, third from the right.

"Thank you, Peter," she was saying. "I'm live here at Trinity College Dublin where a student has been found Infected. The student was found in her dorm in House Seven of student accommodations late last night and succumbed to the Plague. According to reports, the young woman was found in front of her telly, so long gone that ivy had crept in from outside her closed window and nearly concealed the body. At this time, Trinity has not decided whether they will shut down the campus. . ."

The rest faded out, a ringing beginning in Atta's ears

because a photo of the student had popped onto the screen. *Lauren Kennedy* it read under her photo. But all Atta saw was the girl from her class. The one she'd run into weeks ago and seen die that exact way. Covered—picked apart—by creeping ivy.

Gagging, Atta ran to the toilet and threw up bile.

———

Directly after her only lecture for the day, Atta rushed across campus to the Medical Building, hoping to catch Professor Murdoch before class.

After she'd vomited that morning, Emmy filled her in on the rest of the report. She said Murdoch had been on the news with Dean Lynch and the other heads of the medical department. He wasn't in his office, but she found him pacing around the surgical theatre.

The moment he saw her, he shifted toward her. His brows furrowed and he took a step forward. "Are you all right? Do you have a headache?"

Atta regarded him strangely. He must have noted how flushed she was. How anxious. "No, no headache. Do you think they'll close college?"

"No, I don't. It would be unwise and I advised against it."

"Why?"

Murdoch shoved his hand through his hair which was already in disarray as if he'd done that many times since the morning's broadcast. "That isn't how this works. Everyone knows it's not a virus, at least as far as we understand viruses. It doesn't move like one. Her roommate is completely healthy, as are all the other peers she associated with. It would only induce panic in the whole of Dublin to shut down college."

Atta swallowed. Nodded. She was trying to remain calm, but his agitation was feeding hers. "I thought she'd been there so long ivy was growing."

She watched Murdoch look away, consider. "She was a Botany student. Did you know her?"

Atta nodded, barely, her fingertips feeling numb.

"When was the last time you saw her in class?" he asked finally.

"Last week."

"Ivy grows that quickly?"

"Under the right conditions, it can grow eight or nine feet a year." To her own ears, it sounded ridiculous. It certainly didn't grow that much in the span of a week.

"That seems aggressive, doesn't it?"

She couldn't deny that. "It does." But she didn't know where he was headed or what he knew as a consultant to HPSC. "Maybe she had ivy inside her dorm already." She watched his movements. Considered how familiar she felt with his presence in this particular conversation. "What are you thinking?"

His eyes searched her face for a long moment. "Can I show you something?"

"We have class in ten minutes."

"I'll cancel."

"Won't that scare them, today of all days, like you said?"

"Sometimes fear cleanses the soul, Atta. It reminds us to look at the important things we took for granted while at peace." He let his words sink in for a moment. "Come with me."

There might be more magnificent libraries in existence, but none would ever compare to The Old Library. Not for Atta. From the moment she stepped inside, her breath was stolen each time by the sheer volume of 200,000 books, the polished floor, the long, arched ceiling and the busts of academic forefathers observing their children at study.

"What are we doing here?" she whispered to Murdoch as they walked past the busts of Homer, Aristotle, and Plato.

Without answering, he climbed the stairs and Atta followed. Abruptly, he turned into a row of books. Without hesitation, he stopped at a particular shelf and carefully removed a book. He laid it out on one of the narrow standing tables then stepped back and gestured to it.

"Page 419. Tell me what you make of it."

Atta watched him for a moment. He was still so ill at ease that it had her nerves frayed. She'd never seen him appear any other way but brooding or stoic. She approached the desk cautiously, like something within the pages might bite her or release a changeling faerie to take over her body.

The parchment was old and yellowed, and Atta carefully flipped to Page 419. Her lips parted when she saw what he'd meant for her to look over.

It was a detailed diagram of how spores spread, followed by a description of how mushrooms communicate with the plant world around them, through electrical signals in their mycelium. All things Atta knew, but Murdoch . . .

She looked from the pages to Murdoch. "What made you think of this?"

"I've done some consulting on Plague cases. I don't think —" He closed his mouth and ran his hand down his jaw. "I don't think that ivy should have grown like that. And I think the best way to figure out what happened is this." He pointed at the spore diagram. "With your knowledge of Botany, I thought perhaps this would make more sense to you. Why the spore in Patient Zero was so important."

Atta licked her lips and leaned against the standing table, feeling like they took up the entire stall, the two of them and this conversation. "I've been trying to figure that out for the last six years. Since I first read about a spore in Patient Zero." She licked her lips. "You asked me why I'm at Trinity—"

"And that's why, isn't it? Why you blend Morbid Arts and Botany?"

Atta dipped her chin, feeling overwhelmingly emotional that he'd pieced together her interests, and she couldn't place why.

Murdoch ran a hand through his hair again, mussing it up even more. He reached for the pocket of his cord blazer and pulled out his glasses. Putting them on, he nodded toward the book. "Will you write down all you know? Put it in a report for me?"

Dumbfounded, Atta blinked at him. He was standing so close to her that she was finding it a little difficult to breathe. "Yeah. I mean, sure. Yes, I can do that."

His smile, though small, was real and true as it curved his lips. "Thank you, Atta."

He turned from her, selecting another book from the shelf. It was very near the one he'd removed for her to look at, so she assumed it was similar material, but her mind went elsewhere as he flipped a page.

"Oh my god." She said it softly, but he turned in alarm, taking one step toward her.

"What is it? Your head?"

She screwed up her face at him. Why did he keep asking her that? "What? No. I know why you've looked familiar since I met you."

Murdoch went still as one of the marble busts lining The Long Room. "Oh?" The word was tight. Forced out through his teeth.

"You would have been going for your doctorate when I was in undergrad, right?"

He bent his head to one side, calculating, then shrugged. "My doctorate was '78-'83. I took a gap year to live in Italy before beginning postgrad in '78."

"Yes!" Atta almost shouted, thrilled to finally have figured it out. "I was studying at that table right over there." She pointed across the gallery to a stall on the other side. "I had my Folklore exam the next day, and you were there"—she pointed toward the end of that stall—"reading." She looked at Murdoch, smiling, and she thought she saw his gaze drop to her lips before he met her eyes again. "You never did sit down. You just stood there, like you are now. Like you always do when you read. One hand in your pocket until it's time to flip the page." She laughed with a fondness she didn't know she held, and he froze in place again. "It was rather annoying, actually."

There was something searching about his gaze and she tried not to let her smile fade, but it was difficult the longer it took him to respond to her.

"Professor Murdoch?" she ventured after a moment.

"Sonder."

"I'm sorry?" Her heart slammed against her ribcage as soon as he said it.

"Please, call me Sonder. I'm not really your professor and I've asked you here to help me with something as a peer."

Her palms were suddenly feeling clammy, so she curled her hands at her sides. "All right, then. Sonder." She tested his name out on her tongue and he swallowed, his throat bobbing, then he nodded.

"Very well."

ATTA

As soon as the sun set, Atta rushed to Achilles House and banged on the knocker. Gold Stitch answered immediately as if he'd been waiting for her.

"Meet me at the petrol station down the way."

"Do you realise half of what you say sounds like you're an axe murderer?"

"It's good I don't use an axe but a scalpel then, hm? Less painful."

Atta snorted.

"I'll meet you there in ten minutes." He closed the door and she was left doing what he said. Again.

On the drive to the petrol station, she considered talking to him about what she and Murdoch had been researching that afternoon. *Sonder,* she corrected inwardly, suppressing a tingle up her neck. The two of them had to be in contact, at least minutely. Atta wasn't foolish enough to believe Sonder's consulting didn't include information trading with the head of Achilles House. He probably knew who Gold Stitch was and all about the flora found in Stage 3 Infected bodies. She couldn't very well ask Sonder that, or it would reveal a whole host of her own secrets. Sometimes, she entertained the thought that the two men were in league together, perhaps even one and the same. It made sense for how sullen and bossy they both were.

That train of thought flitted away when she pulled into the station and saw Lauren Kennedy's roommate leaning against her Volkswagen, smoking a cigarette. She recognised her from the broadcasts and couldn't help but feel a deep sense of sadness for the girl. Kathryn had been the one to find Lauren like that, dead-eyed and consumed. Atta couldn't fathom what that was like. Sure, she saw the deceased every day of her life, but she'd never stumbled upon someone she loved that way.

What if Kathryn had been at their dorm and not home visiting her new niece as she'd told the newsreader?

The thought gave Atta a horrible, brilliant idea.

She recognised Gold Stitch's car but didn't realise until a few moments later that she'd never actually seen it before. Though, she was convinced people looked like their cars and pets. The lead anatomist of a masked secret society driving an olive Ford Capri from what looked like the 1960s was almost comically fitting.

She parked near him but selected a spot with a streetlight and he had not—ever in the shadows. Atta locked her car and slid into his.

"Do I look like my car?" she asked by way of greeting.

"Excuse me?"

God, she wanted to rip that stupid mask off. "Do I look like my car?"

The mask rotated in the direction of her car, goggles shining. "Em. I suppose so?"

Atta huffed. "Never mind. I think we should look at a different cadaver than the one we found last night."

"Why is that?" He pulled out onto the main road.

"Because I don't know what Stage 4 is, but I think it's Lauren Kennedy."

Gold Stitch's head snapped toward her. "No."

"So you know about her."

"Obviously I do."

"Then let's take her."

"That's a death sentence. We can't thieve a body from under the Society's nose, Atta."

There he was using her name again, damn him.

"We should at least go collect a sample."

He sighed so heavily she had to stifle a chuckle because he sounded like he was about to say, *'No, I am your fatha'* to Luke Skywalker.

"All right."

"*All right?*" Atta squealed.

That low, thunderous rumble of a laugh of his sounded in his chest and Atta's cheeks heated. "Do you know where she is?"

"As a matter of fact, I think I do."

She noted that he wasn't wearing gloves this time, and her attention snagged on his hands as they gripped the wheel.

Atta didn't know her way around Dublin as well as she should, but she definitely knew they weren't headed to college.

"This is a café," she said blandly when he pulled into a car park. "There are Infected bodies under this café?"

"No." He got out of the car and leaned his head back in. "But you've got the underground part right. Come on."

Atta climbed out and followed a masked man onto a

secluded walkway into a dark, wooded area. One of these days, she was going to pay for being so trusting. Or was it reckless?

"Where are we going?" she whispered, stepping more quickly to walk next to him.

"You'll see."

A tree rustled above them and Atta gasped, grabbing Gold Stitch's arm and squeezing it to her chest before she realised what was happening. An owl glided out from the branches near the top, swooping down past them and into another tree with a *hoo*.

Realising it wasn't a monster or villain or anything else that goes bump in the night, Atta let out a breath, then noticed she was clutching her masked man's arm like her life depended on it. She looked up into his goggles and dropped his arm, stepping away abruptly. "Sorry," she murmured, rubbing at the back of her neck.

He said something, but it was too low for her to make out behind the mask.

They continued walking until the trees spit them out at a side entrance to a stunning building of towering stone. Atta looked up at the spires, the arched windows, the utter, sacred beauty. "This is Saint Patrick's Cathedral."

"It is indeed."

To her complete astonishment, he pulled out a skeleton key that looked like it belonged to Dracula and shoved it into a lock. "It might be time for that Society history lesson," she whispered at his back, so nervous that she kept scooting closer to him.

They crept inside, and Gold Stitch locked the door before striding purposefully to a cupboard of some sort Atta couldn't see for how dark it was. He pulled something out, and she heard him strike a match a split second before the flame ignited, and he lit a gas hand lamp. "You really don't believe in torches, do you?"

He chuckled. "Secret societies like to dabble in the arcane and ominous." His words were punctuated by him handing her a plague doctor mask he pulled down from the cupboard. "Put this on. I don't think we'll run into anyone, but just in case."

She followed him to a great wooden door, wishing very much that they were headed into the sanctuary proper, though she knew that was highly unlikely. As expected, the door led to a set of steep stone steps that descended down and down. So far down that it didn't make a great deal of physical sense.

"Are we going underground?" she whispered when the steps turned into broken cobbles, then dirt.

"Quite far underground."

Atta thought he was revealing an awful lot for not even letting her know his name. She wasn't about to say so, though. "About that history lesson . . ."

He glanced at her, the tunnels growing so narrow their beaks were in danger of touching. Her foot kicked something that skittered down ahead of them into the shadows, but not before she could tell it was the skull of some small mammal.

Finally, Gold Stitch spoke. "Agamemnon Society began long ago as a group of comrades who wanted to do academic research outside of regular societal norms without becoming pariahs, mostly hidden behind the HPSC."

It was difficult for Atta to see with the heavy, oblong mask and she tripped more than once, trying to listen to his story.

"Most of the founding members wanted to research medicine, though the only way to truly understand the human body was to cut into it. Most saw this as disturbing, so the

Society formed quietly and made deals with morgues and gravediggers to procure their subjects."

They rounded a corner, the tunnel widening enough that Atta was no longer brushing shoulders with him.

"Eventually, the Society grew to all manner of outcasts, men and women. Poets, authors, free-thinkers. It was a beautiful thing here in Dublin."

"*Was*?" Atta questioned.

"You're a clever one. Yes, the early days were filled with innovation, breakthroughs, and wonders in all manner of academia you can imagine. Slowly, new members and those who gained entrance by blood—an inherited seat, if you will— began poisoning everything the Society stood for. By the time I joined—my seat was inherited and also earned—the Society had become rife with in-fighting and corruption. Even politicians weaselled their way in and began trying to control everything, to use the Society for their agendas."

"Then why be in it at all?" she pressed, engrossed.

"Not everyone in Agamemnon is corrupt, and the opportunities it affords are vital to what I do. Sometimes things have to be reformed slowly from the inside."

Atta reached out and grabbed his bicep to halt him before they went any further. She felt his arm tense, and she let go. "Why are you telling me all of this?"

"Would you like the truthful answer to that question?"

"As opposed to a lie? Yes, please."

She watched his mask move as he looked everywhere but at her.

"I don't know," he finally said, the words hardly audible. "I think I'm tired of looking for a cure, for reform, on my own."

"But you said not everyone in the Society is like that. You have Achilles House. The broader Society."

"You can be surrounded by people and still be alone, Atta."

She could see her birdlike mask reflected in his goggles in the lamplight. "I understand that." Possibly better than most.

"Tell me you haven't been digging alone for years, too."

"I have."

"Then let's figure out what in hell is really going on, hm?"

Atta dipped her beak and they rounded one last corner. Gold Stitch opened the door to what felt like another time. Two giant stone braziers blazed with fire at the foot of a short set of stone steps. *Everything* was stone. Save for the skulls and bones that made up the cave walls.

"*Jesus*," she whispered in awe, descending the steps to have a better look.

The huge door closed with a heavy thud and Atta jumped, turning to see Gold Stitch flanked by two enormous stone-carved reapers on either side of the door, featureless, protective, with their hoods up and arms outstretched, waiting for the dead.

"Sorry." He said, jogging down the steps to meet her. "That door doesn't close quietly, I'm afraid."

"This is where Agamemnon Society meets?"

"It used to be, in the beginning." He pointed to the curved walls of bones. "Society members' coffins are buried empty. We are set aflame on an altar here and our bones are taken from the fire before they become ash." He gestured to the cavelike walls Atta was just realising were inlaid with–

"*Human* bones," she breathed, spinning a small circle, taking in the ossuary, like a miniature replica of the Catacombs of Paris.

"Yes. We make up the walls here."

Without waiting for her to respond, he led the way forward, down another tunnel, shorter by far than the last. It opened up into an identical chamber, only everything was made of marble instead of crude stone. When the door shut, Atta turned to see if the reapers were there, too. In that updated inner sanctum, the reapers were marble masterpieces.

Atta wondered how they managed to get so much pristine marble underground but didn't have time to contemplate it because her guide was already entering through another door.

She ran to catch up, ripping off her mask as soon as she made it inside the clinical space. She expected Gold Stitch to reprimand her, but he didn't. He, too, was taken aback, standing stock-still in front of a body on a metal autopsy table. The body of Lauren Kennedy. Wrapped in crawling ivy.

Atta dropped her mask to the cold floor and walked forward, her mouth agape and breath fogging in front of her, ever so slightly. Lauren's head was too far up. Unattached from her spine.

Atta bent to look closer, marvelling at the stems growing within the flesh like veins, the petiole and buds protruding from her skin. "They're completely embedded," she said as Gold Stitch came to stand next to her.

"They look like they originated from inside her body," he mused.

He was right. Atta rushed to a wall of small drawers, opening and closing them quickly looking for—

"Here." He handed her a pair of surgical gloves and slipped a pair on himself.

Together, they peeled back the flesh at the incision site with forceps, immensely grateful Lauren hadn't yet been sewn back up.

"Someone will be back soon," he said, grabbing a pair of surgical scissors. "She's not been closed properly and there is no way they'll leave her alone here for long. Not like this."

Atta reached for a set of tweezers, pushing and prodding the vines in the chest cavity, looking for the root, the beginning of Lauren's demise.

She and Gold Stitch sucked in a breath in unison when they found a mushroom sprouting.

"Her heart," Atta whispered, then looked at Gold Stitch. "How?"

She ripped off her glove.

"What are you doing?" Gold Stitch's voice was urgent.

But she didn't answer. Instead, she gently touched the mushroom cap.

This time, she *almost* expected the migraine. Was almost ready for it.

Ivy, thick and wild, crawled up marble pillars. It looked like ancient Greece but draped in a golden haze—like an old Jean Harlow movie. At the end of the row of pillars sat a throne of twisted branches, dotted in unidentifiable flora. Colours her eyes had never seen. There was a glimmer, like gossamer wings. Then there were fangs in her face, dripping with blood. Atta gasped as the creature lunged for her, hissing. Everything went black, then she was back. Looking at Lauren's body, Gold Stitch's hands around her waist, holding her upright.

"*Atta?*" He sounded almost frightened like he'd said her name many times already.

"Migraine," she managed to get out and he let her go, a

hand still at the small of her back to steady her as they both looked down at the black spore dust on her fingertips.

In the distance, a giant door thudded shut. Atta just had time for her eyes to go wide before Gold Stitch had her by the wrist.

"Hurry," he urged her. "Hide." He bent and retrieved her mask, shoving at her chest. "Go!"

Heart pounding in her ears, Atta searched in a panic for a place to hide. Any place. There at the back of the lab, she saw what had to be a supply closet. She'd just jumped inside it when she saw the exam room door open through the sliver she'd left hers cracked. Whoever it was wore a mask just like the one in her hands. She tried to make out what was being said, but the voices were too muffled by the leather and steel.

SONDER

"Murdoch," Lynch drawled, the stiffening of his shoulders the only indication he was surprised to see him there.

He hoped to god Atta was too far away to hear them. Surely she suspected him by now. He'd already shown her all this, doomed her anyway. Why not doom himself along with her? Take off the mask.

"What brings you here so late?"

Sonder pushed nonchalance into his tone as he bent over the poor Infected girl. Dead girl, he supposed. "I needed tissue samples and was unwilling to wait for them to be brought to the House." He held up a specimen jar and looked at his colleague, goggles to goggles. Oh, the things they hid behind their fucking masks. "What brings you here?"

"It's not every day we have a Stage 4 in our midst," Lynch said, though he wasn't looking at the cadaver. "I thought I'd come see it before they dispose of it."

It. The neuter pronoun made him sick. She'd been a living, breathing person.

Lynch clasped his hands behind his back like a totalitarian dictator and strode closer, careful not to get too close, sully his pristine coat or his lily-white hands.

Sonder almost snorted at the thought. No, Lynch never did the dirty work himself. Never had.

He suspected the man looked rather green beneath his mask. Just to spite the fecker, Sonder used a nearby scalpel to cut far deeper than necessary and plucked out a piece of the heart. Black blood oozed from the tissue as he held it aloft just long enough to make Lynch shudder before he placed it in his tube and sealed it.

"Where will they take her?" Sonder ventured, looking as inconspicuous as possible, taking another sample from the lung and reaching for a syringe to draw a vial of blood.

"There's a plot at Trinity Cemetery that's been waiting for a Stage 4."

Black blood filled Sonder's syringe and Lynch turned away. "Are you about finished? I need to complete my notes."

Sonder popped the cap closed and put the specimen in his jacket pocket. "Of course. I only need one more thing." His hands developed a small tremor as he retrieved another vial while Lynch looked over some paperwork. He had no idea how to get Atta out.

Carefully, he used a pair of surgical shears to snip a piece of the mushroom stalk, pulling out a bit of the root—mycelium she'd called it. Storing them in a vial, he hoped it would be all Atta needed. He slipped all the tubes and vials into the interior pocket of his coat and discarded his gloves.

"Is there a back door out of here?" Sonder asked, grasping at straws. "I've got to take a piss."

Lynch laughed. "It's a long way up, in'it?" He pointed to a

dark hallway behind where Atta was hidden that Sonder had never noticed before. "That way, I think. Should lead up to the groundskeeper shed."

Now Sonder just had to figure out how in the hell he was going to sneak a woman out of a closet. He hadn't been the type to sneak girls up into his room as a lad, so he had no frame of reference for hiding one and getting her out. Damn, she did make him feel young again, he had to grant her that. He considered for a moment what Atta would do. Probably distract Lynch with some asinine idea, half-cocked.

"Do you smell that?"

Lynch looked up from his notes. "Smell what?"

"Kerosene. The braziers?"

"Oh, fuck." Lynch tossed his notebook to one of the metal tables and rushed out.

Sonder darted for the closet, pulling Atta out by her wrist and hauling her out the back.

When they made it through the tunnel and outside, they were both pulling cool air into their lungs, leaning up against the side of the groundskeeper shed.

And Atta was laughing, aglow in the moonlight, her hair a mess of tangles. He almost took off his mask right then and there.

But he didn't want to risk being the reason she stopped laughing.

As it turned out, he was, anyway.

————

"*No.*"

"I went in there with you," she was shouting at him. "You *took* me in there, you brooding eejit. I should be there to look into the findings with you!"

Fucking hell she was beautiful when she was angry. But not as beautiful as when she laughed.

Sonder shook his thoughts loose. She might not be his student, but she was still *a* student and he was a professor. And she'd already almost passed out on him twice. He shouldn't have involved her as much as he had. He'd wait for the paper she said she was working on. Her research. Then cut this off, whatever *this* was. It would have to be enough.

"No," he said again with more conviction than he felt.

"But—" She was standing in the petrol car park, her indignant face lit by the overhead car light as she tried again to convince him to let her come to Achilles House with him.

"Goodnight, Atta." He reached across the car. "Pleasant dreams." And closed the door in her face.

She shouted several unseemly things at him through the window before finally retreating to her car.

He didn't drive away until she got in and drove off in the direction of Trinity.

It wasn't until he pulled up the long cobbled drive of his estate and checked his pockets that he realised she'd stolen one of his samples.

Atta

"**B** *loody bastard.*"

It had been her mantra for the last three days. She'd hardly slept, hardly eaten, and even bit off Emmy's head when she tried to make her leave her room to go to Mulligan's with her and the lads. She'd spent every free second she wasn't in class or at work studying the mushroom and mycelium sample she'd stolen off Gold Stitch and compiling all of her research over the last six years into something resembling a proper scientific journal.

It had begun as a compilation for Sonder—what he'd asked her to do that day in the library—but it had quickly become an obsession. An obsession not only to understand the Plague but to make sense of what was happening to her. Why she was seeing visions and hallucinations. Why she had seen something that truly happened after the fact.

Despite having asked for the report, Sonder hadn't mentioned it again and had been oddly formal and distant since she'd last seen him. In fact, she was adding him to the Bloody Bastard column too, because he'd sent her to fetch coffee.

Something he hadn't done since the day they bonded—or so she thought—over the autopsy of the murdered woman. When she'd proven she was no man's vapid waitstaff.

Just for being a fucker these last few days, she was going to get him a paper cup. He *hated* takeaway cups—said they turned too flimsy and *had no class about them.*

She stomped the rest of the way to the teachers' room, surprised to see Emmy and Marguerite Vasilios there.

"Atta!" Emmy said cheerily. "She lives! Frankenstein's monster lives!"

Professor Vasilios laughed without looking up from her newspaper and Atta cracked a tight smile. "Clever," the professor murmured, looking as flawless and exotic as ever.

"What are you two doing way over here in this building?" Atta asked, ignoring the jab.

Emmy tapped a pen to a pad of paper in front of her. "Marguerite has been invited to try out her group therapy on Dr Frankenstein's students like we talked about."

Atta ground her teeth together. Sonder had failed to mention that to her.

"Emmaline," Vasilios censured lightly, looking at them over her open newspaper for the first time, "you really must stop calling Professor Murdoch that."

Atta found the oldest paper cup of the bunch, the one already wonky at the lip, that had been touched by who knew how many hands, and filled it with the stalest, sludgiest coffee. "Well, I'll be seeing you," she said snippily and left the lounge, Emmy looking at her like she'd lost her mind.

Sonder was highlighting a passage in a book when she stormed in, and she noted that he covered the pages with a file folder when he saw her.

"Ah, coffee."

She slammed the cup down, some of the hot liquid sloshing out of the lid's spout. "Here."

She turned to leave, but he was around the desk in a flash. "Atta, wait."

Crossing her arms, she stared up at him. "What?"

"You seem perturbed with me."

Was she? Angry at *him*? Or was this all residual anger at Gold Stitch?

"No," she said finally. "It's been a rough few days. That's all."

"Are you having headaches?" he pressed, his brows knitted together in the middle with concern.

Atta's arms dropped to her sides. "Why do you keep asking about headaches? How do you even know I get them?"

She swore there was a flash of panic in his eyes before he smoothed out his features. "Gibbs mentioned it."

"*Gibbs*?" There was a dull ringing in her ears. She wasn't even aware Gibbs knew about her migraines. They must be affecting her more than she thought. "As in my roommate, Bernard Fitzgibbon?"

"Yes. He mentioned you suffer from migraines and I've seen you, I don't know, wince on occasion, like you're overcome by one."

Liar, liar, liar, a voice in her head sang. The one that sang to her of Wills-o'-the-wisp and hawthorn trees. *Liars we hate, the liars we ate, under the hawthorn tree.*

Atta shook off the voice. "I didn't realise you knew Gibbs well enough to gossip with him," she said mechanically, crossing her arms.

His lips pressed into a thin line. "It wasn't gossip, Miss

Morrow. He's assistant to my colleague," Sonder clarified, a challenge in his voice. A razor-thin something dancing between them.

"I know that." She toed the line.

They stared at one another for a moment before Atta cleared her throat. "Well, as it turns out, I *am* having a bit of a migraine coming on, and I work at the morgue tonight, so I'd like to rest this afternoon, if that's all right. I heard Professor Vasilios is taking over your lecture today, anyway."

"You work at the morgue tonight?"

She cocked her head to the side. "I do. . ." she answered slowly, eyes narrowed.

"I'll see you Friday, then."

Atta left, headed for her dorm, for her research, one thought on repeat in her mind like a skipping record: Sonder didn't have any classes on Fridays.

ATTA

B ent over her desk, peering at the mycelium plucked from Lauren's heart through her hand lens for the thousandth time, the early morning sun streamed in to illuminate the hyphae.

Atta jotted notes in her journal next to her sketch before placing the mycelium on wax paper, folding it over to keep the network safe.

A knock came at her door.

"Come in," Atta said, shoving a book over her mess of notes. She almost had the research paper ready. Almost.

Gibbs came in looking sheepish. "What are you working on over there?"

Atta set her lens down and twisted in her chair. "A paper on the effect of urban climate on flora." In truth, she'd hardly touched any of her true assignments in days. She was going to be surviving on crappy coffee for another week, it would seem.

Gibbs nodded noncommittally. "Hey, sorry I snitched about your migraines to Murdoch." He shrugged his shoulders up to his ears. "I was just worried about you, and you've stayed locked in here most days, and you keep strange hours, I just—"

"Thanks for your concern, Gibbs." She felt bad for the lad. He had a heart of gold, but he didn't think through his words very often. "I really do appreciate it."

He smiled, genuine but still a bit on the nervous side it seemed. "I know we're all cramming for midterm exams right now, but some of us are going out to Mulligan's for some much-needed time to blow off steam tonight. Emmy and Dony are in and I think they're bringing a couple of friends. I invited Imogen, too." He looked at his shoes, a little grin on his face.

"You still talk to Imogen?" Atta asked. She couldn't help but root for Gibbs's happiness, but she wasn't sure Imogen was it.

"No. Not really. I saw her in the dining hall yesterday and sort of panic-invited her."

Atta suppressed a laugh. There was the Gibbs she knew and loved. "Are you panic-inviting me now?"

He looked stricken. "No! I really want you to come. I think you could do with a break."

"Thanks, Gibbs. Yeah. I'll stop by."

Gibbs's smile stretched across his entire face. "8:00."

He bustled out and Atta returned to her research. If she skipped her morning classes, she could get it done. Get it to Sonder before her 3:00 lecture and be somewhat freer to enjoy the pub with the gang. She really did need some time off. Not as much as she needed more mycelium and mushroom samples, though.

Atta cursed. One thing at a time.

By the time noon arrived, she'd only left her room to refill her coffee and tea on a rotation, make herself drink a glass of water, and once to use the toilet.

She cited her last resource, closed all the books scattered across her bed, floor, desk and windowsill, and threw on a Trinity hoodie that belonged to Emmy. Rushing across campus, she was breathless and more than a little flushed from the cold wind when she burst into Sonder's office.

He looked up when she entered, his face breaking into surprise before a smile crawled across his lips. She'd never seen him smile like that and it was then that she realised she herself was smiling like a maniac and he was probably mirroring her.

Proudly, she handed the thick research journal to him with a flourish. "I've done it."

One eyebrow raised, Sonder took the bound stack of papers, his eyes on her instead of the research. "I've never seen you so. . ."

Her smile fell. This was a moment of academic achievement for her. A moment of *scientific* achievement. Shouldn't there be a marching band or fireworks? Not a bemused professor who wasn't even looking at her paper? "'*So*' what?"

"Dressed down."

Confused, Atta looked at the hoodie she'd thrown over brown corduroys from days ago. "Oh. Well, I haven't done much but work on that research so *look at it,* would you?"

He smirked and put on his glasses.

She watched, pacing, chewing her thumbnail as he read, scratching at the rough stubble on his chin and taking notes here and there.

"Atta," he said after a few pages without looking at her. "Please stop fidgeting or go wait in the corridor."

"Sorry," she mumbled and busied herself looking at the busts of William Rutherford Sanders and Elizabeth Garrett Anderson. Thrice he told her not to touch anything, and thrice she didn't listen.

Finally, Sonder took off his glasses and leaned back in his chair. "This is—"

He shook his head in what she thought might be dismay? astonishment? and she came to sit across from him.

"Jesus. It's brilliant," he finally finished.

She blinked twice before she could manage words. "Thank you. I'd like for you to turn it in to HPSC. I think it could help."

Sonder baulked, sitting forward and covering the paper almost protectively. "*HPSC*? No. You can't—" He broke off, shaking his head vehemently. "Atta, you can't show this to anyone."

She sat forward in her chair. "You just said it was brilliant."

"It is."

"Are you worried I won't credit you? Because I did." She pointed at the page open in front of him. "Just there."

"Credit?" Sonder huffed a humourless laugh. "No, I'm not worried about getting credit." He glanced at his watch. "When is your next class?"

"3:00."

"Let's go get some tea, then. Shall we?"

As they strolled across campus, Sonder clearly wasn't as anxious to have this discussion as Atta was, and they talked of the group therapy session his students had taken part in a few days prior instead.

"Marguerite seems to think my students need psychiatric help after performing autopsies." He smiled again and Atta noticed she was beginning to look for those smiles. Glimpses behind a dark curtain.

"Do you think they got anything out of the session?"

Sonder shrugged, holding open the campus coffee shop door for her. "Maybe. I think it helped them decompress together—remember they aren't alone. That was my aim in agreeing to the thing in the first place, anyway."

All the natural light flooding in through the windows made the weather feel less dreary.

"I think we've had you pegged all wrong, Dr Frankenstein."

Sonder laughed, full and real. It was so sonorous and infectious that every female in the café looked in their direction, and Atta couldn't tear her eyes away from him. "Let's not let that get out." His gaze met hers, a smirk playing at one side of his mouth. "I like being spooky."

"You're a regular Fox Mulder."

"A what?"

Atta laughed. "It's a new American show on the telly my roommates watch. I take it you're not one for much television, either."

"No, not really." He unwound his scarf and tucked it in the crook of his elbow. "I do *enjoy* films, I just don't have much available time for them. Television programs, on the other hand, don't much interest me."

They reached the counter and the pretty girl behind it smiled dreamily at Sonder. "I'll have black tea and whatever the lady here will have. Put it on my tab."

"Certainly, Professor." The barista eyed him with barely concealed lust, but Sonder didn't seem to notice.

Atta ordered a dark roast with a dash of cream and a sprinkle of brown sugar, feeling Sonder's eyes on her the entire time. He'd found a little secluded table in the corner and was indeed watching her when she turned around. She suddenly hated that she was in crumpled trousers and a stained hoodie. When was the last time she washed her hair? Oh god, or brushed her teeth?

She sat across from him, self-conscious. A moment later, the barista brought over his steaming tea and bent over way too far to pop the lid on the cup. Atta snorted at the young woman's blatant display of her cleavage. But Sonder didn't notice, he was looking at Atta.

"What's so funny, hm?" he asked as he pulled off his jacket when the girl walked away frustrated that he hadn't paid attention to her.

"You didn't notice all the women in here looking at you?"

Confused, his attention swept across the café. "No, I hadn't. I thought you said everyone was scared of me." He took a sip of his tea.

"They are, but that doesn't mean people don't also think you're—and this is a direct student quote—'*fuckable in the most scholarly way.* '"

Sonder choked on his tea. Atta laughed and he straightened his tie, clearing his throat. "Well then."

The girl brought Atta's drink and fair slammed it down in front of her. Atta bit back another laugh, as did Sonder, but colour was visible high on his cheeks above his scruff.

"Aw, he's flustered," she teased.

"Not by her," he muttered, fiddling with the lid of his tea. "I hate takeaway cups," he changed the subject and cursed, removing the black plastic lid from the paper and polymer cup.

Atta saw her opportunity and pounced. "Why can't I show that essay to Achilles House?" she said without preamble.

"Jesus, you're terrible at segues. How do you even know about *Achilles House*, hm?"

Atta's face heated at her misstep, but his eyes were glittering as he watched her like a wolf tracks a trapped hare.

She settled on not answering. "I worked hard on that, Sonder. It's the height of my academic achievement"—she moved her hands erratically as she spoke—"something I've worked six years on."

"That's clear. It was thoroughly researched and profound." He sniffed the tea sans lid.

"Then—" She broke off and shook her head. "I don't understand."

"My point is, not everyone in academia is like you, Atta. It's a very political world and you're orbiting too close to the sun here."

"I'm not naïve enough to have missed that," she snapped, "but—"

"Go on." He sipped at his tea, watching her over the rim of his cup. "Actually, I can't do this." Sonder sat up straight and began looking around. "I need this in a real cup. It's part of the reason I come here, they serve drinks in *real* cups."

Atta suppressed a chuckle, some of her frustration dispelling. "You're dreadfully neurotic."

"I never said I wasn't."

"What if we walk and talk? Then you have to have a takeaway cup."

"I like that idea, but you're mistaken." He rose and took her coffee.

"Hey!"

"I'll be right back." He returned a moment later with two steaming mugs. "Now, about that walk."

When they made it outside in the cool, leaf-strewn air, Atta jumped right back in. "Are you just trying to steal this research from me and use it as your own?" she accused him only half-playfully.

"Oh, so you don't trust me," he shot back, "but you trust a government entity?"

"Aren't you *part* of a government entity?"

His attention snapped to her, his jaw ticking.

"You're a professor at a public college," she clarified, studying his profile.

His shoulders visibly lost some of their tension. "Ah. Public-private partnership, as it were."

Atta frowned down at the dark pool of coffee in her mug. "I know academia can be a political place with hierarchies and corruption like any other faction of society, and I stand by my point earlier this semester that a cure will be handed to the elite first, but don't we *all* want the Plague eradicated? We have that common goal, at least."

He looked at her sidelong. "Do we? Are you certain of that? Or is it a power struggle to see who gets the glory for curing it?"

She clamped her mouth shut and walked on past the library, cradling her already lukewarm mug in her hands.

"My point is this: the things you have pieced together are not safe in the wrong hands."

"And you believe HPSC and its Society are unsafe?"

He stopped and faced her, Atta mirroring him. "You're suggesting that the spore in Patient Zero was foreign flora of unknown origin acting as a biotoxin and spreading. Becoming *more*."

"Becoming the control centre for a fastidious pathogen that needs the correct conditions to thrive."

Sonder licked his lips and looked off in the distance. "It's genius, Atta, but dangerous."

She abandoned her coffee on a bench beside them and stood straighter. "Is that not what you also suspected? Why you took me to the library and asked for my thoughts in the first place?"

"Of course it is." He set his nearly full mug on the bench next to hers.

"Then *what*, Sonder? What's the point if we don't use this knowledge for good?"

He swore and looked around them quickly before grabbing her wrist and pulling her into the shadows between two buildings, her heart catching in her throat.

"What if I wanted to show you something?" he pressed. "Something I've been working on myself for the last six years."

She had to crane her neck to look up at him. He was so close she was nearly backed against the stone wall, his breath mingling with hers. "I would say yes."

He took a step away. Ran a hand through his hair. Looked at her intently. "All right." He bit his bottom lip, eyes darting around the shadows. "All right," he repeated. "You'd better get to class. We can continue this later."

Confused by his sudden onset of nerves, Atta merely nodded and walked back out into the watery daylight.

"Atta."

She turned back, unable to make out his features in the shadows, his tall, lithe body ensconced in darkness feeling familiar.

"Where did you get the samples you had taped in your research?"

A little moth took flight in her abdomen, an aftershock of a migraine sprouting in her skull. "A friend gave them to me."

Sonder chuckled. Low. Deep. Velvety.

Atta froze.

Oh fuck. She knew with absolute certainty where she'd heard that toe-curling laugh before.

"Have a nice evening, Atta." He shoved his hands in his trouser pockets and strolled further into the shadows.

Mycelium: the vegetative structure of fungi, comprised of *hyphae*—tiny branching cells.

Microscopic threads called mycelium, in nature, create an underground communication network with other plants, exchanging nutrients, water, and even warning signals with each other. This same principle is at work within the specimens infected by the Irish Plague. The original spore manifests in the heart or lungs, sprouting into a mushroom, then uses mycelium to command the growth of flora throughout the body.

-Excerpt from *The Plague Treatise of Ariatne Morrow*, circa 1993

ATTA

Atta was late to the pub.

By the time she arrived, the gang was on their third round of drinks. Emmy was getting giggly and Dony was flirting with Imogen. Gibbs was looking sombre about the whole thing, trying not to glance at Imogen every time the conversation between him and Lucas, one of Dony's mates, lulled.

She felt bad for the lad and picked the seat next to him after ordering a gin and tonic at the bar.

"Hi, everyone," she said, slipping off her coat and scarf to drape them over the chair.

"Are you wearing makeup?" Imogen asked without saying hello, her face screwed up like she'd sucked a lemon.

"Em, yeah." Atta fidgeted. "Are you?"

Emmy sniggered into her pint and Imogen scoffed, flipping her hair because she obviously had on loads of makeup. The lads were clueless.

As the evening progressed, the looser Atta's shoulders

became. Eventually, the conversation turned to her being grilled by the others about Sonder.

"I heard he has a belfry at his mansion filled with bats," Imogen burst in.

"I heard he dabbles in necromancy," Lucas offered.

Emmy flopped a hand around like a dead fish. "Atta says he's broody but a normy."

Atta had not said any such thing and found she didn't believe he was anything of the sort. She did, however, feel a strange, burning need to protect him, so she left it at that.

The conversation shifted back to exams, who was seeing whom, and other meaningless topics.

"Speak of the devil, if it isn't the dark lord himself," Dony slurred suddenly.

Emmy whistled low and long, and Atta whipped her head toward the direction they were staring. "I've never seen him in all black. *Jesus*." Emmy gaped openly, and Atta had to struggle not to do the same.

If Sonder Murdoch was the dark lord, her soul was begging to be burned to ash. He sauntered his way through the pub, dressed head to toe in black and looking like a wraith. Like the masked man she willingly committed dark deeds with.

It couldn't be. There was no way *Professor Murdoch,* in all his rigidity, was the same man breaking into graveyards and showing her around a skull and bones secret society. *But that laugh. . .* The one that crawled up her chest and left her breathless. It was the *same*, she was sure of it.

Gibbs looked down into his drink, offering Atta a much-needed distraction from the heat coursing through her body. She was about to ask him if he was all right when Sonder spotted her, moving toward their table like there was a magnetic pull between the two of them, causing her heart to go into a fit of palpitations.

"Oy!" Dohmnall shouted, waving his arm around like a buffoon. "Dr Frankenstein!"

Emmy shoved him in the shoulder while Gibbs barked at him to shut his mouth.

"Jesus. . ." Imogen's mouth fell open as she stared at the professor, to the point Atta worried she'd drool on herself.

"Good evening," Sonder said amiably when he approached, carrying a whiskey. "Last hoorah before midterm exams, ye'?" He looked at everyone, saving Atta for last and holding his gaze on her a second longer than was called for. She very nearly broke out in a sweat.

"Ye'," Dohmnall confirmed loudly. "We have to with you bastards running us around like whores on your errands."

"Woahhhh," Emmy grabbed Dony's arm and squeezed hard. "Sorry, Prof. He's a bit stressed."

But Sonder only smiled. "Kelleher is an arse of the highest order. Next round is on me. I'll tell them at the bar top."

Cheers went up around the table, all except for Gibbs, who found his Guinness particularly interesting, and Atta, who couldn't stop staring at Sonder's lips. Judging by the smirk tilting them, he fucking knew it, too.

"Gibbs." Sonder dipped his head to the lad, then turned those piercing hazel eyes on her again. "*Atta.*"

Holy hell. To her tipsy ears, her name sounded like forbidden honey on his tongue.

"Jesus," she murmured without realising it, looking down at the table, and she heard him chuckle and say, "*Have a good night,*" before walking away.

"I need food," Atta announced to the table. "Now."

Emmy ran to the bar to order two baskets of chips for the table and two more rounds.

Atta consumed none of the alcohol and almost all of the chips along with a litre of water, trying to sober up. For the rest of their time at the pub, Sonder sat across the way at a table with Marguerite Vasilios and a few other professors Atta didn't really know. But every so often, he would glance her way and smirk. Once, he even lowered his hand to his side and motioned for her to turn around. Had she been staring? Of course she had. He looked so devastating, and the alcohol had burned off all her sensibilities.

By 11:00 she was fairly sober and still sneaking glances his way. Jesus Christ. She was *actually* falling for a professor, wasn't she?

"I need some air," she told the group who wasn't paying her any attention, and left the table, tugging on her coat.

When she passed Sonder's table, he wasn't there any longer. Stupidly, she hoped she'd see him outside. See him get in a car and go in the opposite direction she would be headed once she'd sobered enough to drive to Achilles House.

The street was still alive with people and lights and laughter. She curled her arms around herself and snuggled her nose into her scarf, watching them bustle past, wondering if life would soon change. There was one piece of the puzzle they were missing. Atta could feel it. Feel how close they were to understanding how the Plague moved. Perhaps if they studied live patients instead of dead ones. . .

A hand touched her back and Atta jumped. "Jesus, Dohmnall, you scared me."

"Sorry about that, love. I saw you come out here and

thought maybe you needed company." He did not remove his hand from her back and she squirmed a step away.

"Thanks, I'm good. Came out here for a bit of peace."

Dony was a good guy, really. But a salacious flirt when sober. Drunk, he was hard to reason with.

"Aw, come on. You know there's a spark between us, doll." He stepped closer and Atta stepped back. He wouldn't back down, and Atta found herself trapped between him and the wall of the lounge bar next door.

She put a hand to his chest. "Dony. Stop. You're sloshed." He reached for her, and she jerked back.

A hand from nowhere lashed out, catching Dony by the throat and pushing him backwards.

A dark figure stepped out of the shadows, disconcerting plague doctor mask in place. "No means no," he spat at Dony.

Relieved at his arrival, Atta laid her hand on Gold Stitch's arm. "He's drunk. It's all right."

"No, it isn't. He should learn to hold his fucking liquor better." He pushed Dony with enough force that he hit the sidewalk on his arse, several passersby with wide eyes giving them an even wider berth.

Dony hurried to his feet, sobering up quickly. "What are you? One of those secret society freaks?"

Atta's heart pounded as she watched Gold Stitch saunter forward, stopping right in front of Dony's face. "If you so much as look at her the wrong way, I'm the one who will make you wish you were dead. That's who the fuck I am."

Dony played it off, acted tough. But he quickly turned and darted down the footpath, headed for college.

"Is your car here?" Atta asked tersely.

Gold Stitch nodded once.

"Good. Let's go."

SONDER

As soon as the door to his car shut, she twisted in the passenger seat, whirling on him. "You bloody bastard!"

"Oh, come on now. You're not that big a fan of fucking *Domhnall*, are you?"

Fuck. He shouldn't have revealed he knew the prick's name, but he was done with this charade after all they'd talked about today, revealed subtly.

"I don't mean about him, you eejit. I mean about not letting me study *our* specimens."

"That's rich, Atta," he shot back. "You *stole* one from me."

"And yet I have no idea what happened with the others, do I? Are you even going to tell me?"

"I'd planned to take you to see the Stage 4 gravesite after I dropped my friend at home, considering she didn't bring her own vehicle, but here we are." He threw his hands in the air. "Now she's abandoned at night."

Atta looked like he'd dumped a cold bucket of water on her. "You were out on a date?"

Heat lit in his chest. Was she envious? "Does it matter if I was?"

"No." She crossed her arms and faced the dash. "Did you wear that stupid mask?"

"What do you think?"

He watched the calculation on her face as she tried to work out all the times she'd glanced at him throughout the night with that look that was driving him out of his skull. He could walk it all back right now if he wanted to. Make her believe she'd been wrong about who he was.

But *fuck*, he didn't want to.

"She is a friend," he said softly, and Atta turned her face toward him, but didn't look at him directly, her eyes pinned on the steering wheel.

"All right."

Without another word, he pulled out of the parking space and drove them to Trinity Cemetery. She was still quiet. More guarded than she'd been with him in weeks. He wanted to reassure her. Tell her it wasn't a date. That he and Marguerite had ridden together from college and met up with their friends. That he couldn't stop thinking about *her*. Hadn't thought about another woman since the second she walked into his classroom that first time. No. Since the first time he'd seen her at Achilles House with a corpse she'd already opened.

Sonder was no eunuch, but he'd always been focused, driven. Pursued books and ideas and science far before women. They were a means to an end, a way to sate his primal hunger, not woo and build a life with. Atta was different. She appealed to every sense he had and never knew was there.

He turned off his lights and parked in the same spot as last time, hidden by brush.

He looked at Atta and she was peering out into the dark, but she ran her tongue over her bottom lip and he bit back a groan, exiting the car with haste.

"The Stage 4 is—"

"Lauren," Atta said sharply, handing him a shovel from the backseat. "Her name is Lauren."

"Lauren," he amended. "She is buried under the tree, just there." He pointed and was surprised when Atta followed his direction, then whipped around to face him, her eyes wide.

"Under a hawthorn tree?"

"Yes. Is that significant?"

"It was on the coins we found last time. Do you still have them?"

"I do. In my lab at home." He'd been correct about their properties being abnormal, possibly as foreign as the flora.

Her demeanour changed, intrigue slipping in, and he wanted to dive into it. "You have a lab at home, too?" Before he could answer, she went on, her face screwing up adorably in thought. "Didn't you say you wanted to show me something?" She paused, considering. "Wait. No." She shook her head. "Never mind. Come on."

They approached the fresh mound of dirt beneath the tree and bent down in unison. Atta ran her fingers over the soil, inspecting it.

"It's fertilised, just like the others. Bring your lantern in closer." He did as she asked, illuminating a trailing group of mushrooms.

"Like a little cluster of trooping faeries," she mused. "Did you bring gloves?"

Silently, he fished them out of his pocket and handed them

to her, pulling a test tube out of his interior jacket pocket as she donned the gloves.

Carefully, Atta dug at the soil and he wished she wasn't bent over in that skirt. She dug until she plucked up the mushroom, its fungal root system still intact.

"This is exactly what I needed," she said almost reverently. "Fresh mycelium."

He held out the test tube, grateful he'd brought a large size, and she gently stowed their findings away.

She stole the lantern from his grasp and leaned over the place she'd taken the mushroom from. "Do you think it's coming from her, or called by her?"

"What do you mean?" But he already knew. He'd read her research paper three times, after all.

Atta sat back on her heels. "Mushrooms essentially 'talk' to trees by connecting to their root systems through this stuff, the mycelium, which is a network of microscopic threads. It creates a network of communication underground where trees and plants can exchange nutrients and water, all connected. Look." She took his forearm and pulled him closer, but he couldn't see well enough in the low light, not with the blasted mask on.

He reached for the edge of the mask, lifted it from his chin, and she gasped.

"*No.*" She tightened her hold on his arm. "Don't!"

"I can't see, Atta." But maybe he meant that he couldn't see her. Not properly. Not the way he wanted to. In one swift movement, he had the mask off.

Atta's lips parted. Her eyes went wide and glistening in the glow of the lamp. "*Sonder.*" The way she said his name was like a dagger to his heart.

"*Atta*. You're a brilliant woman. You had to know it was me."

She was looking at him with what he'd swear was relief, but then she said, "Of course I knew it was you, but now I have no plausible deniability!"

He huffed a laugh, enjoying how close he was to her. How alone they were. He wanted to take her beautiful face in his hands and learn how that smart mouth tasted. "If we need plausible deniability, we're already fucked, *a stór*."*

Just then, a beam of light passed over their heads. Sonder cursed and pushed Atta down to the dirt, whispering in her ear to stay quiet as he covered her. The beam passed over the grounds, lingering on them once more before disappearing. A clang of the heavy iron gate revealed they were alone again a few moments later.

Rattled, they hurried to his car in a crouch and drove off without the lights on until they were far enough away.

At least they had the mushroom.

At least she knew it was him.

---

* *a stór* (uh stohr)—Irish Gaelic; meaning my darling, or my treasure

ATTA

A t least they had the mushroom.

At least she knew it was him.

"So it *was* you that had something to show me, after all," Atta said coyly after several moments of driving. She hadn't questioned why he didn't drop her off at Trinity. Why they were driving in circles. She didn't want the night to end, and, she hoped, perhaps he didn't either.

Sonder smiled, looking at her across the front seat. It was the freest she'd seen him yet and her heart crackled a little.

"Yes," he said, "but that wasn't it. I'll show you now if you'd like." He glanced at the dash clock. "Though it's late. And better in the daylight."

Atta was incredibly tired, and she didn't relish the thought of facing Domhnall when she got home, but she probably did need sleep, and Dony was likely already passed out.

"Tomorrow?" she posed.

Sonder grinned. "I'll pick you up at 9."

ATTA

S he tried not to overthink her outfit. It seemed silly. She wasn't meeting Sonder for a date, she was going as a scientific peer.

That's what Atta told herself anyway, as she dressed in black trousers and a loose, brown cable knit. This wasn't a peculiar date with an unmasked man and it wasn't her assisting a professor.

Taking one last look in the wardrobe mirror, she nodded resolutely and grabbed her satchel. She had just enough time to snag a cuppa from the coffee and tea cart on the green before Sonder met her.

But when she opened the door to her room, Domhnall was standing there, his fist poised to knock. Instinctively, Atta backed up.

"Aw, fuck. I'm sorry, Atta."

"You look like shite." She crossed her arms.

"I feel like it too. I keep getting glimpses from last night. I was an arse to you, wasn't I?"

"You made a very determined pass at me, Dony. Even after I said no."

He rubbed at the back of his neck. "Fuck. I'm so sorry." His contrition seemed genuine, but that didn't excuse him.

"You need to stop drinking if you can't control yourself. You're going to end up hurting someone."

He looked at his bare toes, but she kept going.

"All it takes is one fuck up and you've destroyed not only someone else's life but your own, too."

"You're right. I don't want to hurt anyone. Least of all you."

"Just"—she put a hand on his shoulder—"get a handle on it, yeah?"

"Ye'. Thanks, Atta."

She moved past him. "One and done or don't drink at all, all right?"

"Deal."

She smiled, but Dony didn't.

"I have some glimpses of a masked man threatening me. Was that real?"

She should have lied. But it wasn't her nature until recently it seemed, and she didn't get a lie out fast enough.

"Are you mixed up in one of these secret societies?"

"No," she said firmly and it was mostly true. "But I don't answer to you, Dony. So drop it."

He held up his hands in a show of surrender. "All right."

Atta grabbed her keys and rushed out the door, irritated she didn't have time for coffee anymore.

Sonder was behind the Medical Building where they'd agreed to meet, leaning against his Capri and smoking a cigarillo.

He hadn't seen her approaching and she slowed to watch him a moment, unobserved. It was strange now, putting both men into one, the seamlessness with which she viewed them before she ever knew for certain that they were one and the same.

Professor Murdoch, with his intellect and Morbid Arts. Gold Stitch, with his brooding and secrecy. And yet they were both just Sonder to her—had been for some time, in many ways—smelling of parchment, cigar smoke and spice, talking of academia and the Plague, pissing her off and pulling her back in; sharply dressed, hands ever in his pockets.

Sonder turned then, still mostly in profile, but he saw her and his mouth broke into a smile. He moved toward the back door of the building and stubbed out his cigarillo. "Good morning."

Two cups were on the bonnet of his car, one a porcelain teacup and one a takeaway cup. One empty, one full. He handed Atta the latter, his face scrunching on one side as he thought aloud, "Dark roast, dash of cream, with brown sugar."

Atta took the coffee gratefully, hoping she wasn't grinning like a fool. "Only in the autumn."

"Ah. I'll have to learn your winter order as well then, won't I?"

"It's just black coffee the rest of the year. Dark as it'll come."

"Much easier."

"Thank you," she smiled, lifting her cup.

"But of course." He mocked a ridiculous bow and she laughed.

They climbed in the Capri and Sonder reached over her to open the glove compartment. Another laugh popped out of

Atta. "You have an entire stash of teacups!" She fished around in them. "Three fancy and two plain."

He handed her the one he'd just used. "Three and three to make six. Uneven numbers are appalling."

Atta looked at him in astonishment, then back at the glove compartment. "It's the only thing you have in here. What if you're mugged? Pulled over? Where's your torch?"

"I live in rotation between college, my home, Achilles House, and back. On *occasion,* the pub or the theatre. I haven't much use for any of those items to be in my car because I don't find myself in those situations. A useful cup, however, has proved invaluable in my daily life." He opened the compartment between their seats to produce a flask and a cigar case. "Along with these."

Atta laughed. "You are so strange."

"Says the woman who got in the car with a masked man in the middle of the night and went to a graveyard. On more than one occasion." He set his face in a comical frown and shrugged, pointing between them. "Pot, kettle."

"All right, all right," she waved him off, closing the glove compartment of drinking vessels. "You've made your point. Now, where are we going?"

"You, darling, will find out when we get there."

She wasn't sure why he'd begun calling her that. Perhaps it was only something he typically said to his friends, but it made Atta's knees weak every time. When he'd said it to her in Gaelic. . . She'd almost swooned.

The drive was long, and somewhere after Marlay Park, the city dropped away, the autumn trees shrouded in fog and mist. The road turned winding, and Atta felt as if she were leaving the world as she knew it behind.

Eventually, they pulled onto a long gravel drive and drove through an ornate, wrought iron gate with a filigreed 'M' there in the middle.

Atta had her fingers curled on the door, knuckles and nose pressed to the glass. Just about everything was dying, prepared to protect itself for winter, but the misty grounds were astounding.

She heard Sonder chuckle at her astonishment.

"Hawthorn trees," she said, her breath fogging the glass. "A whole grove of them." They were vibrant with dying leaves and blood-red berries.

"Yes," Sonder said as the gravel turned to cobblestones. "They've been on these grounds since before the house. My grandmother didn't believe in cutting down a hawthorn, nor did my mother after her. She said it was bad luck. That the—"

"Faeries would be angry," Atta finished for him.

"Yes." He was looking at her strangely. She could see his reflection in the window and she turned to face him. "I thought my matriarchs were just superstitious."

"Superstitions and fairytales all originate from somewhere. Did you know that most supposed fairytales can be found in ancient civilisations that had no contact with one another and the tales have only minor variations?" She shrugged. "Same with religious stories."

Sonder stopped the car. "I did know that. Again, from my mother. How did you know that?"

Atta looked at her thumbnails. "My undergraduate studies were in Folklore and Religion. I did my thesis on the overlap between the two." He looked surprised and she wasn't sure why. "Didn't you have that in my file?"

"I never read your file. It seemed an impersonal, gross

THE EXORCISM OF FAERIES 189

oversight of a person's character to shove highlights and lowlights in a folder and call it fact. I would, however, give my left arm to read that thesis."

She heard his words, but they flitted away in the gloomy fog because she finally looked through the windscreen to see where they had stopped.

"Home, sweet home," Sonder said, opening his door.

Atta climbed out, eyes trained on the most stunning house she'd ever seen. A Gothic manor befitting a Brontë or Radcliffe novel, all dark, bloody stone and black spires. There was even a turret and a stone balcony. She could envision Emily St. Aubert leaning over the side to catch a glimpse of her beloved Valancourt. Any moment, Heathcliff would stomp through the hawthorns, materialising in the fog and calling out to Cathy.

"It's a bit vintage," Sonder broke into her thoughts, "but it's home."

The cobblestones leading up to the manor were broken, like jagged claws coming up from the ground. Sonder produced a set of keys strangely incongruous with the old house and unlocked the heavy front door. The moment her foot passed over the threshold, Atta swore the house pulled in a breath, as if it were surprised to see her.

The feeling was mutual.

Sonder led her through the foyer of dark wood floors and wallpaper of midnight florals. He hung the keys on an antique brass hook by the door and took off his coat. Once it was hung on the rack, he offered to take Atta's, and she slipped it off, making slow work for her marvelling.

Quietly, he led her into a room that took her breath away. One entire wall was made up of mullioned windows, interlocked with whorls of black ironwork. The rest of the sitting room was a masterpiece collection of art and oddities that would rival the Louvre or the Vatican's archives. The walls were a charcoal so dark they were almost black, but there was almost no space between the shelves and paintings to see it.

Atta stopped first at a painting of a woman from behind, standing alone on the beach in the light of the moon, then onto one of a man, blurred, his face buried in his hands. She could feel Sonder quietly watching her, letting her soak in his home.

She wondered vaguely if he let women do this often—see inside his inner sanctum.

But all those thoughts drifted away when she passed one of two floor-to-ceiling bookcases to pause at the portrait between them. It was almost as tall as she was and at least four times as wide. A stoic man, very nearly identical to Sonder, but younger, stood next to a lovely woman. The epitome of romance she was, in her olive dress, her auburn curls draped elegantly over one shoulder. Where he was stoic, she was radiant, her smile the kind that could light up any room, and Sonder had her captivating hazel eyes.

"Edmund and Olivia Murdoch," Sonder said softly. "My parents."

Atta turned to face him, gauging the sadness in his voice. "They—"

"Died of the Plague."

Atta's heart cracked. "Sonder, I'm—"

He held up his hand to stop her, a gentle smile on his face that didn't reach his eyes. "It's all right. I suppose my obsession with the Plague makes more sense to you now."

She nodded, turning back to the portrait to give it another look before moving on. She came to a massive sculpture of a nude woman, her head thrown back in pleasure or agony, it was difficult to tell. Her arms were limp at her sides, a kneeling man holding onto her waist and shoulder with all his might, muscles straining, his head bowed against her abdomen as if he were holding her to the earth.

It moved Atta to tears. "What is this?" she breathed.

"Ruperto Banterle's *Fleeing Soul*. A replica." Sonder came up next to her. "The true piece stands sentry over the Monumental Cemetery in Verona." They stood in silence for a few moments, looking at the sculpture that felt as if it were alive.

After several moments, Sonder finally said quietly, "I like to think her soul was ascending, and he couldn't bear the loss of her,"

"So he attempted to hold her here with him," Atta finished, feeling the same sentiment when she looked at it.

Sonder made a sound of acknowledgement deep in his throat and wandered off to the other side of the wide room of gilded baubles and ornate rugs in deep hues.

"Would you like some tea? It will give you more time to peruse while I make it." He said it like a joke, and he was smiling when Atta looked over her shoulder at him. She had the most peculiar feeling, looking in his eyes across the room, as if she was becoming the heroine of a Gothic novel.

It thrilled her, though a warning sounded in her heart that those never end without tragedy.

Ἁμαρτία.

Hamartia.

To err, to have a tragic flaw.

With Sonder standing there in his childhood home, looking at her, she knew in her bones they were both hamartia embodied. The main ingredient for a tragic end.

"Tea sounds nice."

As soon as he left the room, she felt cold, rubbing her hands up and down her arms.

With one last look at the sculpture, she followed the direction Sonder disappeared in, passing a room of deep green silks and an old, square grand piano, as well as a billiard room before finally locating the kitchen.

Sonder was lighting an ancient gas stove. "Did you tire of Banterle?"

"Never."

"There are many more sculptures around the grounds. I'd be happy to show you. My mother had *The Abduction of Persephone* copied, quite illegally, and placed in the garden. It was always a crowd pleaser, though the artist obviously fell short of Bernini."

He'd rolled his shirt sleeves up in her absence, the muscles in his forearms shifting as he filled a kettle with water and placed it over the blue flames.

As he pulled down a tea tin and filled two teacups with leaves, the earthy scent of it filled the space between them where Atta sat at the butcher block island. "Why Folklore and Religion?" he asked her conversationally.

Atta chewed on her lip, considering. "Part of me wanted to teach. Or write. But, I think really it was all because I know that the grieving need a new perspective, a different sort of hope." A line formed between his brows as he listened intently. "There's darkness found in hearth tales and the Church, but they all know that part already. They've seen it in the eyes of their dead. But there is also whimsy found in fairytales and hope found in the spiritual."

Sonder took the kettle from the stove before it could give

its full self-important whistle. "I've never looked at it that way," he said, pouring the water into their teacups, his face obscured by the steam. "You have made me think outside of my normal reasoning on several occasions."

The steam chose that moment to dissipate and the way he was looking at her sent a rush of heat up her neck.

He slid one of the cups across the island to her and she wrapped her fingers around it, relishing the warmth.

"Are you cold?" he asked, watching her hands. "This old manor is dreadfully drafty."

"A little, but I'm all right."

He lifted his tea and gestured to her with his other hand. "I'll show you around while I light the hearths."

He first took her back down the corridor that looked as if it belonged in a Victorian period drama and into the room she'd seen with the piano. It was a lovely thing, all old, carefully carved wood, and she was beside herself when Sonder set his teacup on the lid and sat on the bench.

"Any requests?" he said over his shoulder with a grin.

Atta lifted her chin in challenge. "Requiem in D Minor, K. 626."

Sonder's grin turned wicked and wolfish before he spun back to face the piano. His fingers moved over the piano effortlessly, the haunting notes a balm to her very soul. It felt like magic, like one of those ethereal moments that makes one feel simultaneously filled to the brim with joy and drowning in despair because you know there will never be a moment exactly like it ever again.

He stopped after just a minute as she knew he would. The piece had never been finished.

"A Requiem Mass. How fitting." He smiled. "Thought you could throw me off with that suggestion, didn't you?"

"Ye', ye'. Toot your own horn later, Murdoch."

His laugh made even her fingertips tingle. "Did you know it was never completed?"

"I did."

His eyes squinted. "You never cease to surprise me, Ariatne Morrow."

Atta looked at her shoes as he rose and came toward her. "What's next on our grand tour?"

"How about the library?"

She paused, and it took him a couple of seconds to realise she wasn't following him out into the hall. "You have an *actual* library?"

"One thousand books constitutes an official library. We have three."

"*Three thousand*, you mean?"

Sonder chuckled and grabbed her hand to pull her along. "Come and see."

Oh, he had not been exaggerating. "Jesus of little Nazareth," she whispered, spinning in a small circle to try and soak it all up.

Sonder was watching her, leaning against the doorframe. "I take it you like it."

"I could *live* here." She craned her neck to look at the top row of books high up into the vaulted ceiling.

"Then you might enjoy this—" He pushed off the wall and strode to a corner where Atta's gaping hadn't reached yet.

"Are you kidding?"

He pulled a floor-to-ceiling ladder on a track across the rows of books. "I'm not much of a kidder, *a stór*."

Her attention snapped to him with the endearment he'd taken to calling her. "Do you need a live-in librarian?"

Sonder laughed, a full, deep laugh and she thought her heart might explode.

They spent the next hour pulling down stacks of books to show one another and discuss them. It wasn't until a grandfather clock in the corner tolled 1:00 that Atta realised how hungry she was. She was about to mention they should find sustenance when a glass case of baubles caught her eye.

No, they were little filigreed glass vials in various shapes, colours, and sizes, danging off the end of dainty chains.

"What about this one?" she heard Sonder's voice from across the room, then his shoes on the wood floor as he approached from behind. "*The Celtic Twilight.*"

"On my shelf in Briseis," she said over her shoulder.

"Ah." His voice was nearly at her ear. "My mother's collection."

"What are they?" Atta ran her finger over the wooden edge of the wide, velvet-lined case.

"Lachrymatories."

Atta looked at him. "Mourner's tear bottles?"

"Clever woman. Yes, my mother said they were not only a way to remember the dead but a great form of protection. She set about collecting these over the years. Here." He gently opened the lid to the case and selected one of the bottles, a deep amber one with filigreed vines crawling up from the bottom all the way to the ornate cap. The beautiful bottle swayed on its chain. "Turn around."

Too stunned to argue, she put her back to him, moving her hair over her shoulder when he unfastened the clasp. His arms came around her, his proximity, the cloying scent of him and his chest so close to her back making her head spin. Gently, he fastened the necklace, his knuckles grazing the nape of the neck, and Atta had never been so grateful she hadn't worn a turtleneck in all her life.

"There," he said and softly touched her shoulders to spin her around. "It suits you." She looked up at him, at a loss for words, and he cleared his throat. "Well, I'd better show you why I brought you here, hm? We'll need our coats."

"Did your mother stay in the green room at Briseis House?" she asked as they walked back through the manor.

"Yes, she did. My parents both stayed at Briseis, as did I. My family has a long history in that building and the Society."

He didn't ask her how she knew, or why she asked, and Atta was grateful.

Bundled up and huddled in their scarves against the cold Irish wind misting them with rain, they made their way across the grounds. The garden and grove were shrouded in a great deal of fog, too difficult to make out much, but off in the distance rose a massive, old hawthorn tree. Its branches bore no leaves, jutting like jagged arms into the mist, its trunk a mass of twisted wood, a hole gouged out of the centre like an open chest cavity.

"The hawthorn," she said, voice raised against the wind.

Sonder looked to where she pointed, adjusting his scarf over his ears. "Ah, that one is the oldest on the grounds, but it's not the one I brought you here to see."

A moment later, Atta was stunned speechless again. A structure of frosted glass and intricate black metalwork towered above them, nearly as tall as the manor itself. He opened the door that was truly a work of art itself and Atta spotted . . . plants. So many plants.

"Is this a greenhouse?" she asked in disbelief.

"It is, indeed. Have a look." He held open the door, and she stepped inside, forgetting the cold in the unnatural warmth, in the presence of wild flora she'd never seen. A veritable jungle of it. Vascular plants similar to ferns clustered on the ground, several different types of creeping plants crawled along the walls and glass roof, florals in inhuman colours dotted the beautiful chaos, and there, at the end of an overgrown path of stones, was the barest hint of a tree trunk visible, and a skeletal arm, held aloft by vines.

ATTA

"What is this place?" Atta said on an exhale, her pulse loud in her ears. She tore her eyes from the scene and looked to Sonder.

"Ah." He'd removed his coat and stood with his hands in his trouser pockets, looking more nervous than when he'd taken her into the shadows and said he wanted to show her something. "Well, some would say this is the last vestige of my sanity unfurling." Sonder ran a hand through his hair, a grin tipping up the corners of his lips. "But I call it research."

Gingerly pushing back overzealous vines, Sonder ushered her toward the tree trunk, another twisted hawthorn she noticed as they approached it. Two sets of bones were held there, nearly invisible for the flora, but a sliver could be seen here and there, the skeletons side by side like lovers entombed in vines.

"This is the epicentre," he explained. "It all seems to originate from this body, all these vines and flora. When you wrote that paper on mycelium and its connectivity to the rest of the whole, to other plants, I began to think perhaps that's what this place is."

Atta reached out to brush her fingers along a dark violet bud, its stem entwined around the radius bone of the corpse Sonder was referencing.

This time, the migraine began at the crest of her skull, blooming like a flower, making her sway on her feet. She tore her hand away before Sonder could notice, but not before she saw the woman from her room. The one in bed, in agony, her veins turning black. The one from the giant portrait in Sonder's sitting room.

"Why have you shown me this?" she asked him in awe.

"Because I believe this is the final piece you need. To understand how to be rid of the Plague."

Atta started. "Me?"

"Yes, you. There is something we're missing and I believe the secret is in the flora. We both know this isn't natural. Lungs and hearts and other organs don't sprout flowers. They don't grow things foreign to our"—he moved his hands, pacing back and forth in front of a woody, perennial plant—"our *planet*."

Atta's pulse beat strong in her palms, her throat, her chest.

"I'm no botanist, but I know these aren't natural. That fresh graves don't bloom like this and push bodies up from the depths of the soil when they've been buried *properly*. Atta—" He ran his hand over his jaw, then his hair, making it stand up in places. "What if—" He stopped again.

"Say it, Sonder."

He paused his pacing. Looked her dead in the eye. "What if the Plague victims aren't infected?"

"What do you mean?" She'd toyed with mad ideas, of course she had. But they were just that—*mad*.

"There's something more to this. It doesn't follow how viruses and diseases work. It isn't contagious, it selects humans seemingly at random. What if it's not an infection or disease at all? But something else?"

"These are the ravings of a madman, Dr Frankenstein."

"Of course they are. But it makes sense, doesn't it?"

It did. *Jesus*, it really did.

"Sonder, where did you get the cadavers for this?"

"This is the part where you may run for the hills. Have me arrested. Hell, *committed*."

"They're your parents, aren't they?"

He nodded somberly. "They are."

Her heart broke for him. For his parents. For all the beauty their deaths caused. Because it was nothing but Juliet's kiss, Macbeth's decapitation, the murder of Desdemona. Achilles mourning Patroclus. "Sonder, I'm so sorry."

A gale howled outside. He sank onto a stool, looking older and yet somehow younger. "I'm sorry," he said quietly. "I've never shown this to anyone before."

Atta approached him and slipped her hand into his. Immediately, he clasped his fingers around her palm like a lifeline. "Let's go back to the main house," she said.

A bit rattled, he led her through the grounds, the wind whipping her hair until it stung her face. Back inside the drafty house, he still held onto her hand and led her to a room that made her heart ache even more. If she thought his Trinity office was a severe, academic haven that encapsulated him, his study at home was downright draconian. It was a living memoriam of Sonder Murdoch with its black, panelled walls, masculine leather and dark wood furniture, and a full wall of specimen jars, various organs floating in ethyl alcohol.

Sonder squeezed her hand once, then let it drop. He poured two glasses of whiskey at the sideboard and sank into a worn leather chair, holding one of them and handing Atta the other. She took it but abandoned it on a side table to light a fire in the hearth, realising they'd been so engrossed all day that they'd only lit the one in the library.

When the fire was roaring, illuminating all the angles of Sonder's face, she came to sit on the coffee table in front of him. "Tell me what happened."

He tipped the dregs of his whiskey into his mouth and unbuttoned his collar.

"I was living in County Cork, preparing to return to Dublin. I'd just gotten the position as Professor of Morbid Anatomy after I presented the board with an embalming fluid of my own design that preserves the body for a few days longer." He rubbed at his eyes with thumb and forefinger. "It provided anatomists and pathologists with more time to perform an autopsy, that's all."

After refilling his drink, he went on. "This was a little over six years ago. I planned to return to Trinity and begin my career, but then I received a call from my father. He wanted me to move back here to Murdoch Manor. My mother was ill, and he was worried about her. She wanted me here. Naturally, this terrified me. My strong-willed, brilliant mother, who'd all but shoved me out the front door to explore the world, to find a life that made me happy, was asking me to be by her side—under the same roof again.

"I told the Trinity Provost and the Dean of Medicine, Lynch, that I would be living outside Dublin proper rather than in the rooms set aside for me in the city, and they agreed. By the time I made it from Cork to Dublin—" He took Atta's untouched glass of whiskey and drained it, setting it back on the table with a crack. "I'd never seen a live person appear dead before. One look at my mother, and I knew she had days left, if that. I stayed by her side constantly. I tried to save her, I—"

Atta squeezed his hand, her heart sinking because *this* was probably why he hated being called 'Dr Murdoch.'

"She woke twice. Once to tell me she was glad to see me, that she loved me and my father. The next time, she was terrified. Unrecognisable. *We* were unrecognisable to her." He ran a finger around the rim of his glass. "That night, she passed." He cleared his throat. "I came downstairs to call the coroner. When I went back up, I found my father dead next to her, tears still on his cheeks. He'd drunk a vial of my new embalming fluid." His voice hitched on the last word, and Atta wrapped his hand in both of hers. "It killed him instantly."

She didn't think words would suffice. There was nothing for her to say. Nothing that could make such an unspeakable pain feel less of a burden. So she stayed silent, holding his hand, and he let her.

"She always said she wanted no wake. Only to be buried under the old, twisted hawthorn. So that's what I did. I buried them side by side. Two lovers in one grave to feed the grove."

He held her hand fast and they stayed that way for a while before he pulled away, gesturing to the necklace of his mother's he'd put on her earlier. "She would have liked you. Same *take no shite* spirit and wild, brilliant mind."

He reached out and took the vial in his fingers, his knuckle brushing her breastbone. The heat of his hand sent shivers up her spine. Gently dropping it back against her chest, he stood and pulled off his undone tie. "Come on."

"Where are we going now?"

He reached over his messy desk to grab a notebook and

pen, handing them to her. "You've heard my sob story. Now let's get you the notes I know you're itching to take."

How did this man know her so well after only a couple of months? It was as if he could see inside her soul.

She took the writing materials gratefully and followed him back toward the Hawthorn Grove. Before they made it outside, he stopped at a closet that was larger than Atta's entire room. He handed her a woollen peacoat that smelt like him because they'd left theirs in the atrium. She put it on and snuggled into it, while he put on an almost identical one in a deep green.

The sun had sunk lower in the sky, the temperature dropping drastically when the wind had blown in earlier. Clouds were gathering quite heavily, but it didn't yet look like a dousing rain. They went into the magnificent atrium of ironwork and glass, immediately shucking their coats and laying them on top of the other two.

"I didn't realise you knew how to cultivate plant life like this," she said, flipping past his anatomical notes to a fresh page in the notebook.

"I don't." She glanced at him. "Not at all. This has all grown completely on its own."

"But the temperature is tepid. Perfect conditions for flora like this to grow." She looked around, but it didn't actually make sense. "There are no heating lamps in here."

"As I said, the corpses began to flower before I knew what was happening. By the time I came to visit their graves, this was already well underway."

Atta furiously took notes, walking around the greenhouse, stepping close to some plants to sketch them, touch them. Most were somewhat similar to things she'd seen before, but just like the flora they'd found in Lauren and all the John and Jane Does, they weren't completely identifiable.

She gently fought past a mess of nearly sea-like fronds, approaching where the bones of Sonder's mother lay, pushed up from the ground, nestled against the old hawthorn tree.

She knew it was her and not her husband, because there was a beautiful ring on the bone of her left ring finger. The ring Atta had seen in her portrait. She turned to Sonder. "Do you mind if I—" She gestured with the pen toward his mother.

"Not at all. Do what you need to do."

Atta just caught him turning away though, as she bent over the arm, following it up until she could just make out the rib cage, covered in mycelium and moss. If only she could see the heart. Or where the heart had been. It had to be the epicentre, not just the body as a whole—the mycelium control centre.

Gingerly, she used her pen to prod at the tiny fungal root system responsible for all the foliage. After a few moments, she managed to make a small opening and could see through the left side of the rib cage.

Atta gasped. The heart was still there, over six years later. Black as pitch and covered in congealed blood that was so thick and coarse it had become fertile soil for the mycelium. But it couldn't be. . .

"Atta?" Sonder called from farther away than she thought she'd left him.

Her hand slipped.

She should have worn gloves.

That was her last thought as the pain seared across her eyes, everything going green, then bloody black and glaring white.

A woman. A beautiful, frail woman. Olivia Murdoch writhed on her bed of white linens stained with her infected

blood. She called out a name. For her son. The vision shifted—
the white glazing into a forest of fog and snow-covered ferns.
Silver teeth like daggers lunged for her throat.

Atta released her grip on Olivia's rib cage and staggered
back, becoming entangled in vines.

Sonder was there in a second, cutting them away with a
machete. "No!" she cried, but he was already through them,
reaching for her. She heard the hiss. Heard the voice in her
head.

*Slash their hearts and gouge their eyes. Give us what is
ours in time.*

"Are you all right?" Sonder hauled her backwards to a
pathway clear of bramble.

"Yes. I'm fine." She put her hand to her chest. "Oh, no!
Your mother's necklace. The chain broke." Atta rushed back
into the mess of vines, Sonder on her heels.

They both stopped dead in their tracks. They needn't search
for the small vial at all. It had fallen against the stones and
smashed, the Tears of the Grieved spilling onto a leaf that was
withering, decaying before their very eyes.

"Let's get out of here." Sonder took her hand and pulled
Atta along until they were back out in the open, cold air.

Atta clutched the notebook and Sonder's coat to her chest,
letting him pull her into the house and lock the door.

SONDER

He hid the tremble in his fingers. "Let's get you home." There was an attempt at a smile, but he knew she saw through it. Too much was in his mind, his soul.

Poetry wasn't in life; it was in what we've made of the past, lending it romanticism instead of watching it burn and lie in the ashes. He shouldn't have brought her into this, this girl made up of poetry and bones, flowers and viscera, everything beautiful and meaningful in life.

Atta retrieved her sachel, and they quietly drove back toward Dublin proper. It was comfortable with her. The silence always had been—both of them lost to their thoughts. God knew they had so many of them, all of the time, like a dark sea they could never get their heads above. In a way, he thought that might have been what first drew him to her. Like a moth to flame. He was so close now he could feel the heat of it, but it wasn't him that he was worried about getting burned.

Sonder took the long way, the tumultuous waves of his thoughts pulling him toward the sea without him realising it until they were nearing the coast. The sun had fully set when he pulled into a car park overlooking the harbour, and Atta finally looked at him.

"Where are we?"

"Dun Laoghaire. The stand here has excellent fish and chips." She followed his line of sight to a little ramshackle hut of a place that had stood the test of time. "You haven't eaten."

"I could eat." Her smile was small, but it tugged at his heart.

Huddled in their coats against the sea breeze, he ordered two baskets and two Guinness.

"What's happening out on the beach?" Sonder asked the man who took their order.

"Oy, it's Samhain," the man yelled over the wind and raucous people flooding the shoreline. "Said they want to do a big bonfire and the whole gambit."

Sonder took their drinks and met Atta at the picnic table she'd found sheltered by a large rock. She thanked him but kept her eyes on the water. "It's Halloween," she said. "I almost forgot."

"They're about to light a bonfire out there."

A few bites into their fish, the fire roared to life, and all the crowd with it, donning their masks and passing around beer and food.

"Ah," Atta said on a sigh. "That's better."

Her face was lit in a warm glow. "The fire or the food?"

"Both." She smiled. "The company isn't half bad either."

"Atta, listen—"

But she held up a hand. "No. I don't want to hear your regrets about letting me in, or how this is dangerous or we're too close to the sun."

"I'm not—"

"That's what you're going to say, isn't it? Something along those lines? Because you might be brooding and mysterious to the rest of the world, but not to me. Not anymore. And this is bigger than us. Do you really think revolutions don't begin with one person? One act? Do you really think change can't be accomplished by two people? According to some, one man saved the entire world, past, present, and future. According to some, the Storming of the Bastille began the French Revolution, Shakespeare changed the English language, and the Beetles altered music irrevocably. Things would be different if people weren't so fucking scared all the time but let their fear propel them instead of paralyse them."

Sonder stared at her, her hair blowing in the wind and making her look like an apparition. A dark faerie queen. *Jesus Christ*. He was falling in love with her.

"*Well*," she pressed with no small amount of sass, "what do you have to say now?"

"What do you propose we do first, All-Knowing One?"

She scowled at him but relaxed her shoulders. "We need a live patient."

"Atta—"

"Stop it. *Stop that*. Stop trying to talk me out of things."

"Would you let me finish a goddamn sentence at least?"

"Fine." She crossed her arms, turning her chin away, and he tried to remain irritated with her, but couldn't with the way she looked in his coat.

"That might take some time. We know the signs of the Plague, but not until it's too late."

Atta shivered, and he took off his coat, wrapping it around

her shoulders until she was drowning in two coats too large for her. "Let's get closer to the fire," he suggested.

"Too many people. Can we just head back?"

Sonder felt a pang of disappointment. He knew it was cold and late, but he wasn't ready to say goodnight yet. "Sure."

Back in the Capri, he blasted the heater until she stopped shivering, and she went back to their conversation. "I know the signs are typical until it's too late, but what if we can speak with an Infected person before they pass? Take notes. *Try* something to save them?"

Sonder gripped the steering wheel tighter. "I do have notes I took in my mother's last days, and I can compile all my notes from research at Achilles House as well. If we look at all that with what I've written studying in the hawthorn atrium and your research. . ."

"We could be well on our way to fitting the pieces together. But I still think we need a live patient."

"I'll see what I can do."

He pulled into the car park. Atta reached for the door handle and offered him a wry smile. "You don't have to watch me walk in. I don't think anyone else has plans to kidnap me but you."

Sonder snorted. "And yet that eases none of my worries for your safety. Oh." He reached into his pocket, pulled out a flick knife and handed it to her. "Here. In case that bastard Dohmnall comes near you again."

"These are illegal," she said, but took it nonetheless.

"So is raping women, but the fuckers still try it."

She frowned at him but slid it into her—his—jacket pocket. "Goodnight, Sonder."

"Sweet dreams, Atta."

ATTA

They needed a live patient. That was the missing link.

Atta sat back from her microscope, the mycelium pressed between two pieces of glass. She'd been staring at it all day, trying to compile as much as she could to compare it with Sonder's research. He'd thought the hawthorn atrium was the missing puzzle piece, and perhaps he was right, but after seeing his mother's heart still intact, only changed, she knew their only hope was to also study a live Infected patient.

What if they're not Infected, Sonder had said. But then what?

It made sense, but she couldn't see the connection, the end, the common denominator. It had been a week since she'd gone to his house, since they'd agreed on their next steps, but they'd both been too busy, her with midterms and him with ridiculous errands for the Society. She hoped one of those errands would lead them to a live patient.

Exams were through, but Atta had a shift at the morgue tonight. If there wasn't a cadaver there that was at least a Stage 3, they were going to have to head back to the Trinity Cemetery and lift one somehow. All of their previous bodies were rotting despite Sonder's special embalming fluid.

Turning away from her botany notes, Atta strode to her bookshelf and pulled down her books on folklore and ancient religions. Somehow, all of this had to connect to her visions—it had to. For years, since that first migraine hallucination, she'd written them off as just that—hallucinations. But after Lauren Kennedy had perished the exact way Atta saw, and she'd seen into the past to watch Olivia Murdoch die, she couldn't deny there was something more to it all.

Atta felt foolish flipping through the pages of fairytales and religious nonsense, and yet, she knew it all stemmed from somewhere, some kernel of truth. Finding the kernels was the difficult part.

Frustrated, she tossed W.B. Yeats's *Irish Folklore and Fairy Tales* onto her bed and picked up *Religious Tales of Woe* by Rupert Rosenthall, thumbing through the pages, using the book like a damn Magic 8 Ball. "Give me something," she whispered, remembering an old fairytale rhyme. "*Pure in heart, keep a stayed mind. Seekers find what's lost o' mine.*" She'd just selected a page at random when Emmy's voice rang out in the sitting area, followed by their front door slamming shut.

"Attaaaa," she sang. "Oh, Ariatne, dearest!" Emmy's head popped in Atta's doorway, her face set in theatrical despair. "The rain is absolutely gushing from the clouds. If I go to the library to study on my own, I'll die. Please join me."

Atta laughed, already grabbing her satchel and shoving books into it. "All right, give me two minutes."

"Thank you! My saviour, my gloomy little cloud. I'll be your sunshine if you'll be my rain."

"You're a disaster, Em."

Emmy laughed. "I think I'm more suited for sunny Venice than I am dreary Dublin."

"Dublin isn't dreary, she's melancholic. Her sunshine is in her people." Atta tapped Emmy on the nose. "Like you."

"Yes, yes, I'm amazing." Emmy started helping Atta gather her study materials, throwing a couple of pens into the satchel while Atta put on her shoes. "Do you need this one?" Emmy pointed a finger toward the book Atta had just opened, then bent in to look, her face twisting in horror. "Christ, that's ghastly."

Atta tied the laces of her Oxfords and stood from the bed to see what had bothered Emmy. "Oh." She marked the page with a dried sprig of lavender and closed it. "That's a chapter on possession."

Emmy wrinkled her nose. "Cute."

They left the lads a note to meet them at The Buttery for a bite to eat before afternoon classes and headed for the library, where Atta suggested a certain row and a certain desk where she'd unknowingly first laid eyes on a certain professor nearly a decade earlier.

Emmy complained about the rain ruining her hair for at least three minutes before someone from the next row stomped over, told her to hush, and she finally pulled out her study materials, both of them sinking themselves into their work.

Atta went directly to the page she'd marked after her fanciful fairytale poem quotation, discovering it was a chapter on possession she recalled from undergrad but hadn't paid much attention to other than what was needed for her exams.

The photo that had disturbed Emmy was a painting depicting Sister Palmerín, a nun who was possessed after Urbain Grandier, a Catholic priest, made a pact with the devil.

The poor nun was prostrate on a small bed, terrified, while a winged demon floated above, only visible to her.

Atta read on, stopping to look over the images of the alleged pact between Grandier, Satan, Leviathan, Astaroth, and several other minor demons.

The next page had her blood running cold the moment she set her eyes on it.

In the painting, a woman was on the floor, her back arched, her eyes rolling back. A priest stood before her, a shining icon of Mother Mary illuminating a burst of small, winged demons that had erupted from the woman's chest. Atta held the page to the light, noticing for the first time that the woman's veins were black, crawling up her neck like vines. Her chest was split open where the beasts had flown out, and her heart was not an anatomically correct organ at all but a bloody rose.

Adrenaline flooding her veins with ice, Atta crouched closer to look at the demons. They almost looked like little trooping faeries, only they had horns.

She let out a gasp. What if they weren't demons at all?

"I have to go." She grabbed all of her things in one sweeping motion, holding them close as she rushed out of the library, Emmy calling after her.

Everything was soaked by the time she made it to Sonder's office, and she rushed in, dripping all over the floor.

He stood from his chair so quickly that his coffee cup fell to the floor and shattered. "What is it? Are you hurt?"

She didn't answer. Breathing hard, she slammed his door shut with her foot and dropped everything to the floor, crouching on her knees and spreading it all out.

Sonder joined her on the floor. "Atta, what's going on?"

She still didn't answer. Instead, she flipped to the painting. Pointed at the beasts. Looked at him.

"Atta, *what is it*?"

"What if they're not demons but faeries?"

"You're not making any sense. . ."

"What if the Plague is not an infection but a possession? What if they're not Infected, but Inhabited?" His brows pinched, but she ploughed forward. "Think about it. The strange coins, the flora. . . Where is it *from*?"

Sonder's mouth dropped open. He looked from Atta to the painting, lifting the book so he could better see it. "The veins in her neck. . ."

"Look at her heart."

"Holy hell." He sat back on his heels. "Atta, this is madness."

"But you think I'm right."

"I–" Shock was writ across his features in harsh lines. "Yes, I do."

"We need a live patient, Sonder. A live Inhabited."

"First we need to understand *why*. What they could possibly want with us and how they select us. We need another cadaver, too."

"Sonder."

He looked at her, his surprise and awe dripping down into confusion when he saw her face. "What is it?"

"It's something I didn't tell you. About your mother's heart. And—"

She looked away, but he took her chin in his fingers and gently pulled her back to meet his eyes. "It's all right."

"It's about my migraines. I think— I think I saw Lauren

Kennedy die before it happened. And I saw your mother in my room, laughing. Then, I saw her dying."

A thousand emotions passed over his face. Fear, anger, astonishment. "I don't understand. Like a— Like a medium?"

She hadn't considered the word for it. Hadn't had time to even think of what the connection was. "I don't know." She scrubbed at her eyes. "A faerie medium?" A wild laugh popped out of her. "Maybe."

"What about my mother's heart?" Sonder ventured, switching gears.

"I see it still intact, only blackened."

Sonder's eyes went vacant, then there was a flash of something she couldn't decipher. "That's impossible."

"They are, perhaps, human souls in the crucible—these creatures of whim."
-W.B. Yeats, *Irish Fairy Tales & Folklore*

ATTA

S onder had their newest thieved body open on his makeshift examination table in the solarium.

They'd had to hurry, digging as quickly and as quietly as they could manage under the cover of night in Trinity Cemetary. They'd dumped a corpse from Gallaghers' into the empty grave, but they'd only been able to fill the dirt back in hastily, without nearly the precision they would have liked. If anyone came in daylight—presumably the same person whose light they'd seen on the grounds at night—it would be obvious someone had tampered with the grave.

On the drive to Sonder's manor, Atta had the idea that they should have made it look like an animal had gotten to the grave. Maybe it would appear that way, anyway. After all, who would dig up dead bodies? What was done was done, and they'd hauled the body into Sonder's laboratory.

After they'd run between the lab and the atrium, clear across the house and grounds thrice to tell one another something regarding their separate research, Sonder moved his endeavours to the hawthorn solarium with Atta.

Sonder cursed, wiping black blood on his leather butcher's apron. He said the leather kept the blood from seeping onto his clothing so he didn't have to wear *hospital-grade rubbish.*

"What is it?" Atta asked, glancing up from her inspection of a *unipinnate* leaf.

He was wiping in between his fingers, having not bothered with gloves. "Damn. I've gotten some on my sleeve." He had them rolled all the way up his forearms and she wondered how deeply he'd reached into the chest cavity. "See, this is why I always wear black at Achilles."

"Did you find anything of significance?"

"No." He sat on a chair they'd dragged in, brushing the hair out of his eyes with the back of his wrist. "I don't understand why some of the bodies flower and others don't. The presence of the flora must be why Agamemnon is burying them."

"Planting them," Atta clarified and Sonder tipped his head to one side, considering.

"I suppose you're right. But why? Why the flowering, why the possession at all? Is the flowering happening as a failure of the possession?"

Atta stood up and brushed off her plaid trousers. "In my. . . *visions,* let's call them, I've seen glimpses of a strange place. It's beautiful with all manner of flora, but there is always decay slipping in."

Sonder scrubbed at the stubble on his jawline, and for a split second, Atta was distracted by the thought of what it might feel like against her fingertips, her lips. "Are you suggesting that their world is crumbling?"

She hadn't been suggesting that, but now her mind spun with the idea. "And now they want ours?" She poised it like a hypothesis to gauge his reaction.

He was silent for a long moment, lost in contemplation. "Are they trying to inhabit humans to *be* us, or. . ."

Atta let out a small gasp. "'*Humans in the crucible*.'"

"Come again?"

"'*Humans in the crucible*,'" she quoted again. "It's a line from W.B. Yeats's treatise on Irish Folklore. "It always stuck with me."

Sonder rose, a light flicking on behind his eyes. "Atta, what is a crucible used for?" He moved his hands as he spoke, beginning to pace. "In science, in alchemy. What is a crucible used for?"

Excitement skittered up her spine. "To heat, to melt down—"

"*Why?*" he urged her, ever the professor begging for his students to locate the answer themselves.

"To make something new." As soon as the words were out of her mouth, they locked eyes. "Sonder," she ventured. A question. A fear. A thrill.

"We have to stop this. I think they're growing more successful."

SONDER

He didn't want to be at Achilles House. He wanted to be locked in a stifling greenhouse with a beautiful woman solving Dublin's problems. In fact, he feared if they didn't, the Plague would spread through Ireland, and though they were an island, who was to say it wouldn't reach further? Across the Irish Sea to Wales, across the Atlantic to Canada or New England?

Instead, he was standing over a Stage 1 corpse, some of her blood still red, and making false observations for a Society he hadn't trusted in a long time.

"Hey Prof," Gibbs said from his doorway. "Lynch is in, and he wants you to take a look at the new arrival."

"And he sent you, did he?"

Gibbs looked at his shoes. The lad had been awfully strange with him since that night in the pub. "I was on my way up the stairs." He shrugged.

"All right. I'll be right down."

Sonder waited for Gibbs to leave, heading in the direction

of the data office before he left his lab and descended the steps to the chill chamber. It was empty, save for several stiffs in their metal drawers and one laid out on an autopsy table. Sonder put on his glasses and looked her over. She was young, early twenties. Nothing was significant about her body at all, save for the small amount of what appeared to be menstrual blood on her upper thighs. If he didn't know any better, he'd say this person hadn't died of the Plague—of possession—at all. Surely she had, or why would the body be brought there for study?

Sonder donned gloves and took a vial of her blood—still healthy crimson. He made to return to his lab to look at it under a microscope, but he noticed something. The cadaver's nails were caked with a substance. Lifting her hand, he inspected it, unable to tell what it was aside from seeming to be something earthy. He decided to use a spoon scraper to pry some out and deposited it into a clean specimen vial. Perhaps he would be able to decipher what it was under his microscope, or he could see if Atta might know.

Vial in hand, Sonder returned to his lab, but the moment he stepped inside, the hairs on the back of his neck stood on end. Something was different. Slowly, he walked around the room, trying to recall how everything was positioned—what someone would want inside his office. But everything incriminating was at home. Or with Atta.

Except her research paper. And her thesis he'd been looking over.

Oh fuck.

Sonder rushed to his desk, searching frantically for the papers. When he found them, he sank into his chair with relief, heart hammering in his chest.

But then he noticed a smudge. Looking closer, he noticed it was ash from a cigarette. The lowest form of nicotine—the kind he never partook of.

ATTA

29 NOVEMBER 1993

The trees were nearly bare and most students were suffering from burnout. They walked to classes slower, studied less, partied less.

Atta thought the latter was a good thing. Without knowing how the possession victims were being chosen, it seemed a better idea to stay holed up inside, alone. But that hadn't seemed to make a difference for Lauren, and it wasn't practical. There was no need to scare everyone. Thus, she and Sonder had kept their research entirely secret the last few weeks. She wouldn't say they'd had any breakthroughs, but that was how science went and they were on the right track, researching what might drive a Fae spirit away. Once they gained access to someone currently Inhabited, they could test out their theories. And Atta had a plethora of theories.

She dropped her satchel on the floor of the Briseis House common room on Third and sank onto the couch next to Gibbs, who was playing some Nintendo game.

"How goes it?" he asked her without looking away from the telly.

"It goes. Want a soda?" She reluctantly rose from where she'd just plopped, realising she was parched.

"Sure. Club Orange, thanks."

She grabbed a Club Orange and a Cream Soda and handed Gibbs his.

"Oh, hey," he said, smashing the buttons on his controller. "You had a message from your advisor. I guess Lynch wants to speak with you, as dean that is."

Atta's hand froze, soda halfway to her mouth. "Lynch? Why?"

Gibbs shrugged, "Didn't say. Just said to be there when you can."

Atta left her drink on the table in front of the sofa and rushed to the student services building, trying not to panic. She'd done everything they'd said. She'd done her TA work and taken as many shifts at the morgue as possible so she could pay the rest of the tuition her TA position didn't cover. She'd even scrimped on meals so she hadn't used up all of her allotted food privileges as a TA.

If they wanted more money, or they'd found out she was spending more time with Sonder than was strictly appropriate, she'd figure it out—she had to. Surely it was all unrelated. Lynch was the dean of the college her TA position was under, but not her actual master's program.

No. It was unrelated, and everything would be fine.

The secretary at the front didn't take her to Mrs O'Sullivan's office, but directly to Dean Lynch. The young girl announced who she was and swept past Atta, back out into the corridor. Lynch regarded her with a look she couldn't pinpoint, but every nerve in her body was on alert. She'd never seen him more than a passing occurrence here and there and had never noticed his sunken eyes and thinning hair.

"Miss Morrow. Please, sit."

She didn't want to. She wanted to run.

He was a large man, and she suspected he was the type to wield it with little grace. Crossing his hands over his protruding belly, he leaned back in his chair. "Miss Morrow, it has come to my attention that you have been traipsing around the college's private grounds at night. Is this true?"

Atta was stunned. Didn't all students walk around the grounds at night? There was no curfew at Trinity. "I don't understand, sir."

"In particular," he punched every consonant, "the cemetery that is strictly off-limits for a myriad of reasons."

Oh no. She felt as if she might cry, or explode. "I—"

"What's worse," his *s* came out like a hiss, "is that one of the graves was disturbed on the very night you were seen there."

Oh god. She was going to throw up on his desk.

"Tell me, Miss Morrow, what does a young Botany grad student need with a graveyard, hm?"

"I—" *Jesus, get some words out. Anything!* A voice unlike her own oozed out of her, calm, collected, slick as oil. "You might not be aware, but I was raised above my parents' mortuary, and I find solace in cemeteries. Walking there, I noticed some pretty flowers, and I picked them. But I did not disturb a grave, sir. The deceased are sacred, especially those who perished from the Plague."

One of Dean Lynch's eyes twitched. "Be that as it may, the provost and I have come to the difficult conclusion that this transgression is unforgivable. You are hereby expelled from

Trinity College Dublin and I want you off the property tonight."

Atta gaped at him like a fish. "You cannot be serious!" She knew her tone hit a hysterical pitch, but she didn't care. "I have kept my grades up. I've worked my arse off to pay my tuition. I walk through a graveyard, and you *expel me*?"

"Do not take that tone with me," he snarled, flopping forward in his seat. "This is a serious matter and you are lucky I don't press charges against you for trespassing!"

Atta stood in a rush. "I can't believe this. This is— It's—"

"I don't believe for one second you picked bloody flowers and I doubt you'd like for me to look any further into it. Would you, Miss Morrow?" His voice had gone eerily quiet, all his anger dissipating like a ghost.

"You're a bastard," she hissed.

"Leave!" he boomed, rising from his chair as quickly as his anger resurfaced. "Before I have security escort you out. Pack your things. You are *through* here."

Atta's eyes stung with unshed tears of fury, of anguish. She wanted to run or lie down and cry. She didn't know which. Everything was a blur, a fog. She found herself back in her dorm without memory of getting there. She stood looking at all her things. All her assignments splayed on her desk, the books in little stacks all over the floor where she'd left them, Sonder's coat still hanging on the wardrobe door because she kept forgetting to return it, or didn't want to. Her watery eyes landed on her TCD mug on the desk and then reality hit her. She dropped onto her bed and wept.

Emmy heard her eventually. She came in, rubbed circles on her back, and waited for her to explain. When she did, Emmy exploded. Furious on behalf of her friend.

Eventually, Gibbs got Atta to drink some water, murmuring that Lynch was a prick.

Dony returned with boxes, looking like a sad, silent pup.

Together, they quietly packed up her things, the silence punctuated by one or another of her roommates voicing their dismay. It was freezing and drizzly out, but they helped her load her car and hugged her goodbye.

"This is just a blip," Emmy whispered when she wrapped her arms around Atta and squeezed her tight. "All a misunderstanding. We'll figure it out."

Gibbs wouldn't look her in the eye, but he hugged her neck. "Where will you go?"

"I– I don't know." And she didn't. Galway was so far from everything she was working on. From Sonder and her friends.

Dony lightly punched her in the shoulder. "Mulligan's isn't on campus. Meet us there once you get settled in a few days, ye'?"

Numbly, Atta got in her car and drove.

SONDER

S onder ripped off his tie, unbuttoning the first few buttons of his shirt. What a fucking mess the day had been. He poured a glass of whiskey and lit one of his most expensive cigars. Sitting in a chair his mother would have skinned him for smoking in, he took a puff, exhaled, let the smoke envelop him as he looked at the sculpture Atta was so enamoured with.

He heard the sound of gravel crunching beneath tyres and looked at the clock. It was half past eleven. Setting his cigar and whiskey down, he went to the door, opening it to find Atta standing there, a box under one arm and an old carpetbag in the other.

"I'm sorry," she hiccuped. "I didn't know where else to go."

ATTA

S he should just go back to the car. Her face was heated with embarrassment, her ears burning hot. This was way over the line.

Sonder glanced down at her hands and Atta looked dumbly at the bag she carried, then at every item she owned in the back of her car. "I didn't think. This is so inappropriate, I'm sorry."

His attention crawled back up to her face, and Atta wished she had a free hand to swipe at the blasted tear about to escape.

He said nothing. She turned, stepping off the first step and preparing herself to drive back to Dublin proper, to— To where she didn't know. A soup kitchen?

Behind her, the door to Murdoch Manor creaked, and Atta closed her eyes, bracing for the sound of it shutting her out, shutting Sonder back into his crypt, safely away from her impropriety and carelessness. She couldn't bear any more embarrassment.

But the sound didn't come.

Atta looked over her shoulder to see he'd only opened it wider.

"Well?" he intoned, gesturing inside. "Are you going to come in or not?"

Relief flooded her. As soon as he stepped down the steps to take the box and bag from her, she swiped furiously at the hot tears she couldn't stop. Thankfully, Sonder said nothing about them, only helped her inside and commanded she sit in a chair he'd surely just vacated judging by the fresh glass and still-smoking cigar sitting next to it.

He disappeared into the kitchen and returned several moments later with a fancy silver tea service, a glass of milk with a plate of biscuits, and a glass of wine. He set it in front of her, then moved his glass of whiskey to the tray too.

"Have your pick. Comfort food."

Atta laughed, she couldn't help it. He looked as dishevelled as she felt. "None of this is food at all but the biscuits."

He shrugged. "I'll get you whatever you'd like. Crisps?" His expression went from hopeful to sour. "Hm. I don't have crisps. . ."

"Tea is fine," she said, and he poured her a cup before taking the whiskey back and sitting across from her on the coffee table, roles reversed from the day she'd done the same when he was upset.

"You're not going to ask me what happened?" she questioned, stirring a bit of cream into her tea.

"No."

"I showed up at your house in the middle of the night crying, with boxes, and you're not the slightest bit curious?"

He rotated his glass, the amber liquid swirling. "Of course I'm curious, but you'll tell me when you're ready. I'm not one to pry."

Atta squinted at him. "Every bone in your body is made up

of curiosity and a thirst for knowledge. I don't buy that for a second."

He stretched across her to reach his cigar and she held her breath, every nerve within her coming alive with him so close. After a puff of the cigar, he said, "I'll wait all night if it means you'll stay."

All of Atta's teasing and prodding fled. She wasn't certain what he meant by that, and she was too drained to decipher it, too drained to fight off the depression waiting in the wings to devour her. "I've been expelled."

Sonder went very still. His voice was coated in ice when he finally spoke. "Please tell me that is a joke, Atta."

She shook her head, trying to fight off another swell of tears. "No. *Dean* Lynch"—she made a mocking face—"said he knew I was in the Trinity Cemetery. He suspected I had tampered with one of the graves, though he didn't have proof. I told him I just picked a flower, but—"

"How could he know that?"

Atta lifted one shoulder. "Maybe the guard with the torch saw my car or me? Or— I don't know. But they kicked me out and made me leave my dorm as well. I—" She heaved a great sigh, and Sonder stood.

"Well, you'll stay here. I have spare rooms and we will figure this all out in the morning."

"I'm so sorry to put you in this position. If they find out I'm staying here, there could be consequences for you."

"It would take quite a lot to get rid of me."

"But you're a professor, and I'm a student." She looked down. "Was."

"Was," he confirmed and took her teacup, setting it on the tray. "Now you are a woman who needs to crash with a friend."

He took her hands to pull her up. "And we'll sort it all out to make you a student again."

He showed her to a room that bordered on lavish but still tasteful, with dark green walls like her dorm room and a huge four-poster in the middle of a plush floral rug. It had its own private lavatory, and Sonder told her it was just down the hall from his room in case she needed anything. He even brought in all her boxes and helped her put some of her clothes away, and then he stole one of her books and made her laugh.

He left for a few minutes and came back with the milk and biscuits. "I'll get you proper food tomorrow, but promise me you'll eat at least a little."

She promised, and he bid her goodnight.

Exhaustion weighed heavily on her mind, body, and soul, and the bed was the most comfortable she'd ever been in. Sonder was right. They'd figure everything out in the morning.

Soon, she was fast asleep, dreaming of faeries and mythical lands of woods and flora, jagged teeth and rotting bones.

SONDER

When he thought Atta might be asleep, he knocked lightly on the door and opened it. She looked like a painting of a Faerie Queen, lying there in that bed surrounded by clouds of duvet and pillows. The very moment he confirmed she was fast asleep, Sonder grabbed his keys.

Rage buzzed under his skin, his headlamps two beams in a dark haze of fury. He didn't even turn off the car when he pulled up to the stately brick and column place housing a common-faced demon.

Sonder slammed the knocker repeatedly, then pounded his fist against the door when no one answered. He was seconds away from breaking the damned thing down when he finally emerged.

"Sonder?" Finneas Lynch blinked blearily at him from the doorway. "It's three o'clock in the morning. What are you doing here?"

"How *dare* you expel one of the most brilliant minds Trinity College has ever seen?" he spat through gritted teeth.

Dean Lynch sighed. His hand dropped from the door handle as he stepped outside in his dressing gown to meet Sonder on the footpath. "Is this about Miss Morrow?"

"Of course it is. She's brilliant, Finneas. This is ridiculous."

"She was trespassing on private Trinity property in the middle of the night," he shot back, his face sallow in the porchlight.

"All part of the collegiate experience, wouldn't you say? How many times have all of us trespassed? Done something stupid during college?" He couldn't possibly think this excuse would hold.

"Not where there were *Plague corpses*, Sonder."

He threw his arm out, his voice rising louder. "Maybe she simply wanted a stroll through a graveyard."

Lynch stared him down. "With a shovel?"

Fuck.

"She wasn't alone, either." The dean's eyes narrowed, his winning hand splayed out between them.

Two could play that fucking game.

"You know damn well this is about that fucking paper she wrote." Sonder snarled, taking a step forward, meeting the bastard eye-to-eye. "Did you really think I wouldn't notice you and your lackeys rifling through my things? You're fucking scared."

"I suggest," Lynch snapped, jowls shaking, "that you leave my property, Dr Murdoch, before I begin to look into *why* you are so viscerally opposed to the expulsion of this *imbalanced* student."

The threat to Atta hit him square in the jaw as hard as any fist could. He should rip his throat out, right there.

But if he said one more word right now, made one more argument, he'd only make things worse for Atta.

Instead, he turned on his heel and drove away.

ATTA

The scents of bacon, black pudding, and coffee roused Atta from sleep. The best night's sleep she'd ever had, if she were comparing. And then it all came flooding back, in the gut-punch way unique to the liminal place between dreams and wakefulness the morning after a tragedy.

Numbly, she dressed in tweed trousers and a thick, cable-knit turtleneck and tried to recall her way back to the kitchen, letting her nose guide her.

Sonder was at the island, whipping a bowl of something with a whisk. There he stood, heartstoppingly handsome in a white collared shirt, the top two buttons undone, showing the barest hint of his chest. Over it, he wore an open knit jumper, deep grey and ribbed. She couldn't help but think what it would feel like to snuggle into his chest, for him to wrap those long arms around her and make her feel safe. His stubble had grown out considerably since they'd begun sinking all their time into their work, and the hints of grey were a little more noticeable. He heard her shuffle forward, looked up, and smiled, a curl of hair falling over his forehead. Her heart was horribly, horribly at risk with this man.

"Good morning, *a stór*."

Oh, she was in so much trouble.

"Coffee is fresh." He gestured to a shiny silver pot next to a fancy coffee machine on the far counter. "Bacon and eggs are ready. Black pudding is just about there. I thought I'd try my hand at blueberry muffins, too. You seemed to like the ones from Buttery."

Atta's stomach flopped at the mention of him noticing her favourite muffin, just like he'd noted her coffee order. "Sonder, this is too much. I don't want to put you out."

He frowned, then poured a cup of coffee for her, sliding it across the butcher block where she took a seat on a stool. "It's my fault you were in that graveyard at all."

"Ohhhh, so you're trying to absolve your guilty conscience," she teased.

Sonder tried to scowl at her, but there was a smile tugging at the corner of his mouth. "I'm going to make this right. But, in the meantime, you'll make yourself at home here. You have all you could dream of as far as tools and research materials go. Imagine what you can do with uninterrupted time, hm?"

"Your *professor* is showing." He glowered at her and she hid a smile behind her teacup.

"Funny, funny girl."

After he artfully filled brown paper cups with muffin batter and slid them into the oven, he plated their food and came around to sit next to her on a stool. "I have lectures today, but I've told the House I won't be in tonight, so I should be home at a reasonable hour."

Atta listened, chewing a bite of the delicious black pudding and egg, considering how domestic it all felt. Sonder cooking her breakfast, talking about his day and returning home. . . It was nice. So nice that it terrified her a little. She couldn't get used to this.

As they ate, they chatted about what Sonder had read in the paper before she awoke and got in a mild disagreement about a scientific hypothesis posed by one of the Society members to him the week prior, and then the oven buzzed.

"My muffins!" He popped up off the stool and Atta laughed. He'd let her in so much in the last few weeks and she hoped she was doing the same.

Or did she? They both had so much to lose.

Tossing one of the muffins back and forth in his hands like a hot potato and saying, "Oo– hot– hot–" Sonder finally managed to land one on the counter in front of her.

She was still chuckling when he put his plate in the sink and told her, "The house is yours, *stór*. Use it as you wish and I'll see you this evening."

Atta wandered the halls for over an hour after Sonder left, peeking into the rooms they never managed to get to on her tour.

In the opposite wing from her and Sonder's rooms, she found a drawing-room she assumed had been his mother's. It had the same dark, enchanted forest feel of her countenance and the rooms Atta had stayed in that used to be hers.

There was an easel in front of a large bay window that overlooked the Hawthorn Grove. Atta peered out over the trees, their leaves blanketing the ground and their branches bare, the oldest hawthorn standing in the centre looking both menacing and alluring, like Sonder before she knew him. Like Gold Stitch in his mask.

Pulling her attention away from the grounds and back into the house, she looked at the half-finished piece on the easel. At first, it looked like any other woodland, but then she noticed the dark strokes that felt like decay slashing the trees, the plants, the sky.

Flashes of her visions assaulted her in blurred, nauseating swirls. Shaking her head violently, Atta backed out of the room to begin her work for the day.

SONDER

"Atta!" He started calling her name from the moment he closed the front door. "Atta!"

Christ, it felt good to come home to another human. To her. He dropped the grocery bags in the entry and went searching for her.

She wasn't in the kitchen, or her room, not even the library, but there was evidence of her everywhere. A glass of water in his study, a discarded jumper in the sitting room, half a muffin on the counter in the kitchen, and four new stacks of books piled on the table in the library.

Of course she would have her nose buried in her research.

Sonder rushed outside and flung open the atrium door, startling her.

"Jesus, Sonder!" She scrambled to catch the shears she was using before they hit the stone pathway.

"I've found someone."

Her eyes widened. "You found someone."

"A newly Infected—"

"Inhabited."

"Inhabited," he amended, "patient. Her name is Pam McDonough and we can go visit her in the morning."

Atta squealed, dropping her shears to the stones anyway, and rushed him. She jumped with such force that she knocked him back a step. Wrapping his arms tightly around her waist, he laughed, steadying her, and she clasped her hands behind his neck.

Time froze as she pulled back, neither of them releasing their hold, neither of them laughing any longer. His gaze dropped from her eyes to her lips, and he watched as they parted, her breath hot and sweet like honey. He had to blink to clear his vision, his head. She felt so good pressed against his chest. In his hands. Her lips so near to his.

Despite what he'd told her the night before, he was still a professor whose position was in jeopardy. She'd never be able to return to Trinity if he took their relationship further.

Her breasts were rising and falling quickly against his chest, and his body was reacting to every part of her he could feel. He needed to break the spell. Put her down. Take an ice bath.

Atta unclasped her hands and slid down his front, not helping matters as far as all *that* was concerned. She stepped back, looked away.

"We have a lot of work to do tonight, then," she said quietly.

Sonder cleared his throat. "Right. I stopped by Dunnes on my way. Let's get some sustenance and begin. Shall we?"

They took an array of foods into his study, and Atta wheeled in a little antique cart she'd found and stuffed with items she'd been looking into all day. Sonder lit a fire, poured them each a glass of cabernet sauvignon he'd picked up in France in '84, and they set to work.

One by one, she pulled out each item and explained why she thought it would work to dispel the spirit of a faerie, and they both tried not to feel like they were going mental.

"The sample you brought from the woman with a substance under her nails—" She held up a little glass jar. "It was mugwort, a common herb used for many things such as headaches and promoting regular menstruation cycles."

Sonder plucked a grape from a vine on the platter. "I did see signs of menstruation, but I didn't mention it because I didn't want any outside information to influence your determination."

Placing the jar of mugwort back on the cart she seemed very fond of, Atta agreed with him. "I would say she was probably using it for that purpose, at least. It's vastly outdated, but some people just prefer the old ways, I suppose. However, mugwort was also used to keep evil spirits at bay, especially on Samhain."

"Intriguing."

"Very." She turned theatrically to her cart of curiosities and back again, holding a—

"What, pray tell, is that thing?"

"This is a smudge stick. Watch." She produced a prickly sort of potted plant in a violent shade of fuschia. "I detangled this from the main mycelium, but it seems to be growing its own network since I've done that. I've been documenting its progress all day, but note what happens when I do this. . ." She held the smudge stick out and wiggled it. "Light, please."

Sonder hid a smirk and produced a box of matches from his

pocket, dong as the lady requested. Soon, the space between them filled with a long, steady stream of earth-scented smoke. After a moment, she held the plant close to the stream of smoke floating up toward the ceiling and the plant visibly shrank away.

"What in hell?"

"Keep watching." Atta forced the plant closer, and it shrivelled up, just as the other plant had when the Tears of the Grieved spilt on it.

"This is a huge breakthrough, Atta."

She gave a little pleased smile and set the plant to the side. "It will grow back. These plants are far too evolved not to, but the mugwort apparently worked on the newly Inhabited woman you took the sample from. She may not have known what was going on, but it worked."

"But she still died," he considered aloud, taking a sharp bite of an apple.

Atta's shoulders slumped as she chewed on her bottom lip. Jesus, that was distracting.

"The mugwort must not stop the Inhabitation, but slows it down."

"So we need a way to— What?" He couldn't help being a teacher to his bones. "What happens in a classic exorcism in Catholicism? The priest uses what to hold the demon?"

"Usually holy water or salt."

"All right. And then what is used to drive it away? To officially exorcize it?"

Atta was slower to answer this time. "It's a series of things. That is exactly the train of logic I've been following, but they're not demons. I have some ideas, but I don't think we'll know for certain in this case until we have a test subject."

"And we need to know how to contain it—the faerie—or it

could very well just find someone else. That might be what's happening when the human host dies, the faerie is simply finding a new, suitable host."

"That makes the most sense." She looked down at her hands, her dark nail polish chipped. "But why has the hawthorn atrium ecosystem thrived?"

"Perhaps because I gave it the shelter it needed," he ventured.

Atta stood from the floor, where he always seemed to find her working rather than at a desk or a table. He adored that about her.

"I don't think that's it. I think—" She broke off, contemplating. "I think it thrived because it had two hosts. One Inhabited prior to death—"

Sonder sat up straight. "And one after."

Atta nodded, looking sombre. He didn't want her to feel like she couldn't venture where she needed to because those cadavers were his parents, but he also couldn't be completely honest about them. "Go on," he encouraged her. "Say what it is you're thinking."

"I don't know what I'm thinking yet, but it's significant, the pair of them. Don't you think?"

Sonder nodded and Atta sat back down, talking about how plants thrive and what they need from the soil. After a while, he missed everything she said because, with the glow in her eyes from the fire, the wine suppressing his inhibitions, and *her* —Ariatne Morrow—sitting cross-legged on the floor of the room he'd worked, laughed, wept, *lived* in his entire life in a jumper of his she'd found on his desk chair, speaking of everything with such passion and brilliance, he knew, beyond a shadow of a doubt, that he would sacrifice anything, *everything* for her.

"Are you even listening to me?" he finally heard her say sharply. She popped a cube of cheese in her mouth. "Are you drunk?"

"Only on you." The words were out before he could stop them.

She pouted, her brows furrowed with skepticism. "Go to bed, Murdoch."

ATTA

"**M**aybe this was a bad idea."

A terrible, horrible, foolish idea.

Atta and Sonder stood looking up at a run-down apartment building with cracked walls and a door lilting off its hinges. Inside flat C6 was a woman in her mid-forties. Sonder's sources said she was fine one day, then not the next, and the deterioration had been swift after that.

Truth be told, neither of them was certain what they would face. They weren't sure anything they'd done to protect themselves, or the supplies they'd brought with them would work. It was highly likely they'd be laughed out of the flat and have to go into hiding somewhere off the Amalfi Coast. Actually, that didn't sound half-bad. Sonder in only swim trunks, lying on the beach, sipping cocktails.

Stop it.

"This isn't a bad idea," he reassured her. "We do what academics do. We go in there, test our theories, and we learn. There is no failure here today, no matter the outcome. Understood?"

"Yes, Professor Murdoch," she droned in her most irreverent tone.

"You might want to watch that smart mouth, Miss Morrow."

Heat licked up her neck, despite that it was hardly the appropriate time for such things. "Or what?"

Sonder opened his mouth and damn her, she wanted to know what he was going to say, but the front door buzzed and a voice came over the intercom.

"Come on up."

Plague Doctor masks firmly in place, they strode into Sunny Hills Complex—which was neither sunny nor remotely near a hill—and rode the lift up to the third floor. A baby wailed inside one of the flats and a couple was in a shouting match in another. Flat C4 had a very distinct odour wafting from it, and C5 sounded like they were shooting a porno inside.

"Classy place," Sonder muttered through his mask. They'd taken other precautions besides the masks, electing to wear vials of Tears of the Grieved around their necks, pure iron rings —because faeries notoriously hate iron—and ornate crucifixes on iron chains around their waists. They had no scientific data to prove the crucifixes would be effective protection, but Sonder thought it gave them credibility. Atta thought it looked ridiculous. She'd told him at least five times that they looked like creepy priests in plain clothes, but he didn't listen. In fact, he seemed to find it amusing.

Sonder knocked on the door to C6, and a young man answered. Atta would have pegged him around eighteen or nineteen. "I was told by some lady at the hotline that you'd be by in masks." He looked them up and down with a grimace.

Sonder nodded. "Yes. May we come in?"

"Not so fast. She told me you'd pay."

This had not been mentioned to Atta, but Sonder pulled out a wad of pounds and handed it to the lad. "Now may we come in?"

He stepped out of the way, counting the money. "Have at it. She's as good as dead if it's really the Plague."

"You don't seem too broken up about it," Atta observed and the lad pulled a face, shrugging.

"She's not exactly been the best mam, you know? This Plague is doing me a favour."

Sonder went rigid, but Atta was still collecting data. "I'm sorry to hear she wasn't there for you in the way you hoped. Can you tell me what sort of person she is?"

"I told ya', she's no good. I'm not exactly a fecken saint, but I wouldn't choose fuck buddies over my kid his whole life."

Atta stored the fresh data in her tired, *tired* brain. "I'm sorry. That's not fair. Would you mind directing us to where she is?"

He threw a thumb over his shoulder. "Second door on the left. See yourselves out when you're done." And he walked out the way they'd come in, leaving them alone with an Inhabited woman.

"All good?" Sonder asked her softly.

"Yes."

He led the way to the room they'd been pointed to and knocked. No one answered, so Sonder slowly turned the knob and went in.

The stench hit her first, square in the stomach. Like foul soil and crops gone bad, the sickly sweet of turned meat.

"Jesus," Sonder whispered under his breath.

The woman was on her back in a filthy bed, needle tracks up and down both arms, the veins collapsed. The doctor in Sonder kicked in, and he pulled gloves from his coat, slipping them on quickly. "She needs naloxone. An IV."

"We have to face the Inhabitation first. Then we can get her help."

Sonder nodded and let her arm fall. "Her veins are black. She's at least Stage 2. Maybe you should—" He gestured toward the woman and Atta was grateful he didn't finish the sentence. She already knew what she should do.

Slowly, and with trembling hands, Atta approached the woman, whispering soothing nonsense, a faerie poem she'd heard as a child. The woman didn't stir, but something in the air did.

"Light the black candles," she said over her shoulder.

Sonder did as she requested and stepped back.

"Get the smudge sticks ready, but don't light them until I say." With a deep breath, Atta let her fingertips touch the woman's bare wrist.

The pain wasn't as deep this time, but it began at her temples, slipping behind her eyes. A woman, young and beautiful but selfish. There were flashes of skin and hands and carnal pleasures, each sweat-slick body tangled with hers different from the last, the cries of a child off in the distance, alone, on his own. Just as he'd said.

Atta ripped off her mask and forced the images to the back of her mind, focusing on maintaining contact, but willing her mouth to form the words she'd prepared. A variation of an exorcism prayer limned in fairytales and folklore.

"As smoke alights on the Fae,
so are they driven away;

as wax melts before the flame,

so the wicked perish;

gone in light of day—"

She felt the woman arch her back and Atta opened her eyes. The Inhabited patient was nearly floating off the bed, arms splayed at her sides, her mouth set in a silent, horrible scream Atta could feel in the marrow of her bones. "Light a smudge stick," she whispered.

"Keep going," Sonder urged, doing as she instructed him.

Atta moved her hands to the woman's chest, keeping her pinned to the mattress.

"We drive you from this place,

whatever you may be,

unclean sprite,

all the wicked Fae,

all infernal invaders,

all to leave this day."

She heard Sonder gasp and her eyes flew open again, just as the woman dropped back down to the bed with a thud, limp as a corpse. There was a terrible screech, so loud and vicious Atta had to cover her ears. Sonder stood eerily still, his eyes wide, but appearing unaffected by the sound. At some point, he'd removed his mask as well, and his face was locked in horror and astonishment. Trembling, she followed his line of sight.

Her hands dropped to her sides as she took in the scene.

The Inhabited woman was leaking black blood from her nose, her eyes, and from her mouth crawled a being. Small, no larger than Atta's palm. Devoid of flesh, made up of bone and gossamer wings, it clawed its way over the woman's lips, its bones clacking against her teeth.

"Palo Santo," Atta whispered, afraid to move, for the creature had its sightless eye sockets trained on her, head cocked to one side.

She heard Sonder strike a match behind her. Smelt the citrus and smoke. Then he was pressing something burning into her hand. The creature—the faerie, she realised with a roiling in her gut—rose unsteadily to its feet upon the woman's breast, on her nightgown soaked through with sweat. Its wet wings unfurled, trembled like a moth drenched in water.

In one swift movement, Atta lifted the burning Palo Santo stick in front of the creature. It screamed and thrashed. The stick was burning fast, too fast.

"Trap it!" she screamed at Sonder, but he was already there, a carved-out lantern in hand they'd brought for this very hope, as small as it had been when they prepared it.

The creature clawed at the woman, its sharp talon fingers slicing her abdomen open, but the blood was red. Beautiful, glorious, crimson red as it spurted on Atta. She jumped onto the bed, swinging the palo santo stick, connecting with the faerie's back, sending it flying into the lantern. Sonder closed and locked the door, the creature hissing and flailing in the black salt at the floor of the lantern—its cage.

"Will it hold?" Sonder urged, sweat trickling down his temple.

"I don't know!"

She hadn't thought any of it would work, not in truth. She'd thought they would fail. Be back at the manor licking their wounds. Now they'd trapped a goddamn faerie that crawled out of a woman's throat.

Sonder thrust the lantern in her hand. "You can do this." Then he was dashing toward the bed, throwing off his coat and rolling up his sleeves so quickly he popped the buttons off his cuffs. They bounced across the floor toward her feet and Atta just stood there, thinking how strange that the two buttons were all she could see.

She didn't understand what was happening, the chaos paralysing her. But then she saw the woman convulsing, Sonder using all his medical training to save her. He was talking to her, pulling her toward him to lay on her side as she vomited black bile all over the bed, the floor.

The lantern, too pretty to hold such a monster, swayed in Atta's hand, pulling her out of her stupor. The thing—the faerie —was clawing its way up the side of the glass toward the vents in the ornate roof. It hissed and bared its sharp teeth and Atta stepped back, but she was still the one holding the lantern, so the creature came with her. Then it started to flicker, the entire creature. It began to smoke, turn into some sort of vapour.

Atta gasped, fumbling for the black salt in her pocket, managing only a dusting in her grasp, but it was enough. She threw it through the vents onto the faerie and it went solid again. Atta dropped to her knees, rifling through the bag they'd brought, pulling out the binding rope. She wasn't sure it would work, but her research had led her to this moment, and she had to try.

Working as quickly as her shaking fingers could manage, she set to tying a Celtic knot around the cage, across the latch. She could hear Sonder talking to someone urgently, then the slam of a phone down on the receiver.

"Hurry, Atta. We need to be out of here before the medics arrive."

"I only need one more, across the top."

He looked over his shoulder at the unconscious woman,

then rushed to kneel next to Atta. He removed the other binding rope and deftly began tying another Celtic knot around the top of the cage. "Will this hold?" His breath was hot on her cheek.

"It should bind it in place, but I don't know for how long. I should have spent more time—"

"Now is not the time for regrets." He took the lantern and pulled her up. "That woman is still breathing and free from possession because of you."

She looked up at him, her bottom lip wobbling. His face fell and he hauled her roughly against him with one arm and kissed the top of her head. "We have to go."

ATTA

Atta cradled a cup of tea in her hands. She hadn't taken a sip, but she relished the warmth against her fingers. Still, an hour later, she was chilled to the bone.

That *thing* floated in its hollowed-out lantern cage on the coffee table, wings moving so quickly they were just a blur.

"We need to move it," Sonder said gently.

He was right. Who knew what it was taking in. If it could report back somewhere. "Keep it away from the hawthorn." Her voice came out rough, haggard. "Away from your parents."

She didn't have to explain. Sonder knew as well as she did that it needed a conducive environment to maintain its strength, to thrive.

He rose and silently picked up the cage, holding it out in front of him as he left the room.

When he came back, he told her he'd put it in the wine cellar. Deep underground, but without the mycelium of its species, it wouldn't have a way out. At least she hoped that was true.

The phone rang, and Sonder looked puzzled for a moment before going to answer it.

Atta couldn't hear the person on the other side more than the distant hum drum of a voice.

"Gibbs," Sonder finally interrupted. "Slow down."

Atta turned, still living in a daze. Gibbs? Why was Gibbs calling Sonder at home?

"Yes, I understand."

He hung up and returned to Atta's side. "Gibbs?" she asked.

Sonder sighed. "The short truth is that he is in the Society, Achilles House specifically. I'll explain when I get back, but I have to go to hospital. The Inhabited or, I suppose, *Uninhabited* woman is in a terrible state of drug withdrawal, and her son called Gibbs—"

"Your informant?" Her brain was finally catching up.

"One of them. He called Gibbs and said she was alive but he needed help."

"You can't go there as you," she protested.

"I know. Gibbs told him he was sending someone. He didn't tell the lad I was the man he met today."

"I'll go with you," she said instead of *I don't want to be alone*.

Sonder seemed to be in heavy debate with himself inwardly if the crease between his brows was any indication. "I don't want to leave you alone with that thing."

"But someone needs to keep an eye on it," she finished for him. "You're right. I need to figure out how to hold it indefinitely. We can't waste any more time on that front."

He looked into her eyes for a long moment. "All right. I'll be back as quickly as I can."

Alone, the manor felt cold, as scared as she was. A gale hit the house, making it shudder, like it knew what sat beneath it, in its depths, invading it. Murdoch Manor's new inhabitant.

Atta shivered and went into Sonder's study to steal one of the three jumpers he'd left lying around. With it on, inhaling the scent of him, she felt safer.

Liar, Liar, her insides sang, *trapped in briar, sliced by thorns and tossed in the fire.*

Cursing, Atta stomped to the atrium to retrieve a few more items she needed and two plants she'd planned to research, taking them back to the safety of Sonder's study. She lit a fire and went to the kitchen to make a fresh pot of tea and a sandwich.

Retrieving the sandwich-making supplies, she pondered how peculiar it is that something transcendent, something unparalleled, can take place and yet humans still walk, breathe, move, live the same. Things like hunger and exhaustion should cease to exist in the face of the sublime, the tragic. And yet, there they are. It felt blasphemous.

Atta stilled, a slice of deli meat in mid-air on its way to the bread. "There's a *fucking faerie* in the cellar."

She dropped her sandwich paraphernalia to the plate and made for the cellar door.

Her hand rested on the handle for a moment as she contemplated if she was about to make a grave error. On second thought, she decided to arm herself first. Just in case.

Returning to the cellar door armed with black salt, mugwort, and palo santo, Atta fingered the Tears of the Grieved bottle around her neck and flicked on the light switch, venturing down the stairs. To her dismay, only one dim bulb flickered on, the manor so old and outdated. At the bottom of the stairs, however, she saw a shelf of kerosene lamps. *The Murdochs and their lamps.*

She lit one with a match and held it aloft to take in the space. It was dank and musty, almost entirely made up of shelving holding countless bottles of wine, whiskey, Scotch, you name it. She guessed she was looking at more money than her parents made in five years down there. More than she would have made in ten working at Gallaghers'. At present, Atta doubted she still had a job at all after not showing up for two shifts with no explanation. Alas, she had more important things to worry about than that.

And there it was. A flitting faerie, a trooping creature of the Fae, sitting in the middle of an alcohol shelf next to a bottle of Absinthe—The Green Faerie. It was comical, really, Sonder's odd sense of humour. The bottle he'd placed the creature next to was ornately described as *La Fée Verte*, a naked, green-haired pixie on the vintage label.

Atta moved her lamp to the cage holding a real, true faerie. She bent down to peer at it, looking at it intently for the first time. She should have brought her notebook to sketch it, all the sinewy bone, the flitting, crêpe-paper wings. Part of her wanted to go up and retrieve a journal, then come back down. But the little creature tipped its head to one side, and Atta mirrored its movement. Time suspended, just for a second, two beings eyeing one another. And then it flew forward faster than she could see, slamming itself against the thick glass of its lantern cage.

Atta startled back, dropping the lamp. It smashed to the floor in a thousand pieces, the light guttering out. Regaining her composure, she slowly approached the cage, pulling a handful of black salt from the pouch she'd brought. It was harder to see in the dim glow of the overhead bulb, but she managed to examine the latch. It was held fast, but they needed something air-tight next time. They hadn't known the bastards could dissipate unbodily, though she supposed it made sense. How else would they inhabit humans without anyone knowing?

That was when she saw it. One of the Celtic binding knots had come undone. Slipped free.

Atta swore she heard a laugh, dark and sinister before smoke began rising from the grates at the top of the lantern. No. She stepped back. Not smoke. *Vapour.*

The faerie was escaping.

Atta wildly threw black salt at the vapour, reciting broken bits of her prayer, her spell, her enchantment—whatever the hell it was. Sparks flew from the vapour where the salt hit, like the dancing embers above a blaze, but it wasn't stopping it. She didn't have the smudge sticks or palo santo lit. No black candles. No binding knot.

A hiss came at her ear and she screamed, a blinding, excruciating pain burying her skull in agony. Atta bent over, the vision so strong it took her breath away.

The Hawthorn Grove.

Faeries as far as the eye could see, wings flitting against fog, sharp teeth bloody, bits of flesh and flora in their gaps.

Atta hit the cold floor of the cellar, a strange tinkling meeting her ears before she felt the bite of a cut, and everything went black.

SONDER

"Yes, that's exactly what I mean."

"But, sir. . ." The Head of New Days Rehabilitation gaped at Sonder with a look somewhere between disbelief and sheer confusion. "Sir, it's an astronomical sum, and I was under the impression you don't even know the patient."

"Dr Reyes, I'm trying to cover, in its entirety, a full-length rehabilitation for a patient who willingly checked herself in today. The wise thing to do would be to take the money and begin treatment."

Eyebrows still halfway to his hairline, Reyes finally agreed and accepted Sonder's money. He was back in his Capri without having to speak to Ms McDonough or her son again. As it turned out, Ms McDonough hadn't taken all that much convincing to check herself into New Days. She was beside herself with gratitude for having survived such a traumatic experience and wanted to turn a new leaf.

Sonder had been worried she'd somehow remember his face, though she'd never opened her eyes while he and Atta were there, but she'd said nothing of the sort, only gone on and on about her guardian angels. *That* was why he slipped out without saying goodbye.

The sky was a slate grey when he returned to the manor, promising a heavy downpour. The house was quiet and he called out for Atta, wondering where he'd find her this time. Hopefully, he would find her curled up asleep after such a wild morning. With that as his hope, he checked her room first, but the bed was in an empty disarray. His study was also empty, so he ventured down to the kitchen to check there before heading out to the atrium. Chuckling at her recurring disappearing act, he noticed the cellar door was ajar. And the half-made sandwich on the butcher block.

Dread coated his gut.

Flinging open the cellar door, he bellowed her name, rushing down the stairs. He saw her in the dim light of the overhead bulb before he'd even made it all the way down. She was crumpled on the ground, a wet pool of something next to her.

"No, no no no." He knelt beside her, trying to understand what happened. He touched the liquid, bringing it to his nose. "Oh thank fuck," he exhaled when it was only lamp oil.

With two fingers on her neck, he felt for a pulse, relieved to find it was steady. He pulled her shoulders and head onto his lap, bending to quietly say her name in her ear, not wanting to startle her. Had she just fallen down the stairs? Tripped and hit her head? She didn't stir, and he searched the shelf for the faerie lantern. It was there, intact, the door closed.

"Atta, wake up. *Please.*"

Nothing.

He brushed the hair back from her face, cradling her in his arms. "Wake up, darling."

She began to stir, her eyelids fluttering open. The barest hint of confusion knit her brows before she winced, grabbing at her arm. Sonder helped her upright, inspecting her arm the best he could in the dank space. "You've a cut and your arm is covered in lamp oil and glass shards. We need to get you upstairs."

But Atta's mouth dropped open, looking behind him. Sonder spun around. "What? What is it?"

"It's gone." She stood and ran to the faerie lamp. "Oh no. No, no, no! The faerie is gone!" She put her hands to either side of her face, the gash on her forearm visibly oozing. "It's going to Inhabit someone else. What have I done? The knot, it was loose, and I tripped and fell, and—"

Sonder came forward and scooped her up.

"What are you doing? I'm fine! Put me down, Sonder," she protested as he carried her upstairs.

"You are not fine, you're bleeding everywhere."

"But the faerie!"

"We will sort it out."

"You always say that." She wiggled free of his grasp before he made it to the sitting room. "I'm fine."

Sonder snatched her wrist and inspected her arm in proper light. "I don't think it needs stitches, but at least let me clean and bandage it."

Atta was looking at the gash with her nose scrunched, most likely realising it was worse than she thought. "Fine."

She sank down onto the sofa and he returned a few moments later with a med kit.

"I let it get out," she said quietly while he knelt in front of her and cleaned the cut, wiping the oil from her arm.

"What happened?"

"I wanted to see the faerie, maybe take some notes and begin studying it, but it turned into that vapour, and I panicked. I did think quickly enough to throw some black salt, but it wasn't much, and when it rushed the side of the cage, I startled backwards and fell."

"Did you hit your head?"

"No, I don't think so. I don't recall a vision, but I must have had one if I passed out."

He tried to be as gentle as possible wrapping her arm.

"I'm not going to break," she teased, and he looked up into her eyes.

"You're all right?"

She held his gaze. "I swear it."

He could feel the flutter of her pulse in her wrist beneath his fingers where he held her. Her gaze dropped to his lips, just for a second, and the pulse in her wrist began to beat faster. Sonder could feel his blood begin to heat. She was so close. . .

She tucked her bottom lip between her teeth, and he tracked the movement with his eyes.

"Atta." His voice had gone low, gravelly. Hungry.

And hers had gone breathy. "Yes?" Her breasts were rising and falling rapidly beneath her thin blouse.

"I'm going to kiss you now."

Her gaze dropped to his mouth again. "All right."

Sonder cupped her face in his hands in just the way he'd imagined doing for months. Her eyes searched his in the split second before he moved closer, and then they fluttered shut as he pressed his lips to hers. His heartbeat pounded in his ears, his blood roaring.

One kiss, just one kiss.

But her lips parted for him and all of his control evaporated. He pressed closer, his tongue colliding with hers, his fingers tangling in her hair. Then she was pulling him by the tie, her legs spreading to bring him toward her, against her. He picked her up by the waist, hauling her further back on the sofa, laying her out. Pressing his body to hers, he moved his lips to her neck, dragging his fingers beneath her blouse, up her stomach with its soft curves and warmth. The feel of her skin set him on fire, but then she arched her back, breathing heavily in his ear, her hands in his hair, and he thought he would combust.

"*Atta*," he said on an exhale, "we need to stop." But his words were contradicted by his hands finding her breasts. *Fuck*, he couldn't take it.

"Why?" she breathed, her fingers untucking his shirt, sliding under it, toying with the dip of his pelvis.

"Because— Oh fuck, I can't remember." His mouth found hers again and they were a tangle of limbs, teeth, her fingernails digging into his back. Then she pushed him away and he thought she'd changed her mind, but she only ripped off her blouse over her head and he sucked a breath through his teeth at the sight of her.

He slipped his middle fingers underneath the straps of her black, sheer, *sheer* bra, and let them slide down her shoulders, the bra falling away to reveal her to him. He drank her in, her swollen lips and peaked nipples, her hair a wild mess, her cheeks flushed.

"Jesus, you're beautiful."

She pulled him back to her, her mouth greedy, and he slid his hands under her skirt feeling her arse through her tights.

"*Sonder.*" She said his name like a plea when he trailed kisses over her breasts. He hooked a finger in the waist of her skirt and pulled, his tongue sliding down to her hip, and she let out a desperate whine, lifting her hips.

A bang sounded at the front door.

Sonder's attention snapped to the door and Atta scrambled back, away from him, clutching a throw pillow to her naked chest.

"Who is it?" she whispered.

"Hell if I know." He stood up and they both looked at his very obvious arousal. Atta pulled her bottom lip between her teeth, stifling a laugh. The banging came again, but his blood was roaring just as loudly. He bent down and kissed her roughly, biting that intoxicating bottom lip as he pulled back. Her gaze was heavy-lidded and he could only guess what sort of situation her arousal was in, but Christ, he wanted to find out.

She stood, and he tossed her blouse to her. "*Thank fuck,*" he said when she had to drop the pillow to catch her shirt, and he got to see her again. "Hurry up, *stór.*"

He could have sworn she whimpered when he said that, and then she rushed away down the hall.

Sonder adjusted himself as best he could manage and looked through the peephole.

"Gibbs?" he said, opening the door. "What are you doing here?"

"Why is Atta's car here?"

The lad was finally growing a set of balls. "None of your fucking business. What are *you* doing at my house?"

"Can I come in? It's important."

ATTA

She fumbled with a clean blouse, trying to gather her wits. All Atta could think about was Sonder's fingers dancing along her skin. His mouth on her body, his hands gripping her hips. . .

But she pushed it all away as best she could and straightened her skirt.

It was good they were interrupted. There were more important things happening than the attraction that had been slowly building between them for months.

Stopping first at a mirror in the hall, she smoothed her hair and inspected her bandaged arm before heading back downstairs to see who had arrived.

"*Gibbs*?" She wasn't even off the stairs before she jumped in the middle of whatever it was they were discussing. "What in hell are you doing here?"

Gibbs stood from the sofa looking like a disappointed father. "I could ask you the same thing. Are you fucking the professor?"

"*Jesus*," Atta hissed at the same moment Sonder jumped up from his chair and said, "All right. Time to go, Gibbs."

"No. Wait." He put his hands out. "I'm sorry. I really do have something important to say." He looked at Atta then at Sonder, and she saw Sonder nod once. "She knows everything, then?"

"Just about."

Just about? Atta scoffed. Crossed her arms. "I'd love to be caught up."

"Of course," Sonder directed the words at her. "Let's just hear what the lad has to say first."

"I think Lynch has tapped my phone."

"Wait." Atta put two fingers to her temple. "*Lynch?*"

Sonder turned to Atta, "Lynch is in Agamemnon. Along with Vasilios, Kelleher, and"—he gestured toward Gibbs—"this fecker here, which you knew."

"Hang on. Does that mean Dony and Emmy. . ."

"No," Gibbs jumped in. "I think Emmy is suspicious of Vasilios, but I don't believe she knows for certain. Dony—"

"Is an eejit."

Gibbs shrugged and agreed with Sonder.

"Now you're caught up."

"I don't believe you," she accused Sonder.

She watched his jaw tense. "Atta, let the lad say his piece and we can fill in the missing bits after."

"Ye', this is sort of important. "What time is it?"

Sonder glanced at his watch. "7:03."

"It's already started! Hurry, turn on the news."

"I don't have a telly."

"Christ in a cradle," Atta muttered. "My room has one."

"It does?"

"This is your house, isn't it?"

She caught him shrugging out of the corner of her eye.

The telly was closed in one of the two armoires in her room and she opened the oak doors to reveal it.

"Well, I'll be damned," Sonder muttered.

Gibbs took the remote Atta offered him and flicked it on. A few staticky channels flitted by until Gibbs stopped on a wide shot of a newswoman gripping a microphone.

"That's the flat building from today," Sonder observed, looking at Atta, then Gibbs.

He was right. It was dark out and the building looked less dingy under the cover of night, but it was unmistakably the same place.

"Yes, thank you, Adam. I'm here in front of Sunny Hills Apartment Complex, here to speak with a man who claims his mother was cured of the Plague this morning by two masked individuals."

"Oh fuck," Atta and Sonder said in unison.

The camera panned to the lad from that morning, standing there looking nervous in the same clothes he'd had on earlier, but he'd taken off the cap and combed his hair.

"Lisle McDonough, in your own words, tell us what happened today."

"Thanks, Katie. Always wanted to meet you. You're so pretty on the telly. Better in person."

Katie laughed uncomfortably. "That's so sweet of you. So tell us what happened with your mam today."

"Ye', so, my mam has been sick. Ya' know, coughin' and snot 'n all that for a few days. But then it started gettin' worse. She couldn't remember a thing. Started sleepin' all day, then the wee veins in her arms started goin' black. So I called the hotline, ya' know, the one they tell us on the news to call if ya' think it's the Plague." Katie the newsreader nodded along patiently. "Next thing I know, I get a call from a woman who says she's sendin' someone out to help me. That he's. . . em— Gonna pay me to do a special sorta research or somethin'."

Sonder glanced at Atta, but she couldn't look away from the telly.

"So this man came, and then what?" Katie said into her microphone before holding it back in front of Lisle's face.

"He came, dressed like he was headed to mass, ya' know, in his nice clothes. Except he had a mask on." Lisle gestured in a way that anyone else would think he was miming an elephant trunk, but Atta knew it was the leather beak of a plague doctor mask. "One o' those old scary lookin' ones with the big goggles and bird beak."

Katie looked genuinely interested for the first time. "Like an old plague doctor's mask?"

"Ye'! Just like that. Only he wasn't alone. He had a girl with him. She had a mask too, so I couldn't see nothin' of her face but the rest of her was—" He mimed several vertical waves with his hands that Atta took to mean her curves and she blushed. "Kind o' girl ya' won't soon forget, ya' know?"

Katie laughed awkwardly on screen and Sonder smirked at Atta.

"What happened after that?"

"Well, I don't know. They paid me, I left, and when I came back the medics were there haulin' my mam away, but she didn't have the Plague anymore."

Katie pointed the mic back to herself. "And you have no idea what they did? How she was cured?"

"Not at all, neither did the docs. She had to stay in hospital for a few hours, she's em. . . Had a rough go in life. But then a doc from college came and put my mam up in a rehab facility. Paid for it himself."

"Really now?" Katie was saying, astonished, but Atta was turning her head slowly toward Sonder, her eyes wide and accusing. He winced.

"Well, you had a load of anonymous heroes today, didn't you!" Katie turned back to the camera. "You heard it here first. The Plague *can* be cured and we are doing our best to find these masked heroes and coax them out of hiding so we can eradicate this Plague once and for all."

Gibbs shut off the telly, and they all stood there looking at one another.

"The hotline has been flooded," Gibbs finally said. "What in hell did you two do?"

"We need Marguerite here," Sonder said, ignoring Gibbs and pushing past him. They followed him out into the hall as he stalked to his study and picked up the receiver of a vintage phone Atta had thought was only decorative.

As he dialled, Gibbs sidled up to Atta. "Are you fucking him then?" he whispered accusatorily.

Atta elbowed him in the ribs. "Stop talking."

"It's a fair question," he spat, rubbing at his side.

Whirling on him, Atta spat right back, "Is this why you wouldn't fucking look at me the last few weeks? You're part of Agamemnon?"

Gibbs looked away. "I was going to come find you. Later. Once I figured out where you were, and make sure you were all right."

She was saved from responding when Sonder spoke into

the receiver, and they were both drawn away from their whispered argument.

"Yes, Marguerite. It's Sonder. Can—"

He held the phone back from his ear and Atta could make out the shrill tone on the other end.

"Marg—" He pulled the phone away again, frowning. "*Marguerite,* would you stop shouting?"

He listened intently while Gibbs and Atta looked between one another, Atta on edge.

"Yes." Pause. "I completely disagree." Pause. "Fine. See you then."

Sonder slammed down the receiver.

"Well?" Atta prodded.

"Marguerite will be here in an hour to discuss what's happened."

"What does Marguerite have to do with all this?" Atta asked, finding herself irritated.

"She's tangled in this mess with us now, and we need her help to continue."

ATTA

S he heard Gibbs let Marguerite Vasilios in, but she and Sonder were still in a heated debate.

"We need to go find the faerie before it Inhabits someone else!" Her hand sliced through the air as she attempted to drive her point home for the thirtieth time over the last hour.

"It's a vapour. How are we supposed to locate a vapour?"

She'd pulled him into the piano room to have this discussion and he looked up at her dubiously from the piano bench.

"I don't know, but we have to try." Atta crossed her arms. "What if it's lying in wait for one of us?"

"Then we arm ourselves. Make it impossible to Inhabit us," Sonder argued.

"We don't even know how to do that," she snapped, her nerves feeling frayed after all that had happened that day.

Sonder frowned at her and stood. He approached and placed his hands on her upper arms, sliding them up and down as if to warm her. "This morning was still a success."

Part of her hated that he could read her so well. The other part of her was horribly grateful that she didn't have to explain herself. "I let it get away."

She peered up into his woodland eyes and let them search hers. "You didn't let that faerie do anything. I am all for people taking responsibility for things that happen when the situation warrants it, but this is not one of those situations. For all we know, it was moving the damned thing that loosened the Celtic knot, and I'm the one who did that."

Tears welled in her eyes despite her best efforts, and when one slipped down her cheek, Sonder was there to catch it, his palm along her jaw, his thumb swiping the traitorous tear away. "It's going to hurt someone else."

"We don't know that, a stór," he reassured her, his voice low. "But right now we have to move forward. Success and scientific discovery are not linear. We're still on the right path."

He was right. She knew that much.

Atta sniffled and stepped back from him, letting her analytical brain take charge. "We need to ward the manor. I can do that while you speak with Professor Vasilios."

Sonder nodded once and they strode out to meet Marguerite and Gibbs, who were conversing awkwardly in the sitting room.

As soon as she saw them, Marguerite stood up from the sofa, her distaste plain on her pretty features when her attention landed on Atta. "Miss Morrow," she said icily. "I did not expect to see you here." She shot Sonder a look. "Is this what Finneas is so livid about?"

"You're not here to discuss Lynch, Marguerite." Sonder had slipped into his cool, collected Dr Frankenstein persona as he sat in one of the wingback chairs opposite the sofa. "Please, sit."

"Like hell, we're not here to discuss Finneas Lynch," Vasilios hissed but took a seat, smoothing out the skirt of her expensive two-piece. "He's already on a tirade, trying to figure out who is going behind the Society's back. It won't take him two seconds to discover it's you."

Sonder tilted his head to one side, unbothered, and Atta sank onto the loveseat next to Gibbs, who looked at her with wide eyes.

"*What* are you doing, Sonder?"

"Curing the Plague," he answered simply. "Isn't that the job of *my* House within Agamemnon?"

A sharp, unladylike laugh popped out of Marguerite, incongruous with her polished demeanour. "You know how this works." She gesticulated wildly. "We are their puppets or else we're their *bones*."

Her last words sent a chill up Atta's arms and Gibbs reached out to squeeze her hand once. She offered him a small smile of gratitude as Sonder responded.

"We're already their bones and it's foolish to think we're not. Achilles has always stood as a place that was meant to find a cure. To put an end to this Plague. This has never been about glory or control, not for me."

It dawned on Atta then that he had chosen the name Achilles very carefully. It was artful, brilliant, and so fitting of the hierarchy and relationship between the two, wasn't it? *Agamemnon and Achilles.* And a slap in the face. Things were beginning to make a lot more sense.

"Lynch wants Agamemnon to be the hero," Atta put in, all of their attention swivelling to her.

"As it's safe to assume Rochford does as well," Marguerite murmured.

Rochford? *Why did that sound familiar?*

"In short, yes," Sonder answered.

Marguerite deflated onto the sofa. "Thank god you wore the masks. At least they can publicly attempt to take credit."

"I'm not scared of the Society," Sonder assured her.

"Well, I am." Marguerite pointed at Atta. "And she sure as hell should be. And you!" She looked at Gibbs. "If Lynch finds out you're two-timing him, you're in for a world of hurt."

Sonder rose and poured them all glasses of wine. "We will remain discreet. Lynch is no moron, he already likely knows it's us, but he won't storm the doors. If Lynch is anything, it's a man of tradition."

Marguerite sipped at her wine nervously. "Expect a tribunal then."

Atta and Sonder met eyes, and he answered her silent question. "Agamemnon is still ruled by a council. It's archaic but effective."

"And what happens at one of these tribunals? You said you become their bones."

Sonder took his seat again, setting the wine bottle on the table between them all. "It's not as bad as it sounds."

"Do they actually murder people?"

Marguerite drained her wine and poured another glass. "There are things far worse than death."

Atta and Gibbs chugged their wine in unison. Then Atta stood, her head already spinning from the alcohol and lack of food and her spill earlier. "I have a few things I need to do if you'll excuse me."

Their conversation played on repeat in her head as she

---

moved about the house, discreetly setting out wards. She sprinkled black salt on every windowsill she could find, laid out herbs in various places, and drew the chalk symbols she'd found in one of her textbooks on the doors to the rooms they went in most often. At the door to the cellar, she drew an ancient symbol meant to lock out evil spirits and prayed it would work.

Every time she passed the sitting room, Marguerite and Sonder were deep in hushed conversation, and every time it made her muscles more taut. Somewhere around the time she heard them laughing, she drank a second glass of wine on her empty stomach.

She did hear Gibbs interject here and there that there was no such thing as faeries, but the lad had panic drank—one of his signature moves—and was passed out on the loveseat, curled up like a babe when Marguerite left, and Sonder took Gibbs to one of the guest rooms.

When they were finally alone, he smiled at her, but she couldn't return it. Sonder sighed and pulled her up from the sofa, leading her to his study, where it was warmer with the fire. She draped herself over one of his favourite chairs, and he went to the sideboard.

"You look like someone poisoned your puppy," he said as he poured. "Please tell me what you're thinking so this agony I'm in can end."

Atta huffed a laugh. "You're so dramatic."

He handed her a glass of wine and sat on the arm of her chair. "Please."

Closing her eyes so she wouldn't have to look at him, she said, "You and Marguerite are close." It was an easy thing to observe. They were close in age, highly intelligent doctors, the both of them, and they'd been in a secret society together for years. She rode with him to the pub the night that Sonder showed Atta beneath his mask, and he had planned to take her home.

Cautiously, Sonder said, "We are. We've been friends since grad school. She and Mariana O'Sullivan are all the good that's left of those days for me."

Atta hated what she was about to say, but she was exhausted. It had been a rollercoaster of a day, and he'd just handed her a third glass of wine for the night. "And you've always been just friends?"

One of Sonder's brows rose, and then his face slowly broke into a grin. "Are you *jealous,* Ariatne Morrow?"

He looked so pleased she wanted to smack him. "Don't be coy with me, Sonder," she snipped. "You just saw me *naked.*"

"Ah. No, I saw you *partially* naked, which I plan to rectify."

His words and that smirk sent moths fluttering in her chest. "I'm serious. I need to know where you two stand after what happened between us tonight."

Sonder nodded solemnly. "Of course. Marguerite and I have been friends since our first year of grad school. One drunken time about seven or eight years ago, we ended up in Marguerite's room together—we were roommates, you see, in Briseis House. To be fair, I hardly remembered it then, and I recall almost nothing of it now. That is all. There is nothing there, I swear it."

Atta watched his face. This man she hadn't quite realised she'd fallen so hard for. "One time?"

"One time."

"Am I a '*one time*'?"

He looked wounded, his face dropping. "Atta. . ."

"I'm sorry." She waved a hand. "This is juvenile. I'm just tired."

Sonder took her wine glass and set it down on the table, kneeling in front of her for the second time that night. "Should I tell you then that I can't stop thinking about you? That I haven't thought of another woman since the first moment I saw you outside Achilles House with a corpse you'd cut open yourself?" He took her chin in his fingers. "Or how I have *never* thought of a woman the way I think of you?" He kissed her gently on the lips. "How I thought I was destined to be alone, but it turns out I was *starving* all these years, waiting for you?"

Atta swallowed.

"Or"—he brushed her hair away from her neck and kissed her collarbone—"how many nights I've thought of you while alone in my room?"

Breathing was becoming quite difficult.

"Are you still jealous, *a stór*?"

"Only of the walls of your room," she breathed out.

He laughed against the hollow of her throat, his stubble tickling, and her toes curled. "Would you like to see the walls of my room, then?"

The moment the door closed behind them, Sonder had her pressed against a wall, his mouth on hers, his hands roving over her body. Atta pushed at his chest, refusing to break their kiss as he walked her backwards toward the bed. They fell on it in a heap of limbs and he chuckled, that deep laugh that had been under her skin for months. Every place he touched was set aflame as they sloppily undressed one another.

He laid her out, slowing down, savouring her until she

thought she couldn't take it anymore, his lips exploring, their skin colliding.

Sonder moved atop her and whispered in her ear, "Are you certain?"

"Please," she confirmed breathily.

He needed no coaxing. He slid inside of her and sucked in a breath through his teeth. "Fuck, Atta."

She gasped, arching her back and driving her fingers through his hair, watching the way his brows knit, looking at her as if he might consume her.

After a moment, she stopped him, pushed him down, and climbed on top. His hands gripped her hips, pulling her forward and pushing her back. His control snapped, she saw it in his eyes the second before it happened, and he rolled her. Nimbly, he stroked her, kissed her breasts, whispered how beautiful she was.

"Sonder, please," she begged and he shuddered.

"Anything for you, darling."

He moved inside her again, and she arched her back, moaning, and he let out that low, rumbling laugh, her whole body vibrating with it. But then he began a rhythm that felt so familiar it was as if they'd done this countless times. Loved each other countless times in countless other lives, other realities.

Sonder wrapped his arm around the small of her back and pulled her up to sitting, never severing their connection. He held her to his chest, her hair draped over his shoulder, his breath hot on her neck, rising and falling on his knees, driving into her.

"Atta," he breathed when she was close, tightening around him. "Look at me."

She pulled her head from his chest as he held her up, gripping her waist. She looked into his hazel eyes and came. Her head fell back, her body on a whole other plane of pleasure, and she felt Sonder come within her as he kissed her breasts.

The second time was sweeter, slower, lingering. A savouring and an acquainting.

They collapsed together on his bed, and he held her tucked against his chest as if he never wanted to let her go.

SONDER

I t felt like he'd barely closed his eyes when he awoke to the sun beginning to rise, as he always did.

Atta was curled against him, her arm wrapped around his middle. He kissed the top of her head, relishing the floral and rain scent of her. She let out a little sigh in her sleep, and he regretfully detangled himself, slipping into a pair of lounge pants to venture down to the kitchen for a glass of water.

Gibbs was already awake, there at the stove making coffee, tea, and porridge.

"Where is Atta?" he asked after handing Sonder a newspaper. "She wasn't in the room where her stuff is at."

"Don't worry about that. You look frazzled, lad. What is it?"

He handed Sonder a note in his perfect handwriting. "Already had three calls since Marguerite got the line diverted. It's up and running this morning. You can see one patient this afternoon."

Sonder set down the newspaper and glanced at the name

and address of the Infected person—Inhabited, he corrected inwardly. "It's a posh part of Dublin this time."

Gibbs nodded his agreement and Sonder set to pouring tea for himself, coffee for Atta. "There's still no clear rhyme or reason with this Plague."

"Not yet. But we're close."

Without another word between them, Sonder carried the teacups up the stairs to his room.

In the doorway, he stopped.

She must have sensed he'd gotten up, because she'd turned over in her sleep onto her stomach, her arm reaching over to his empty side, giving him the most glorious view of her body from behind. He leaned against the doorframe watching her for a long moment. Warmth flooded his heart at the sight of her naked in his bed, bathed in golden, watery sunlight beginning to stream in from the window. They were either in for the ride of their lives or a hellish nightmare.

Quietly, he set the cups on the nightstand and lowered himself onto the edge of the bed. She didn't stir, so he brushed the hair from the side of her face with his fingertips. When that didn't work, he smiled devilishly to himself and began trailing light kisses from her arse all the way up to her neck. By then, she was smiling, her eyes still closed. He pulled away, and she opened her eyes, then rolled over.

Sonder wanted to sketch her, paint her, sculpt her. Immortalise her just like that, clothed in nothing but the sun and the scent of him.

"Good morning," she said groggily and he handed her the coffee.

"Rise and shine, darling. We have another faerie to exorcize."

Her eyes widened. "But we're not ready."

Seeing a potential disaster before it could take place, he took the coffee back from her, as it was perilously close to sloshing all over the bed.

"Then we will prepare."

"We don't even know how to contain a faerie with finality." She threw her arm out toward the window. "I *lost* one back out in the wild!"

"Then let's figure it out. First, though I don't relish the thought of it, Gibbs is downstairs, so you might want to get dressed." He bent and pressed a kiss to her breast.

Grumbling, Atta rose and picked up the first item of clothing she came to—one of his collared shirts. She put it on, buttoning only one button just below her breasts, and Sonder officially had another image of her seared into his brain quite pleasantly.

In fact. . .

He abandoned his tea and followed her.

ATTA

Sonder had rather abruptly interrupted her shower, pressing her against the glass, one leg wrapped around his hips.

Even washed clean and dressed in sheer tights, a sensible brown skirt with a black turtleneck and an oversized tweed blazer, she was still dizzy with the way he made her feel. She'd never been especially good at compartmentalising, but she would need to be now. At least, that's what she told herself as she tied her Oxfords and went downstairs.

Sonder was sitting at the table with Gibbs, Sonder with a newspaper open in front of him, Gibbs munching on a piece of toast. When she entered, Sonder's eyes slid up from the paper to her, and Atta felt her cheeks heat, remembering all the ways he'd explored her last night and locked eyes with her in the shower again this morning as she came.

"Ah. She lives," he said with a smirk.

Gibbs looked at him, crumbs falling onto his chin as he said, "You realise you feed into the Dr Frankenstein rumours on a regular basis, right?"

Sonder chuckled, and judging by Gibbs's brows rising to his hairline, he'd never heard Sonder laugh before. "It's amusing you think it isn't on purpose, Gibbs."

"Fair." He shrugged. "When you climbed in my window to force me into making sure Atta was okay, I decided you couldn't be all bad." He slid a glance in her direction.

Atta pushed her lips together in a frown, brow wrinkled. "I have several questions."

"All of which I'm happy to answer"—Sonder folded the newspaper and set it on the table—"but we really do need to get to work." He gestured to a plate of food. "Eat up and let's get busy."

Atta sat and dug into the colcannon and fried eggs. "Did you make all this?" she asked Gibbs with her mouth full.

He bit into another piece of marmalade toast. "I made the eggs and the toast." He pointed his toast at Sonder who was looking at them both with some measure of distaste. "He made the colcannon."

Sonder brushed crumbs off his newspaper with disgust. "Would it be possible for the pair of you to chew and swallow prior to speaking?"

Atta laughed, shovelling in a bite of the most amazing colcannon she'd ever tasted. "This is what we get for having breakfast with a grumpy old man, Gibbs."

"All right, have your fun. I'm going to the study." He stopped to fill a cup with steaming hot tea and left.

"So," Gibbs started, "you and the prof, huh? You can't deny it anymore."

"I didn't deny it. I just said it was none of your business."

He nodded a little solemnly and fiddled with his fork. "This is all pretty mad, isn't it?" He wiggled his fork in the air in a circle. "All this Fae Plague stuff. I'm still not sure I believe it."

"Fae Plague," Atta mused, her appetite diminished. "That's a good name for it."

"I calculated your probability of success today."

Atta straightened. "Do tell."

"I already talked to Murdoch about it, but he's optimistic." Gibbs pulled one of his ever-present flip notebooks from his pocket. "The Infected—"

"Inhabited," she corrected and Gibbs looked at her. "You need to be all in or all out."

He nodded skeptically and pushed his glasses up his nose. "I'm trying, but I need facts. To see things with my own eyes."

Atta could understand that, but she didn't agree. "The most incredible and inexplicable things in life can't be seen, Gibbs."

The sigh he heaved aged him. "I trust both you and the prof. I'm just—"

He looked out the window and Atta followed his gaze to the foggy Hawthorn Grove. For a split second, a glimmer came out of the mist, making the twisted hawthorns look full and vibrant, lush like spring.

"I just need some time," Gibbs said, pulling Atta's attention back.

"That's understandable. What's there in your notebook?"

"Oh." He looked down at his scribbled notes. "Projections. Your probability of success today with the . . . Inhabited." He flipped a page, looking more like a detective than a scholar. "The patient is a Stage 2, but I looked at Murdoch's notes last night and I think he'll be at Stage 3 by the time you arrive. Most don't live past Stage 3 for long."

Atta nodded her agreement, filling a teacup.

"I placed your probability of success, based on the factors of a newly Stage 3 patient and the results from your prior. . ." He trailed off with a grimace.

It took Atta a second to decipher why. "Sonder told you we called it an exorcism, didn't he?"

Gibbs scrunched his nose. "He did. Showed me the giant crucifixes, too, and a pair of monk robes he wants to convince you to wear."

Atta baulked. "No fucking way. No."

"I think it was a joke."

"Thank goodness." Atta sagged against the back of her chair. "The crucifixes were ridiculous enough. When did you two have time for all of this?"

"You take *really* long showers. Frankly, there's a lot more hot water in the suite now that you've moved out."

"*Rude.*"

Gibbs smiled for the first time all morning. "We do miss you, though. Especially Emmy."

Atta fiddled with the handle of her teacup. "I need to call her."

"Well," Gibbs shifted the subject back, "I've pegged your probability of success at between 53 and 56%."

"But we still have time to raise that probability." Not that Atta lived by *probabilities*. Where was the whim and wonder in that? "I already have some methods I was studying that I believe will give us more success."

"Like?" Gibbs prompted, not convinced.

"We learned that the faeries, at least the kind we encountered, can dissipate into vapour—that's how they're Inhabiting people. Therefore, they have to be contained in something air-tight. Stage 3s are more dangerous, of course, but I think Black Tourmaline mixed with Wormwood will do the trick."

Gibbs blew out a disbelieving breath. "You act like this is a fairytale, Atta."

She ground her molars together, trying to be patient with his doubt. "All of Folklore is grounded in some truth, Gibbs. You need to expand your realm of thinking. What if we are the myth in their world, hm?"

Something burned in her chest, her fingertips. Her teeth hurt, felt pointed against her tongue.

"What if there are other realms or worlds out there, and the Fae are dying? They've heard tales all their lives of a world where humans walk around destroying their planet, destroying each other, and the Fae decided the humans didn't deserve this place. That they would take it for their own?"

The burning left as suddenly as it had come, her fingers feeling like they'd fallen asleep. She tasted copper in her mouth, on her tongue, and a wave of dizziness hit her.

"Woah. Are you all right?"

She reached across the table for the cup of water Sonder had left behind and took a sip. "I'm fine."

"That was, em. . . Some speech."

"It's just a theory," she said shakily. "Let me show you what I mean about the Black Tourmaline and Wormwood."

They rose together and Gibbs followed her to the back all-season porch. "Where are we going?"

"Have you been to the greenhouse?"

"No. I've only been here a handful of times and Murdoch was always crotchety about it, kicking me out as soon as I gave him whatever it was he needed dropped off."

She stopped, considering Sonder may not want Gibbs

anywhere near his parents or even their research. "Perhaps we should bring Sonder along for this. I'll go get him."

Gibbs plopped down on a lounge chair and pulled out his notebook. "I'll be here."

Atta opened the door to the kitchen and Gibbs said, "Hey," so she turned back. "He looks different when you walk into a room."

"Different?" She cocked her head to the side. "Different how?"

"Happy."

Atta didn't know what to make of Gibbs's comment. It made her feel a thousand different things she didn't fully comprehend and had no time to ponder.

Sonder was bent over his sketchbook in the study. "*Stór*," he said when she appeared in the doorway. "Come look at this."

He pushed back from the desk and let her have his chair. As she looked at his remarkable anatomical sketch of the faerie they'd caught, he lit a cigarillo and perched on the edge of the desk. "I had to do it by memory, and I don't know what their organs are like."

"It's all assumption at this point, but this sketch looks exactly as I remember the faerie." Atta ran her finger over the wings Sonder had drawn to look like they were in motion.

He puffed on the cigarillo, blowing the smoke out slowly. "Where is Gibbs?"

Atta stood and rounded the desk, Sonder pulling her between his legs. He slung an arm around her lower back and her heart did a somersault. "Waiting for us. I wanted to show him the Black Tourmaline and Wormwood effect on a plant in the atrium."

Sonder licked his lips. "I don't want anyone but you in there." He said the words gently, but she knew his stance was firm. Sonder Murdoch was not a man who wavered.

She reached up and pushed the hair from his face, relishing the feel of it between her fingers. "That's why I came to ask. I'll pot a sample and bring it here." She wiggled free of his arm but he grabbed her wrist and pulled her back, kissing her hard. She could taste the spice and smoke on his tongue, feel his grip on her waist and the softness of his knit jumper beneath her palms, but resisted the urge to melt into him. "We have work to do, Professor."

"Ní mhaireann solas na maidine don lá."*

Atta swallowed hard. She loved way too much when he spoke Irish to her in that tone. "Yes, and that is exactly why we need to get moving," she said, putting space between them. "There are lives at stake."

Sonder's brow quirked up. "You're quite right." He put his cigarillo in an ashtray to burn out. "You are also quite distracting. I'll be better behaved, on my honour."

"Thank you. Now, you occupy Gibbs while I pot a specimen."

---

* *(*Nee war-in sul-is nah mawd-in-ye gun law) *No morning's sun lasts all day; an Irish Gaelic saying meaning: life is finite, enjoy it while you can*

ATTA

G ibbs blinked at her where she stood with a dripping
bottle still poised to spray a fern. "Atta. Please don't
take offence to this, but are you seriously going to
walk into a patient's room and squirt him?"

"We're not trying to look grand," she spat. "We want
effective." She gestured roughly to the plant that had gone from
wilted to steaming to a dried-up husk.

"I'll grant you it appears effective." He stood, shoving his
hands into the kangaroo pouch on his Trinity hoodie. "Nothing
left to do but drive you lot there, then."

The three of them must have looked completely mental in
their plague doctor masks, pulling up to a fancy house in a
Volvo. Their appearance didn't seem to deter the woman who
came rushing out as soon as Gibbs's tyres hit her drive.

She was an average middle-class wife in Chinos and a knit
blouse, but she was clearly beside herself. Mrs Byrne rushed
for Atta the moment she exited the car, her lip wobbling and
eyes watery.

"Oh, thank goodness you're here. You must hurry." The

woman pulled Atta along so quickly she almost tripped, Sonder on their heels.

Before they even made it through the lavish entryway with its polished floors, it wasn't difficult to understand why she was in such a rush. The Inhabited, Mr Byrne, bellowed from wherever he'd been stored to await his final moments.

Atta exchanged a look with Sonder, cursing that she couldn't make out his face, and they all picked up their pace, climbing the stairs two at a time.

"Oh my. Oh Jesus," Mrs Byrne cried. "What's happened? He hasn't made a sound in days. I–"

Outside the door of the sick room, Sonder gripped Mrs Byrne's shoulders firmly. "This is where you trust us to do what you called us here to do. Go outside. Get some air. Do not come in, no matter what you hear." Tears streamed down her face. "Do you understand?"

The poor woman was shaking, looking from Sonder to the closed door and back, but she nodded.

"There you are." He gently squeezed her shoulders and turned her around, back toward the stairs.

Whether it was the screaming or curiosity that drew him, Atta didn't know, but Gibbs had ventured inside the house and was standing at the foot of the steps.

"Go with my friend, there. He'll keep you right as rain, yeah?"

"Okay." The word was barely a whisper, but she made it down the stairs, only looking back twice.

Gibbs, bless him, wrapped his thin arm around Mrs Byrne and ushered her back out into the drizzly afternoon.

Sonder ripped off his mask and Atta did the same. There was something bordering on fear in his eyes, and she had little doubt the same was reflected in hers. "He's screaming," she said stupidly, but it made Sonder's face change.

It was Professor Murdoch who looked back at her. "The plan has not changed. You are well equipped for this. Trust your gut."

Her gut was afraid. Roiling. "First things first," she said to Sonder, forcing her back ramrod straight. "I need to see what I can sense."

"I'm at your command, darling."

She nodded once and took hold of the knob, inhaling deeply before she twisted it and opened the door.

Nothing in all the world could have prepared her.

There was no saving this man. Not when his chest was ripped open by the feral growth of flora, sprouting right from his lungs, his heart.

Atta moved forward quickly, not allowing herself to think. To feel.

Sonder rushed to the man's other side, scalpel in one hand, black salt in the other.

It wouldn't be long. His lungs were a tangle of viscera and vines already crawling up the wall.

"If you see vapour," Sonder said, "get your mask back on or get the hell out."

Atta tuned out the screams and refused to feel the writhing of the Inhabited man. When this was over, she could feel. Mourn. Retch. Console a widow who was outdoors praying they could save a man already sentenced to die. But right now, she needed to focus.

Calming herself and closing her eyes, she reached out and let her fingers rest along the inside of his arm.

Behind her eyes, the pain and buzzing began, spreading to

the back of her skull. She couldn't see anything. But she could hear. A voice like a child of lily-white innocence, but it felt wrong. Off-kilter.

Cut your eyes, one at a time, scoop them out and make them mine.

Atta gasped.

"Close your eyes!" she shouted at Sonder over the patient's screams.

"But the vapour!"

"Now!" she commanded.

"Atta, what's happening?" he shouted back.

"I can't see, but I can hear it—smell it, even."

"Smell it? Can you track it, then?"

"I'm not a fucking hound!"

"We have to do *something*."

He was right. They had to do something. If the Inhabited man perished, the faerie would leave. If Sonder's parents were the blueprint, the faerie would need both its host—the soil— and a living person—the nourishment.

Oh god, they hunt for pairs. Mrs McDonough and her son. Lauren Kennedy and her lone roommate. Sonder's parents.

Eyes still squeezed shut, she listened, followed the voice of the girl, followed the scent of loam and petrichor. There. Beneath the screams of a man being ripped apart by flora, was a pixie faerie, tucked behind the heart, already dissipating into vapour. "Tourmaline," she shouted. "Behind the heart, hurry!"

She felt Sonder move next to her, his practised anatomist's hands sliding into the open chest cavity. The girlish voice turned to screams that joined Mr Byrne's.

How were they to trap it with their eyes closed? Atta panicked in the split second before the solution came to her. It needed to be immobilised. "Get me your embalming fluid in a syringe. Keep your back turned!"

A moment later, she felt Sonder place a syringe in her left hand, and she jabbed it into the place the faerie was hiding. At first, she thought she must have missed, but then the scent turned cold. Not gone, not lost, but like the first frost over dead leaves.

Mr Byrne's cries turned to whimpers.

The pixie's to sobs.

The sort used to lure in a kind heart, only to devour it.

"It's immobile," Atta said. "We can open our eyes. Just don't look in its face."

Fighting back a bout of terror that she might be mistaken, Atta opened her eyes slowly. Sonder, who apparently had more confidence in her, already had his eyes wide open, his hands desperately trying to staunch the black blood oozing from Mr Byrne.

"End this," she told him. "He can't be saved."

Sonder only gave her the briefest of nods, a pained look in his eyes before he used his scalpel to slice the heart irreparably. The last breath, the first Mr Byrne ever took when he was free of his mother's womb, left him.

There was no longer any need to rush. Something about that fact was what caused the first fissure in her heart. But there was still no time for that. Not yet.

On wooden legs, Atta bent to retrieve the open specimen jar next to their satchel filled with the embalming liquid of Sonder's own design.

"Move the heart," she directed Sonder, who reached into the chest again. "Careful of its eyes," she warned. He nodded and looked away, moving the heart just so. "A little more to the right," she instructed, hoping the faerie was still in the same position she'd sensed, so that her eyes would meet only its bony feet.

There they were, skeletal. Tiny.

She pushed away a leafy frond with her fingers, pinching at the creature's phalanges with tweezers. Still as stone, as if it were frozen or taxidermied, it slipped free from Mr Byrne and Sonder let the heart go. He moved to hold the specimen jar for her, but his hands were too slick with blackened blood. Cursing, he wiped it on his coat and managed to get a grip on the jar. Very carefully, Atta slipped the faerie inside.

Sonder closed it, and they stood back, watching in awe as the embalming liquid sizzled. The faerie twitched and went still again. Dead. Frozen in time. It was a scientific success. It was miraculous. But Atta looked at Mr Byrne's body. Thought of his wife. And the success felt hollow.

While Sonder slipped off his ruined coat and called the medics using a phone down in the kitchen, Atta collected samples of the flora that had crawled up the wall behind Mr Byrne as they'd worked. It had all but taken over the ceiling, too, the fan drooping like a weeping willow.

"Shall we?" Sonder asked quietly from the doorway and Atta nodded, pulling a sheet up and over Mr Byrne.

They gathered their supplies and walked outside to alert Mrs Byrne of her husband's death.

ATTA

tta sat numbly in the car, barely registering where Gibbs was driving to.

She'd been so dissociated that, at some point, Sonder made Gibbs pull over, and he climbed in the back seat with her.

"Talk to me, *a stór*."

"If only we'd been there sooner."

She watched his chest rise and fall in her periphery as Dublin proper passed by. "You can't do that to yourself." His words were so gentle it made her want to weep.

"But if we'd left earlier. . . We were—" She abruptly cut herself off, unsure if it was out of embarrassment, shame, or not wanting to say anything that would lead him to believe she regretted what they'd been doing that morning. "We were frivolous with our time this morning."

He brought one of his arms around her and scooted her until her thigh was flush against his. "No, we weren't. We'd only just heard of this man at all, and we showed up exactly when we were asked to. Twelve minutes early, actually." She rested her head on his shoulder, staring ahead at the back of Gibbs's hair. "Just because someone else is dying doesn't mean the rest of the world has to stop living. That would spit in the face of the days they did have. Don't get lost in if-only's. Today was not a total failure. You trapped a faerie—for good. We can study it now."

"They hunt for pairs."

Sonder stiffened and Gibbs caught her eyes in the rearview. "Pardon?"

She picked at her thumbnail. "The Fae. To be fully successful, they need a host and then another person to provide the nourishment. Seed in the soil—the sacrifice—then a living host to make it flourish. Ms McDonough had her son, Lauren had her roommate, and Mr Byrne had his wife." She didn't mention Sonder's parents, not with Gibbs around, but one glance at his face showed he was adding them to the list as well.

"Atta, then you saved Mr Byrne's wife. That faerie was almost successful. You saw how close it was. And now *we're* one step closer to figuring out why this is happening and how to stop it."

"Atta has a theory," Gibbs piped up from the front seat.

"Oh?" Sonder looked at her with one brow raised.

"You didn't tell him?"

Atta glared at Gibbs in the rearview. "I'm beginning to think they aren't just possessing people. It isn't that they want to walk around as us in the flesh, but they want our world." She let her words sink in as Sonder's brows furrowed, but he remained silent. "I think their world is dying."

She didn't need to explain why she thought that. Gibbs didn't know about her visions, and he already thought the two of them mental enough. "The reason they're using flora is to make a suitable environment for their species."

"*'Humans in the crucible'*," Sonder quoted.

Atta nodded. "Humans are the soil."

They rode on in silence until Gibbs pulled up to the treeline outside Achilles House. "I have to gather some things Lynch asked me for." He tossed Sonder the keys. "Be back in a couple of hours and I'll take you home."

The pair of them climbed into the front seats and it reminded Atta of their nights spent in her car or his Capri. He took her hand in his as they drove, a comfort and balm. It wasn't until he pulled into campus that her anxiety came flooding back.

"I'm not supposed to be here."

Sonder took the keys out of the ignition. "Have you gotten this far by following the rules, Atta?"

"I could be arrested if Lynch finds out I was here."

"He won't call the Garda. I told you, Agamemnon functions by council." He squeezed her thigh right above her knee, and she was momentarily distracted, but it didn't last long. "But this is Trinity business, not Agamemnon business."

A sad smile lifted the corners of his mouth. "Darling, it's all the same. You weren't expelled because you traipsed through the cemetery. You were expelled because your ideas scare the Society. *We* scare them. If we eradicate this plague separate from Agamemnon, then we disembowel everything they've done."

"The public may not know Agamemnon's name, but we all know of the secret society that claims they've made great strides for Ireland," she argued.

"But they've never before claimed they would do away

with something like this, something so massive. If they aren't first, the public will lose their faith. HPSC will take a hit. *Politicians* will take a hit. "

"Good," Atta punctuated the word.

Sonder ran a knuckle down her cheek. "But not for them. We threaten their foundation."

"They're going to figure out it's us. Me, at least."

"Probably."

"And what will we do?"

"We'll figure it out."

"*How?*"

"I don't have the answers—right now. But I will." A sly grin spread across his face, and she knew it was intended to make her laugh, but it didn't work. "We've only just begun doing whatever it is we're doing. We're still figuring out what that is. And while we figure it out, failures will come. The Inhabitations will continue to come; the Society will continue to come. *We* have to continue to come forward. Not give up."

After a long moment of silence, Atta gathered her resolve. "All right."

"There she is." He smiled and leaned across the car to kiss her cheek. "I want to show you something."

The campus was quiet, even for a Sunday. Very few students milled about and they spotted no other faculty as Sonder led Atta to Freeman Library.

Several students were hunched over desks trying to finish up assignments at the last minute. There was an ache in Atta's chest as she passed them. She'd been so busy down the rabbit hole of faeries and exorcisms that she hadn't paused to consider that she should be one of these students.

Christ, had it only been a week since she'd been expelled? It felt like ages and no time at all.

Sonder walked to a door situated in the back corner that Atta had never noticed before and produced one of the several keys on his chain, letting her inside.

The tiny room was a mess of disassembled books. A work table stood in the centre with an apparatus of wood and screws, surrounded by spools of thread and other materials, and it sandwiched a bare-pages book within its wooden slats.

"Is this a bindery?"

Sonder closed the door and walked around the work table. "This is where I come when I'm trapped on campus but need to get away."

"You bind books when you're upset?" she teased, secretly pleased that he had cheered her up.

"I do. It's just mindful enough to keep your mind empty." He shoved his hands in his pockets. "I also play banjo." He smiled, his cheeks turning pink above his beardline.

"What?" Atta sputtered.

"When I'm upset, I play the banjo."

"Oh, I have to see that." She felt her face stretch with a wide smile.

"Come here, and I'll first show you how to bind a book."

As he'd said, the process took just enough concentration to leave her mind blank, save for the thoughts his hands on hers brought about as he guided her in certain steps.

"Do you think Gibbs is through yet?" They'd re-bound an old, tattered copy of *Jane Eyre* and Atta was feeling quite a lot more grounded. "We need to get that faerie back to begin studying it." The footwell of the car was probably not the best place to keep a mythical creature.

They'd only been outside Achilles House for a few moments when Gibbs came rushing toward the car, looking over his shoulder anxiously as if something were chasing him.

"We need to go," he whispered harshly, fumbling with the door to close it. "Atta, get down."

She wasted no time ducking in the backseat, and Sonder wasted no time kicking up gravel as they sped off.

"What's happened?" he questioned when they were out on the main road and Atta popped back upright.

Gibbs took off his glasses to wipe them on his shirt. "You need to get to Achilles as soon as you can. Your absence has been noticed, and Lynch is on a warpath. Word is already spreading about the death this afternoon. They sent Vasilios to speak with the widow and field any news crews that decide to show up, but they're on the lookout for who's fucking with Agamemnon's precious reputation."

"I'll drop the pair of you off at the manor and head straight in," Sonder said diplomatically.

Atta bit her lip, thinking through everything being said. The risks still seemed as if they were outweighing the rewards, but in her heart of hearts, she knew that wasn't true.

The prize, the prize, that fairytale voice hummed, *always comes with sacrifice.*

SONDER

"You need to get your House in order, Murdoch!" Spittle flew from Lynch's mouth as he paced Sonder's lab in Achilles. "You can't possibly believe I don't know these charlatans have originated here, under your eye."

"Who's truly upset here, Lynch? The Agamemnon Council, or your pride?"

Lynch crossed the room and stood toe to toe with Sonder, only he was shorter by a few inches. He had to look up at him just enough to cause one side of Sonder's mouth to lift smugly.

"I ought to shut this place down immediately," Lynch threatened.

"Aw," Sonder mocked. "But then how will you get all the glory for the eradication of the Plague, hm?" He took a step forward and Lynch took one backwards. "How is your Trinity Cemetary going? Seeing any growth in your specimens?"

Lynch ground his teeth together. "You do what this House is funded to do, and that is *it*."

Sonder slipped his hands into his pockets and quirked his

mouth to one side. "See, I thought Achilles was funded to cure the Plague, but now I'm standing here thinking you just wanted me to feed you data for your own gain." He *tisked*. "For shame, Finneas."

The dean's face was turning a mottled red. "The moment I find proof it's you under that mask, you're finished."

Sonder closed the distance between them and bent over to make them eye-level. "I'm shaking in my trousers."

Lynch stormed into the corridor and Sonder let out a breath. Sinking into his desk chair, he ran a hand through his hair. His lab phone rang and he answered it on the first ring. He loathed the sound of telephones ringing.

"Murdoch."

"Someone here to see you, prof," Walsh's nasally voice came over the line.

"Send them up."

Marguerite rushed into his lab a moment later and shut the door behind her.

Sonder rose and moved to stand near his wall of chemicals and instruments. "What is it?"

"I redirected as best I could." She looked haggard. "The woman, Mrs Byrne, was so distraught about her husband's death that she was inconsolable, and no one could understand a word she said. I acted as her therapist, turned all reporters away."

"Was the Garda phoned?"

Marguerite shook her head. "No, thank god. Only the Society coroner. All the widow said about the two of you is that you did all you could. I followed it up with '*he was too far gone to the Plague*,' and that was the official statement that went out to the media. They were still camped outside her house when I left."

Sonder removed his glasses and pinched the bridge of his nose. "Where did the coroner take the body?"

"Saint Patrick's. Some of the higher-ups want to have a look, and then I'm told he'll come to you here at Achilles."

Sonder scrubbed a hand down his jaw, relieved he and Atta had gotten a good look before the corpse could possibly be tampered with prior to releasing it to him. "Thank you, Marguerite."

"Of course." She adjusted the strap of her purse. "I'd better get back to my office. Emmy is supposed to help me this evening and the phone has been ringing off the hook. If she answers it, I don't know what I'll tell her."

"Ringing off the hook as in media requests, or loved ones of Inhabited patients looking for us?" Sonder questioned.

"Both." The cadence of her voice came off as more than just frazzled. He shouldn't have involved anyone else in this bloody mess.

"Fax me what you have to the manor."

"Sonder," there was sufficient warning in her tone, and he knew what would come next. "This is a dangerous game you're playing." Her lips pursed into a thin red line, a slash against her smooth, tanned skin. "In more ways than one."

Ah, she meant Atta. "You worry too much." He wasn't about to indulge her suspicions by confirming them. "Good evening, Marguerite."

She frowned at the dismissal but left. He waited a full five minutes before instructing one of the anatomists to clean up the corpse in his lab and prepare for a new one to be delivered. The young lady, Lucy, he thought her name was, hardly had her gloves on before he rushed out the door to check on things at the manor before the delivery.

Atta was on a bench in the hawthorn atrium, three empty coffee mugs around her, when he arrived. Winding his way through her trail of notes and open books was as wild as it was endearing. If either of them was a mad scientist, it was Atta—and he adored it.

Seasoned, old, ancient as he felt, Sonder had never understood desire until she'd walked into his life. He crouched and kissed her tenderly. She licked her lips and tucked them between her teeth for just a second after he pulled back, a flush under her freckles.

"Papers were spit all over the floor of your study," she said.

"Faxes from Vasilios," he responded, but he found himself distracted by something other than her lips and bent to pick up a list she'd made. It wasn't the first attempt, judging by the mass of crumpled and scratched-out papers surrounding her. "*Stages Protocol*," he read.

Atta tucked a pen behind her ear and he took another mental snapshot of her. "It's not set in stone, of course, but a working theory." She looked away. "If we get there in time, that is."

"We need a compilation of symptoms as well," he added. "And to spend more time with the Inhabited's counterpart. That way, the Inhabitation can be recognised earlier, and we can potentially discover how the hosts are being selected."

She stood and walked through her mess of notes and books and potting soil before stooping to pick up a weathered tome he knew to be his mother's, one from the top shelf in the library. "I've been thinking about that," Atta said, pointing to a passage. "Faeries notoriously hate hubris. Lisle stated that his mother is a selfish woman, and I saw that displayed quite erotically in my vision."

Sonder raised a brow at this new detail but refrained from comment.

"And I read on one of those papers Marguerite faxed over that Mr Byrne was a business owner. That led me to flip on the news. They were interviewing some of his employees concerning his death, and he wasn't a very well-liked man." She took up pacing in front of a plant that looked more like it belonged under the sea to him. "Lauren, on the other hand, was a bit snobbish but very well-liked. So I think there is more the Fae are looking for. Another component. They're not just selecting humans with overbearing pride, but that does seem to be something they're considering."

Sonder watched her in awe as she picked up a mortar and pestle, bending down to where he was still crouched on the ground. Burying her fingers in the fragrant mixture of dried flowers, she lifted them up and let some of the yellow and pink blossoms in varying shades sprinkle back down like confetti. Her eyes met his, lit mischievously, and she whispered, "Watch this."

She rose with a bounce and Sonder stood. Like a maiden delighting in the spoils of spring to call forth the Fae Folk, Atta sprinkled a dusting of the dried flowers onto a bulbous plant that looked tropical to his untrained eye. As soon as the floral confetti made contact, the plant's vibrant petals withered. Another sprinkle and the plant was scorched, as if it had dried out in the summer sun.

Atta smiled at him and lifted her mortar. "St John's Wort, Yarrow, and Rue."

Sonder looked from her wide grin to the withered blossom and back. "Have I ever told you that you're a genius?"

She preened at him and he realised he'd do anything for that smile. "No, but you've danced around it," she said coyly. "Nice of you to finally admit it. Admission is the first step to recovery."

He slowly closed the distance between them, wrapping his arms around her waist. "And what am I recovering from?"

She looked up at him and he could see a graphite smudge on the tip of her nose, ink stains on her cheek. "The hit to your ego. Knowing that I'm smarter than you."

He knew she was only teasing, but he had begun to wonder if she was right. Not that it bothered him in the slightest. He lightly kissed the smudge on her nose. "Mm. All the more reason to get you reenrolled at Trinity, then."

Atta's face fell and she took a step back, breaking his hold on her. "That's not funny."

"I'm not trying to be funny, Atta. I mean it."

"You just said earlier that it's likely the Society will have it out for me."

"It's possible only Lynch has it out for you."

Her brows furrowed. "He's a *dean*. Even more damning for me."

"If we can find success in this, eradicate this Plague, they will all have to eat their own words. They won't have a choice but to shout your name in the streets and give you the highest accolades."

"I don't care about all that," she snapped, folding her arms over her chest. She looked exhausted. He should tell her to sleep. To eat. But instead, he opened his stupid mouth to begin an argument.

"I'm not talking about accolades, Atta. I'm talking about your future. Your life. Grabbing those bastards by the balls and making them respect you, give you back your education."

"None of that matters if all of Dublin becomes a playground for the Fae, Sonder."

Atta snatched her coat from the worktable and stormed out of the atrium.

Stages Protocol:

Fae can be exorcized in one of four ways,
depending on how deeply Inhabited the human is.

Stage 1] Burn Mugwort & Palo Santo Smudge
Sticks
*Note: This only drives out the Fae spirit, it does
not destroy it.

Stage 2]
1. Drive the spirit out with Smudge Sticks and
Black Candles, singing various Fae Hymns
2. Dispel it with crushed Black Tourmaline
3. Inject appropriate embalming-level serum

Stage 3] Stage 3 Fae must be dealt with using all
the above, but they are much stronger and can still
Inhabit unless Black Tourmaline is mixed with
Wormwood and the exorcist is guarded with
Protection Oil and Tears of the Grieved

Stage 4] TBD

ATTA

She was too pissed at Sonder to play assistant.

To his credit, he hadn't asked her to, but if they were going to attempt another exorcism before it was too late to do so, the faxes Vasilios sent over needed to be sorted and a plan put in place.

Atta sifted through the gathered stack and sorted them into piles on the long table in the library. *Inhabited*, *Media Requests*, and *Misc*. Then, she sat back in the stiff wooden chair and blew the hair out of her eyes.

"I do not have time for this."

She phoned Gibbs instead. He loved organisational tasks. An hour later, he was at Murdoch Manor with takeaway and a scowl. "You realise I'm not your assistant, right? Or Murdoch's, *technically*? I have fucking Lynch breathing down my neck, and that's who I work for."

Atta took a bag of food from him and pulled out a chip. "You're here, aren't you?"

"The disrespect, I swear." But he stomped in and slammed the door shut. Once he'd deposited the food on a shelf in the library that Atta had relieved of its books days earlier, Gibbs looked around at her piles. "Eat and shower. I'll handle all this."

"Bless you, Bernard Fitzgibbon."

"Ye', ye'. Go away. You stink."

"I do not!"

"Yes, you do. You smell like death and cigars. Murdoch's signature scent," Gibbs groused, shoving a chip in his mouth and fussing with the faxes.

Atta couldn't help but smile, even if she was peeved at Sonder. She took her food and left Gibbs to his work, but she heard him shout, "What the hell am I supposed to do without any damned call-back numbers!"

That was his problem for now. Atta chose the hawthorn atrium to eat, mostly out of curiosity. They'd had copious amounts of alcohol, tea, and coffee near the organisms but never food. Presumably, the flora itself wouldn't react to human food, but what sort of scientist would she be if she didn't test things out?

While she ate, Atta placed bits of food here and there and recorded where she'd put them. Then, she forced herself to sit still and finish eating without working at the same time.

Her brain, however, never shut down. She sat munching, staring at the hawthorn, contemplating the way she could sometimes see Olivia Murdoch's heart still there, still beating, when it was long since lost to faerie growth. It still didn't sit right. It didn't make *sense*.

Her appetite sated enough, Atta discarded the majority of her food to the side and wove her way through the overgrown vines and flora masking the hawthorn—the bodies—from view.

It was dark enough outside and the flora so thick that she couldn't quite see clearly beneath the plants, like being under a willow tree at dusk, but Atta didn't need her eyes for this particular curiosity.

With a deep inhale, she gently moved the creeping plant winding around Olivia Murdoch's ribs and placed her hand on her moss-covered sternum.

The pain was so great it snatched her breath away and made her knees quake.

But then she was gone. Out of her body. Locked in her mind. Only for a second before she was *elsewhere*.

An enchanted forest spread out before her, all emerald trees and lush florals glowing in the mist and moonlight. The moss beneath her feet looked soft as down, like the euphoria of spring grass between her toes, but Atta couldn't feel it. And she was not alone.

A woman in a white nightgown with long, flowing hair wandered through the trees, brushing her fingertips along their twisted trunks. She was barefoot, too, her nightgown blowing in a breeze Atta couldn't feel. The woman was young, maybe a handful of years younger than her, but she could only make out the gentle curves of a young woman's body and her profile, nothing more.

A twig snapped under Atta's feet and the woman turned around, her wonder turning to fear in her wide, hazel eyes.

Sonder's eyes. Olivia Murdoch's eyes.

Atta froze in place, at least she assumed she did, because the trees stopped moving past her and Olivia turned back around, headed deeper into the fog. Atta followed Olivia again, all the way to a hollowed-out trunk, where she reached inside and withdrew the most beautiful book Atta had ever seen. A tome of the deepest olive green, its lettering gilded and gleaming.

Olivia turned around, looked from the book to Atta and said in a sing-song voice, "Welcome to the Faerie Wood."

With a gasp so deep she nearly retched, Atta was back in the atrium, her ice-cold hand pulling away from Olivia's sternum.

No, she hadn't yanked it back. It was almost like it had been *pushed* back.

Rattled, shaking, Atta stumbled her way from the flora and out of the greenhouse, back to the main manor.

"There you are," Gibbs met her in the hall to her room. "I have a few more calls to make, but most of the Inhabited patients we received calls for are lower stages, so there is some time to stagger them out." He looked down at his calendar instead of at her, and she was grateful. "The first appointment will be tomorrow at 10 a.m. That's a Stage 3. There will be two tomorrow. The second is at 3 p.m., and that Inhabited is a Stage 2."

"Right. Yes, that's perfect." She brushed past him, stumbling a little.

"Are you all right?"

"Fine. I think I just need to shower like you said and go to bed."

Gibbs checked his watch. "I'd better make those last few calls and head out."

"See you, Gibbs."

She didn't recall much from her shower, or changing into a nightgown and slipping into bed.

Sleep claimed her the moment her head hit the pillow, dreams pulling her under. There, in the hazy world of sleep,

Atta moved through the mist, something calling to her. She soon found herself in a wood unlike any she'd seen before. The grass was lush beneath her bare toes, lusher even than she'd expected. Trees bent and swayed in a gentle breeze, stunning flora dotting the ground, the vines, the bushes. But sometimes, in this dream, when she would blink, the forest would fall away to reveal a wood of bramble and decay. Of twisted hawthorns and sharp teeth. Always, there was a beating of wings, but the creatures moved so quickly she couldn't make them out.

Somewhere off in the distance, a woman sang.

Tik, flick, tick
The clock keeps time with the candle
Until they all get sick
Wax slides down the gilded stick
And the Fae invade with bramble

Atta followed the voice, led by the moonlight through the treetops and a jumble of lights bobbing through the branches.

Ghost lights.

Wills-o-the wisp.

The woman's voice faded away on the last word, dissipating into the mist and fog. Atta had made it to a clearing of moss and mushrooms, a lovely tea set laid out on a stone. Without thinking, she approached the teacup and felt its side, though she needn't have done so because a tendril of steam curled into the crisp night air from the tea.

"Hello?" she called out, but she was only met with a chorus of giggles, a chorus of hisses.

She spun in a circle, enjoying the wood, the moss beneath her feet and the twirl of her nightgown. It was then that she saw the old, twisted hawthorn, the one visible from the bay window in the kitchen of Murdoch Manor. The one that whispered for her to come closer.

Here she was, and she answered the call, walking forward to press her palm against its trunk, the bark rough against her palm.

There in a hollow, where creatures had surely burrowed to protect their young, she felt a hum, deep in her bones.

Reaching into the hollow, the forest flickered, going barren, dark, and so very cold.

Atta started, but with a blink, it was the mystical grove once more. All she felt in the hollow was dirt, bramble, and the bones of small animals.

Dig, o' child of the wood.

Dig, and bring us what she thought she could.

So Atta dug. She dug in the hollow until one of her nails broke, until her fingers hit leather, old and cracked. Standing on tiptoe, she reached down as far as she could and pulled out a tome. Forest green like the trees at night, pages limned in gold, and a spine cracked from use. She ran her filthy fingers over the title. *Into the Faerie Wood.*

She lifted the cover, the leather protesting, and the forest fell away again. Atta blinked, but it did not correct itself this time. Dark clouds blocked out the moon, the Wills-o-the-wisp blinking out. She moved away from the hawthorn, back toward home. Where was home? Fear licked up her spine as something flew past her face, gnashing its teeth. The tree branches bent, reaching for her, grasping at her nightgown, her hair.

Atta ran, her breath loud in her ears, the book clutched to her chest.

She tripped, landing with a thud in the dirt, banging her knee on a rock.

Something grabbed at her arm, talons scraping, fangs biting. Thousands of wings surrounded her until they felt like a gale of wind. The book was nearly tugged from her grip, but she wrenched it free, falling back into the dirt and sharp bramble. Her necklace, the bottle of Tears of the Grieved, clanked against her teeth, the pain reverberating up into her skull.

The tears.

Atta ripped the necklace free from her body and smashed it on a rock.

Hissing, steam, then silence.

And Atta ran.

Hard and fast.

SONDER

It was nearly dawn before he made it back to the manor to find thirteen sticky notes from Gibbs plastered throughout the house.

I fed Atta, on the kitchen door.

I'm not a maid, on a stack of discarded jumpers he'd folded.

I'll pick up more milk, on the fridge.

Among other things.

A very detailed schedule sat on his desk next to a glass of whiskey and a fresh cigar Sonder had not placed there, along with a note that read: *I'm not your fucking secretary.*

Sonder chuckled, wadding up the note, and tossing it in the rubbish. He really needed to give Gibbs a pay rise. Reclining in his desk chair, he held up the whiskey in a silent thanks to Gibbs before taking a sip. It burned down his throat and into his empty stomach, liquid gold to push out all the stress of the day before he would face the music in the morning of the beautiful woman who was furious with him. He picked up the cigar and found another note, folded over and over until it had been concealed by the cigar. Taken aback, Sonder tossed the cigar onto a stack of research papers and unfolded the note.

Atta was acting strange tonight.
I was worried to leave her.

Sonder shot out of his chair and tore down the hall toward her room.

The lights were out, but her door was slightly ajar. Quietly, he opened it and ventured in. In the light bleeding in from the hall, he could make out her form on the bed, fast asleep. He didn't want to wake her but needed to know she was all right.

With his eyes still adjusting to the dark, Sonder knelt down by the side of the bed. Atta's features were fuzzy in the dim light, but they still made him smile. Before he could think better of it and the possibility it could wake her, he leaned in to kiss her temple and run his fingers down her hair. She smiled in her sleep and sighed, the sight warming his cold, dark heart.

He stood, satisfied she was all right, and squeezed her hand before leaving her to sweet dreams.

Out in the hall, he felt something on his hand and looked down to see traces of soil on his fingertips from where he'd held onto her briefly.

Sonder chuckled to himself. Atta never truly slumbered, not when there was work to be done.

But a chill slithered up his spine at the thought, and he went to chase it away with the fire of hearth and whiskey.

ATTA

Atta sat up in bed, unsure for a moment where she was, expecting bramble and bones.

With a few blinks, she recognised her room in Sonder's manor, her heart rate slowing. She'd had the most peculiar dreams.

Groggily, she stretched and stood from the bed, recalling all the work that needed to be done before the first exorcism appointment. She hadn't seen Sonder last night either and wanted to ensure everything was all right after their argument.

On her way to the wardrobe, she caught sight of herself in the looking glass. Sucking in a breath, she stumbled backwards until the back of her knees hit the bed, forcing her to sit down. She was covered in dirt and blood.

Tears of fear welled in her eyes as she pulled up the sleeve of her nightgown to look. It couldn't be real. The dream. The nightmare. It couldn't.

But there was the evidence, etched out in claw marks up her arm, and teeth marks on her wrist, next to the healing cut from the broken lamp.

With horror and trembling, Atta rose on unsteady feet and looked around the room.

There, next to a tea set she'd seen before, was the book.

Into the Faerie Wood.

———

"There she is." Sonder smiled at her over his newspaper, a sight she was growing fondly used to in the mornings. Immediately, he folded the paper and gave her his full attention. "I'm sorry about yesterday."

"Yesterday?" she asked, distracted.

"Our argument."

"Oh, right." Atta sat across from him and began buttering toast without thought. "It's nothing."

He was studying her intently. "Are you all right?"

She should keep her mouth shut. Say nothing. Figure out what happened first. But she looked up from her toast and into his eyes. He'd been what she was running back to from the Faerie Wood. And his mother had been who she'd followed in. Atta didn't understand what it meant, but it wasn't right to carry it all alone.

Was it?

"I found a book," she half-lied.

"A book?"

"Em, sort of a strange book. I think it belonged to your mother."

Sonder sat forward in his chair. "What kind of book?"

"A collection of fairytales. *Into the Faerie Wood.*"

Sonder's face contorted. "But my mother lost that book

when I was a baby. She complained about it all the time. Where did you find it?"

To lie or not to lie? Atta settled on a variation of the truth. "In the Hawthorn Grove."

Sonder's brows rose. "Tell me you didn't go out there alone at night."

Affronted and afraid, Atta started. "It's just a grove of trees." Wasn't it?

"What of the foxes? The stags? It's not safe alone at night."

She needed to start the day over. Her belly was on fire or ice, she couldn't tell which, her blood *itchy*. "We have a lot to do before we go to our next exorcism. I need to catch you up on my work from last night."

Sonder studied her face for a long moment, but Atta refused to flinch, refused to look away. "All right," he finally said and rose. "What's that on your cheek?" He came forward and swiped at it softly with his thumb. "Dirt?"

She'd forgotten in her dizziness to bathe. Atta tugged at the long sleeve covering the bite and scratch marks. "I might need a bath."

The concern in his eyes set a guilt in her heart. "I'll come with you." Her brows rose and he chuckled. "Not like that. I'll bring what we need to work on and we can discuss it while you bathe. You look as if you could use a long, comforting soak."

Tears welled in her eyes at his thoughtfulness and her desire not to be alone. "I'd like that."

When she made it to the master bathroom with fresh clothing and *Into the Faerie Wood*, Sonder had the water running, the bath nearly overflowing with bubbles.

"I might have over-poured." He shrugged apologetically and gestured to the tub. "It's all yours. I'll go grab a stool."

The water was deliciously warm, stinging her cuts and soothing her sore muscles from her fall. Sonder returned with a stool just the right size to put him at eye level with her. He sat, one leg crossed over the other, elbows on his knee, and flipped open *Into the Faerie Wood*.

As he read her fairytales, Atta closed her eyes, pressing her neck against the lip of the tub, and let his voice drown out her fears, keeping her arm hidden beneath the bubbles.

ATTA

The next exorcism was gruesome.

A Stage 3 headed straight for Stage 4.

Jesus. His eyes.

"His eyes," Sonder echoed her thought. "Hornets."

"Vulture Hornets," she breathed out, but there was no such insect in Ireland. They were devouring his eyes, burrowing their way in while the poor man was still breathing, scavenging on the soft tissue as the man lay unconscious.

Sonder lifted his mask and withdrew a vial.

"Be careful," Atta warned when he reached out a gloved hand and plucked one of the hornets from Mr Whelan's eye socket with tweezers. It wriggled and buzzed between the metal prongs holding it captive, and Atta leaned in to inspect it. "It's almost iridescent," she mused.

"Is it from there, do you think? The Faerie Wood?"

They exchanged a look before their attention was pulled back to the patient regaining consciousness. Atta jumped to his side as Sonder stowed away the hornet. She slipped her hand under the bedsheet, grasping onto the man's ankle. Her head fell back, and she just caught sight of Sonder jumping to her side to hold her up before her knees buckled and her eyes rolled back into her skull.

Atta was instantly in the Faerie Wood. Lush, magnificent, wild. There was an ornate looking glass danging from a willow tree and in it, Atta saw a man. Mr Whelan, young, whole and smiling, his little brother by his side. They sat beside a babbling brook, their trouser legs pulled up to their knees, feet in the cool water and fishing poles in their hands. Mr Whelan took a bite of apple, catching his brother looking at it longingly. He smiled at the lad and relinquished the entire thing to him without fuss.

Atta's heart warmed at this fraternal show of love. But the scene was interrupted by an infernal buzzing. She only had time to register the sound before the hornets were on the younger brother, drawn in by the sweet, crisp scent of the apple. They attacked with a vengeance until Mr Whelan yanked the apple away, shoved it between his teeth and pushed his little brother into the water. The hornets immediately turned on him. Young Mr Whelan threw the apple as far into the woodlands as he could, then dove into the water to haul his brother out. There on the muddy bank, he rocked him, smoothing down his wet, downy hair.

The scene faded, turning to Mr Whelan and his brother as they were now, older but still inseparable, the younger trying to feed the prone Inhabited man soup, his hands trembling, his eyes watery. "Please, Brother. Please eat. You have to."

Atta reached out and took one step forward. The trees around her were on fire, Fae of all kinds screaming. Atta covered her ears, but one of the Fae got through, screeching at her, pulling her hair until she thought her neck would snap.

"*Mine! Mine!*" it hissed in a tongue she somehow knew but had never heard.

The buzzing invaded her skull and she covered her ears, gasping back to the present. "Cover your ears!" she shouted to Sonder, but he was already ripping up a portion of his shirt, shoving twisted bits in her ears. She clamped her hands around his until he was through and shoved pieces into his own ears.

Everything was muffled, but Atta could still hear the screeching, the buzzing. "*Mine, mine, mine,*" on repeat until she finally understood.

"He's not yours!" she bellowed, dousing Mr Whelan with bits of iron-infused moonwater, but a vine coated in black blood and dislodged viscera was snaking out of his nose, his mouth. He arched his back, writhing on the bed, gagging.

"Syringe!" Sonder shouted, and they both moved. "Sing, Atta!"

And she did. In a language she'd never spoken until she was a ghoul in the corner, a spectre on the ceiling, a woman outside her body.

A mist lifted off the vine, like fog off a lake in the morning, and Sonder bound it with black salt while Atta solidified it, shoving the needle toward its tiny jugular. The faerie twisted free, only a fraction of the Yarrow and iron fluid making it into its body. But it was enough for Sonder to reach out and snatch it.

With his teeth bared, he gripped the writhing, gnashing faerie with his gloved hand. "Jar!"

Atta already had it open, and he shoved the creature inside. Instantly, the hornets dropped dead, falling in small heaps in Whelan's bloody eye sockets.

Hot. She was too hot.

Sonder fastened the lid on with no embalming fluid to kill it this time. They wanted to study it alive. Moving.

Dizziness washed over Atta and she sank to the floor. She heard Sonder say her name, but it was muffled by more than the strip of his shirt shoved in her ears.

The next thing she knew, he was crouched in front of her, ripping off her blazer, shoving a bottle of water in her hands.

Something pulled his attention away and he stood, his face marred with indecision, looking from Mr Whelan on the bed, to her. In the end, he chose her. He pulled her to a wall and propped her up. Took her water and doused what was left of the hem of his shirt in it and pressed it to her forehead, taking the strips out of her ears.

"Atta." The fear in his voice pierced her heart but he was a mirage and she couldn't answer. "Darling, please talk to me. What is it? What's wrong?"

She didn't know. But there was a shimmer clouding Sonder, making him blurry, and all she could hear was, "*Mine,*" hissed in that ancient Fae tongue.

"No," she managed. "Not yours." The fire in her bones roared and she stood up, finally understanding what was happening. "Not yours," she growled in its tongue at the shimmer above Sonder's head. "*Mine.*"

It popped, like a soap bubble, and everything returned to focus, Sonder's terrified eyes, his heaving chest, Mr Whelan moaning on the bed.

"Whelan!" she let out, rushing to his bedside.

Sonder followed, opened his medical bag, and set to work, but he kept watching her, question in his eyes.

"I'm all right," she told him gently, and he took a shuddering breath. "I'm all right."

"Jesus, you scared me." His tone broke her heart and sealed it all back up in tandem.

She stepped to him and put a palm to his face. "Focus on Mr Whelan. I'm all right. I promise." But it was the second of too many lies she knew would come.

He kissed her forehead hastily and poured all his attention into Whelan.

The hornets had vanished with the spray of Yarrow water, but Mr Whelan's eyes were gone—gaping black holes of blood —but it wouldn't kill him.

"He's in pain," Sonder announced, "but his vitals are good. Go get his brother."

Atta donned her mask and did as instructed, trying her best to prepare Whelan the Younger for what he was about to see.

"He'll need to go to hospital to ensure there is no damage to his organs. And"—she halted him outside the bedroom door —"you should know that his eyes are. . .gone." Fuck, her bedside manner was not what it should be. "But he's going to be okay."

If the sight of his brother frightened him, he didn't let it show, but rushed to his side, gripping his hand.

"I've given him a sedative," Sonder explained, scrawling out the name of it on a slip of paper. "You'll need to tell the medics what it's called when they arrive and tell them to check his lungs, heart, nose, and throat."

"Nose, throat, heart, lungs," Mr Whelan repeated out of order, his nerves causing his eyes to dart around, landing on his brother's eye sockets.

"Among the obvious things," Sonder finished solemnly.

"Right. Thank you. Thank you both so much."

"No thanks is needed, mate." Sonder squeezed his shoulder and gestured with his head for Atta to follow him out.

They barely made it down the stairs before Sonder dropped his medical bag and lifted both their masks, searching her eyes. "Say it again," he demanded, his voice tumultuous. "But only if it's true."

"Sonder, I'm all right." She laid her palm against his cheek again and he leaned into her touch.

"I've never been so scared in my life, Atta." He fitted her mask back on and donned his own, but he wouldn't let go of her hand as they lugged all their supplies out to Gibbs's car.

"Well?" Gibbs jumped on them as soon as they got in. "How did it go?"

"Another success," Sonder told him plainly.

Atta clutched the bag housing a jar with a live faerie in it as they passed the wailing sirens of the medics on their way to tend to Mr Whelan.

The anatomical structure of the Fae mirrors that of humans, though on a much smaller scale, and situs inversus. It stands to reason that this gives them insight into the human form, and is potentially why our species has been selected as the root.

-Excerpt, *Collection of Faerie Findings*, Dr Sonder Murdoch, PhD, circa 1993

SONDER

"There are several things to note." Atta had a pen sticking out of her mouth, distorting her words.

He hadn't let her out of his sight for the last few days. It felt like she was sand about to slip through his fingers if he looked away.

They'd had six more successful exorcisms since Mr Whelan, and they were riding high. He knew he needed to make an appearance at Achilles House—that Lynch would expect him to autopsy at least one of the bodies and that there was no way he hadn't begun to put together his absence with the *cures* all over the news. . . but Atta.

There were jagged cuts on her arms, healing now. She'd told him they were from falling in the grove, and it felt like a half-truth.

She'd seemed fine. Happy, glowing, eating. She'd even crawled on top of him the night before and again that morning. She'd felt glorious in his hands then, alive and real and *his*. They'd lain there in the wintery morning light discussing their findings of the live faerie sitting in the cellar, and she'd had an idea, left his bed stark nude and returned with a towering stack of books against her breasts and climbed back into bed with him. He'd decided that would be the painting he made of her, standing there nude with her books.

Still, something wasn't sitting right. Like a stone in his gut. Achilles awaiting the downfall of his Patroclus. Could he have stopped it if he'd known?

"Are you even listening to me, Professor Murdoch?"

Her face was contorted with ire. Even her smart mouth was there in typical fashion, but he couldn't shake the feeling that something was wrong. She'd spoken in a strange language that day at Whelan's. Trembled and looked terrified of what she saw that he couldn't.

"No," he said, pushing away all the darkness. "Tell me again."

She rolled her eyes and straightened behind his desk. He'd offered it to her and taken the coffee table so her back wouldn't hurt being hunched over.

"The Dryad Faeries seem to be the ones with the highest rate of success, which makes a great deal of sense. They're quite close to a successful Inhabitation, and they're also the ones choosing their hosts more selectively."

Intellect finally closed the door on his worry and cataclysmic thinking. "I'm listening." Sonder leaned forward, elbows on his knees, brow furrowed.

Her face lit up like it always did when she was lost to her academia. "From what I saw when I touched them, some of the Inhabited were selfish, yes, but some were beyond kind. Self*less*. Protective. In ways that were potentially detrimental to themselves."

"Go on." The professor in him never could be turned off. It

was best to draw out a person's thoughts, not interject one's own.

"The faeries possessing people are all under the same umbrella of Fae, though different variations. Unless we can recruit more people to help us, our focus needs to be on Stage 3 Inhabitations because those all seem to be Dryads, and they're bordering on the success of Stage 4. I'm not sure there's another stage after that, and if there is—"

"Then they've won."

"Possibly, yes. I keep seeing their world vibrant, then dying or completely burnt. They're desperate."

"Your view into their world is astonishing," he mused.

Atta tucked a strand of hair behind her ear, looking self-conscious. This astounded him considering he'd seen, touched, tasted every part of her. He worried there was a corner of her mind she'd shut him out of, and he wasn't certain *why*.

"We have a good list of symptoms here to possibly catch early possessions, but we can't catch everything on our own and shut down the source, too."

Sonder nodded, looking at his own notes and drawings, at the sleeping faerie on the coffee table at his knees. "There is definitely a source. A place they're coming in from."

"We have to figure out where," Atta agreed, her voice far off as she put the pen back between her teeth and was lost again to her books.

Sonder returned to his own work, wondering how Atta would feel about him cutting open one of the faeries. He needed to see inside it.

The sun was rising on the other side of the world, his eyelids heavy when he leaned back in his chair with a glass of whiskey, his third of the long night. Atta was on her stomach, feet up and ankles crossed in front of the fire, flipping through the pages of his mother's book she'd found in the Hawthorn Grove. *In the Hawthorn Grove* of all places. Why had his mother placed it there?

"Anything of note?" he asked, breaking the comfortable silence that had stretched on the last hour or so.

She turned and sat up, tucking a leg beneath her. "No. It's still just fairytales that I can tell." Her face was drawn in disappointment.

"Come here."

She gave him a coy smile, but her eyes glinted with mischief, and she ultimately obeyed.

He looked up at her as she approached and ran one finger down the line of his jaw. The stubble had grown out further than he usually let it, but Atta seemed to like it. Perhaps he'd leave it that way. She pulled her plaid skirt up enough to straddle his lap, just as he'd desperately hoped she would. He set his glass down on the side table and took her arse in his hands as she fiddled with the ends of his undone tie.

Sonder pulled her toward him enough to make her squeal and topple forward so he could catch her mouth with his, but it was her that deepened the kiss.

"Mmm," he said against her hair as she moved her lips to his neck. "Don't we have work to do?"

"You're the one who called me over here," she murmured in his ear.

"And what if I only wanted to discuss fairytales?"

She laughed huskily and shifted her hips. He groaned and she laughed again. "I don't think that's true."

"You know"—he tugged at the hem of her jumper and she raised her arms so he could slip it over her head—"these skirts

of yours drive me out of my mind." He watched the firelight
dance along the curves of her breasts, perfect in that sheer lace
bra, as she left him just long enough to slip off her tights and
throw them over the faerie enclosure.

When she returned to his lap, he slid his hands up her
thighs to feel her silk panties.

"Perhaps the skirt should stay on, then."

"Perhaps it should."

She unfastened his belt and unbuttoned his trousers, all the
while driving him mad with her tongue colliding with his. No
woman had ever made him feel so alive. So desperate for her.
So madly in love. He knew the moment he'd fallen. It was
standing there in The Old Library, holding a book in his hand
as she told him she'd watched him years ago, stand the same
way in the same library. When she'd laughed and said it was
annoying, when he had that first laugh, he knew then and there
he'd set the world on fire for her. Slay a thousand beasts, cure
any Plague, fight to the death. For her. His Patroclus.

He deftly pulled her panties to the side and slid within her,
relishing that he could make her tip her head back like that.
Breathe like that, the ends of her hair tickling the back of his
hands as he gripped her hips.

When they were spent and she lay curled in his lap, this
beautiful window into another world, he lifted her chin with his
fingers and gently kissed her lips. She looked up at him with
those eyes he adored and his heart squeezed. "Do you know
that I'm in love with you?"

She smiled, the sleepy, blissful smile he knew was his. "I
thought that might be the case, yeah."

"You've tangled yourself up in my soul like a vine, *a stór.*"

He dragged his thumb across her bottom lip and she smiled against his touch.

"I'm terrified of this world, Sonder. But I don't fear facing it with you."

He kissed her forehead and she fell asleep, everything he cared about there in his arms.

ATTA
18 December, 1993

Atta woke in the moonlit grove, covered in frost, huddled beneath the old, twisted hawthorn. The Faerie Wood book lay on her lap, open to a drawing of a door.

She was trembling so fiercely she nearly couldn't stand, could hardly hold onto the book as she raced for the manor in nothing but one of Sonder's button-down shirts. She nearly slipped on a patch of frost outside the door but made it inside, tossing the book away from her onto the kitchen counter, and rushed for the shower.

The Irish Independent :

DUBLIN'S MASKED HEALERS NEARLY IDENTIFIED!

NEWLY HEALED PLAGUE VICTIMS HAVE SUNG THE PRAISES OF OUR CITY'S FAVOURITE MASKED DUO JUST AS EVERYONE ELSE HAS, AND THE IRISH INDEPENDENT HAD ONE OF THEM SIT DOWN WITH A FORENSIC SKETCH ARTIST TO CAPTURE A LOOK AT THE DUO FOR THE GENERAL PUBLIC

ATTA

5 JANUARY, 1994

The last fortnight had been a blur of exorcisms, successes and failures, and studying their processes until the wee hours of the morning when Sonder and Atta would crawl into bed together. Sometimes, they would sleep wrapped in one another's arms. Sometimes, they would expend the rest of their energies via their sexual appetite for one another. Sometimes, they would stare at the ceiling and speak in whispers about their fears, their dreams, their lives before they met.

I want to drown in this love, darling, he'd told her one morning when she apologised for hogging the bed.

Every moment with him had become her new most treasured.

Wrapped in a towel, Atta looked in the full-length mirror in her room that was essentially only used as a giant closet now. Her attention was drawn to where she'd tucked a Polaroid she'd taken of Sonder weeks ago and tucked it into the mirror's edge. His hair was in disarray even more than usual because she'd driven her fingers through it just before, his car windows all fogged up. Starving, he'd dragged her out to the city for food and a night for them to be normal. He wore a maroon knit jumper over his collared shirt where they sat tucked in a dimly lit corner booth.

The night had been perfect. No Plague, no exorcisms, no Society breathing down their neck. Only the man she loved hiding his face with his hand when she pulled out a Polaroid camera and snapped his photo. But he was *grinning* behind his blurred hands that only managed to cover half of his face before the flash. The smile that sent peace flooding her heart. The smile of the man she would do *anything* to protect.

"*A stór!*" she heard him call her, his voice climbing the stairs from the ground floor. "Your coffee is getting cold!"

She kissed the tip of her finger and pressed it to Photograph Sonder's lips. "Coming!" she called back and went to dress.

The last vestiges of her trepidation from waking in the grove yet again slipped out of her like faerie mist the moment she stepped into the kitchen and Sonder greeted her over his newspaper like he did every morning. The constant that settled her.

"Good morning, darling."

She smiled, her gaze dropping to the front page of the Irish Independent, and her heart stuttered. A gasp escaped her, and Sonder pulled the paper to his chest, looking down at it.

"Ah, yes. Quite the cover story today, isn't it?"

"Is that a *drawing* of us?" She came forward and snatched it from his hand.

"It is, indeed."

There they were, immortalised in printer ink by sketches that were far, far too accurate for her liking. Sonder was there in his trousers, a button-up, the sleeves rolled to his elbows, and a sweater vest, while Atta was in her signature skirt and tweed blazer look. Thank Christ they had the plague doctor masks on. "Even the shoes are accurate!" she said, her voice hitting a pitch only dogs can hear.

"Lydia Callahan had a very keen eye the other day. She'd be my guess for who spoke to the forensic sketch artist."

Atta was still gawking at it when a loud crash came from the foyer. Sonder was on his feet instantly, Gibbs's voice cutting through the tension. "Oy! Are you lot up?"

"Christ!" Sonder shouted back, storming for the sitting room. "Haven't you ever heard of fucking knocking, you eejit?"

But Gibbs's voice was drowned out by the shrill ringing of the telephone on the wall of the kitchen. Atta answered it just to make it stop ringing, the chaos too much.

"Atta!" The voice on the other end was urgent.

"Professor Vasilios?" she questioned, unsure if she was correct.

"Marguerite, please," she corrected. "But yes. You need to turn on the news immediately."

Sonder crashed through the kitchen door. "We need to turn on the news!"

Atta hung up on Marguerite and followed Sonder and Gibbs to her room, where they repeated the night they'd stood there and first saw Lisle speaking to a news crew about them.

Only this time it was international news.

An American woman in a navy suit sat at a newsdesk, the sketch of Atta and Sonder plastered on a screen behind her. "A pair of masked individuals have spent the last months curing the Plague that has run rampant in Dublin for nearly seven years. No one can verify who they are or how they're doing it. But we at CBS News have spoken to several of the cured patients and they sing high praises for these masked heroes.

Atta's stomach roiled.

Sonder looked away, his lip curled in disgust. "Turn it off."

Gibbs flicked off the television, and they all three stared at each other. "I think we're going to need that help now," Sonder said quietly.

The phone in his office rang and he went to answer it.

Gibbs swallowed hard. "He means for me to start helping, doesn't he?"

Atta nodded, but there was a banging on the front door before she could answer. "Jesus, what is this chaos?" she mumbled. "That's probably Vasilios." But how could she have made it to Murdoch Manor so quickly?

The knock came again, more urgently, and Atta opened the door.

"*Emmy?*"

"*Atta?*"

They traded befuddled looks.

"What are you doing here?" Atta opened the door wider and pulled Emmy inside, shoving down a pang of guilt that she'd hardly kept up with Emmy at all since she'd been expelled.

"I followed Gibbs," she explained, gawking at the manor's lavish foyer. "He's been acting so strange lately. Cagey and dodgy. So I followed him here." She paused her slow circle, mouth agape. "Where is *here*, anyway?"

Sonder came around the corner, and Emmy's eyes widened as she slowly turned them on Atta. Apparently, his presence was a sufficient answer.

"Oh, hello there," he said casually, sliding his hands into his pockets and looking to Atta for an explanation.

"She followed Gibbs here."

"Where the fuck are you two?" Gibbs's voice came from the sitting area. "Marguerite is on the phone *again*."

Sonder growled curses and stomped off. Atta grabbed Emmy's arm and followed him.

"Marguerite?" Emmy whispered, struggling to keep up with Atta's frustrated pace. "Professor Vasilios? Ow, quit squeezing me so hard!"

"You can't just follow people to strange places, Emmy." She gently pushed her friend to sit on the sofa.

Emmy scoffed. "You fucking disappeared from the face of the planet, Atta. I've barely heard from you for two months, and you want to talk to me about being in a strange place?"

Atta sank into a chair. "Fucking hell," she muttered, scrubbing at her tired eyes.

"You all seem very stressed," Emmy said absently, looking at Gibbs and Sonder arguing over who should talk to Marguerite and back at Atta. "Did I walk in on something?"

"Atta," came Sonder's voice as Gibbs stomped away. "A word?"

Atta pursed her lips and looked at Emmy. "Stay here and don't wander off, all right?"

Hands in the air in a show of surrender, Emmy leaned back on the sofa and picked up an old copy of *Laboratory News*, flipping the magazine open.

With one last wary look over her shoulder at her friend she hadn't seen in far too long, Atta followed Sonder into the billiard room.

"Shall I get a candlestick?" he said cheekily as she entered and shut the door.

"What?" she asked, confused.

"We're in the Billiard Room. . ."

Lost, Atta blinked at him.

"The film. . ."

"*Clue*?" She screwed up her face. "Are you making a *Clue* joke right now?"

"Evidently, it didn't land."

"I thought you didn't watch movies."

"I never said that." He shook his head. "Never mind. What is Vasilios's assistant doing here?"

"I don't know. She said Gibbs was acting strange, so she followed him here."

"Right. Well, first things first. My phone call was Lynch."

Atta's heart climbed into her throat.

"He saw the newspaper and the international story."

"Oh fuck."

"The Agamemnon Council and the Trinity Administration would like to hold a private hearing for each of us."

"Please tell me why you're so calm," she demanded, angry that he wasn't sweating or crying or throwing up like she was about to.

"Because there's no sense in hiding who we are now, and there's nothing they can do to us."

"Nothing they can do to us? Sonder, that's insane. There is so much they could do to us."

"Not true." He placed his hands on her shoulders and gently rubbed up and down her arms. "They want the glory. They chose a hearing because it won't involve the Garda and they won't try to stop us. All they want is to try and get us to be their face—give the Society and Trinity the honour of looking like they finally cured the Plague."

"I don't understand how that's good." She didn't mean for her words to come out so sharply, but she couldn't quite help it, either.

"If we can get in their ear, they might let you back into Trinity."

Atta broke away from him. "I told you I don't care about that."

"Atta—"

"*No*. We have more important things to worry about right now." She started pacing, fiddling with the ends of her sleeves. "We need to train help. We need Gibbs and Vasilios as boots on the ground." An idea struck her and she stopped. "Emmy is Marguerite's TA and my friend. Maybe even she could help."

But she could tell by Sonder's face that he hadn't jumped subjects like she had. "Atta, I'm not saying we have to side with the Society or play their games, I'm only saying—"

"We can talk about that later," Atta snapped firmly. She knew her age was showing, her idyllic, naïve mindset, but she didn't care. They didn't need goddamn Agamemnon. They were fucking Achilles.

Sonder sighed but nodded, clasping his hands together in front of him and sitting on the edge of the billiard table. "Gibbs and Marguerite I can get behind. I don't know Emmy."

She grabbed his hand and pulled him up. "Then come get to know her."

ATTA

E mmy blinked at them where they all sat around a table in the library. "Maybe if you explain it one more time. . ."

Gibbs groaned.

"I'm getting tea." Professor Vasilios sighed and left the room.

Sonder scrubbed at his jaw.

"Emmy, it doesn't get any clearer than *it's not a Plague. Faeries are possessing people*," Atta explained, her patience drained.

A mad laugh crackled out of Emmy. "It's just mental, you know?"

Nods passed around the room. "But it's important," Gibbs interjected.

"And we need your help."

Emmy considered their words and Sonder stood. "I have to go." He bent and kissed Atta's cheek. "I'll be back."

He was hardly out the door before Emmy turned on her. "Explain what's going on *there*, right fucking now."

Gibbs snorted and pushed his glasses up. "Isn't it obvious?"

"Oh, the sexual tension could be cut with a *blade* it's so thick," Emmy teased, and Atta pushed her. It was nice to have Emmy around again.

Marguerite came in with a fresh pot of tea. "*Please*. No one saw that tension before now? It's been obvious since day one."

They all looked at Professor Vasilios, and she paused. "What? No one noticed Sonder pining after Atta? His eyes always straying toward her? The fact no one else would have lasted five seconds as his TA?" The other three looked at one another, and Marguerite chuckled. "Oh, you dear young folk. I've sure as hell never seen Sonder like this, not in the ten years I've known him."

"I did suspect there was something there when he climbed in my fucking window to make me monitor Atta's migraines," Gibbs offered.

"You said that before." Atta squinted at him. "What was that all about?"

"Just what I said. In the middle of the night one night, he climbed a fucking tree and came through the window of my room and woke me. He was a mess, worried about your headaches I didn't even know you had."

It dawned on her that Gibbs must mean the night she fainted on Sonder's lap in the graveyard that first time and he'd dropped her off at Briseis.

Marguerite was looking at her intensely, concern in the line of her brow. "You have migraines, love?"

Atta nodded. "That's probably what we need to go over next."

This was the part they hadn't told even Gibbs. He cocked his head to the side in question and Atta spotted something on his shoulder. She leaned in and he backed up, startled at her close proximity. "What are you doing?"

Atta looked up at him with narrowed eyes, then back down at his shoulder. "Gibbs, why do you have long, blonde hairs stuck to your hoodie?"

Emmy gasped, the entire situation making Atta feel like they were in secondary school.

"Oh, em, I—"

Atta reached to pluck one off his shoulder. As soon as her fingers made contact, she knew exactly who they belonged to, and all gathered got a front-row seat to her *migraines*.

Where she used to be blonde and snarky, the young woman had become a hollowed-out vessel with a gaping mouth, the thin trunk of a juniper maiden jutting out of the column of her throat, her eyes sprouting branches lush with frosted indigo berries.

"Atta!" They were all shouting her name when she came to, her cheek smashed against the wood of the tabletop. Marguerite was fanning her, Emmy was panicked, and Gibbs was yelling for someone to call Sonder.

"Stop," she croaked, sitting up. "It's fine. I'm fine."

"I'll get you some water," Marguerite declared and rushed out of the library.

Atta nodded her thanks and turned to Gibbs. "You need to go get Imogen immediately. Bring her here. The Fae have their sights on her."

His eyes were wide as saucers, a tremble starting in his fingers and travelling quickly up his arms. "Wh–what?"

"Imogen?" Emmy screeched. "Your old roommate? What the fuck does that—"

"Go!" Atta shouted at Gibbs. "I'll explain when she arrives."

Gibbs stood so quickly that his chair toppled over and he ran out of the room.

"You're scaring me," Emmy said in a small voice so unlike her.

Marguerite bustled in with the water and Atta took a gulp. "I think Gibbs has been sleeping with Imogen secretly. And I don't get migraines, I get visions."

Emmy's mouth fell open, and Marguerite winced. "For fuck's sake," she muttered. "If Sonder hadn't shown me that jar collection of fucking faeries, I would think this was grounds for a nice, long asylum stay for you all."

"I know." Atta stood, unable to sit still anymore. "I used to think it was all hallucinations, but then Lauren Kennedy died."

"The girl from Trinity?" Emmy asked.

Atta nodded. "Yes. I bumped into her one day before class and got a splitting headache. I saw strange visions of her being consumed by ivy."

Marguerite sank into the chair Atta had vacated.

"And Imogen?" Emmy ventured, her features set in an obvious show of fear of the answer.

"We just need to get her here where we can monitor her. Stop it before it starts. I have wards on the house, and I think they're holding."

"And 'it' is. . ." Emmy cut herself off, but Marguerite answered.

"Possession."

Atta nodded grimly.

SONDER

The Agamemnon Council berated him for the better part of an hour.

After that, it became an amusing match of members defending him and others all but hanging him.

"You wore the mask of this society alongside someone who does not even belong in our ranks," Lynch began his closing remarks. "You defied our protocols by stepping out on your own with some disastrous results."

Some, but not all, Sonder thought.

"What do you have to say for yourself?" Lynch demanded.

All eyes in the chamber beneath Saint Patrick's were on him, and Sonder stood. "All I have done is what my arm of Agamemnon set out to do. Most often, there is no time for red tape and bureaucratic processes. Lives are being saved because of the work of Achilles. Yes, I formed a small, covert unit within, but the results are the same. Lives are being saved, the Plague is losing ground, and Agamemnon maintains its reputation—has kept its promise."

Murmurs went up around the room. Most of the argument

had revolved around whether Agamemnon was being credited with the mounting success or not. The public knew so little about the Society that ran as an undercurrent to the city, but they knew enough, and that meant many members had argued in Sonder and Atta's favour that the masks they wore pointed people to the Society.

It irked Sonder that the effect on Inhabited patients had never come up, save for the mention of their failures—the ones they'd lost.

"I do not stand before you today," Sonder went on, his voice ringing out in the room of marble and bone, "with any desire to claim glory for the success of what's happening. When I lobbied to have Achilles House opened, it was with one goal in mind. The goal of eradicating the Plague has remained my only aim, and I will not stop now. Take all the credit you'd like." He looked each of the eight council members in the eye, then turned to sweep his attention over the Society members gathered for the spectacle. "I only wish to end this nightmare."

Lynch, his face as mottled as ever, stood from his seat, nearly toppling it over. "Then report your goddamn findings! Your process!"

"That I will not do," Sonder responded simply, firmly. "You let me and my team do as we are doing without interference, or we take off the masks. Take off the Society."

"This is an outrage!" Sonder watched the spittle fly from Lynch's mouth, his jowls wobbling.

"Enough!" Trinity Provost Nial Rochford stood, speaking for the first time since the council convened. Even Lynch had to sit down and listen to him.

The Rochford family had led Agamemnon since its

inception. Many had been better leaders than Nial, but many had been far worse.

"We cannot stake our reputation on your processes we know nothing about, Dr Murdoch. Your conduct with a student, no less, has coloured your once rosy academic and Societal character in grey. Tell us your methods, or we *will* interfere, beginning first with your position at TCD."

Sonder did not gape at him or gasp as some of the others did. He'd seen all this coming. Had for weeks. "I'll share our protocol, discoveries, and all our research if you will reinstate Ariatne Morrow at TCD." More murmurs echoed through the council and the audience.

Lynch had his meaty hands in fists on the council table while Rochford's steely grey eyes bore into him. "You have a deal. On one condition. Miss Morrow can come here and pledge her life to Agamemnon and share her research herself."

Sonder's stomach turned. Atta would never agree to that. Nor did he want her to, but she could return to her studies, to her beloved college. She shouldn't have to sell her soul to do it. "You should be kissing the fucking ground Ariatne Morrow walks on," he spat through gritted teeth. "She shouldn't have to dance to your tune to be granted entry back into Trinity, not when she's single-handedly responsible for saving this goddamn city."

Nial Rochford's even demeanour cracked. "Ariatne Morrow is responsible for the deaths of multiple people and a multitude of crimes."

That was when Sonder began to shout, to bellow horrible things at them, cursing them to high heaven until someone dragged him out—Walsh and Mariana, he realised when they made it outside.

Sitting on the cathedral steps, Mariana O'Sullivan laid a hand on his shoulder. "I'm sorry I got you into this mess," she said gently.

Sonder looked up at her, arms slung on his bent knees. "I'm not."

"She'll need to make the decision herself, pet."

Mariana was right. "See if you can get her here."

ATTA

I mogen wouldn't get out of the car.

"What am I supposed to do?" Gibbs shouted.

Emmy had her arms crossed over her chest, and she bent to look into the window, her face twisted. "Did you abduct her or something?"

"I didn't *abduct* her," Gibbs groused.

Marguerite rapped on the window with her knuckles. "Dear, it's quite brisk out here. You can't stay in there all day."

Imogen flipped her off.

Marguerite frowned and delicately crossed the broken cobbles in her designer heels. "Isn't she a delight?"

Imogen shouted something, but her voice was too muffled by the car. Atta approached with little patience. Despite the vision seared into her brain of Imogen succumbing to a Stage 4 Inhabitation, the girl before her was as infuriating as ever.

"What?" she questioned with as much congeniality as she could muster. "We can't hear you."

"This place is creepy!" Imogen pointed through the window at Murdoch Manor.

"This is Professor Murdoch's place," Atta raised her voice so Imogen could hear.

As expected, Imogen wound down the window a crack, unable to resist that juicy detail. "Why are you all at the spooky, sexy professor's house?"

"It's a lot to explain. Would you come inside and we'll do our best?"

Reluctantly, and with quite a lot more coaxing, Imogen made it inside.

Explaining she was a target for the Plague, however, did not go well. Atta could only imagine how it would go to explain it wasn't even a sickness but a faerie that wanted to possess her.

Gibbs was sweeping up three broken glasses Imogen had smashed against the wall before she tuckered herself out with her fit when the phone rang.

Resigned, Atta went to answer it.

"Atta?" A familiar voice came over the line, but she couldn't quite place it.

"Who is this?"

"Mariana O'Sullivan, dear."

Her advisor? What could she want? "How can I help you, Mrs O'Sullivan?"

"You're going to need to come to Saint Patrick's Cathedral immediately. The Agamemnon Council needs to speak with you."

She didn't know where Sonder was and wished she didn't want him there with her as Emmy drove her to Saint Patrick's.

"You look green," Emmy observed.

Atta didn't want to talk about it. "Where did you get this car?" she asked instead.

"Oh, the uh guy I'm seeing. It's his mam's."

Emmy pulled into the crowded car park and Atta nimbly got out. "Hey, it's going to be okay."

Atta bent to look at her friend's attempt at an encouraging smile. "I've missed you."

Emmy's smile was true that time. "Go tell 'em to fuck off."

She'd told Sonder time and again that it didn't matter if the council called on her, that she wouldn't side with them, didn't care, but she was swallowing back too many emotions to count as she approached the side door she'd used with him when they were there in the fall to collect samples from Lauren Kennedy.

"Atta."

The voice came from behind her as she reached for the door handle, and it instantly soothed her frayed nerves.

"Sonder? What are you doing here?" So this was where he'd been all day. Her heart sank, but he pulled her around the back of the cathedral.

"I can't just let your name be raked through the mud."

She looked up at him, a little halo of sun peeking out from the clouds behind his head. "Yours is."

"I don't care about mine, but I do care about yours. They want you to join Agamemnon. If you do, they'll let you back into Trinity. Let us continue the exorcisms without interference." A humourless laugh escaped him and he ran his hand through his hair, then threw an arm out toward the church, rigid. "You deserve for them to know what you're really doing for Dublin. For *Ireland*. For the whole of the fucking world probably. I told them as much, not kindly, I'll admit."

"Did it help?"

His face dropped.

"I'm sorry, Sonder."

He placed his palm on her cheek, his fingers at the nape of her neck. "You, *a stór*, are everything that is right with the world. *My* world. With all the worlds. And don't you dare apologise for it."

"Let's go home."

"You're not going to go in?"

"No, I'm not."

A weak smile curved his lips. "I'll face whatever music there is with you."

Emmy said she needed to get the car back to its owner. Atta and Sonder followed, their fingers intertwined, and gave Emmy a lift back to the manor.

"So," Emmy said when she slid into the backseat, "faeries, huh?"

Sonder squeezed Atta's hand. "How mental do you think us?"

"Just mental enough, mate." She laughed and it dispelled some of the tension. "That ancient council shite didn't take long."

"I didn't go in."

Atta couldn't see Emmy's face, but she pictured her wincing. "What now?"

"We take off the masks," Sonder answered. "We keep going on our own. Do you agree?" He looked across the car at Atta.

"I do."

She didn't hear the rest of the conversation. There were overlapping lullabies on rotation in her head, but not the kind that lull to sleep, the kind that usher in nightmares.

ATTA

S onder and Gibbs made everyone a hearty meal of salad, shrimp, lamb, and roasted potatoes.

Atta could tell he was thrilled to have the house full, but she also knew that excitement would wear off soon, and he'd wish they were alone again as recluses. They all gathered around the massive, polished oak table in Murdoch Manor's formal dining room and came up with their next steps.

To say Imogen wasn't convinced would be an understatement, but they couldn't very well have her wandering about the manor and stumble upon something, or walk on eggshells in their discussions because they'd left her in the dark.

After a dessert of espresso and madeleines, Gibbs handed everyone detailed schedules as Sonder spoke. "Emmy and Gibbs will take all Stage 1s and the stray Stage 2s. Marguerite will handle Stage 2s as long as there is someone to accompany her. Atta and I will do so on a rotation. We will also be handling all Stage 3s and Stage 4s."

He looked pointedly at Imogen. "You will remain in this

house." She opened her mouth, but he held up a hand. "Call foul, abduction, whatever you'd like all you want but you'll be dead inside a week if you choose to be an eejit."

Imogen's eyes went from slits to saucers. "I should call the Garda on the whole psycho lot of you."

Done with her attitude over the last two days and her one attempted escape, Sonder rose and stomped off, returning with the kitchen telephone he'd apparently ripped from the wall if the outlet cover and bits of plasterboard dangling from the telephone jack were any indication. He slammed it down on the table. "Be my fucking guest. It's your death, not mine."

Imogen gaped up at him, a madeleine still between her fingers. "No, thank you," she said meekly.

Sonder ignored her and returned to his seat. "Next schedule, please, Gibbs." Another paper landed in front of each of them, save for Imogen. "This is the schedule for who has the great honour of watching over Imogen and at what times during the night. Nighttime is when we most suspect an Inhabitation attempt."

Imogen snatched a schedule from Gibbs next to her and scoffed. Emmy was looking at the other paper, her nose scrunched. "I'm not so sure I'm ready for this. It says our first exorcism is tomorrow. I literally just started learning two days ago."

"It isn't as complicated as it seems," Atta reassured her. "I could ward the cellar and let one of the faeries out as a trial run if you'd like."

She could tell by Sonder's face that he didn't like the idea, but he didn't fight her on it.

"Sure." Emmy nodded and looked at Gibbs. "It's a good idea."

"Yeah, I guess."

"We'll head down in a few, then," Atta decided.

"I have papers to mark tonight." Marguerite stood, wiping her mouth delicately with a cloth napkin and laying it on the table. "I'll meet you at the first appointment in the morning, Sonder."

Gibbs began clearing the plates, but Sonder waved him off. "Go with them to the cellar, I'll clean all this up."

"Am I free to watch the telly," Imogen sniped with her arms crossed, "or do prisoners not get the privilege?"

Sonder pinched the bridge of his nose. "Someone else please deal with her. I need a cigar."

Gibbs got Imogen settled in her guestroom for the evening and met Emmy and Atta down in the cellar.

When they weren't studying the creatures, they kept them locked away there with a plethora of wards that, coupled with their various levels of embalming fluids, had thus far been successful.

Emmy approached the third they'd trapped alive, using a specially prepared dose of one part Sonder's embalming fluid, and two parts Yarrow, Rue, St John's Wort, iron, and moonwater mixture. It left the creature suspended in mid-flight, but its heart beat and its eyes blinked. Every so often, it managed to gnash its pointed teeth.

Emmy moved down the line to one of only two faeries they'd left almost untouched. "Why do you keep them? It seems dangerous."

"It is," Atta confirmed. "But we need to understand them. I told you our theory for why they're Inhabiting humans, but we still aren't quite sure where they're coming from.

Liar, Liar, trapped in briar, sliced by thorns and thrown in the fire.

The faerie slammed against the glass of its enclosure, startling Emmy. Atta swore the creature laughed. She could hear it clanging around in her skull.

"Can we not let that one loose?" Emmy asked in a squeak.

Atta agreed, electing the quietest of the three live faeries. The one that had sat stoically as Sonder sketched its sinuous body. As Atta documented its sleep schedule. They'd been unsure what to feed the creatures for some time to keep them alive but had eventually found mild success with root vegetables and small rodents. The aftermath of the enclosures had not been pretty and Atta knew they would soon have to embalm these three.

The one who had stoically allowed itself to be studied, eaten with decorum despite obvious distaste, and had yet to make a sound, watched her carefully as she approached. There was something elegant about it. Dignified. Atta's theories oscillated between thinking it was an evolved form of faerie or higher-up in some social ranking system amongst the Fae. Perhaps it was both. They'd exorcized it from their sixth Stage 4 patient, clamping off its near success.

The faerie stood still in its glass cage, and Atta watched in wonder as it clasped its tiny hands together, awaiting her approach.

"Prepare yourselves," she instructed Emmy and Gibbs. "Black salt, Palo Santo, and your Wormwood and Tourmaline serum."

She heard rustling and the clinking of vials behind her as they set up, but she did not take her eyes off the faerie, its too-wide mouth had curved in a smile.

Hello, daughter of many worlds.

Atta staggered back a step. No. That was in her imagination. She was exhausted, that was all. But a laugh echoed within her, vibrating in her marrow.

"How do you coax it out of the body?" Atta asked them.

"One of the Faerie Songs," Gibbs answered.

"Good."

"All right," Emmy said. "Let's get this bastard recontained."

Inhaling deeply through her nose and pushing it out through her mouth, Atta wiped away the chalk ward on the door of the enclosure, lifted the latch, and stepped back.

"Bless you," echoed across her thoughts before the faerie shot forward, pushing the door open and flying out into the dank cellar.

"Be quick," Atta commanded as it flitted about, trapped within the centre of the room where the wards were drawn on the concrete. "This one is subdued, already trapped. You can't slow down in a normal exorcism," she instructed. "What do you use to subdue it to this point?"

"The salt," Gibbs answered, his knees bent, ready.

"Then the Palo Santo," Emmy said as she lit a smudge stick, the smoke and earth scent wafting to the ceiling, the faerie already hissing.

"Good," Atta encouraged. "Next?"

But Emmy was already there, her syringe dripping. "Embalming."

"Wait." Atta held up a hand. "Which version?"

Emmy paused, her brow furrowed. The faerie somersaulted in the air, hissing, steaming, but Atta could feel its laugh in her blood.

"This was a Stage 4," Gibbs recited, "but it's subdued by the Level 4 embalming fluid, making it. . ." He thought for a second. "Stage 3. Level 3!" he declared to Emmy, who traded out her syringe with trembling fingers.

Her hand was still shaking when she encroached upon the chalk circle, close to the living, breathing faerie fluttering angrily at her eye level. Atta's heart was pounding in her chest, and she knew her friends' were too.

"Jar!" Emmy commanded Gibbs and Atta felt a bolt of pride shoot through her.

Gibbs was already there with a specimen jar filled with black salt, waiting.

Emmy darted forward and missed. The faerie chomped its teeth at her and she pulled her hand back, but then she growled and came forward again, shoving the needle in its abdomen. "Bastard," she hissed.

Gibbs darted forward and scooped the falling faerie out of the air, slamming the lid on.

Emmy let out a little cheer and Atta jumped. "We did it!"

"Wonderful!" Atta clapped her palms together once. "Now, you need to transport it into a warded enclosure."

Gibbs nodded too many times and approached the cage with Emmy. She drew the ward quite well and Gibbs said, "All right. On three."

"One. . ."

"Two. . ."

"Three!" they said in unison. Gibbs removed the lid and pumped it forward until the faerie tumbled out, spasming on the bottom of the cage, and Emmy slammed the door shut, locking the latch.

"Ah!" she screamed, giving a little hop. "We did it!"

Atta laughed as she hugged her and Gibbs. "You'll be just fine. Only remember that some might have moved to Stage 3 by the time you arrive, and you'll need to be prepared to cover your ears or look away from the faerie if need be."

"Got it, boss." Emmy saluted.

"Whew. I need a drink," Gibbs sagged.

"I second that."

Atta couldn't argue.

Sonder was on Imogen duty until midnight, so she went and checked on the grump before going out on the all-season porch with Emmy and Gibbs with two bottles of wine. They sat talking and laughing, looking out over the damp Hawthorn Grove until it was Gibbs's turn to be with Imogen, and Sonder carried Atta upstairs.

"Would you lie with me?" she asked him sleepily when he tucked her into his bed.

He smiled at her, her favourite sight in all the worlds. "Of course."

Sonder removed his trousers and shirt, climbing in bed with her, and Atta nestled into the place between his shoulder and chest where her head fit perfectly. After a moment of him silently stroking her hair, she sat up and kissed him. He was intoxicating, more than the wine, more than anything. Not only his mouth but everything about him. His grumpiness, his stoicism with everyone but her, his mind, his dreams, the way he could command a room, the way being a professor was in his very bones, his soul.

His hands were on the small of her back and she could feel her arousal rising low in her belly. She loved those hands, too. What they could do to her, the way they sketched every stray thought he had, the way he used them as he spoke, the way he flipped the pages of a book.

She reached for the dip of his pelvis and Sonder chuckled against her lips, but he gently grabbed her wrist and moved her hand to his chest. "You're too drunk for that, *a stór*."

Atta sighed and relaxed her cheek against his chest. "You know I'm in love with you too, right?" she said quietly, drawing small symbols on his abdomen. Wards, she realised drunkenly.

Sonder kissed the top of her head. "I hoped so."

Silence enveloped them, sweet and thick. The kind when you know the second the moment ends, the world will be waiting to devour you once more.

"I'm not going back to Trinity."

Sonder shifted her so he could look down into her eyes, his features hard to make out in the dark. "No, darling. You're not. But I do believe you're saving the world."

Atta closed her eyes, breathing in deeply the scent of Sonder, the beauty of their love. If he were to die, she'd envy the soil that cradled him in its arms, the flora that sprouted from his bones.

He swooped the pad of his finger down the bridge of her nose tenderly until she fell fast asleep to dreams of faeries calling her name.

ATTA
18 JANURY 1994

The days passed in a blur of success. Even Imogen had begun to help them sort research, fit as a fiddle. Safe. Emmy slid yet another Fae jar onto the shelf in the cellar, pulling down a bottle of absinthe. She turned around, holding it by the neck, and grinned.

"I think we've all earned a little celebration."

Atta's smile was weak. Everything about her was weak. She'd been forgetting things—full conversations replaced with stanzas of Fae poems she'd never read, fairytale songs she couldn't recall a second after they left her.

"I'm sure Sonder has a delightful antique spoon and sugar cubes." Emmy's eyebrows lifted and lowered rapidly. This drew a genuine smile from Atta.

"If the vote is unanimous, we drink." She took the bottle from Emmy. It was the same bottle Sonder had placed their first faerie next to. The one Atta had let get away.

She felt her insides squirm, her heart stutter—something unwelcome rooted there.

"I can agree to that. I'm very persuasive," Emmy preened.

They climbed the stairs up to the kitchen and locked the cellar door. Everyone was scattered across the manor, Sonder just in from a lecture. He was worn as ragged as she was, struggling to keep up his professor duties. There'd been some backlash after they'd removed their masks, news cameras parked in front of the manor, and Trinity students seeking him out, but no one with the power to excommunicate Sonder from Trinity or Agamemnon seemed to find the will to do so.

Emmy managed to gather the fatigued crew on the back porch, claiming the full moon was a sight to behold.

Sonder brought out an entire set of beautiful antique absinthe spoons with a matching dish of sugar cubes, while Gibbs carried out behind him a tray of decorative glasses filled with ice.

It was cold and the drink was cloying, the conversation as warm as the blankets and the fire Sonder lit.

But the old, twisted hawthorn kept signing her name. Beckoning her into the mist.

And Atta couldn't shake the feeling that the clock was running out all too soon.

Tick, flick, tick. . .

ATTA

19 JANUARY 1994

Atta's hand slid toward Sonder in the dark, but he wasn't there, his side of the bed cold.

Something felt eerily wrong. Like doom awaiting an invitation to seep in.

She rose and shoved her arms into one of Sonder's discarded collared shirts. She was still buttoning it as she searched the top floor, headed toward the glow—flickering light bleeding out from his study into the hall.

"Sonder," she said gently when she entered. Still, her voice startled him where he sat hunched over his desk, looking half-crazed.

"You should be asleep."

"So should you," Atta countered. "What are you doing?"

"You *forgot*, Atta." His voice hitched and her heart sank.

"I'm only tired."

Sonder stood, his chest rising and falling quickly. "An entire conversation we had. A very important one. You forgot it."

Atta rounded the desk and put a hand against his

breastbone. He'd been out of his mind for days since she'd forgotten a simple pass of words between them. Though they both knew it was nothing so simple as that.

"Sonder, you know how tired I've been. Dead on my feet." He flinched, and she withdrew her hand. Poor, *poor* choice of words. "Bits are coming back to me. I was only tired."

Liar, Liar, trapped in briar, sliced by thorns and thrown in the fire.

"We need to find a way to know the possession has begun earlier. We have to— to—" He ran his hand through his hair, and Atta closed the distance between them again.

"Those two things are not related, my forgetting our conversation and some of the Inhabited losing short-term memory."

Sonder looked at her lips, his eyes glossy. "I need to know, *a stór.*"

"I'm fine, my heart, my soul." She stood on her tiptoes to kiss his lips. "Cut me open, and you'll see."

That made the corner of his mouth twitch, but she'd never know his response because the night was rent by screaming.

They shared a terrified look and tore down the corridor, Atta clipping her shoulder going around a corner too quickly.

"It's Imogen!" Gibbs met them in the hall past the library, his glasses askew and fear shining in his eyes.

"What's happened?" Sonder asked, moving past Gibbs into Imogen's room.

Gibbs trotted behind. "I don't know. I fell asleep on duty and I woke up to her screaming and convulsing.

Sonder flicked on the light and he and Atta rushed for the bed. Imogen was flailing on the mattress, soaked in sweat. Her eyes were rolled back in her head and she was screaming bloody murder.

"What the fuck is happening!" Emmy's terrified voice came from the doorway.

"Get an exorcism kit!" Atta yelled. "Hurry!"

"And my medical bag," Sonder barked at Gibbs over his shoulder.

When they were alone with the writhing girl, Sonder pinned Atta with his gaze. "They got past the wards."

A familiar laugh coated her skin. "No," she whispered, her vision going spotted. "It was already in." She felt the world spin, Sonder, Imogen, the room a blur. "Check the cellar." And then she was falling, Sonder lunging for her, but the floor was coming at her too quickly.

Then Olivia was there. Here.

Just a young woman, younger than she'd yet seen her. She was singing, swaying amongst the Hawthorn Grove, the trees alive with vibrant leaves. They seemed to sway with her, their branches dipping and bowing. A court worshipping their queen.

Atta, full up with peace and dread, curled onto a warm rock in the sun, her fingers toying with the moss as she watched Olivia approach the old, twisted hawthorn.

"What is it you seek?" the voice from Atta's mind echoed through the treetops.

"Magic and majesty," Olivia Murdoch spoke into the hollow. "More for my son."

Atta couldn't make out the rest of their words, and the sky grew dark, the breeze cold. Olivia shrank away.

Atta rose and turned back toward the manor, but it was different. Autumn. Foggy and crisp. Sonder was outside, arguing with someone. Curious, she darted forward, listening.

It was his father. The spitting image of Sonder today, save for his mother's eyes. They were arguing over her condition. She was sick and Sonder couldn't make it better. His father had called Agamemnon.

Atta moved past them into the manor, floating like a ghoul up the stairs. She went to her room, to Olivia's room, put her fingers on the door and pushed. There she lay, twisted in the sheets, pale as death, crescent wounds beneath her eyes.

"Hello, Olivia," she said quietly and sat down to hold her hand.

Olivia's eyes opened and locked onto Atta's a second before her vice-like grip latched onto her wrist. "You have to close it. Close the door."

Atta gasped horridly, finding herself in a heap on the floor, Imogen still screaming, Gibbs and Emmy throwing salt, spraying Yarrow serum.

Sonder had her face in his hands. "What did you see?"

Atta knew then.

She knew too many things.

All at once.

Like a world of information shoved into her brain until it bled out her eyes, her ears, her mouth. Because someone was in *her*. She'd been Inhabited. And she would not let them take Sonder, too.

"What did you see?" Sonder asked again, fear making his voice catch.

"Patient Zero," she said, her voice croaking too.

Sonder stilled, the chaos behind them continuing. Nothing would help Imogen. Not anymore. They wouldn't get rid of the faeries. But Atta knew how.

"Who was Patient Zero, Sonder?"

His eyes filled with tears and she knew she was right. About them being a tragedy.

Ἁμαρτία.

Hamartia.

The tragic flaw.

Achilles and Patroclus.

"Patient Zero wasn't burned, was she?"

From his lap, his arms around her, their friends screaming in the background, she watched Sonder's throat bob as he swallowed. "No, she wasn't."

Atta pulled free of him. She wanted to hate him. Hate his mother. But how could they have known? He didn't know his mother was the key. That she'd unlocked the door. But she'd never opened it, because Sonder didn't know what was inside his mother, and he'd not followed her true wishes about her burial.

Atta put her palm to Sonder's cheek. "You buried her under the wrong hawthorn tree." And it had saved the world. For a time.

His lips parted, his brows knit together, puzzled. "I don't understand."

"I'll explain." But she wouldn't. "For now, help Imogen. I'll be right back." Another lie.

He could read it in her eyes, she knew that, and she watched terror flash there in his.

"I'll be right back," she lied again. And he let her go.

ATTA

T ears mingled with snot slipping down her nose, but Atta kept on.

She could still hear Imogen's cries of pain, of terror. Hear Sonder bark orders.

This was it. She knew now what she had to do, and she was terrified. Determined.

She didn't know what had connected her to Olivia, to the Fae, to another world, but it was all for this moment. She knew that with a stark clarity that terrified her.

Atta went into her room. Olivia's room. And pulled down the photo of Sonder, his smile making her heart crack. A sob hiccupped out of her, and she wanted to drop to her knees. Turn around and run back to him. Face the slow fade, the cataclysm. But she knew it wouldn't do to run from Fate.

She was a tragedy, and he was her peace.

Atta tucked the photo and a vial of black salt into the pocket of Sonder's shirt, not bothering to change. There would be no point, and Sonder was too wound around her soul to be fooled for long.

The Fae would take Imogen, then Gibbs. Then they would take her and Sonder. Here, at the epicentre of it all.

Olivia Murdoch had begun to open a portal into another world with her fairytale book, *Into the Faerie Wood*. Her death, with her husband's, would have opened the door fully. But Sonder, sweet Sonder, had buried his parents beneath the wrong hawthorn.

What called to Olivia called to Atta, beckoning her to the old, twisted hawthorn, the one that would set them free and doom the world to die. The same faerie scuttled beneath her skin, singing lyrical nonsense, turning her blood to sludge.

But not if Atta closed the door. Locked it. Threw away the last key.

With one last look in the mirror at the newly black veins in her neck, Atta snatched the book from her bedside table and let the Faerie Songs of the Hawthorn pull her toward it.

The foggy wood grew around her, expanded, surrounding her with endless trees.

Terror gripped her heart, squeezed. And Atta took off at a run, afraid she would turn back if she didn't.

Behind her, someone was calling her name. They sounded more frightened than she was. She could feel freezing tears on her cheeks, her throat burning, her eyes stinging.

No, she thought. *Stay back. Stay away.*

"*Atta!*" The voice again, bellowing. It was familiar, that deep, resonant voice.

The tears fell harder, her legs pumping faster.

"Atta, *no!*" The cry was guttural, rife with pure agony.

Lights began flickering in the fog. Blue, like the hottest part of the flame.

Wills-o-the-wisp she heard her own fragmented mind say. *Corpse Flames.*

She darted further into the fog, chasing one. Breath heaving, she pulled out a vial of black salt and ran harder.

A piercing scream filled the misty night, and Atta spun to face it, face the faeries she couldn't see.

Teeth bared, she uncorked the vial. The screeching came again, like a banshee bent on escape.

Atta clutched the vial in one hand, the book in the other, and stomped forward. She could still hear Sonder's anguished cries for her to stop, but he wouldn't be able to reach her. The Faerie Wood had already swallowed her up, gnarled branches tangling behind her, impassable.

She paused, the old, twisted hawthorn in her sight.

Keep coming, daughter of many worlds.

Atta obeyed, a peculiar, terrifying calm washing over her.

She approached the hawthorn, opened the book, and read the last tale, the one they'd never gotten to.

The one of a maiden in search of more for her child. In search of magic and a world where purity and adventure were gods. A world that did not exist past a lie. A trick of the light. An illusion of the Fae. A lure.

The maiden found out the truth too late.

When the last word rolled off her tongue in the language of the Fae, it began to rain, a mirage of light and smog materialising before her.

The door.

Come through, too many voices sang—one within her lungs.

She stepped forward, the forest holding a collective breath, the Hawthorn Grove of Murdoch Manor peeking through.

But Atta had another vial. Around her neck. It had been there for weeks. She saw it in a dream, this moment. It hadn't made sense then. But now it did.

She pulled the cork and tipped the contents into her mouth. It burned her throat, made her eyes water, and her stomach heave. But she kept it down and walked forward through the door.

SONDER

is voice was raw. He'd bellowed for her, screamed for her to stop. But he couldn't get to her.

You buried her under the wrong hawthorn.

It had taken him too many minutes to understand. To grasp the gravity of her statement.

His mother had called the Fae to Dublin. He didn't know how, but he knew it was the truth in his bones. And Atta had figured out how to make it stop.

He'd left the others fighting for Imogen's life and ran around the house, shouting for her, searching for her, but when he saw the missing book from her room, he knew where she'd gone.

Sonder thought his head would explode, his heart would beat out of his chest, his lungs collapse. He'd been lost in a wood that was not his own for what felt like an indeterminate amount of time.

"*Atta!*" he bellowed again, his voice cracking, all used up.

And then the world exploded in white just before a *BOOM* shook the earth, knocking Sonder to his knees.

He covered his ears and closed his eyes, nearly blinded by the explosion.

Another *BOOM* came before the sounds of crashing stones, trees cracking, glass shattering, branches falling, the world being destroyed. His world.

And then everything went silent.

"*Atta!*" he screamed, and he was on his feet, tripping, stumbling through the fallen forest.

He found her body beneath the collapsed hawthorn, still. Too still.

Tears crowded his eyes, his throat, as he fell to the ground next to her, pushing at the hawthorn helplessly. He finally managed to get it off of her, but her chest didn't move.

That was when he saw the uncorked vial around her neck.

"*A stór*, no."

Sonder bent his head over her chest and wept.

ATTA

She felt warm rain on her collarbone, frigid air on her cheeks, but she was numb. She could hear someone crying.

Poor soul, she thought. *Don't cry here. There are no tears in the Afterlife.*

There are no tears in the Afterlife.

Her eyes flew open and she sucked in a gasping breath.

"Sonder?" she croaked.

But he was crying harder, laughing, hugging her, berating her, squeezing her, moving the hair from her face, then pulling her to his chest again.

"You drank the embalming fluid," he accused.

"Only a little."

He laughed through his tears. "Jesus, Atta. What did you do?"

She pulled back to see his face and ran her fingertips over his brow. "Nothing major. Just exorcized myself and closed a portal into another world, once and for all."

He laughed again and squeezed her so hard she thought her ribs would crack if they weren't already. "I still might need a hospital," she managed through his grip.

"Oh god! Of course." He pulled her back and stood, scooping her up into his arms.

They both sucked in a breath when they saw what had been behind them. Murdoch Manor was nothing but rubble. Stones and twisted iron, smoke and destruction.

Sonder ran, jumping over fallen trees and debris, the broken glass and crushed flora of the atrium, over the broken bones of his parents. They shouted for their friends, Atta still clutched to Sonder's chest as he manoeuvred the debris.

"Gibbs!" Atta sobbed, seeing him sitting in the rubble that might have once been the kitchen, rubbing at a gash on his head. "How?" she asked the universe. No one should have survived such devastation.

Sonder set her down on a beam and checked on Gibbs. "I'm fine. Find Emmy and Imogen," he said, his voice hoarse.

Atta heard a groan not far away. "There!" she pointed and Sonder made his way through the rubble, uncovering a piece of the roof to find Emmy there.

"I think my leg is broken," she complained, "but I'm otherwise okay."

A scream drew all of their attention to the other side of the destruction, Gibbs and Sonder both stumbling their way over. Atta could just make out Imogen's blonde head and a manicured hand sticking out of the rubble like a zombie escaping its grave.

"Help! I've been crushed! I'm dead! I've been abducted!"

"*Christ*," Sonder muttered sarcastically when he pulled her free and she was fine, nary a scratch on her.

Atta laughed, full and true, tears streaming down her face. They'd done it. It was over.

One by one, Sonder and the others joined in her laughter, whether from joy or hysteria or both.

ATTA

"I'm going to be late," Atta whispered against Sonder's mouth.

He ran his hands up and down her bare thighs. "I do believe you're the one trapping me here, Professor Morrow-Murdoch."

She pushed off of him, and he chuckled deeply. "I need to make a good impression. These are my first students."

"You saved the world, *a stór*. Even Agamemnon couldn't help but beg your forgiveness and admit your genius."

Atta snorted. That wasn't exactly how it happened. The truth was nothing so romantic as all that, but she had been asked to return to Trinity, and this time as a professor. Her research had become a worldwide phenomenon, and their story a thing of legend.

She wandered naked around their room in the flat they'd rented after their summer-long honeymoon on the Amalfi Coast. She couldn't find the outfit she'd laid out. *Oh god,* she was going to mess everything up before she even started.

Sonder tossed a tweed blazer at her from across the room.

"I had it pressed for you." He pulled on his trousers. "Get ready, and I'll be back with coffee and pastries."

An hour later, Atta's hands trembled as she turned around to face her first set of students at Trinity College Dublin.

"Good morning, everyone. My name is Professor Morrow-Murdoch, and welcome to The History of the Fae Plague. Please open your textbooks to Page One. "

THE END

AUTHOR NOTE

Ireland has my heart. Though this was a work of fiction, and I took certain liberties with the layout of the incomparable campus of Trinity College Dublin (such as making the beautiful Geology Building into the Medical Building and enlarging the park to suit my fancy), I want to extend my greatest thanks to TCD and the Irish people for being such an inspiration to me. I know nothing of my slight Irish heritage save for what my DNA tests revealed, but I feel Ireland is my home, and she and her people call out to my very bones.

Until endless future times,
Jane

SOME WITCHES CAST SPELLS.
OTHERS SLAY KINGS.

AUTUMN OF THE GRIMOIRE

THE SISTERS SOLSTICE SERIES

J.L. VAMPA

AUTUMN OF THE GRIMOIRE EXCERPT

Our burden to take, for History to make.
  -Sacred Texts of Hespa

She was naked in the murky woods, dripping wet. Agatha frowned down at herself, then up at the full Reaping Moon. Unfortunately, it wasn't the first time—or even third—that she had been summoned in the nude. Though, Agatha was usually dry when she found herself suddenly in a new location, not of her choosing.

With a sigh, she turned to find her eldest Sister glaring, lips pinched and one finger *tap tapping* against ghostly pale arms folded across her chest.

A giggle sounded behind Agatha, and she turned once more to see her second eldest Sister appear in the gloom, also naked and dripping wet. Agatha's head tilted to one side as her brows knit together.

"Why are you both naked and *wet*?" Wendolyn demanded.

Agatha's third eldest Sister appeared out of thin air next to Wendolyn, fully clothed in swaths of blinding lemon chiffon and cradling an ancient tome. Seleste looked a bit like a black python devouring a canary.

"I was in a bath, Winnie," Agatha answered drily.

Sorscha sauntered forward, her tanned skin glowing under the moonlight. "I was with a girl on the beach."

Winnie shook her white-blonde head as Seleste, her polar opposite in absolutely every way, smiled sweetly at their two dripping Sisters.

"Come along, then." Winnie intertwined her arm with Seleste's, the contrast of their skin bewitching.

Sorscha slapped Agatha on her backside before gliding after their Sisters, content to remain nude. Sister Spring was rarely clothed, anyway.

Agatha plucked a handful of elderberries from a nearby shrub. With a will of iron and wisps of her magic, she summoned a dress of the same colour from her cottage on the far side of the twilit woodland. The cottage with a perfectly delightful bath—now abandoned. She sighed, slipping the bedimmed violet gown over her head.

Agatha wiggled her toes in the fog, contemplating which of her lace-up boots to conjure—crushed velvet or the ones Sister Winter referred to as *sinister*. The cinnamon and sienna leaves felt delicious beneath her bare feet, so she settled for none.

Agatha trudged onward after her Sisters, wringing out her sopping, deep auburn hair and readying herself for what was to come on this eve—her Autumnal Equinox.

The Sisters Solstice gathered around a blazing fire Seleste conjured, each of them facing the flames from whence their magic came: Wendolyn from the Nord, Sorscha from the Est, Seleste from the Sud, and Agatha from the Ouest.

"I'll not sit here starved, Sisters. I worked up quite an

appetite on that beach." Sorscha raised a brow coquettishly at Winnie. "You pulled me away just as things were beginning to take a delightful turn."

Winnie huffed. "I'll gladly provide nourishment if you'll put some clothing on."

Sorscha whispered and snapped. A blood-red chemise— nearly transparent for all the lace it was comprised of— appeared on her sun-kissed body. Sorscha leaned back on her hands and winked at their eldest Sister. Her familiar, Ostara, wound herself around Sorscha's arm and hissed at Wendolyn.

Winnie wrinkled her nose at the snake. She muttered a complicated incantation from memory and a roasted turkey on a spit appeared over the fire, fat dripping and sizzling on the logs. Agatha and Sorscha ripped off the legs in unison. Seleste unsheathed the long dagger strapped to her thigh and sliced off a chunk of white meat. She ran her tongue along the length of the blade before returning it to its rightful place under her yellow skirts.

Wendolyn sat primly upon the Nordernmost rock, eyeing Sorscha and Agatha. She ran a hand down her snow-white owl's feathers as her talons scraped the boulder. Winnie would inevitably comment on the way they favoured one another, Agatha and Sorscha, with their full lips and plain features; their honey eyes and freckles—she always did. Sorscha's complexion was darker, albeit not nearly as dark as Seleste's, who favoured their father most of all with rich skin and hickory eyes. But Sorscha was the perfect blend of their long-dead parents.

Agatha noted the way she and Sorscha held their turkey portions the very same way. They were similar in many ways, but Agatha found Sorscha to be all she was not. Sorscha's body was lithe and romantic whereas Agatha's was curved and soft. Sorscha sat with her shoulders back and chin high, but Agatha was slouched, the heaviness she always carried bowing her shoulders. The wind blew her hair back, whispers of past Autumn nightmares tickling her neck. Agatha wished she'd brought Mabon for comfort, but he had a treacherous habit of trying to eat Seleste's colossal monarch butterfly, Litha.

"Sometimes," Winnie spoke over the fire, "I'd think the two of you identical if only Aggie did not sink into the dark, and Sorscha did not run wild in her brightness."

How very predictable Wendolyn was.

"The pair of you"—she pointed a long fingernail at her Sisters—"do know it is forbidden to be together apart from our meetings."

Agatha snorted. As if Winnie hadn't mentioned that edict four times a year since they were wrenched apart as babes.

"You can join us next time." Sorscha made a crass gesture. Winnie rolled her eyes and Agatha stifled a laugh. "We were not together anyway, *Your Highness*," Sorscha drawled.

"You can see why one would think that is a falsehood, yes? When you both showed up here indecently? And *wet*?"

"If you would simply set a consistent time"—Agatha glowered—"you would not summon us whilst *indecent*."

"You know it's coming, Aggie. Every Solstice and every Equinox we meet. Why is it so difficult to be prepared?"

"What about the time you summoned us at High Noon?" Sorscha egged Winnie on.

"That was *one* time, and it was well over two hundred years ago."

"And the time you waited until the Witching Hour when the Solstice was nearly over?" Agatha added.

Winnie opened her mouth, but Agatha kept going. "Just set a damn time, Sister." Winnie's eye twitched at Agatha's disrespect. "Here. I'll set it for you. Dusk on the Solstice, dusk on the Equinox." She sank her teeth into her turkey leg and ripped a chunk off, eyeing her eldest Sister.

Seleste's mouth quirked to the side and she lifted one elegant hand into the air, her many bracelets tinkling. "I second."

Winnie's nostrils flared and Sorscha barked a laugh. She adored seeing Winnie and Agatha at each other's throats. "I third."

Winnie begrudgingly took a black tourmaline crystal from the pouch at her hip and let it slip from her palm, falling into the fire. A plume of silver smoke billowed into the twilight sky. "It is done. Dusk on the Solstice; dusk on the Equinox."

"Now," Winnie went on. "Our first order of business." She turned to Sorscha. "It appears a young man just outside your village has been. . .consumed."

Sorscha baulked. "Don't look at me. I haven't drunk a lad's blood in at *least* a hundred years."

Agatha snickered.

"The fact that you have to clarify the last time you drank mortal blood is unsettling." Seleste's words of censure did not match the mirth behind them.

Sorscha shrugged and licked the bones of her turkey leg clean.

Winnie heaved a great sigh. "Please just see to it, Sorscha." Sister Winter turned toward Seleste. "Your Order this Summer went well?"

It bothered Agatha that Winnie phrased it in such a way.

Undoubtedly, it went well. The Sacred Grimoire delighted in giving her Sisters only Orders of wholesome purpose.

"It did." Seleste's glowing smile warmed the wind a fraction, and Agatha felt a pang of guilt for her resentment. "I was sent to a dignitary in Eridon. His wife was with child, and she needed special care for an internal affliction. When it came time for the child to be born, I discovered the babe had the affliction as well." She smoothed her skirts. "A potion distributed methodically to them both, and now lives a healthy mother and a healthy heir." Seleste's eyes twinkled.

Agatha ground her teeth together. Of course Seleste's Order was to heal a newborn babe.

Winnie dropped her chin and eyed Seleste. "And you are certain no one suspected your tincture to be witchcraft?"

For the briefest of moments, a crease settled between Seleste's brows, but she smoothed it away with a sweet smile. "I'm quite certain, Sister."

"Good." Winnie straightened and ran her hands down the sides of her pristine, white bodice. "I trust you are all reading your Sacred Texts daily?" They all nodded, Sorscha with derision and an eye roll. "And you've all had the chance to read Father's journal?" They all nodded again. "Very well. It is time to trade."

Winnie snapped her long fingers, and one of their father's journals appeared on her lap. She looked at her Sisters pointedly, and they all three snapped in unison. A different, worn notebook appeared in each of their laps, and Winnie gathered them all to redistribute them.

Sorscha blew a stray hair out of her face and irreverently lifted the journal she'd been handed. "Why do we continue to read these things?"

Winnie's eyes widened and Seleste looked at her toes. Agatha felt a sting deep in her bosom.

"They're all we have left of our father, Sorscha. Of our coven." Winnie's gaze bore into Sister Spring. "That's reason enough."

"I'll take yours if you don't want it." Agatha held out her hand and Sorscha dropped the journal into her palm before crossing her arms. Winnie seethed but said nothing.

There was a brief lull, then Sisters Winter, Spring, and Summer turned to look at Agatha one by one. Sister Autumn sagged. "It's time, then?"

Wendolyn nodded. "It is."

Agatha stood and shuffled her way to Seleste, taking the gargantuan Grimoire from her. The weight of it in her arms dragged her heart down to the Underworld—precisely the *opposite* of what it should do.

Part of her thought it best to rush and open it—to see what dastardly deed she would be Ordered to commit this time. Part of her wanted to toss it into the blazing fire. Part of her wanted it to take centuries to walk back across their little fireside circle —everything else did.

Alas, it only took a moment to return to her place.

Her Sisters' eyes were unrelenting fire pokers upon her cheeks as Agatha ran her sharp-tipped fingernail down the length of the worn cover. She unfastened the bronze latch, took up the velvet placeholder—nearly black with time—and opened the Grimoire. The familiar script of Belfry—the first Sister Autumn—spelled out Agatha's name on the page before her eyes, followed by the shortest Order she'd ever received. Certainly it wasn't the full command—it rarely was. The rest would follow soon, and with it bring death.

Agatha slammed the Book shut.

Crippling silence filled the air. A hush permeated the Autumn trees, and the fire ceased its crackling. Even nature knew the Grimoire would not be kind to Agatha.

"Well," Winnie pressed, dispersing the aura of stillness like moths off a corpse. "What did it say?"

"You know exactly what it said," Agatha snapped.

"I do not, Sister. You know we cannot see what is written for another until it has come to pass."

"It says the same thing it always does. Can we move on?"

"What has happened to you to fill you with such disdain?" Wendolyn chastised.

"I'm a three-hundred-year-old witch, Winnie. What *hasn't* happened to me is a road far less dark to travel down."

"We're all witches. Don't be dramatic, Aggie. I simply think you could be happy if you'd let yourself."

"Because you're the picture of bliss, Winnie," Sorscha pointed out. Wendolyn stiffened, but she kept her eyes fixed on her youngest Sister.

Agatha's jaw clenched as she looked down at the Grimoire on her knees. "What makes you think I'm not happy?"

"Tell me you do not still think of Ira."

Agatha's eyes ticked up at that. Sparks burst from the fire toward the stars at the sound of his name. Her magic would not soon forget him, either.

"Not fair, Winnie," Seleste's sing-song voice broke in.

"It was nearly a hundred years ago," Winnie challenged.

"You know that's just a breath to us," Sorscha added.

"Ah yes, it's all just a breath. An agonising, horrendous, dreadfully long *breath*, suffocating your lungs until you *drown* on dry land."

The Sisters stared at Agatha.

"Thank you for trying to help, Seleste and Sorscha, but I'm okay. Truly." Agatha turned to Winnie. "Yes. I think of him every time the wind blows cold. So, thirteen times since you summoned me right out of my bath."

"We've all lost lovers, Aggie—"

"*Not like that*," Agatha cut her off, the words catching in her throat. "Now, if you don't mind, I have some packing to do."

"I don't make the rules." Winnie's voice was soft. Almost as if she cared.

But Agatha knew better.

"No, you just enforce them with the tender care of a dungeon warden."

Winnie's rigidity surfaced once more as her hand sliced through the air in time with her words. "It is our duty, our purpose, and our *privilege* to honour what the Grimoire says."

Agatha held up the ancient tome, her knuckles white for how tightly she gripped it. "This Grimoire has done nothing for us. *Nothing*. It's just a damned book."

All three of her Sisters gasped. An ice-cold knot of dread knit together in Agatha's abdomen, but she'd already said the words aloud.

"How dare you blaspheme Hespa! She is our Goddess Three."

"Hespa is not a book, Wendolyn."

Winnie took a deep breath before speaking again. "Please do not be difficult, Agatha."

Agatha laughed, mirthless and wicked. She set her eyes on her eldest Sister and curved her lips into a sinister smile. "Who has the Grimoire called upon to incite wars, Sister? To unleash plagues and kill kings? Is it you, or is it me?" She stabbed a fingernail into her own chest. "Because I am quite certain it is *me*."

Winnie stood, towering over her youngest Sister. "We've all been Ordered to do difficult things, Sister."

Agatha lifted her chin. "Oh, and what was your Order last Winter? That's right—to poison the garden of a village healer. How very malevolent, indeed." Sister Autumn's eyes flashed and the fire guttered out.

"*Disparaître.*"

And Agatha was gone.

MORE FROM
J.L. VAMPA :

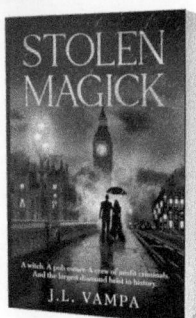

Toil & Truffle
A Gloam
HOLLOW
COZY WITCH MYSTERY
JANE LENORE

MORTAL
MAYHEM
Gloam
HOLLOW
JANE LENORE
2

SOME WITCHES CAST SPELLS
OTHERS SLAY KINGS
AUTUMN
OF THE
GRIMOIRE
SISTER'S SOLSTICE
SERIES
J.L. VAMPA

THE QUEEN'S
KEEPER
J.L. VAMPA

STOLEN
MAGICK
A witch. A pub owner. A crew of misfit criminals.
And the largest diamond heist in history.
J.L. VAMPA

J.L. VAMPA

Jane Lenore (J.L.) Vampa is an author of Fantasy and Victorian Gothic fiction. She lives in the south with her musician husband and their littles who are just as peculiar as they are.

Be sure to follow JL on TikTok - @JLVampa

ACKNOWLEDGMENTS

Thank you, from the bottom of my heart, to my beta readers. Dan (Dónal—who, by the way, is the voice of our beloved Grimm), Cory & Angela (my favorite pair!), Kaylin (my book-gushing pal), and Jen (my IRL book club buddy): this book wouldn't have its sparkle without you all! This one's for you guys. And for Mr. Tramel, as always.

www.ingramcontent.com/pod-product-compliance
Ingram Content Group UK Ltd.
Pitfield, Milton Keynes, MK11 3LW, UK
UKHW010712020625
6183UKWH00021B/114

9 798330 651139